NEVER SUCH INNOCENCE AGAIN

GILES EKINS

NEVER SUCH INNOCENCE AGAIN
Never such innocence,
Never before or since,

4th stanza
MCMXIV (1914)
Philip Larkin.

Dedicated to Patricia, as always with my love.

PROLOGUE

Immutable, as permanent as the earth itself.

We will remember them.

The War Memorial in the village of Ashbrook Stills in the county of Durham, stands at the junction of Whitton Lane and Ashbrook Road. It is a grey granite obelisk, standing proudly on a tiered plinth upon which are laid the poppy wreaths on Remembrance Sunday.

It is some nine feet tall and is inscribed with the names of men from the village and surrounding countryside who died for their country in the Great War of 1914-18.

In 1914, the population of the village stood at 267 men, women and children. Twenty-nine of them are commemorated on the Memorial. Seven more names were added after World War II. Below the list of names, the stanza of a poem reads:

They shall not grow old, as we that are left grow old,
Age shall not weary them, nor the years condemn.
At the going down of the sun and in the morning,
We will remember them.

In 1953, Councillor Mrs Edwardes donated a wooden bench in memory of her husband Percy, a survivor of the trenches whose lungs finally gave out after having been gassed in the Ypres Salient in 1917. The bench sits alongside the memorial; old women, many of the widows of those whose names are on the roll, used to sit to rest there on sunny days as they walked down to the Post Office to collect their pensions.

If you carry on down Whitton Lane, you will come to the rows of miners' cottages built in 1848 when the mine, Pit No 1, was first sunk. The cottages, six rows in all, running from the derelict railway line up to Whitton Lane, are all identical. The front door, which was rarely ever opened except for a wedding or a funeral, leads directly into the two-up two-down cottages with kitchens at the back. An entry passage, serving four houses, leads into the backyard where the privy used to be, and where the back gate leads out onto the back lane.

The streets are all named after Queen Victoria and her family.

At the top, naturally, stands Victoria Street with Albert Street next (never very popular), followed in quick succession by Edward Street, Alice Street, Alfred Street, and Helena Street. They stopped building then, because No 2 Pit proved to be so wet and thin-seamed as to be unprofitable.

The pit head buildings, which were a couple of hundred yards beyond the cottages, have been dismantled for some years now. The tall stone engine house, with the dragon-breathing steam winder that drove the huge fly wheel and cable drum (built in 1852 by J.C. Joicey of Newcastle upon Tyne), was a masterpiece of Victorian industrial engineering.

Next to the engine house stood the heapstead building, standing directly over the mineshaft with the great spinning headstock pulleys guiding the cables that sent down the cages full of men, and brought up the tubs full of coal from the depths below. It was thought that those pulleys would turn forever; they seemed moulded into the earth, immutable, as permanent as the earth itself.

The spoil heaps have been grassed over now, and a stand of new trees follows the line of the railway tracks that used to carry the coal to the Penshaw Staithes on the River Wear or the Dutton Staithes on the Tyne, there to be loaded onto colliers and shipped all around the country, to East Anglia and the Thames, and across the North Sea to Scandinavia and the Baltic.

The pit cottages are still there, but the spirit that lived with them died with the closing of the mine; they are still cottages, homes even, but they are homes without soul, the very reason for their existence died years ago.

The 'Green Tree' pub is still there on Whitton Lane, at the bottom of the hill that leads up to the village of Bitchburn, too small to be even called a village, merely a single street of houses by what used to be the Queen Mary Drift Mine, also long since closed. The names of the dead of Bitchburn are also commemorated on the Memorial.

Number 2 Ashbrook Road is the first house on Ashbrook Road and is where Mrs Ida Cantley used to live. Ida, who died in April 1995 when she was 98, had lived there ever since her marriage to Jackson Wragg in 1913, moving two doors up the road from number 6 where she had been born in 1897, Queen Victoria's Jubilee year. Widowed in 1916, when Jackson had been killed on the Somme, she married Fred Cantley in 1924 and was widowed again in 1929, when gas exploded in No 1 Pit, killing 17 miners.

Ida lived alone for the best part of 65 years. Her children had long since left home and scattered far and wide. Only her youngest daughter, Mary, used to visit regularly, every two months or so, but Ida did not feel lonely or neglected.

She had her memories and as she sat by her front room window, she could see the War Memorial without even turning her head. She drew great comfort from it; even after more than 75 years, it solaced her to know that Jackson Wragg's name had not been forgotten.

Her tears had long since dried but the pride she felt for the fallen lived with her until the day she died. When the Boy Scouts, Freemasons and old soldiers stood to observe a minute's silence by the Memorial on Remembrance Sunday, her heart seemed fit to burst with pride and it was as well to have a hankie tucked in her sleeve, as the tears sparkled at the corner of her eyes.

Ida had known that she had not much time to live; the hard winters seemed harder to get through than ever before, but the prospect of her death had not dismayed her. She knew she would be re-united with Wragg and Cantley, who had been good friends to each other and good, if brief, husbands to her, and after she had gone, the Memorial would live on forever, of that she had no doubts.

The Memorial would live on forever.
At the going down of the sun, and in the morning,
We will remember them.

PART ONE

ONE

July 1914

'I hope it may'nt be human gore.'

Mary Blackett Garforth dozed fitfully in her chair. She was desperately tired, in fact she could hardly remember a time in her life when she had not been tired, no, not just tired, exhausted to bone-weary numbness, drained to a point beyond fatigue. Possibly as a child maybe, but even then, she would have had to help her mother look after her brothers and sisters, carry the water for her Dad's bath, help with the washing and the baking, run errands and black the stove.

At 13, she had gone into service at 'the Big House' as Exham Hall, ancestral seat of the Lords Exham, was known, and life as a 'tweenie' had not been conducive to leisure or an excess of sleep either, especially when old Mrs Lankester, the master's mother - in-law, had still been alive, as vicious an old bitch as ever had been; nothing could ever be right for old Mrs Lankester. No matter how hard you tried, she would always find fault and box your ears, she made you bend over her bath chair and keep still as she smacked her leathery hand, full tilt, at the side of the head.

'Take that, girl, and if you can't do better next time, you 'll be all the sorrier for it'. Or worse still, she would smack her walking stick onto your knuckles, often until they bled.

She had been hateful and petty, and Mary had been glad, no, *ecstatic*, when she died, and even though she prayed hard for forgiveness for harbouring such un-Christian thoughts, nothing could replace the relief when the old witch was finally laid to rest in the family plot. 'And good riddance to you', Mary had thought as the coffin was lowered into the grave. All the staff had been allowed two hours off, without pay, to attend the funeral and had stood, heads bowed, at a discreet distance, away from the graveside and Mary could bet every single farthing she owned that not one of the other gardening or domestic staff felt sorrow or grief at old Mrs Lankester's passing.

Things were better after that, when she became Lady Exham's personal maid, still tired, of course, but tiredness was simply a way of life and she remained as maid to Lady Exham until she died in an accident in 1897 when following the Hunt— trying to put a 3'0' horse at a 4'0' fence was how Mr Brindley, the butler, had put it in his usually sneery way, curling his lip as he spoke, his moustache crawling up into his nostrils like a hairy slug.

Butter wouldn't melt in Brindley's mouth above stairs, bowing and scraping and licking the master's boots until his tongue was as black as a coal scuttle whilst, below stairs, he hadn't a good word to say for any of the family. He was forever asking Mary to go into the cellar with him, but Cookie said she knew what he was after and told him to keep his wandering hands to himself.

Then, in 1898, Mary had married Jack Garforth and moved

down from Exham Hall to Victoria Street. Then, she had really learned what tiredness meant.

She was Jack's second wife and he had come with a ready built-in family, Jack himself, Joe the eldest boy, Daniel, Mary Margaret, always both names together, as if they were joined into one, Mary-Margaret. No one could remember how Mary Margaret came to be called that; she wasn't christened that way, as though it were a double name like the gentry sometimes did, it had just happened.

Margaret Mary followed and then there was Harold, sneery, thin, creepy Harold, burning with sullen resentment at the world, who always seemed to be somewhere else, or at least his mind was. She tried to love all of Jack's children as her own, but there was something unlovable about Harold; the way he looked at her reminded her of Brindley at 'the Big House'.

Mary did not like being in the house alone with Harold. He never did anything untoward, never touched her or said anything you could take exception to. It was just the way he looked at you —with red bitterness in his eyes—and it made her feel uncomfortable to be near him.

After Harold, there came Edgar and her own especial favourite of Jack's children, the wondrously dreamy Eleanor, so pale and ethereal and fragile that Mary had kept her at home far longer than was normal, stopping Jack from letting her go into service, claiming she was needed at home.

This was only partly true. Mary always needed the extra pair of hands around the house, but it was more than that. Eleanor was … what was the word? Simple? Not in the sense of stupid, but innocent, naive, untainted by the world, as trusting as a lamb amongst wolves. Mary felt that Eleanor would bruise too easily if left to fend for herself … bruise inside where the hurt was always so much the greater.

There had been three other bairns: John, Jack's first born,

Edward and Sophie, but all had died in infancy. Losing those three children had been too much for Jack's sickly first wife, also called Mary. She had simply been worn out and had died giving birth to Eleanor.

Mary always wondered if something had happened during the childbirth that had left Eleanor the way she was; perhaps the cord had got wrapped around her neck, starving her of oxygen. They said that that could cause simple-mindedness, but there again, Eleanor wasn't simple-minded exactly.

At least, not in the way you thought of simple-minded children, not like Jimmy Poskit from Alice Street, twisted and garbled, forever touching and playing with himself, leering at you as he did so, a bit like Harold, only more so. And come to think of it, Jimmy wasn't the only Poskit boy who was a bit feeble-minded, a bit peculiar. Sammy Poskit, who was married to Ethel Whittaker as was and lived on Whitton Lane, he was a few lumps short of a full coal scuttle as well.

Then, there were her own children, Nicholas, the apple of her eye, who had won a scholarship to the grammar school and would never ever have to work underground like his father or brothers and for that blessing alone Mary gave Thanks every night.

And lastly there were the twins, Isaac and Saul, 13 years old now, and up to every conceivable bit of mischief imaginable. Their father had taken his belt to them on more than one occasion and would no doubt do so again, but nothing seemed to have much effect. They would take their beatings, dry their tears and, within minutes, be up to their tricks again, as artful as a barrow-load of monkeys.

Still, Mary thought, 'I would rather have them as they are, safe and above ground, than going down the pit, but soon, too soon, they would be 14 years old, no longer boys.' Unless she could find some way out of it; down the mines they would go. The prospect filled her with dread that clogged up her heart.

Often, all too often, there were deadly collapses, gas explosions or flooding. The pit was always hungry for men; it devoured men with ferocity that was almost Satanic. Too many men had been maimed and killed for any mother to be sanguine about her children working in the mines.

Mary nodded off again for a minute or two, and then she woke with a start of disorientation. She had felt herself about to slip into a deep pit, a dream she had had over and over recently, and it terrified her, believing that it portended a great disaster, and to a miner's wife that could only mean a collapse or explosion underground.

She shuddered in trepidation. 'Someone walking over my grave,' she whispered fearfully and pulled her shawl tighter about herself. She was cold as well, even in the height of summer; those dead chill hours before dawn could be frigidly bitter.

Mary stretched to ease the knots on the muscles of her neck and back. Yesterday had been washday, the most tiring of all days, hours spent hunched over the washtub, as sheets and linen and thick black coal encrusted pit clothes were scrubbed and battered on the washboard, boiled and beaten with the poss stick, rinsed in the rinse tub, twisted and mangled damp-dry, the kitchen filled with a dense, almost gelatinous fog compounded of sweaty clothes and steam and soap fumes, a sour-sweet brume that caught in the throat and stung the eyes.

Line after line of washing had crisscrossed the back street, the whole street bedecked with washday bunting like a fleet of galleons at full sail. Then, it had rained, so all the clothes had to be swiftly dragged off the lines and brought in to join the piles of still damp and wet clothing waiting to go out on the line. The skies cleared up and, with Eleanor's help, they had strung out the laundry once more, only for the coal cart to come around, so back inside went the still wet washing, to join the ever-growing pile again.

She thought she would never get any of it dry and, in fact,

there was still a load drying on the clothes horse in front of the range; the boys' school shirts and underwear hung over the brass rail under the mantle shelf and yet more hung on the drying rack suspended on pulleys from the ceiling, a gallows liberally strewn with flannel shirts and grub-grey vests, long johns, short hogger trousers, neckerchiefs and wool stockings, dangling like executed criminals hanging from a gibbet.

By the time she had got all the washing hanging somewhere to dry, there had been Jack's dinner to fix when he came back from the 'Green Tree' and then, later, Edgar's dinner and break-time sandwiches to fix before he went on night shift.

Harold had come in from afternoon shift at ten and needed his bath and dinner, there was ironing to do, and it had been well after midnight by the time she had finished, bone weary, back aching, hands with the dead white skin of a drowned corpse, eyes bleary and smarting, wanting nothing more than to fall into her bed and sleep for a week.

But she could not, Jack was on morning shift, starting at four and she would have to be up and about by three o'clock to get his breakfast ready and prepare his bait, the sandwiches for his break. They were always strawberry jam sandwiches, sticky jam to lubricate the back of a throat made as raw as a harsh file by the coal dust.

She squinted up at the clock nestling between a forest of brass candlesticks on the mantle-shelf, peering through the night-gloom, trying to read the time, but could not and had to get up from her chair to hold the clock close to her face. 'Ten to three,' she said to herself. 'Well, I'm up now and may as well stay up.'

And feeling her bladder suddenly full, she padded across the backyard to the privy, wrinkling her nose as ever at the smell. No matter how often she scrubbed it, no matter how much carbolic was used, she could never get rid of the smell, the smell of stale urine and fetid dankness that seemed permeated into the very fabric of the whitewashed walls.

As she hoisted her skirts, the cold air on her bare legs and thighs sent a shiver through her body, rattling the bones inside her goose-pimpled flesh.

The night air was still, as if buried under a quilt of silence, an eerie silence; even the sound of her urine tinkling into the bowl seemed deadened, mute, and Mary shuddered again, portents of disaster casting icy fingers up her spine.

'Somebody else walking on my grave,' she said aloud, needing the sound of her own voice to break the spell of heavy, woven silence.

Back indoors again, she warmed herself over the dampened down coals in the range, washed her hands in the stone sink and swiftly made up Jack's sandwiches before going into the front room to wake him.

The big four-poster bed seemed to fill the whole room, and she looked longingly at it again, feeling her eyelids weighting down from just thinking about sleep. She might catch an hour or so in the rocking chair after Jack had gone, but Edgar was on night shift and would be home at six, ready for *his* bath and breakfast.

Harold was on two o'clock shift, the boys Isaac and Saul had to be got off to school, and Nicholas to the Grammar; she would have some time to bake and prepare dinner, by which time Jack would be home again.

Jack was a small compact man, as strong and wiry as a bull terrier, and he seemed lost in the big four-poster bed, like a baby curled up in the corner of a cot. He was snoring lightly and, as she looked down on him, Mary felt a surge of affection for him run through her like static electricity. He had been a good man to her, better than she deserved, a good husband and provider who had been there for her when she had needed someone—*desperately* needed someone.

Life with Jack had been hard, would remain hard, there was no denying that, but the lot of any miner's wife was hard, but when he had a good cavil, a good thick seam to work at; money was adequate, he didn't beat her as some men beat their wives, and he was not much taken for the drink. A pint or two at the 'Green Tree' to wash down the dust, but that was all, and who would deny him that?

Reaching over, she shook him by the shoulder. 'Jack. Jack. It's time.'

'Uhhh? What?'

'Time, Jack. Time!'

She could see him struggling to wake, coming up through the layers of sleep, coming up from the depths as if coming up from underground in the mine cages. He yawned and stretched and coughed and sneezed and farted, all at the same time, and then rubbed at his eyes before swinging out his legs from under the covers and sitting up straight.

'Aye, right then Mary. Be with you in a minute,' he said as he stretched again. 'You get us me breakfast on, though I doubt you've a deal left.'

'Bread. There's always bread, you know that. And I've still got a bitty bacon rind and fat. I can fry it up with your bread. And you've got jam for your bait.'

'That'll do grand, Mary. And choose us the book, will you?'

'Owt special, pet? I'll put it by your plate?'

'Nay, you choose. Right, best be getting on I suppose, else Billy Bedlam will be here, and the day has yet to come when I'm still in my bed when Billy comes by.'

Even as he spoke, they could hear a cry at the head of the street, 'LAD AWAAAY. UP. UP. LAD AWAAAY. GET UUUP, GET UUUP. UP, UP,' as Billy Belledame, better known as Billy Bedlam, the caller, came down to rouse those men on early shift.

Mary put on the bacon rind and bread to fry together, glad she had been able to eke out that last piece of flitch. The miners had been on strike, coming out in sympathy with the building workers, and although the Union had sent a delegate to the Institute to explain it to the men, and Jack had tried to explain it to her, Mary could not understand, refused to understand, why she should have to put her family on short measures out of sympathy for the building workers. Times were hard enough when Jack and the elder boys were working, let alone when they were on strike.

Two weeks they had been out and even now they had gone back, had been back for 10 day,s there was no money in the house. They would still not get paid until Saturday, which meant four weeks without a penny coming in. And for what? Going on strike to improve your own lot, that she could understand, striking to get a better rate for the coal produced, since the men at the face were paid 'by the weight of mineral gotten' as the Act put it, *that* she could understand, but to strike, to make her children go hungry merely to help some unknown building workers in another part of the country? That she could not accept, and it still made her angry to think about it.

She poured a big mug of tea, set his fried bread and bacon on a plate, leaving it by the hob to keep warm, and crossed over to the wooden bookshelf on the opposite wall. Jack liked to read for 10 -15 minutes before going to work. 'Sets me at ease,' he had told her. 'Gives me something to think about, some'at to mull over in my mind when I'm at the face. Why, you'd go daft else, nothing to take your head up with, nothing to think on except the hewing.'

He had a full set of Dickens, green morocco leather-bound, gold-embossed, that he had found in a bookseller in Durham. They had not been new when he had bought them, years and years ago, not even secondhand, third- or fourth-hand maybe, but they were his pride and the day would not go past that he did not read from them. He liked for Mary to pick a volume at random and lay it by his place and he would open it at any page and read for a while.

Mary did not think he had ever read a book the whole way

through, but that did not matter to him. The three or four pages he read before his shift would last him the whole day as he turned over the phrases and characters in his head; in his mind's eye he could see Little Nell or Mr Bumble the Beadle, Pickwick or Micawber, Jacob Marley, Wackford Squeers, or Bill Sykes, and with them in his mind to keep him company, the hours underground hacking at the coalface soon sped past.

Mary didn't even look at the titles as she reached up and took the first book that came to hand and laid by his place, next to his mug of tea.

Jack came back from the privy, his braces dangling from his waist, washed his hands and splashed water into his face, and sat down as Mary laid his breakfast in front of him. He opened the book where it would and began to read, tracing the words with the forefinger of his left hand, mug of tea held by the other, munching his bread to the rhythm of his reading.

'Is there more tea, Mary?' he asked shortly.

As she bent over to fill his mug, the close written words of the pages seemed to leap out at her, and she almost dropped the tea pot in shock. 'Something will come of this,' she read. 'I hope it may'nt be human gore.' And the horrible premonitions she had earlier, swept over her once more, like a tidal wave of ice, shudders of panic clattering at her heart.

'Which, which one is that, Jack?'

He put his finger in the pages to mark his place and folded the book over to read the spine. '*Barnaby Rudge*. Why, you want to read it? Here, take it now, time I was off, anyhow.'

'No, I just wondered, that's all.' She hesitated, wanting to hold him tight to her, to feel his strength and for him to tell her she was being foolish, but she could not. 'Take care Jack,' was all she could say as she walked with him to the back gate. No miner's wife would ever let her man go without seeing him off, no miner's mother would ever fail to see her sons to the gate, as the possibility that it might be the last time they ever saw them was all too real.

Mary, the black wings of her premonition hovering over her like a monstrous bat, tried to blink away her tears; she could not let Jack see her like this, she could not disgrace him front of his workmates, and especially she could not disgrace him in front of Nellie Spearman, who lived next door. She had a nose for gossip like a rabid bloodhound and would be certain to make something out of the sight of Mary crying at the gate. What Nellie didn't know, she would guess at, well, *invent* would be a better word and in next to no time, all manner of stories would by flying round the village, sped on their way and nourished by the spite of Nellie's vindictive tongue.

'Morning Nellie, morning Charlie,' she managed to say with a smile, the words like choking feathers in her throat. 'Ta-ra then pet,' she said to Jack, laying her hand on his arm, desperate for a (final?) touch on him.

'Aye, be seeing thee, lass. And tell Isaac and Saul, if I hear they've been in trouble again, they'll be feeling me belt to their arses. Soonest they get working down the pit, the better, where I can keep an eye on 'em, the young buggers ... they'll have no time for their tricks then.'

Jack pulled on his flat cap, tugged at the peak to settle it squarely on his head, and fell into step with Jim Comby and Charlie Spearman, the sound of their hob-nailed boots ringing off the cobbles and echoing around the morning damp walls of the back passage.

Mary watched him for as long as she could without inciting comment from Nellie Spearman and then hurried back indoors to kneel by the side of the bed, praying for Jack to be kept safe, unable to rid herself of the hard knot of tension that weighed on her stomach and heart like a ball of iron.

She was so tired that not even the hard clogging weight of apprehension could stop her from nodding off and as she dozed in her chair, waiting for Edgar to come in from night shift, something Billy Bedlam had said a few days ago coming to mind. Billy had claimed that war was coming, said he could smell war in the air. He had said it even before that Grand Duke Ferdinand had been assassinated on June 28th, nearly two weeks ago, shot in some place that nobody had ever heard of, somewhere across the other side of Europe, but then everyone knew that Billy was touched, had been for years.

Mary hoped that it would not come to a war. She had a brother, Norman Blackett, an infantryman in the Royal Durham Regiment. She could hardly remember Norman, Mary was seven years old when he had run away from home at the age of 13, choosing, like so many boys, the apparent glamour of the Army to the rigours and danger of life underground. Even when he was home on leave, she barely saw him.

Even though he lived a mere 16 miles away, at Mangdon Heath on the other side of Durham with his wife Olive when not in Barracks, she doubted if she would recognise him if he were to walk through the door that very minute. Even so, blood was blood, thicker than water and war could mean he might have to go and fight, and so she added a little prayer for Norman as well.

But the idea of a war involving England was nonsense anyway. Who on earth cared what happened to some Grand Duke or other? It made no sense, no sense at all, to say that war would reach England, even if a few Serbs and Austrians and Hungarians did get to fighting in the Balkans or Bosnia, or wherever. *How could that possibly affect us?*

No, Billy Bedlam was touched and that was the end of it.

Billy Bedlam's name was obviously a corruption of his surname, Belledame, (which he claimed was French and swore that his ancestors were aristocrats fleeing from the French Revolution and the guillotine, but why the offspring of French aristocracy came to be Durham miners was something Billy had never been able to satisfactorily explain). Some said he was called

Bedlam because of the noise he made when calling the shifts, others said it was because he belonged in Bedlam, an asylum for the mentally insane (Bedlam, in itself, a corruption of Bethlehem).

Whatever the case, no-one disputed that Billy had never been the same since there had been a collapse of the north-east boards back in 1894. Billy had been working as a putter then, moving full and empty tubs up and down the roadways of the mine. Hearing the rumbles and the screams as the tunnels began collapsing behind him, he had scrambled headfirst into a small side passage, and screamed and screamed in helpless terror as the roof caved in around him, entombing him as the coal dust wrapped around his face, clogging up his eyes and nose and throat. He thought he would die of suffocation and screamed again, wishing he had not been so stupid as to dive into the passage; at least, if he had been crushed, it would have been quick and painless, not this, not to be slowly suffocated in coal dust as his air ran out.

The collapse could not have been total, or else there was a bigger air pocket than he realised because Billy Belledame was dug out alive 27 hours later, almost crazed with thirst, his throat a raw mass of emery-papered flesh from screaming and the dust.

He did not speak for nearly a month, and then only in a whisper. His hair had turned as white as the snow on the high valley sides in January, and when he walked in through his door, his wife thought him a ghost and screamed and fainted. He never went underground again, could not even bear to go near the steel stairway that led to the cages at the pit head.

It was thought that Billy's vocal cords had been ruined forever and it had been Abel Poskit's perverted idea of a joke to suggest to the Under Manager that Billy be given a job as caller.

When he heard of this, Billy had just smiled, taken a deep breath and yelled out, 'You bugger you, Abel Poskit,' in a voice fit to wake the dead. He grinned again and said simply, 'I knew the bugger were there somewhere, just didn't know where to find him.'

Billy had been a caller ever since, but even though he'd found his voice again, no-one doubted but that he'd left his wits in the dust underground, for who but a fool can claim to smell war in the air?

TWO

Gone off the same night, following the drum.

As Jack Garforth and the other miners walked across to the pitheads to start their morning shift, Jeb Fulcher eased open the warped back door to his tied farm cottage and slipped out into the dark pre-dawn stillness, a stillness that wrapped itself around the row of mangey labourers' hovels of Highfield Farm like a cold wet cloth.

As the name might suggest, Highfield Farm stood high on the south, facing slopes of the valley and was still buried in deep shadow as Jeb climbed over the dry stone wall at the corner of the houses and dropped down into the fields, and skirted past the herd of Shorthorn cattle that were the pride of Highfield. Jeb sometimes fancied that Hector Whitehead, the owner of High-field, thought more of his Shorthorns than he did of his wife and children—certainly he spent more time with them and seemed to take more care of them, forever checking on them and writing up all the details in his stock book.

Scurrying crabwise downhill towards the copse at the base of the valley, Jeb hunched over like a mole-skinned Quasimodo in the hope that this would make him less visible.

Jeb Fulcher was a stout, stunted man with disproportionately long arms and the gnarled appearance and complexion of an ancient olive tree. Clumps of mousey hair grew on the top and sides of his head like clots of marsh grass in a swamp, and the most prominent aspect of his face was a great hooked nose, standing out from the blandness of his face like a granite outcrop on a sandy plain. He thought this nose to be a noble ornament, Romanesque, patrician even, the distinguishing feature of an imposing visage, whereas everyone else simply thought that he had a big conk and called him Nebbie Jeb or Jeb the Neb behind his back.

Jeb the Neb crossed over seven more fields, eight more walls, so that by the time he reached the copse, he had left Highfield property and was onto Exham lands. As always, he felt a little grim smile of satisfaction creeping across his face; Jeb loved to poach from His Lordship, even though it would mean a heavy fine or even prison if he were ever caught. He had nothing against His Lordship, it was simply that his elder brother Samuel, miserable old bastard that he was, was Lord Exham's head gamekeeper and Jeb was always eager to get one over on him. Jeb and Samuel had never got on, even as children, and even though they still lived barely four miles apart, they hardly ever saw each other and could barely speak civilly to each other when they did.

There had always been trouble between them; they had been forever scrapping in bloody-nosed scuffles over nothing, nothing that is except the fact they did not like each other, had never liked each other, and never would like each other. Blood might be thicker than water, but in their case, the fratricidal gore was curdled—thick-sour and rancid.

Samuel had left Highfield Farm at 14 to go and work for Lord Exham as an apprentice gamekeeper and, ever since, Jeb had taken perverse pride in poaching on Exham land, poaching from right under his brother's nose, setting wire snares along the rabbit runs, lifting a pheasant or two from here and there, and always taking grouse from the high moors beyond the dale before the 12th July, the glorious twelfth when all the nobs came to stay with Lord Exham and shoot.

Jeb reached the edge of the copse, and stood very still for a good five minutes, listening for alien sounds that might indicate gamekeepers, not that he expected there would be, Samuel had not caught onto him yet, but caution and sharp ears were the hallmarks of a good poacher and Jeb Fulcher was the best in the valley.

'Aye, no doubt bugger Sam's still ploughing that scrawny chicken-necked bitch of a missus of his, else snoring his big gob off,' Jeb said sourly to himself and, satisfied at last, eased himself silently into the copse, moving as smoothly as a shadow over polished marble, and checked out his snares.

The snares were loops of wire tied to a peg, driven into the ground, and strategically placed along the rabbit runs that criss-crossed the woods, inviting the bobtail beasts to garrotte themselves as they scampered along the dung-pellet strewn paths.

He was in luck, three of his seven snares had taken, a fat doe, pregnant by the feel of her belly, a long-legged leveret, which was a surprise; hares normally kept to the open fields but perhaps this youngster had been driven into the copse by a fox on the prowl. The third catch was an exhausted buck, which had somehow managed to ensnare himself by his back leg. Struggling to get free from the tightening wire noose, the big buck had all but flayed his leg down to the bone. Fur and matted blood were liberally spread around in a circle about the snare.

'Lucky all that thrashing about and the smell of blood didn't bring that vixen in from Bottom Hollow to see him off,' Jeb thought as he snapped the rabbit's neck with a crunch that seemed to echo deafeningly loud around the thick murky strakes and tree trunks of the copse.

Well pleased with himself, Jeb gathered up all his snares, stuffed the catch into the deep poacher's pocket of his coat, and hurried back up to Highfield as the dawn light spilled more brightly across the fields.

He was later than usual this morning; normally he was back indoors well before the dawn crept over the valley crown, but he had slept until well past four. Too much cowslip wine last night had befuddled his internal clock, but he had dared not leave his snares in place. 'Even blind-bugger Sam couldn't miss them,' he thought as he slipped back through the door of the cottage, still fairly certain that he had not been spotted.

Jeb, the second son of Thomas and Millie Fulcher, had lived in the tied cottage at Highfield Farm all his life, and never envisaged anything other than dying there. His father, Thomas, had been taken on by Hector Whitehead's grandfather as a 14-year-old and he had lived there all the remainder of his life, taking Millie Winslop as his wife in 1878 and raising seven children in the cottage, all on 8s a week, farmworkers wages being reduced from 11s in 1889.

The cottage had been all but empty of furniture back then and remained so now. The living room floor was still scrubbed brick, although Jeb was less fastidious about scrubbing it than his mother had ever been. The same peg rug, made from scraps of old cloth pegged onto sacking that his mother had brought with her as a dowry, still lay on the floor, although it would have defied anybody's powers of description and imagination to say what colours it had originally been.

There was a broken legged table propped by a piece of wood, a single hard chair where his father had sat to eat whilst everyone else squatted on the floor as best they could. To this ensemble, Jeb had added an old wooden rocking chair that had been thrown out of the cottage two doors down when old Martin Handyside had died.

Off to one side of the living room was a larder with four or five rude wooden shelves, the shelves never contained much more than a stale loaf of bread, a packet of tea, crinkle-skinned apples, potatoes, swedes and, if he had been lucky with his snares, a rabbit or two.

The cottage had no water, no gas, no sewers, and if it rained heavily and the wind blew from the north, not much of a roof either.

Through to the back of the cottage there were two bedrooms, one in which the children had slept and one where his parents and the youngest baby had slept, and even now Jeb still slept in that same bed he once had shared with his siblings. The bed his mother and father had used was still in the other room, a room that Jeb had only been in but once or twice since his mother had died there in 1911, his father having died the winter before.

The third son, Jubal, had been a soldier in South Africa, enlisting in 1897 when a recruiting Sergeant had passed through by Bishops Shilton on a recruiting drive. Jubal had taken some cattle to market there for old Mr Whitehead and had signed on immediately, arranged for the money from the sale of the cattle to be sent to Highfield, and had gone off the same night, following the drum. He came home only the once afterwards, in 1900, just before shipping out to South Africa.

He had caught a ride from the station on the milk-cart and walked through the door, resplendent in a bright scarlet coat, just as if he were returning from Bishops Shilton market that same day, instead of three years later. His mother had kissed him on the cheek, but his father looked up once, grunted, 'How do, Jubal? Is't cold out?' and carried on laboriously reading his newspaper.

A few days later Jubal left to re-join his Regiment and ship out to the Cape. His mother and sisters had watched him walk away, watching him all the way until he was out of sight at the bottom of the hill. Jubal survived all through the Boer War, but then caught a fever. Jeb never could remember exactly which fever it had been, ent-errick or ant-eric, something like that, which Jeb presumed was some form of exotic disease caught from African ants, and he died in 1902.

Jacob, the youngest boy had worked alongside Jeb in the fields, starting in 1890 as an 11-year-old boy, earning half a crown a week for 70 hours labour, Jeb, bigger and six years older, was earning 4s 6d, but then he had to work on Sundays as well.

One day in 1902, when Jacob was 23, he had an argument with Hector Whitehead about not being paid when laid off because of bad weather. He tossed his spade aside. 'Bugger this for a fucking lark,' he said and walked off. The next anyone heard from him was in 1909, when he wrote a five-line letter from India to say he was in the Army with the Norfolk Regiment. How he ever got into the Norfolk's his letter did not explain.

All three of Jeb's sisters had married and left home and so, when his mother and father died, he remained alone in the cottage, and even though it was intended to be a family dwelling Mr Hector allowed Jeb to stay there as a gesture for all the hard work he and his father had done over the years ... at least until another farmhand with a wife and family came along.

Jeb hung up his catch in the larder, munched a piece of stale bread, after first breaking off the mouldy bits, and then swilled out his mouth with cold water from an earthenware jug before setting out for his day's labour in the fields.

THREE

Gnawed at his vitals like a rat at a granary door.

Just as Mary nodded off again in her rocking chair, hoping to catch a few minutes quiet nap, the back gate clattered on its hinges and the weary scrape of hob-nailed boots echoed across the yard and splintered the sharp silence of her sleep like a broken mirror.

'Morning Mam', Edgar Garforth said as he clumped in from night shift and hung up his cap on the back of the door. 'Is me bath ready?' he asked and turned away to unlace his boots, thinking how tired she looked, but then she always looked tired, and he gave no further thought just how drawn and exhausted Mary really was.

'It'll not be but a minute, pet. Bring us in the tub. Some water's already hot and I'll put some more on an' all.'

Wearily, she dragged herself up, holding her aching back, her knees creaking in protest, but glad of something to do to take her black-cloaked mind off her worry about Jack.

Edgar brought in the tin bath from the backyard, where it had been hanging up on a nail on the side wall by the privy and set it in front of the fire. Mary poured the hot water from the pans on the stove and set more pans of water on the stove to heat up. When the bath was ready, she draped blankets over cords hanging from the ceiling to screen Edgar off as he bathed.

After he had bathed, and finished his breakfast, Edgar slowly climbed up the steep narrow stairs to the front bedroom. He kicked the twins, Isaac and Saul, out of the double bed; they would have to get up soon for school anyway. Harold was lying diagonally across most of the bed and Edgar unceremoniously pushed him over to make room.

'Watch what tha's bloody doing, buggerlugs, else tha'll get a clip round your ear'ole,' Harold grumbled, still half asleep, supposing that it was either Isaac or Saul who had shoved him.

'Who're thee calling buggerlugs?'

'Oh, it's thee, is it Edgar? Still, who does tha think you're pushing?'

'Get yourself over, Harold. Man comes in from his shift, he wants to get some kip, not bugger about with thee trying to find room.'

'You've got stacks of room, man,' Harold grumbled in a whiney voice, but he moved over anyway as Edgar, in clean long johns and vest, climbed into the bed, ancient springs creaking in protest, and settled down to sleep on the lumpy horsehair mattress.

Harold would soon be up in any case, before he went on his shift. He liked to take his rod and go down to the river, hoping to catch a trout or two for his supper before the sun got too high and the fish stopped feeding.

Even though tired after his long shift down the mine, sleep would not come to Edgar; he tossed and turned and, eventually, with a grunted curse, Harold got up and pulled on his trousers and shirt and clumped downstairs, banging the bedroom door loudly as he did so.

'Bastard,' Edger hissed through his teeth after him, and turned over again to try to find a more comfortable lie.

Edgar still could not get to sleep, his mind seemed incapable of accepting the fact that his body was tired, and no matter how much he tossed and turned in the bed, it remained uncomfortably lumpy. He plumped out his pillows again and wrapped one around his head but the hard morning light filtering through the tiny dormer window still seemed blinding and every tiny noise took on deafening proportions.

He kicked off most of the covers and lay with only the top sheet over him, but that made no difference. Despite eyes heavy with fatigue, and the solid ache in his back and shoulders from pushing loaded tubs of coal up and down the underground roads, sleep still refused to come; it hovered shyly around the outer limits of his consciousness, like a reluctant dance partner.

He turned over again, bouncing down hard into the mattress, and heard the clatter of the headboard rattling against the wall. 'Bloody shitting hell,' he mumbled to himself angrily, his frustration only adding to his unsettled mental state, as his brain, as if super-charged, fizzled and popped like soda water bubbling over the rim of a shaken-up bottle.

Edgar Garforth was just 18 years old; his 18th birthday had been a month or so ago, in May, but even so he had been down the mines for more than four years and now worked as a 'putter' with George Hindle, whose son, William, was engaged to Mary Margaret.

But until a place became available on the coalface as a hewer, that was as far as he could go, and a place only became available through death or retirement and, even then, it might not go to Edgar. Many other men had been down the mine longer and had far stronger claims to any hewers' job coming free. Edgar could be working as a putter for 20 years or more before getting onto the top paid job. He might never get to be hewer.

Jim Comby, his Dad's putter, was nigh on 45 years old and would likely now never get to be hewer.

'Damn it,' he thought. 'There's got to be more to life than pushing a bloody tub of coal up and down the mine for the next forty sodding years.' He desperately wanted more than that from life but had no idea how this might be achieved, or even what it was he wanted to achieve. He simply knew, deep inside, that life was cheating him, that there had to more to man's existence than that. Frustration gnawed at his vitals like a rat at a granary door and the more he thought about it the worse it became.

But things were stirring in the air—he could feel it—there was an almost intangible sense of excitement, a crackling zest, like far off lightning … excited talk of war … a sense that after what might come, things would never be the same again and Edgar was determined to be part of that change.

Whatever it was.

Eventually, as it had to, the fatigue of hard physical labour took over and Edgar drifted off to sleep, stretching out fully in the luxury of for once having the bed to himself.

FOUR

In a dank dark cellar with the rats and the bats and other troll-like things.

Sleeping arrangements for all the children was a problem, not just for Mary, but for most of the families in the village—the problem the same, too many children in too few rooms. When they had all been small, it had been less of a headache, they could all sleep in two beds, topped and tailed, but even though Joe and Daniel were married and left home, with kids of their own, Mary still worried about how to fit the rest in two small upstairs rooms. There was hardly room to swing a cat around, let alone house eight children, especially since Harold and Edgar and the girls, Mary Margaret and Margaret Mary were all full grown, and even Eleanor at 16, coming on 17, was now a young woman in full bloom.

Mary solved the problem as best she could. It was easier when Harold and Edgar were on different shifts and Mary Margaret was to be wed next week, that should help, but it was unavoidable that brothers and sisters had to share the same room, the same bed, and she worried about it at times.

Not that she thought anything had happened, or that it would happen but, just to make certain, she made sure that whatever sleeping arrangements were current, Harold was never ever in the same room as the girls.

Which meant that Harold, Edgar, Isaac and Saul slept in one room, in one bed, and Mary Margret, Margaret Mary, Eleanor and Nicholas slept in the other. Which was all very cosy, and the girls did not mind a bit, but Nicholas did get so terribly embarrassed at times, because no matter how hard you tried, with three full grown girls in the same bed, it was difficult not to occasionally brush against a plump breast or firm buttock, or touch a leg or thigh, especially if a nightgown got rucked up in the night— and then what to do with a raging erection that always, always came on at the most embarrassing times, and particularly in the morning when he had to get up to go to the privy? He dared not use the buckets that everyone else used at night.

Nicholas loved his half brothers and sisters, except possibly for Harold, loved especially Eleanor, would most probably die for Eleanor, but he never felt a part of the family in the same way that the other children seemed to. He thought it might because he came from a different mother, but the twins were fully accepted. They were not isolated on the periphery of the family as Nicholas felt that he was.

Sometimes he felt like a lodger, living and eating with the family, but still outside of it, tolerated, but still not kindred. He could only suppose that it was because he was the brainy one, expected to do better than become a miner, and because of that, remained outside the close bonds that the pit produced in a family.

Nicholas knew that Harold despised him for his cleverness, knew that Harold sneered at him for his books, calling him a four-eyed sissy-freak and a crybaby mother's boy, afraid to go down the mine and do a real man's work, yet at the same time he was resentful that Nicholas had the chance to better himself.

Harold had always been spiteful to him, even as a child— used to kick his shins under the table until they were bruised black and blue, or spit at him when he thought no-one was looking, or twist his arm in an Indian rope burn, or stick nettles and thistles down his shirt, and the more Nicholas fought back, the more Harold would hurt him, and there was very little that a boy could do against another who was five years older than you, five years bigger than you.

And to tell tales to Mam or Dad only made it worse, would only result in a bigger beating the next time.

Even now, with Nicholas at 15 and Harold at 20, he could feel an animosity pouring out from Harold like molten lava, willing him to fail, bitter that anyone should rise above him, wanting to smash whatever he himself could not have, wanting to bring the world down to his base level, to the lowest common denominator.

What Nicholas did not know, what nobody knew, except that in the deepest regions of her sub-conscious, Mary might suspect that Harold had once tried to kill him. He had still been a baby, only a few weeks old, and Harold resented the intrusion that Nicholas brought to his life. His new stepmother, Mary, had at first taken an interest in him that his real mother, always sick, always tired, always too ill to bear him much mind, had ever done. For the only time in his life, Harold had felt wanted, had not felt that the world wished he were not there.

The new baby, the hateful, puling, demanding new baby had changed all of that. There was no time to spare now for stories about Goldilocks and the Bears, or Little Red Riding Hood or his very own favourite, the Three Billy Goats Gruff (always hoping that the ending would one day change, that for once, just for once, the Troll under the bridge would get to kill and eat Big Billy Goat Gruff). The other younger children, Edgar and

Eleanor, had always been around in Harold's memory, had the same mother, and were therefore not intruders brought into the house from outside.

When Nicholas arrived, Harold felt he had become invisible, and the more he did to make himself visible, scratching on the walls with coal, pulling on Mary's skirts all day long, smearing clart on the privy wall or kicking a tin can around the yard when the baby was trying to sleep, the more he seemed to be pushed aside. 'Not now Harold, I've got to feed your brother' or 'Don't do that Harold, the baby is trying to sleep' or 'Harold, you just go and clear up that mess while I see to the baby.'

Always, always, always, the baby seemed to be in the way and to Harold the answer was obvious: the baby would have to go.

Five-year-old Harold waited until his sisters were out on errands and Mary had nodded off in her rocking chair, and then he stealthily slid past her and into the front room, where *it* lay asleep in the crib. He looked down at the sleeping babe, his heart beating with a bubbling excitement that was almost over-whelming.

The crib, with curved end panels so that it could be rocked back and forth to sooth the thing to sleep, had been handmade by Jack Garforth from odd bits of planking and wood scrounged from here and there and painted in a baby-blue colour, with a silly picture of a soppy lamb at the head that his Mam had painted. If it had been Harold's bed, he would have wanted a picture of the troll, whatever a troll might look like.

Grandma Blackett, his new Grandma, had made a flat firm pillow and quilted a cover for the thing, and Harold gently lifted the pillow from under Nicholas' head and placed it over his face, but it did not look right, it looked too obvious and Harold had enough animal cunning to realise that a small baby could not possibly drag a pillow up over his own face and that questions would be asked and fingers pointed, and he did not think that a mere strapping from his father would be his punishment. He would be taken away and locked up in a dank dark cellar with the rats and the bats and other troll like things.

He glanced anxiously back into the kitchen where Mary still dozed and scurried back to the crib, put the pillow back under Nicholas' head and then rolled him over and turned him face downwards into the suffocating folds of the feather filled pillow, holding the back of his head and pressing him down. Nicholas snuffled and scuffled. Harold could feel him kicking and fighting for air, his muffled cries and grunts deafening to his ears. He pressed harder, wanting to thrust the hateful thing right through the mattress. Nicholas was really kicking and wriggling now, and Harold was surprised just how much strength he possessed.

Something, possibly some deep-rooted maternal warning bell sounded in Mary, or maybe through the folds of half-sleep she simply heard Nicholas' smothered whimpering; whatever, she woke with a start, knew instinctively that something was wrong and hurried through to the front room.

Harold heard the clatter of Mary's chair rocking on the kitchen floor and quickly stepped back from the crib, just in time, as Mary ran through and picked Nicholas up, blue-faced and gasping, holding him to her as he fought to get air into his lungs.

She saw Harold, guilty-faced, toe scuffling in the corner, unable to meet her eye.

'What are you doing in here, Harold? You know your Dad doesn't let you in here.'

'Nothing, Mam.'

'Don't give me "nothing."'

'I … I heard the babby and come to see he were OK.'

'How long have you been in here? You been in here long?'

'No, Mam. I come in just now.'

'If you're lying to me, I'll tell your Dad. And you know what he'll do to you; you won't be sitting down for a week.'

'No. Honest Mam. I heard the babby, just now, came to see if he were right. Honest. You ask anyone, ask our Eleanor. She'll tell you, honest.'

Nicholas was crying lustily now, and Mary held him to her breast, shush-shushing him, rocking him in her arms, patting the back of his head. Harold was lying about something, she knew that, but refused to give substance to the dark lurking suspicion that he might have been trying to do something to Nicholas. After all, he's only five for goodness sake. What could a five-year-old do?

She looked hard at him once more. Again, he refused to meet her eye. He had definitely been up to something and all she could think of was that he had been looking for money to steal. Jack sometimes left his small change on the sideboard and had thought once or twice before that pennies and the odd sixpence had gone missing (actually it had been Daniel, stealing money to buy cigarettes, but neither Jack or Mary ever discovered that and always and forevermore blamed Harold).

'Have you been stealing? Shall I tell your Dad on you?' she demanded, scowling at him. 'Tell him you've been after nicking money?'

'No Mam, honest, I weren't,' he squealed, the prospect of being reported to his dad for stealing, which he hadn't been doing, was only slightly less horrifying than being taken away and locked in a cellar with the rats and the bats and the trolls. His Dad would skin him alive, and he burst into tears, knowing his new mam had a soft heart and was a sucker for tears. 'I only come in to see the babby. I ain't been nicking. Honest I ain't. Honest,' he sobbed.

'Are you sure? Truthfully? And remember, God will punish you if you lie.'

'Yes, Mam, I'm sure. God's honest truth. I've not been nicking. Never.'

'Get on out of it then. And don't let me ever catch you in here again. Else you will be answering to your Dad.'

'Thanks Mam. Thanks … er … is the babby all right?' he asked hesitantly as he sidled out, trying to keep out of arms reach. His new mam might be a soft touch, but she was quite capable of boxing his ears for him; she had done it more than once before now.

'Aye, just a bit of wind, eh?' She held him up to peer into his face.

And Nicholas, who knew no better, said nothing.

Mary kept her barely formed suspicion well hidden, never giving it voice or thought again. Nevertheless, sub-consciously or not, she never allowed Harold to be alone with Nicholas, or Isaac and Saul when they were babies, ever again.

As for Harold, he knew he'd had a lucky escape, and knew he that would never get away with it again either and so contented himself with making Nicholas' life a misery whenever he had the opportunity.

FIVE

I thought thee were about to bring your lungs up, an' all.

Jack Garforth had finished the kerving, undercutting of the coal-face and hewing out the base of the seam, chopping out a foot-high groove at the thrill or floor of the mine. Now, he was cutting the vertical grooves at each side of the mass he wanted to bring down.

It was a poor cavil that he and his team of 'marras' had pulled this quarter, drawing a narrow unyielding seam, wet bottomed, with the ceiling barely 4'0'high, and it was desperately hard work to make up good weight, the headroom too low to swing the pick effectively.

He sat back on his small stool, called a cracket, taking a short breather, wiping the sweat from his brow with his arm. Jack Garforth was now 57 years old, a nuggetty little man with great strength in his shoulders and arms, but his back was bent from years of crouching in thin, confined coal seams, his shoulders hunched from stooping through low mine tunnels for all his working life and, as the years passed, it became harder and harder to relax the knotted muscles in his neck and shoulders and legs at the end of his shift.

The pit had been his life for 45 years, *45 years*, and if he ever thought about it at all, it seemed barely yesterday since he had started work as a 12-year-old boy, trying to hide his nervousness as he climbed into the first deck, the lower deck, of the cage, his lamp clutched tight, as if it were the only lifeline to the surface again.

His heart was in his mouth as the cage started its descent to the depths below and he remembered his terror as the cage seemed to hurtle out of control down the mineshaft, the slimy-dank impenetrable, heathen, shaft walls rocketing past at such speed that it seemed impossible, inconceivable, that it could ever slow down, could ever stop before it smashed them to bloody pulp on the shaft bottom. Or what if there were no shaft bottom and they carried on falling, hurtling through the pitch-black, malevolent void forever?

He had closed his eyes, trying not to scream out his panic, no longer the cocky self-assured youth going off to work like any other man, but a very frightened 12-year-old boy who had been afraid to hug his mother goodbye that morning in case everyone thought him soppy, but he wished above all wishes he could give her that hug now.

God answered his prayers and the cage suddenly slowed and stopped, and the miners began to slide out. 'Follow on, then lad,' Thomas Bears, the miner next to him said, nudging him with a sharp elbow to the ribs.

'I dun'naw where t'gan. Dun'naw what t'do,' Jack answered in a small voice, unsure of himself, forgetting all that he had been told at the surface, knowing he had made a fool of himself, knowing they would sack him for bollocksing up on his very first day and then what would his Dad say? For losing his job before he had even started? Except he would probably say nought but reach straight for his belt and tan the arse off him.

Jack's dad was a man short on temper, short on words, but long with his belt. Jack felt very close to tears.

'First day down is it, then lad?' Thomas Bears had asked, not unkindly and led him over to where the fore overman stood checking all the lamps. 'Another little canary, for you, Wilson.' He turned to Jack, standing very small and subdued beside him. 'This here's Wilson Wragg, you know him no doubt, because he lives near to thee on Helena Street. He's the fore overman, got too big for his boots for my way of thinking, but think nought on it. He'll take care on thee. Gan canny then lad.'

Wilson Wragg. Why did all the Wragg family have first names like surnames, Jack asked himself when thinking back. There had been Wilson Wragg, the fore overman. Pearson Wragg, who had caused a scandal by leaving his wife and running away with Miss Appleby, the Sunday School teacher. Then there was Jackson Wragg, married to Ida Pearson and living on Whitton Lane. There had been Pringle Wragg, Gardiner, Robson, and Haswell Wragg, and even a daughter called Scarlett Wragg, so named because her father Richardson Wragg had been a soldier, a trooper with the Heavy Brigade under General Scarlett in the Crimea. She had married an Irishman, Padraic O'Hara, and emigrated to America, and were now living somewhere in the South.

Be that as it may, Wilson Wragg had told Jack to go with a lad called Will Barnwell, who set him to work as a trapper, opening a closing a ventilation trapdoor to let the putters and the drivers with their pit ponies through.

Jack had knocked his lamp over, and it had gone out and he had spent a very long, very miserable, very lonely, and very dark first day as a miner. He had worked as a trapper for nearly a year before Wilson Wragg sent him to go with another lad and learn his job.

It was the time he enjoyed most in all his years in the pit because he was working with the pit ponies, known as galloways. He had Freddie, his own pony, his very own galloway to work with, shunting the tubs of coal to the shaft for the on-setter to load onto the cages and taking the empties back for the putters.

It was a wondrous time for Jack; he loved his galloway more than any other creature that ever came into his life. At the beginning of each shift, he would collect him from the white-washed stables at the pit-bottom, always with a titbit or two for him from his breakfast, or maybe an apple scrumped from Quantrill's apple trees, and the day never seemed too long when he was working with his pony.

It all but broke his heart when the Deputy moved him on from driving the galloways and onto a team at the face. At first, he worked as a putter, serving the hewers with empty tubs and taking away the full ones, and then after a collapse at the south face which had killed nine men, he was made up to hewer. And had been one ever since.

Jack worked at the vertical grooves again, cutting at the coal with short, heavy chops, unable to get into a position to get at it properly. He worked rapidly for a few minutes before he had to stop to take breath, feeling his chest heave from his efforts, panting in short desperate gasps to drag more air into his lungs, trying to keep his mouth closed and only breathe through his nose and prevent coal dust from getting to his chest, even though he knew the dust would take him away someday soon anyway. At times he felt so short of breath, he thought he was suffocating, as though his lungs were full to bursting with choked up dust. And when he coughed!

Even as he thought about it, he could feel a rasping wheeze tickling at his chest, growing to a tightness cramping his breast-bone, and he turned to cough into his hand, a dry harsh cough, raking the back of his throat like claws.

The paroxysm grew worse, lung-bursting hacking coughs that pulled and tore at his stomach muscles, tears streaming from the corners of his eyes as he thought his chest and heart would explode from the strain. At last, the spasm slowed, and Jack wiped the tears away and hawked noisily to the side, feeling the thick phlegm slimy on his tongue, yet gritty from dust.

'Jesus, that 'un were a bugger, and no mistake,' he gasped to Jim Comby, his marrow, the putter who kept Jack served with empty tubs and took the loaded ones away.

'Aye man, I thought thee were about to bring your lungs up, an' all.'

'Might as well. The buggers are no bloody use to me no more.' Jack hawked again, trying to clear the vile taste left on his tongue. 'Jim, you got any tea left? Mine's all done.'

'Aye, Jack, hold on.' And, after a minute or so, Jack felt Jim pass him his mash-tin, a white enamel jug with a cup-shaped lid. Jack poured out a mouthful of cold milk-less tea and swilled it around his mouth, feeling tea leaves catching in the gaps in his teeth like mackerel in a purse-seine net.

The sharp tannin of the tea tasted fresh and clean to Jack's sour palate, and he swirled it around his tongue again, savouring the acidic, faintly metallic taste before swallowing it down. 'Thanks Jim, I needed that.'

He hooked a few tea leaves from his teeth with the tip of his tongue, spat them out, stretched tight with his elbows scrunched into his waist to ease his aching neck, cramped and knotted from working for hours in a crouching position, eased his hogger trousers out from his crotch, and picked up his windy pick. 'Right, yer bugger,' he addressed the coalface. 'Let's be getting you down and out the fucking way.' Quickly, he chopped away to finish the vertical cuts.

Taking up his hand drill, he adjusted the height of the stand and jammed it between the thrill and the ceiling, tightening the threaded shaft as tight as he could with the tommy bar to hold it in place, and then slotted in the drill, positioned the cutting bit where he wanted the shot holes and began to turn the cranked handle, swearing under his breath as the bit at first refused to take. 'Come on you little fucker,' he muttered. 'Take, you useless bastard, take.' Grunting between clenched teeth, he felt the bit spinning without cutting.

He placed it again, hoping to find a softer patch of seam. This time the bit took, and Jack slowly drilled the shot hole, grunting with the strain of working bent double, which made it hard to get enough leverage on the crank, the sweat on his palms making it difficult to get a tight grip on the handle.

At last it was done, the shot hole about a yard deep, and he withdrew the drill, unfastened the stand, folded it up and put it to one side. Adjusting his carbide lamp to get a better view of the hole, he blew out the loose dust, sneezing as the fine powder tickled his nasal membranes, and then blew his nose into his fingers and flicked the snot away, where it hung on the wall like a small green-black grape.

The hole was then packed with black powder squibs, which Jack had brought from the powder magazine on the surface. He put in the pricker and sealed the hole; it was illegal to use anything other than clay for this, but clay was hardly ever available, so the miners used the only other obtainable material, which was of a similar texture and consistency to clay. Jack undid his belt, unhooked his braces, dropped his trousers, squatted down and defecated at the side of the works.

Holding his breath against the noisome, enclosed stench, which smelled almost as bad as Jeb Fulcher's midden, which said something, Jack scooped up the clarts, and sealed up the hole. Rubbing his hands in dust and wiping them on the walls to get rid of as much of the shit as possible, he then pulled out the pricker, which left a hole through to the powder, and inserted the final squib, and after clearance from the Deputy, carefully lit the fuse, standing well back.

Many a miner had had accidents with the black powder like that, to be left burned and scarred. Jack's neighbour, Charlie

Spearman, bore a vivid blue powder burn on his face, a patch on his cheek like crumpled blue cloth which, when combined with his straggly brown beard and red nose, gave him the angry appearance of an intemperate cross-eyed mandrill.

After the explosion, which echoed around the chambers like a thunderclap, Jack, coughing and spluttering in the thick choking dust, trying to breathe with his handkerchief clapped tight over his mouth and nostrils, barely waited until the dust had stopped swirling before picking up his shovel and began to load the empty tubs.

Paid only by the weight of coal recovered, it made no matter how much lay on the floor; all of was totally worthless until it been loaded and weighed, and Jack shovelled with a fury, closing his mind to the pain in his back and the ache in his lungs, trying to remember what he had read that morning from *Barnaby Rudge*, but for once it had escaped him. All through his shift he racked his brains, but not one single word came to him and, unable to lose himself as usual in his Dickens, the shift seemed endless.

SIX

The black ball of apprehension that still lurked, like a stalking predator.

Mary Garforth had finished her morning's work and was just taking a short nap in her chair again when she heard the back gate latch click open and the squeal of hinges, thinking as she always did, 'I've told him time and time again about oiling them hinges, every day the same,' but knowing she would say nothing else about it.

Jack Garforth stumped in.

Even through the coal grime on his face, Mary could see that he was grey-faced and worn, ragged with exhaustion, but her relief at seeing him alive was like a dam of warm water breaking over her and she ran to embrace him, unmindful of the dirt on him. She needed to hug him to her. 'Jack, Jack, I'm so glad to see you, I've been so worried.'

'Worried? What's thee been worried about then, lass? I've not seen you like this afore.'

'I just had this bad feeling all day. Worried. It's been sitting heavy on me, all day. I felt sure something was going to happen, all day I've been listening, expecting the siren to sound at any minute. Every time I heard loud voices, I thought it was somebody about to say that the pit had gone off.'

'Thee always was a silly little kitten, Mary.' He chucked her under the chin, and she smiled at the childish endearment. 'You just stop worrying your silly head. Nowt's going happen lass, not to me, not to the lads. Not to anybody. Right?'

'Aye, Jack, pet. If you say so.' But reassuring words could not drive away the black ball of apprehension that still lurked, like a stalking predator, in the pit of her quivery stomach. 'If you say so,' she repeated, not believing a word of it.

'I do say so. So, let it out your mind and give us a hand with these bloody boots, me back's an absolute bugger today and I can hardly bend for it.'

'Aye right, pet. And your bath's ready and when you've done, I'll rub some liniment in, if you'd like.'

'Aye, that'd be grand, pet. Then I'll rub some on thine, eh Mary? Us old buggers should take care on each other.'

SEVEN

The growing bleakness in her soul.

Joe Garforth, Jack's eldest surviving son, put down his knife and fork, took another sip of tea and picked up the *Daily Sketch* again, quickly scanning the headlines before throwing it aside. He had finished his shift at two o'clock and now felt restless and irritable, checking the time from the clock on the mantle shelf every minute or so; it was now just gone a quarter past three.

His wife, Lizzie, came over and took away his plate. 'Do you want anything else, Joe? Another cuppa?'

'No thanks, Lizzie love, I'm away down the Institute in a minute and if I have more tea, there'll not be no room for ale.'

At that, Lizzie pursed her mouth tightly in disapproval, pressing her lips into a thin-cut scar of displeasure. Like all the other miners, Joe had been on strike, and Lizzie did not appreciate the fact that the children had to live on bread and potatoes while Joe still had money for beer.

Not that she approved of drink anyway. The sermon at the chapel on Sunday had made it very clear that strong drink was the work of the Devil; she had explained this to Joe, as reasonably as she could, but he had only told her to 'getaway on out of it' and asked if drink were the work of the Devil, 'how come Jesus turned water into wine at the wedding in Canaa?'

She couldn't answer him directly, but she would speak to Mr Evenham, the rector at the chapel, as he would certainly have the right answer, and was sure Joe would take notice if she could only explain it properly to him.

Before her marriage to Joe, Lizzie used to be a Wesleyan, and went to the chapel in Scranton, where she had lived, and carried on going there for a year or so after her wedding, but recently she had been going to the 'Primitive Methodists' on Ashbrook Lane in the village. It was more convenient, for one thing, and she had found in its fundamental doctrine a puritanical austerity that complimented the growing bleakness in her soul.

Marriage to Joe had not been the bed of roses she had been led to believe it would be when they had been courting.

Not only did he drink, and more and more often at that, but he wanted to indulge in fornication more often than she deemed necessary. She had done her duty by him and acceded to his demands when they were first wed, after all it was her Christian duty as a wife and she had fulfilled it, bearing him three children in as many years, but his loathsome, unwholesome advances continued, almost nightly, especially when he was in drink, pawing at her, sour-breathed and heavy handed, as he would be tonight, no doubt.

The dumplings and gravy of his dinner were sitting heavy in Joe's stomach and he belched slightly, drawing another scowl of disgust from Lizzie. 'That's all she ever seems to do. Whatever I do these days, she takes monk on about it.'

He thought how much she had changed since they had wed. She had always been a bright-eyed lively girl, sparkling like soda, that was what had first attracted him to her, but Lord how she had turned since then. She seemed to have lost all glimmer of humour, all the colour seemed to have drained away from her personality, so much so that she was almost a different person altogether. She even looked smaller and thinner; she was a dried-out husk of the young girl she used to be, like an old woman.

They hardly ever laughed together and were forever at it, like squabbling starlings, as Lizzie needled and goaded him, prodding at him all the time with the sharp side of her tongue. 'Whatever it was that gets up her nostrils all the time, I wish she would spit it out.' And she never wanted to know in bed anymore, turning away and curling up tight with her back to him. 'She never used to be like that, the three bairns were proof enough of that.'

The children in question, or at least the two youngest, Sophie, nearly two years old, and George, 11 months coming on 12, (Mary, the eldest at three and a bit was across the yard, playing with Alice Tunstall, who was nearly four), were crawling and capering around the floor, under your feet as usual, but Joe didn't mind that; he found a peace and comfort with his kids that he no longer found with Lizzie and he looked fondly down at them.

Sophie seemed intent on exploring the inner reaches of the coal scuttle and had smeared coal dust through her shock of yellow-gold hair and across her face, sticking to the jam around her face like a crust, as George seized hold of Joe's trousers and precariously hauled himself upright, let go and, with his arms swirling like a windmill, fought for balance and, suddenly finding equilibrium, stood beaming up at his dad, overcome by the magnitude of his achievement.

Joe scooped him and held him over his head, tickling his ribs as George gurgled and squealed in delight and Sophie abandoned her search for whatever in the coal scuttle and scurried over to him. 'Me Dad, me Dad. Me.' And he set George down again, holding him under the armpits until he had his balance and let him go, at which he promptly forgot how to stay upright and collapsed back onto his bottom with a soft plop.

Sophie squirmed up onto Joe's lap, there to be soundly tickled, before he set her down in turn.

'Right then, Lizzie, I'm off.'

'You going to be long?' The vinegar-sour scowl was on her face again.

'As long as it takes.'

'And how long's that likely to be? All day, no doubt, but you'll be back here before you go on shift, expecting your dinner on the table.'

'It won't be all day. I've never been and gone and left you all day, you know that. But like I say, it'll take as long as it takes.'

'Aye, as long as the money lasts out, you mean, and with the kids supping on dry bread and scrape again.'

'There's always been food for the kids, and don't you say it otherwise.'

'Aye, and who puts it there? Who has to skimp and scrape and make do and go without whilst thee's got money in your pocket for ale?'

'Don't go on at it all the time, Lizzie. A man's got a right to a beer or two, working like a dog as I do. You don't go short, none of you do.'

'Well, you certainly make sure that you don't go short, I'll give you that; you always make sure you take care of yourself.'

'Leave it alone, woman, why don't you?' Joe muttered as he brushed past her, feeling the heat of anger flaring in him like an opened furnace door. He stumped out across the backyard, slamming the gate hard behind him so that it rattled back and forth on its hinges, and turned down along Exham Lane, as if heading into the village proper.

However, at the junction, he turned right instead of left and took the Etherington Road. Once past the edge of the village, he climbed over the drystone wall at the side of the road and hurried across Quantrill's fields, heading up Marley Hill, towards West-field Copse.

The shade of the trees in the copse felt cool after the bright sunlight, and he shivered slightly as the sweat on his back chilled under the sharp, black shadows. Taking a path that ran off to the left, into the depths of the copse, Joe walked on steadily, noticing how the dense woods seemed to muffle sounds, how even the birdsong and insect buzz were muted, deadened by the weight of shadow.

At the far side of the copse, where the path leads out into fields overlooking the Top Road, he stopped and looked around, making sure that nobody else was about, before turning back and nodding his head towards a patch of deeper shadow under a clutch of high standing sycamore trees. A young woman stepped out from beneath the trees and ran over to him.

'Why aye, Joe, I thought you were never coming, pet. I'd all but given up.'

'Sorry Ethel, love. Only Lizzie were going on and I thought it best to let her have her say. It only poisons her up, otherwise.' he said as Ethel Poskit slipped her arm into his and pressed it against her full, heavy breasts.

'Well, ne'er mind all that now. Forget about her and give us a kiss and let's get on. Heaven knows how I've been aching for you these past days, Joe. Aching!' And she led him back into the shade where she had been waiting. They kissed hungrily, and Jack could feel himself growing hard against her. She broke the embrace and sat down on the sheet she had already spread out, and held out her arms to him, her eyes sparkling with antic-ipation.

'Come down 'ere, Joe, I've got some'at for thee.'

'Where's Sam this afternoon?' Joe asked as Ethel pulled him down alongside her.

'In with his pigeons. You know Sam … once he gets inside with his blessed pigeons, nowt'll get him out 'til dark.'

Joe lifted her skirts and ran his hand up the inside of her smooth thighs and into the leg of her drawers as she arched her hips to meet his probing fingers.

'Tell you what, lass,' he whispered, 'once I get inside thee, nowt'll get me out again 'til dark, neither.'

EIGHT

Like lemmings scrambling to get the best view of the sea from the cliff tops.

The Garforth twins, Isaac and Saul, grinned at each other across the width of the classroom, devilment in their eyes. Even though they had long been separated, no longer sitting together as being too disruptive in class, they still worked together on that intuitive level of perception that twins often have, sometimes changing places and claiming to be the other.

Isaac showed Saul his cupped hand; he had a hard pellet of paper, the size of a large pea, which he had chewed and compressed into a solid ball. Saul nodded and grinned again, pointing with his finger at the back of Stephen Wilson's neck. Hidden below the lip of his desk, Isaac wrapped a thick rubber band around the thumb and forefinger of his right hand (he was lefthanded, Saul righthanded, and as mirror-image twins, it the only obvious difference between them), slotted the pellet into the loop of elastic and drew it back with his left hand, took quick aim and fired.

The pellet zipped across the room like an angry hornet, missed Stephen Wilson's neck altogether and hit Tommy Grandle smack on his cheek. With a squeal of sudden pain, he jumped to his feet. 'Bloody 'ell,' he shouted, rubbing his face vigorously, 'some'ats stung me. Bloody wasp or something.'

'Sit down, Grandle,' said the class teacher, Mr Byers.

'No, honest sir, some'at hit me. Here, on me face, doesn't half sting.'

'Sit down and stop making such a fuss, Grandle. Most likely, it's only a fly or something. Any excuse to disrupt the lesson.'

Molly Hindle, seated on the other side of the aisle from Isaac, raised her hand—'Please sir, it was—'—only to be silenced by a warning glare from Saul.

'Yes, Molly. you wanted to say something?'

'Er, no, Mr Byers.'

'You had your hand up.'

'Just to say it was … er … a wasp, sir. A wasp. I saw it.'

'Alright then Grandle, it was a wasp. Now, will you sit down and let us get on with the lesson? Even though it might well be one of the last ones most of you will ever have?'

'Sir,' Tommy answered, barely appeased, and as he sat he found the pellet on his desk. He was about to say something else, realised where the attack had most likely come from, turned around to look at Saul, who grinned wolfishly at him, daring him to say anything. Tommy subsided back into his chair, contenting himself by merely rubbing his cheek in pained resignation; like all the other boys in the class, he was afraid to cross the twins, who were a formidable combination in playground fistfights.

At last, the bell went for the end of the lesson, the end of the day.

'Right,' shouted Byers. 'Put your books and pens away quietly. No banging of desk lids."

Which, of course, resulted in a tremendous clatter. Some boys (not Isaac and Saul, who knew they would be under espe-

NEVER SUCH INNOCENCE AGAIN

cial scrutiny) banged their desk lids three or four times. Then, Molly Hindle let out a piercing scream. 'Aaaahhhh. A mouse! A mouse! Someone's put a dead mouse in my desk. Get it out somebody, please, oh God, get it out!'

Isaac and Saul didn't even look at each other. Saul had found the little dead rodent out the back earlier on and slipped it in Molly's desk just before class had started. Isaac hadn't known that Saul had done it until now, but immediately the telepathic bond with his twin told him that it had been him and he knew that any sort of reaction would result in a visit to Proctor's study for the pair of them and at least six strokes of the cane on each hand. And their Dad would be told, which meant a thrashing from him as well.

Molly was still screaming and panicking, Byers was ineffectually trying to regain order and placate Molly at the same time. 'You boy, Garforth—never mind Molly—Isaac, Saul, whichever one you are. Be quiet a minute, Molly, after all the thing is dead. Did you put that mouse there, Garforth? Do stop crying, Molly. If you did, it's Mr Proctor's study for you. Oh, for goodness sake, Molly. Never mind. You, Saul, Isaac, whichever one you are,'—pointing a bony finger at Isaac—'just get the creature out from Molly's desk and then get out of my sight, the lot of you. The quicker I am rid of you all the better.'

Children, 12- and 13-year-olds, almost 14-year-olds, boiled out of the classroom like lemmings scrambling to get the best view of the sea from the cliff tops. Within seconds, the room was deserted, apart from Molly and Isaac who had gone over to Molly's desk and lifted the dead mouse out by its tail.

'Urghh. Don't show it to me, put it away,' she squealed as she shivered and shook in horror. 'Don't let me even see it. Oh, I can't stand mice, it makes me ill to even think about 'em.'

'It's' all right now, it's gone,' said Isaac who, having nowhere else to put the mouse, had put it into his trousers pocket, where it nestled amongst a dirty hankie, three marbles, two clay ones and a glass alley, his rubber-band catapult, two farthings, a dog-end, and a considerable amount of dust and fluff.

'Thanks Isaac, ugh, makes me ill, it's stupid, I know, but it just makes me feel ill.' And then, realising that there was at least a 50% chance that Isaac had been the one to have put her through such torment, she backed away. 'It was you what did it, weren't it? You, else Saul.'

'It weren't me Molly, honest,' Isaac answered, noticing for the first time how pretty Molly Hindle had become, how her blouse had suddenly, and very nicely, started to fill out, and he blushed, in case she had seen him looking. 'It were Saul. I'm sorry, I didn't even know he were going to do it. Else I would have stopped him.'

They walked slowly toward the classroom door.

'You know,' Molly said, 'you and Saul being twins, and twins is supposed to be the same as each other, and when you swap places and Mr Byers can't tell which one is which? I can, always.'

'How come? Even our dad gets us mixed up sometimes.'

'You're nicer.'

'Aye? Getaway on out of it.' But pleased, nevertheless.

'It's true. If it had been Saul what'd picked the mouse out from the desk, he would've tried to wave it under me nose, or stuff it down the back of my dress. You didn't.' She giggled, a little girlish giggle, but the coquettishness behind the laugh was all woman. 'What's it like having a dead mouse in yer trousers pocket?'

'It's' alright. Better than having a live one, I suppose. Least it can't bite.' And they laughed together, rather more loudly than the comment warranted.

Saul was waiting by the gate as they walked over, a furious scowl on his face as he saw Isaac with Molly.

He took Isaac's arm and led him away, and Isaac was suddenly quite sorry to leave Molly's company.

'Tarrah then, Molly,' he called over his shoulder to her.

'Tarrah then, Isaac. See you tomorrow.' Molly waited until he was a few paces further on. 'Isaac!' she called and as both twins turned around, to his absolute and total mortification, she blew him a kiss.

'What're' doing with her?' Saul hissed angrily at Isaac. 'She were going to blab to Byers on thee, man.'

'Nay, she weren't. Anyhow, I like her,' Isaac answered defiantly.

'Tarrah then, Isaac. See you tomorrow then, Isaac,' Saul mimicked in a falsetto voice. 'Thee's going soft, Isaac. You'll be holding her hand to school next.'

'Who you calling soft?'

'You, you bloody big soft Jessie.'

Isaac flung himself at Saul, seizing him in a headlock as Saul pummelled at his legs and back before throwing them both to the ground, where they rolled and wrestled about in the dirt, scuffing up small tornadoes of dust and grass stalks.

Exhilarated by the sheer joy of scrapping, their argument was soon forgotten as the boys rolled and heaved and scrambled at each other, looking for wrist and arm and head locks, first one, then the other gaining advantage until, finally, Isaac caught Saul with a shoulder butt to the stomach and knocked him flat on his back and jumped astride his chest, pinning him to the ground. Saul wriggled and heaved, trying to shake Isaac off, but he couldn't, Isaac was able to hold tight onto Saul's shirt and kept him held down.

'Who's the big soft jessie, then?' Isaac panted.

'Thy art, buggerlugs,' Saul answered, barely able to speak for laughing.

'Who?' Isaac demanded again, rubbing dirt in Saul's hair and face.

'All right then, buggerlugs, we both are. How's that then, thee and me both, bloody big jessies.'

Knowing he would get nothing more than that from Saul, Isaac rolled off and the two boys laid side by side, panting from their exertions.

'She were still going to blab on you, Molly Hindle,' Saul said at last.

'Aye, I suppose she were really. I still like her though.'

'She's growing tits, that's why.'

'Wha'dya mean? Get away out on it, man,' Isaac answered, but blushing nonetheless, because he had been thinking about those enticing shapes inside Molly's blouse.

'Ask her nicely and she might let you feel 'em,' Saul leered, sensing he had struck a nerve.

'Don't you talk like that about her,' Isaac said, clenching his fists, ready to fight again. He felt angry, without really knowing why, except that he didn't want Saul to talk about Molly like that.

Saul, noting Isaac's reaction, said nothing, but he would store the information away for future use, just in case.

'What'll us do now?' he asked after a minute or so.

'Whadda want to do?'

'Don't know? Play footie?'

'No, it's too hot. Let's go home and get us catties and go hunt starlings, else rabbits or some'at.'

'Aye. Right. Up on Marley Hill. Loads of rabbits up there.'

They got up and set off home to get their (prohibited) catapults, hidden away under a loose slate in the backyard, prohibited ever since they had been shooting at tin cans on the privy roof and had broken the windows of Nellie Spearman's upstairs window. After thrashing the boys, Jack Garforth had put the offending weapons out with the rubbish, but Isaac had rescued them and stashed them away.

At the end of Exham Lane, Isaac suddenly broke into a sprint.

'Last one home's a big jessie, buggerlugs,' he shouted, and maintained his lead all the way to Victoria Street.

NINE

Small and bouncy and ebullient, like a puppy.

'Go on then, what did 'e say? Proctor? 'Ow many did you get?'
   'None.'
   'Bloody liar! Go on then, show us your hands,' Jamie Strawbridge demanded of Nicholas Garforth as he came out the side
door into the playground. 'Go on, show us. Nobody gets sent to
Proctor and comes out without strokes of the cane.'
   Jamie Strawbridge, inevitably known as Strawberry Jam or
Jammy by his pals, or Jamface by his enemies, was Nicholas'
closest friend, although Nicholas always felt that it was Jamie
who wanted to be friends with him, rather than the other way
round. He was small and bouncy and ebullient, like a puppy
bounding around a bigger dog wanting to play, and sometimes
Nicholas found him tiresome, infuriatingly infantile, and wanted
to smash his moon beam face, just because it was there, but
knew if he did, Jamie would only come bouncing back up again,
like a Kelly doll.

'I told you, I weren't caned.'

'Bloody liar, you must have been.' And he took hold of Nicholas' hand and pressed his thumb into the flesh of his palm and along his fingers, watching Nicholas' face, watching to see if he winced in pain, as he would have to if Proctor had caned him. 'Bloody Hell, you jammy sod. Last time I went to him, I got four. On each hand.' Aggrieved by what he saw as an injustice, everybody got caned when they went to Proctor, it was as immutable a law of nature as high tides at full moon.

'I didn't go to Proctor. Parsons didn't send me. Just give me a telling off, said to take more notice in future.'

'Bloody hell, he must be soft on thee. I mean, that rubbish you were spouting, it was dead obvious you hadn't been taking a blind bit of notice. I mean, he weren't talking about what you said at all, nothing to do with Walter bloody Scott and that other … whatever you were on about.'

'Jane Austen.'

'Aye, her.'

They had reached the gates of the Grammar, and as he always did, Nicholas looked over to the gates of the girls' school, hoping to see Sarah Treddle waiting for him, but she wasn't, and he felt a pang of disappointment, but then he shrugged. 'What the hell? I'm not really bothered anyway.' But he knew that he was.

'Nicky,'—he hated being called Nicky—'Nicky, you want to come round my house?' Jammy was asking. 'We can do some-thing. Play. Muck about. Whatever you want.'

'Nah, s'okay, but thanks. Got to get on back home, got my jobs to do, you know, else me Dad'll go spare.'

Jammy looked disappointed, almost distraught, but even if he didn't have some chores to do, Nicholas would have made some excuse, a diet of too much Strawberry Jam could be a bit wear-ing; sticky and cloying.

He said cheerio to Jamie and set off home, immediately

picking up a good fast pace. It was a long way back to Ashbrook, even taking the shortcut over the railway lines and across the lower fields by Becksdale Woods.

TEN

It most definitely was not a man-eating tiger.

Catapults tucked safely in the back pockets of their baggy well-patched grey shorts, the twins slunk out of the bottom end of Victoria Street before their mam could see them and call them back in to do jobs or run errands.

At the end of Ashbrook Road, they turned up Whitton Lane, heading towards the Church and then Marley Hill. As they walked along past the row of houses, they both looked at each one and nodded.

'Buggerman,' said Isaac.

'Aye, the buggerman,' responded Saul.

'BUGGERMAN, BUGGERMAN, BUGGERMAN,' they chanted softly to each other, like a tribal war cry. 'BUGGER-MAN, BUGGERMAN.'

Mrs Jim Comby, who had been cleaning up at the vicarage, looked askance at them as they marched past by her, heads down, so intent in their chanting that they hardly seemed to notice her, not quite sure that her ears had heard what they had. She shook her head and carried on, muttering under her breath what a handful they were and how Mary Garforth had always been too soft on them, thankful that they were not her children; her boys, Johnny and Ronnie, would never ever use language like that. Which goes to show how little she knew.

Outside number 22, the twins stopped and checked up and down the road, making sure that there were no tittle-tattling adults around to go telling tales to their mam and dad, bringing retribution about their ears, or to be more accurate, across the seat of their pants.

Satisfied the coast was clear, Saul took out his catapult and hammered hard on the door with the base of it, making little quarter-moon dents in the painted wood as Isaac pushed open the letter box and shouted through it as loud as he could. 'BUGGER-MAN, BUGGERMAN, BUGGERMAN. COME OUT, COME OUT WHEREVER YOU ARE!'

Laughing like drains in a cloudburst, the boys ran off as the door opened and Earnest Sowerbutts stood on his doorstep, waving his stick at them. 'BUGGERS. BUGGERS. Come back here you little buggers, come here you buggers! BUGGERS. BUGGERS.' Which was how he got his name and, for years and years and years, kids have been knocking on his door and running away.

Their merriment lasted almost all the way up Marley Hill and whenever the laughter showed signs of running down, like a clockwork mouse, it only needed for one or other of them to wind it up again by saying 'Buggerman' or 'Come back, you little buggers' or to shout 'BUGGERS, BUGGERS' as loud as he could across the affronted fields to reduce them to helpless fits of giggles again.

But even the best of mischief palls after a while, and after one or two false starts, the clockwork finally did run down for good. Besides, the serious business of finding ammunition for their catties was in full swing as each boy filled his pockets with small stones.

Small round pebbles, 1/2' or so in diameter were the best, but there were not so many of those to be found on the road and they had to make do with sharper, angular pieces of gritstone. The best place to find round pebbles was obviously by the river and they knew a short stretch, where the stream widened out and shallowed where you could find the perfect catty stone by the bucketful, by the barrow-load, but what they now had would be effective enough, if only they could actually hit something.

A magpie sitting on the wall swore at them as they went past and they both quickly drew a bead on him and fired—and both missed—their stones crossing in front of him and zipping past on either side. He twitched his black and white tail feathers contemptuously at them and laughed, swore again, and then flew off in great disdain. The boys didn't mind too much; after all, everybody knew that magpies were immortal and could not be killed.

Then Saul wanted to shoot at some cows. 'Let's get 'em. Right up the arse, watch 'em run.'

But Isaac wouldn't let him. The thought came to him that Molly wouldn't like it and it suddenly seemed important to be in good favour with her. He knew she could not see him, but somehow thought she would know anyway.

Climbing over the wall, they set a large stone on top of the wall and used that as a target, but neither hit it, although Isaac struck the wall just in front of the target and claimed that as a hit, but Saul wouldn't allow it.

Very quickly tiring of that, they continued over the fields towards Westfield Copse, occasionally stopping to stand close to cow pats and shoot into those, watching the cowshit and flies leap into the air in a soggy brown fountain, like shell shots, as the stones smacked through the thin outer crust of the dung-plop.

Coming up to Westfield Copse, they thought they might start

a rabbit although, in reality, chances of hitting a speeding rabbit were zero. They'd have a job even if the beast were tied helpless to a stake 6'0' in front of them. Or, if they couldn't find a rabbit, there were always starlings and other birds in the trees to shoot at. And miss.

They skirted round the edge of the Copse, keeping as quiet as they could (which was not very, 13-year-old coming on 14-year-old boys in hob-nail boots were not built for stealth), catapults loaded and a half cock, imagining that they were stalking a wounded man-eating tiger through the steaming jungles of Africa; their knowledge about the habitats of feline carnivores was not very extensive.

Saul was leading the hunt as they cast wary glances from side to side, Isaac covering their rear, as man-eaters could spring out from any direction. They rounded another clump of bushes when Saul suddenly held up his hand and held a warning finger to his lips, catapult still held tight in his hand, nearly poking his eye out in the process.

'What?' mouthed Isaac.

Saul motioned him forward with a jerk of his head and pointed into the trees. At first, Isaac could not see what he was looking for, and when he did see it, he could not believe what he was looking at.

It was a man's backside, naked, white-fleshed, thrusting.

'Whaaaat?' he mouthed again.

'Sssshh!'

Then he noticed the legs wrapped around hairy thighs and wondered how anybody could get their legs into such a position behind themselves like that before realising they had to be someone else's legs.

Saul put his mouth close to Isaac's ear. 'It's a courting couple. Fucking!'

Isaac looked again. He knew the word. Knew what it meant. But what he could see did not seem to correspond with what

Tommy Heslop had told them. He claimed to have watched through the bedroom keyhole and seen his married sister, Mavis, doing it with her husband when they had been first wed and still been living with her mother. Tommy said that Peter had been sitting on the edge of the bed and Mavis had been sitting on top of him, but then Tommy Heslop always was a bloody big liar, and nobody could believe a word of him.

He looked again, fascinated and excited; he could hear grunts and groans and wondered if it was supposed to be painful for the girl and then something about the shape of the man's head, the jut of the neck and shoulders, told him just whose backside it was, and he backed away suddenly, beckoning Saul with him.

'Bloody Nora,' he whispered, 'it's our Joe. He'll bloody kill us if he knows we been peeking on him.'

'Joe? Our Joe? *Brother* Joe?'

'Aye. Come on, let's gerroff before he catches us.'

'Are you sure?'

'Look for your bloody sen.'

'Nay, I'll take thy word for it. Who's that with 'im, then? It's not Lizzie. It'd not be church mouse Lizzie doing aught like that.'

'I dunno. And I'm not going to hang around and find out, neither. Thee knows our Joe, he'll bloody kill us, man. Bloody well murder us. Specially on aught like this.'

'Aye. You're bloody right there, and no mistake.'

'Come on, let's bugger off, sharpish. And keep it bloody quiet, man.'

As quietly as they could, Isaac and Saul backed away and as soon as they thought they were a safe distance away, broke into a run. Danger lurked in those woods and it most definitely was not a man-eating tiger.

ELEVEN

Doing as we shouldn't ought to be doing.

Ethel Poskit hooked her ankles around Joe's legs again and then grasped his buttocks tightly, wanting to hold him deep within her, arching to meet his thrusts when, through the luscious mist of her ecstasy, she thought she heard noises, rustlings, footsteps. She froze, tapping Joe urgently on his back. 'Joe! Joe! there's someone here. I can hear some'at, somebody around, watching.'

'What?'

'Ssshhh. Listen,' she whispered, 'there's someone nearby. I can hear them.'

Joe stopped in mid-stroke and listened … for all of five seconds. 'Nay, you're dreaming lass,' he said before thrusting deeply again and Ethel groaned with the sudden pleasure of it, clasped him close and was soon lost to the delicious insistence of his rhythm, feeling the climax rising in her, rushing to overwhelm her, and they both came, more or less together, he for the second time, she for the third.

They lay clasped together for a minute or two, panting,

before Joe raised himself on his hands and slowly withdrew from her, lingering the clench of her about him for as long as he could. When he finally pulled out completely, Ethel gave a little sigh, a sough of deprivation and then stretched out fully, luxuriating in the afterglow of orgasm.

'Oh Joe, if I were to die now, I'd die a happy woman.'

'You're some woman anyway, Ethel Poskit,' Joe responded with a smile. 'D'you know that? Thy Sam's a lucky man. Aye, a right lucky man.'

Ethel grimaced at the mention of Sam's name as Joe got to his knees, still between her outstretched legs. He bent down to tenderly kiss the soft flesh of her inner thigh and as he moved over, he slowly ran his hand up the length of her leg and cupped her mound, feeling their combined juices sticky in her pubic hairs. She wriggled slightly as he parted her wet labia and slid his first and second fingers into her, needing to feel the warmth of her again.

She closed her legs tightly, trapping him. 'I love you, Joe', she said quietly, looking up intently into his face. 'I do. Really, I do. And not just because of what we do … what we've just done. I love you so much, I could die when we're not together.'

Embarrassed, Joe tried to move away, remove his hand, but Ethel reached down and held his wrist, keeping him trapped inside her. 'I don't want you to say 'owt you don't mean, Joe. I mean, don't say you love me, not if it isn't true, just so you can carry on with me like his. I'd still let you do it, pet, I'd still want you to do it … even if you said the only reason you ever saw me was because I let you … do me. I love you so much, I'd still want you to do it, even if you hated me.'

'I don't hate you, Ethel love, don't go thinking like that. I think you're a grand lass.'

'But you don't love me?'

'I didn't say that,' he said uncomfortably, finally extricating his hand and starting to put his clothing back together, pulling his underwear and trousers up from around his ankles.

'You don't have to say it, Joe. That you love me. You don't have to say anything. Just let me love you, that's all I ask.'

Joe stroked her neck, and she turned her face into his touch. 'It'd make me proud to have you love me, Ethel. I mean that. Proud. And I do want to see thee often as I can and not just for this, either.'—lightly touching her pubis again—'You're a grand lass, Ethel. A grand woman, a lady and I wish you were mine. Aye. Properly.'

'I am yours, Joe. I'll always be yours.'

'Aye, like this maybe. Furtive. Starting at shadows. Lying to Sam. Lying to Lizzie. I don't like that, not one bloody bit. The deceit. I wish things were different, that's all I can say. I wish it could be different—proper. Then, perhaps, I could love you as thee deserves to be loved—not like this hole in the corner business.'

'I'll settle for what I can get, Joe. If the only way I can get even a part of you is like this, I'll take it.'

'Even though we both know it's not right?' he asked gently.

'I love you Joe, and love knows no right or wrongs. Least-wise, not *my* love. I know I shouldn't love you, but I do. I know we shouldn't be doing this, but we do, and we will again, so there's the end of it.'

'And Sammy? What about Sammy? Don't you love him? You must have loved him to marry him?'

'No. I never loved him,' Ethel replied matter-of-factly. 'I don't even know why I married him, and I knew I'd made a mistake as soon as I'd done it, but as my ma said, I've made my bed and now I've got to lie on it. That doesn't mean to say that Sammy is going to lie on it with me though.'

'He doesn't …?'

'Not much. He'd rather be with his pigeons, I reckon, and I don't give him no encouragement, you can be sure of that. I wish

69

we'd met before Joe, before I married Sam. Even if you'd still been married to Lizzie, I would have kept myself for you alone.' Ethel sighed quietly. 'Sometimes the world is so unfair.'

'The world's not meant to be a fair place, is it, Ethel, love? Here we are, both with the wrong spouse, you with Sam and me with Lizzie, and there's nowt we can do about it, is there? We're stuck with it, and as much as I don't like doing it to Lizzie, after all, it's hardly her fault, but no doubt we'll be up here again before long, doing as we shouldn't ought to be doing.'

Joe had finished straightening his clothes and fastened up his fly buttons and now was adjusting his braces over his broad shoulders.

'Nay Joe, it's not a fair world, is it? But, as I've told you, I'll settle for what I can get. Except I can't hardly look Lizzie in the face without I'm thinking it shows.'

'Talking of Lizzie, I'd best be off. Stop by the 'Tree', couple of pints, else she'll be wondering why I don't smell of ale.'

'Tha'd best make sure you don't smell of me an'all.'

'I'll get me'sen a wash at the 'Tree', aye.' He stood up and brushed himself down and then held out his hand to Ethel. 'You coming, love? Though we'd still best go back different ways.'

'No pet. You gan on, I'll stay on here a while. I want to fix it all in my mind—everything—the look of you, the touch of you on me, *everything*, so's I can remember it and think of you all those lonely nights when you're not with me.'

'Aye, right then, love.'

'When'll I see you again, Joe? Make it soon. I just die inside when we're apart.'

'I'm on afternoon shift next week. What's Sam on?'

'Early.'

'Next Monday morning then? About 10? Unless it's raining.'

'I'll come anyway, even if it does rain. Just in case you had come, and I'd missed you.'

He bent down and kissed her lightly on the cheek. 'Ta-ra then, Ethel love. Take care.'

'And thee.'

She waited until he had gone a few paces. 'I love you, Joe Garforth.'

He stopped and stood with his back to her for a good few seconds before turning around. 'I love you an' all, Ethel Poskit.'

TWELVE

The dreary lives of the impecunious or of the miner.

Nicholas felt hot and sticky. Even though it was late afternoon, the sun still had a lot of heat left in it and the baked dry ground was throwing convected heat back into the oven-hot atmosphere.

He stopped to wipe his brow again and pull his sticky sweat-soaked shirt away from his back and armpits. He had grown too big for it and his perspiration made it chafe him even more under his arms and on his biceps. His feet felt tight-swollen and molten hot in his boots, but he daren't take them off; he knew he'd never get them back on again, because they were getting too small as well.

The events of the extraordinary English lesson kept coming back to him. He still couldn't really begin to believe it—the mere fact that he had not been sent to Proctor was amazing enough, then that incredible after-lesson scene with Parsons. He definitely could not begin to believe in that...and then his unconsidered and totally unexpected (to him as well) revelation about wanting to be a writer.

'I think that I would like to become a writer, sir.'

Parsons had said nothing for some seconds as Nicholas furiously scrambled around in his mind, trying to find out where that idea, that bizarre thought had come from.

'A writer, eh? A scribbler of words,' Parsons had said. Then he paused, as if trawling through the sea of quotations in his memory, casting his nets far and wide to find a suitable fish, but coming up, wanting on every throw, fishing in empty waters. No Biblical bream, no Shakespearean sardines, no poetical pilchards, and even mixing metaphors didn't help; like Mother Hubbard before him, Parsons still found the cupboard bare, and so resorted to repetition. 'A writer, eh?'

'Yes, sir. At least, I think so. Not sure really why I said that, but aye, I think I would like to be a writer.'

'Like Sir Walter Scott. From your learned dissertation it was obvious you approve of Walter Scott, if not of Jane Austen. An interesting monologue, by the way, Garforth. Of very little to do with my lesson, but of interest nevertheless, and if nothing else, it did display invention and imagination.'

'Thanks ... sir', he added as an afterthought. The whole situation had become so bizarre that Nicholas found difficulty in relating it to a normal pupil/teacher relationship any longer. 'No, sir, not like Scott, me to be a writer, I mean. I do like Scott, or rather I used to, but I don't think he ... relates any more to me ... me and my kind, I should say.'

'Explain.'

'Well, sir, writers like Scott ... and Jane Austen ... they write, or rather wrote, for people like them. I mean Scott, he was a Sir, wasn't he, and Jane Austen, she wrote about posh people in big houses down South...? But that doesn't mean owt to folk like me. For all it means to folk like me, she could be writing about native tribes in ... Africa or on't moon. It doesn't ... relate to us, nor we to it, but there's a lot of folk like us and nob'dy has ever written about people like me. Poor people, miners and such.'

'Dickens? He wrote about the poor. London poor.'

'Aye, but he wasn't of them, was he?'

'His father was imprisoned in the Fleet for debt.'

'Yes, but he were still … middle class, weren't he? Still on the outside, looking in, as far as being one of the poor, I mean. What I am trying to say, sir, is that I couldn't write about knights and kings, or posh folks down South or in London, because they're not real to me, but I could write about things I know. Poor people … miners and such.'

'Unfortunately, Garforth, the people who buy books are not likely to be much interested in the dreary lives of the impecunious or of the miner. I fear that a poor boy who writes books about the poor is likely to remain a poor boy.'

'But it's reality, sir.'

'Deluded fool. People do not buy books for reality, Garforth, they buy books to escape from reality.' And then the quotational fish began to leap, like spawning salmon, back into his mind. 'There is an apt proverb—fine words butter no parsnips. Profound words, Garforth.'

'Err, yes, sir. St Matthew?'

'No, boy. Scott, your erstwhile mentor, Garforth. Sir Walter Scott.'

Nicholas said nothing further. He could not express it any clearer than he had already tried to, but he knew what he meant, even if he could not properly explain it and, after a moment or two, Parsons merely said, 'Perhaps you are the common or garden variety dull boy, after all, Garforth. That behind your blank mask there is only yet another blank mask. Go, boy, be off with you. Perhaps my disappointment in you will not be as great as I fear.'

'Yes, sir. I'll be off then.'

'Go, bind thou up yon dangling apricocks.'

'Er … yes, sir. Of course, sir. Goodnight, sir.'

As quietly as he could, Nicholas slipped past the classroom door and closed it behind him as Parsons, lost in himself, began to quote the monologue from *Richard II*: 'Let's talk of graves, of worms and epitaphs…'

THIRTEEN

A brightly painted carousel with prancing horses and cockerels.

After Joe had left, Ethel lay there quietly, eyes closed, thinking of him, head on her forearm, listening to the buzz and hum of insects, still naked from the hips down, skirts hiked up around her waist. She seemed to have forgotten her earlier suspicions that there had been someone around. If there had been someone around, he would have had a fine view of Ethel as she lay there, legs asprawl, exposed and luxuriant, and it was not until some insect—a midge, a horsefly or mosquito—bit or stung her on the thighs that she had actually pulled her clothing down, no doubt trapping there-in whatever it was that had been lunching on her flesh.

She had been thinking of Joe and everything else tended to pale into insignificance.

Joe! The strength, the depth of her love for him was so over-whelming, so overpowering, that she knew that she would die without him, would want to die without him.

She had met him at the Miners Gala last month in Durham.

Was it really only last month? It seemed like a lifetime ago. Met him to fall in love with, that is. Of course she had known him around the village, ever since she had moved there from Bishops Shilton after her wedding, knew him well enough to say 'good morning' and 'good evening' and 'how is Lizzie, Mr Garforth?', that sort of thing, but it was at the Gala, and after, that she had fallen in love with him, fallen in love so deeply that it was frightening. Her heart simply seemed too frail to hold all the love she felt.

Gala Day. The greatest day of the year for any pit village. Everybody went to Durham for the Gala. The whole village community went. Shops closed for the day as shopkeepers and assistants joined in the march to the station to catch the train to Durham.

Long before six o'clock in the morning, it seemed as though the entire district had congregated beside the pit as kids too excited to have slept the night before raced round and round, the groups of miners and their wives lifting their hats and bidding each other 'good morning', and 'grand day for it' and 'hope the rain keeps off', self-conscious, all in their best clothes, trying not to get coal dust on them.

The Colliery Brass Band warmed up in the corner by the engine house and then, at the signal from John Longden, the bandmaster, the band began to play 'Onward Christian Soldiers' in earnest and after a hesitant pace or two and a shuffle-footed skip to get in step, set off to march through the village, then up the hill and along the top road to the station at Scranton, to catch the special train to Durham.

Kids marched in step alongside the band, swinging their arms in great self-importance, and as the procession passed through the eagerly waiting streets, more and more folk would join the procession, Hamelin-like, swelling along the road like an army on the march, complete with camp followers and stragglers.

When they arrived at Durham, the station was a bedlam,

with trains arriving every few minutes from all over the county, a milling throng of tens of thousands, the biggest single annual gathering of people in the county, a great outpouring of miners and miners' families, whole mining communities, forming behind their band, banners jostling like battlefield pennants. Many of the banners, too many of the banners, would be draped in black in memory of miners killed during the year. They all waited their turn to march through the city streets, streets lined with people by the thousand, through the market square, over the Wear Bridge with the great Norman cathedral and castle looking on from the heights and down to the racecourse.

All the shops in the city closed and put up their shutters, and down at the racecourse, traders were banned. Everything had to be bought from the different chapels that set up tents and sold tea and stotties and scones and cakes to raise funds.

Ethel had lost Sam, her husband, early on. He had got no further than the alehouses in the market square, never would get any further than the alehouse. For some, Gala Day was a great beer day and Sam would have to be all but carried home. Some would not get home at all, leastwise not on that particular day, and those with long memories could remember Harold Ives; he had taken almost a week to get back, only to find that his wife Ida had changed the locks on the doors and put all his things in a couple of old orange boxes out in the backyard. She relented eventually and let him come home, but always made sure she kept a tight grip on him whenever next they went to the Gala.

Ethel slowly wandered around the stalls and tents dotted around the edge of the racecourse, bored and restless. The heat of the day was heavy and humid, oppressive, as though a thunderstorm were brewing its mischief in the distance, and she wished that it would hurry up and arrive and clear the air.

An energetic bowler-hatted, red-faced Union official with a thick walrus moustache was up on the platform, giving a speech about labour solidarity, but he kept on looking down at his notes and mumbling, and no-one could really hear what he was saying.

Not that Ethel was really all that interested anyway; the speech was boring enough when you could hear it, let alone otherwise. After all the official Union and Labour party speeches were done, the various associations and societies would take their turn, the Labour College, the Good Templars and others—it was going to be a long, long, day for oratory.

Ethel had been with her sister, Bridget, and two of Bridget's friends, but had become separated from them when they stopped to look at a needlework display. She was not worried, everyone, or almost everyone, would meet up again later, in time to catch the train back home.

Over, across on the other side of the course, away from the raised stage, some rides and swings had been set up for the children. There was a brightly painted carousel with prancing horses and cockerels, shuggy swings with brilliant red and yellow gondolas and spiral ropes to pull on and make the swings go higher and higher, flying chairs where all the girls squealed in mock terror and pretended not to like it as they held down their flying skirts. There was a Punch and Judy show, coconut shies, together with ice-cream, lemonade and candy floss stalls and a barrel organ with a bad-tempered grinder and a worse-tempered monkey. Even as Ethel watched, one boy got too close and the beast leapt onto his shoulder and pissed down his back.

She wandered slowly through the fairground, smiling at the children as they squealed and laughed and ran about in joyous droves. She and Sam had no children of their own, for which she was profoundly grateful. Not that she didn't like children, she did, but close proximity with the Poskit family had left her with no doubt that there was something inherently unstable in the Poskit bloodline, not only the obviously mentally subnormal Jimmy, but all the Poskits seemed to be short of a chair or two in their mental furniture, and Sammy's grandmother, dead now this past year or more, had actually been known as Doolally Lyla. No, whatever it was that was wrong with the Poskits, she did not want to pass it on to her children, even though it would mean she must remain childless.

A flatbed Vauxhall truck bounced and jounced across the rutted track, almost pitching the flat-capped gaggle of waving men onto the grass as Ethel walked back towards the tea tents.

'Nice cuppa, aye, hinnie?' the large-bosomed woman at the tea stand asked and Ethel nodded, suddenly feeling thirsty and not a little faint as the heavy heat had taken more out of her than she had thought.

'Make that two cups, would you, pet?' said a voice at her elbow. 'Afternoon, Mrs Poskit—Ethel. Managed to lose Sam, I see.'

And she turned to find Joe Garforth at her side, and she felt a sudden little flutter of attraction running through her, like a shiver, and then dismissed it as the heat, a hot sweat—but knowing that it wasn't.

'Oh! Hello, Mr Garforth. I didn't see you there—'

'Joe,' he interjected. 'Joe, call me Joe. After all, I've known thy Sam all my life.'

'Well, alright then. Joe. Like I say, I didn't see you standing there. Give me quite a start.'

'Aye, well, sorry about that, didn't mean to startle you.' Joe looked around. 'As I said, you seem to have lost Sam?' Taking both cups of tea and passing one to Ethel, he handed the tea-lady 2d in payment.

'Why, thank you, Joe,' she smiled, looking up at him. 'He's very tall,' she thought, 'much taller than average, broad-shouldered, good looking in a roguish, piratical sort of way.' And she noticed how his hair, thick and curly, swept up from under his cap and over the stiff white collar of his best shirt, and then she blushed and told herself she was a married woman and not to be noticing a man's appearance like that.

'As for Sam,' she said, 'aye, well, he never got no further than the alehouses in the market square.' She wondered if she were being disloyal to him by saying that.

'That sounds like Sam alright, proper beer day is Gala day, and I'm right relieved that's the way of it.'

'Relieved?' she asked, sipping her hot tea.

'Why, aye, relieved it's you what's lost him, not the other way about. Wouldn't like to think of Sam Poskit losing an attractive woman like you. Be criminal would that, downright criminal.'

'You shouldn't say things like that, Mr Garforth, after all I'm a married woman. And you a married man.'

'Nothing to say that a married woman shouldn't be attractive. Nor that a married man shouldn't think so.'

'Thinking it and saying it out loud are different matters, though.'

'Tha' means I should think that you're pretty but say that thee's ugly?'

'You shouldn't be thinking anything of the sort. What would your Lizzie think, hearing you say things like that?'

The woman serving the tea stared at them both and sniffed in loud and obvious disapproval, and Joe and Ethel looked at each other and smiled and tittered.

'Me sister,' Joe explained to disbelieving ears and then took Ethel's arm, and she felt a tingle, like electricity, running through her spine. 'Come Ethel love, let's move on. Round here, there's ears flapping so much, you'd think she was trying to fly.'

'Disgraceful! You ought to be ashamed on yourselves, the pair of you, married folk an' all. Disgraceful.'

'No more disgraceful than you trying to pass off this slop as tea.' And Joe up-ended his cup, spilling the tea onto the grass, and then took Ethel's cup from her and did the same, and handed the dripping cups back.

'Well, I never!'

'Aye, missus, I can well believe that, miserable old bat like you.'

As he led Ethel away, she again felt that tingle run through her. 'You shouldn't speak to her like that. What if she says something?'

'Aye, sorry love. I know I shouldn't 'ave, but she was getting to me. After all, it's none of her business and what with her big flapping ears and nose getting so long, I thought she was going to turn into an elephant at any minute.'

'An elephant!' Ethel giggled and looked back at the stall where the tea lady was standing, hands on substantial hips, chins thrust out, glaring at them. 'Well, we'd best be careful … looks as though she's about to charge.'

Joe pivoted, held his bent loose arm against his face like a trunk and then reared it skywards, trumpeting as he did, so that Ethel collapsed in giggles again.

'Joe, stop it. Stop it. Everybody's looking.'

'Well let 'em.' He cupped his hands to his mouth like a megaphone. 'It's open season on elephants,' he called to the half dozen or so people gaping at him in amusement. 'Get your tickets here. Open season on elephants.'

'Joe, come on,' Ethel insisted, still giggling, taking his arm and pulling him away. 'Come on, before she says something.'

'Aye, maybe you're right. But who's she going to say owt to?'

'Well. Sam. Else, Lizzie.'

'How can she? She don't know 'em from Adam.'

'Suppose not. Where is your Lizzie, anyhow?'

'Well, I doubt she's in the alehouses with your Sam. She don't hold with drink, you see? Probably, she's still at the temperance meeting, tried to get me to go. Some chance I'd say.'

They spent another hour or so together, Ethel taking his arm as if it were the most natural thing as they strolled around the periphery of the racecourse, by unspoken understanding avoiding the most heavily congested areas, where they might be seen together.

They spoke easily together, Joe making her laugh with his silly jokes and extravagant gestures, and Ethel could not remember when she had so enjoyed herself, been so at ease with a man, certainly never with Sam Poskit. She felt herself wanting to be with Joe again, knew she was falling in love with him and tried hard to fight it. She could have walked away, she knew, but the growing ache to spend just one more minute with him was overpowering and she dreaded the time when they would have to part, afraid that she might never be able to be with him like this again. Eventually, as it had to, that moment came.

'Well then Ethel, love. I'd best be off,' he said as they stood facing each other, not touching. 'Lizzie'll be out by now and I've left the bairns with me mam and she'll be beginning to wonder an' all.'

'Aye, of course. And I'd best go find Sam, else he'll be so much in his ale he'll not be able to walk. I've really enjoyed myself Joe, really, I mean that.' She was desperately hoping that he would respond, would want to see her again, whilst telling herself once more that she was a married woman and should not be thinking like that.

'Me an' all. You know, I didn't think anything on it when I came over to you at the tea tent, just being polite, as you might say, to a neighbour. But I have, really enjoyed it.'

Joe looked down at his feet. 'Ethel, I'd like to see you again, if I might.'

Her heart leaped at his words.

'I can talk to thee, you see, I feel able to … open up with you, like I can't do with Lizzie no more. We just get to argy-bargy about everything … and … and I would really like to see you again … just so's we can talk … all proper and above board. If you'd like to, I mean.'

'I'd love to, Joe. I was hoping you'd ask and didn't know how to let you know.'

'Really?'

'Why, aye.'

Joe took a deep breath, suddenly nervous; he could hear his blood pounding in his ears. 'How about one afternoon? I'm on early shift next week?'

'Yes, that'd be fine by me, Joe.' Her mouth was suddenly dry, as though stuffed with feathers.

'Monday?'

'I can say I'm going over to me mam's. Sam'll know no different.'

'We'd best meet somewhere private ... not because of anything, you understand ... anything improper ... but folk ... they talk.'

'Westfield Copse?'

'Aye, Westfield Copse.'

Westfield Copse it was. They met on the Monday afternoon as planned, Ethel feeling more excited and more nervous than ever in her life before. She spent ages looking through her meagre wardrobe of clothes, trying to decide which dress made her look prettiest, all the while telling herself that she should not be making herself look pretty to be seeing a married man.

When they met, both were so tense they could hardly speak, the carefree delight in each other seemed to have been left behind in Durham, and both of them cursed themselves for behaving like a fool, convinced that the other would not want to see them again, and it was not until Joe stumbled and barked his shin on an overgrown hidden stump and hopped around in pain that they were able to relax again, to be as they had been.

It was on their third clandestine meeting that they first made love, although sexual tension had been building up like a bonfire between them; when they touched hands, it was as if sparks of static electricity were arcing, flesh to flesh, so powerful as to be

The river was her numinous home, sanctuary for a restless soul.

Her rambles took her farther afield as well, up over Marley Hill and Westfield Copse, where she knew a big dog fox had his lair (not very far away, in fact, from where Joe Garforth was wont to slide into the moistly warm and welcome depths of Ethel Poskit), or across the river on the other bank, up towards Wardley Woods, where there was a sunken hollow, surrounded by old wise oaks, called Tanfield Hollow.

One magical morning, she had seen a pair of badgers there, gambolling and frolicking like romping children and she had watched spellbound for what had seemed an age, before the male had either caught her scent or heard the rustlings as she changed her position slightly. With a grey, silver-black blur, they were gone, and she never saw them again.

Not so very long ago, she had cried when she heard that the gamekeeper, Sammy Fulcher, had led a badger hunt one night and set the hounds onto a pair of badgers they had cornered and tore them to shreds. Afterwards, Sammy had paraded the bloody masks in the public bar at the 'Green Tree' before being asked to take them out.

Not that anyone had objected to the hunt; it was just that the masks were still dripping blood and the smell was getting the pub dogs excited. Eleanor never knew if they had been her badgers, but it felt as if her own children had been murdered, had been torn from her heart and butchered before her eyes.

Nobody understood how she had felt, not Mary, her step-mother, who had comforted and held her as she sobbed out her inchoate heartache and anger, not her father or sisters, not Nicholas, although perhaps he came closest to realising that it wasn't simply that a pair of beautiful creatures had died for man's enjoyment that had been so upsetting, it was that the idyllic peace of her inner sanctuary had been foully desecrated— simplistic illusions violated—that paradise had been raped.

She got over it, of course, but the window it opened into the brutality of man's dark soul never left her, and she never went back to Tanfield Hollo. She could not bear the fact that it might have been those same beautiful badgers that had been ripped apart in the fangs of Sammy Fulcher's dogs, those beautiful, pure creatures that had given her such a magical, privileged feeling that perfect morning.

Now, crossing over the stream by the dam stones, Eleanor headed upstream, following a faint footpath that ran through the lower of Quantrill's fields, keeping a careful eye on a herd of cows ruminating in the near corner, tails swishing; they watched her with brooding bucolic stare, regarding her with such a single-minded purpose that it was disconcerting.

Glad to leave them behind, she climbed the stile and, keeping the twinkling river to her right, made her way to her favourite place, her secret place, her desert island, as she liked to think it.

It was a shallow hollow, some six feet deep, as perfectly symmetrical as though a giant had dropped a 20' ball-bearing into the soft, pliant earth. Lying some yards away from the river-bank, it was screened from the river itself by a stand of young willow trees; tall grass clumps, sedges, thick-clotted thistles and nettles obscured the approach from along the river, and yet the depression was hidden from the far side simply because it was a hollow, grassy bowl so serene and silent, so overpowering in the feelings of peace it brought her that Eleanor thought it bewitched, magical, a fairy circle.

Magic was a concept she could readily accept, a belief in a naturalistic primitive magic, the magic of the ancients, the magic of the winds, not the magic of witches and spells, sorcery and devil's pacts, black cats and succubae; for Eleanor, it was the pure magic of being young and alive on a beautiful summer's afternoon.

She stood at the very edge of the lip, raised herself high on tiptoe, spread her arms slowly wide, and closing her eyes, breathed in deeply and slowly, smelling the clean beauty, feeling the peace wash over her. She felt uplifted, as if she were flying, as though the birds were transporting her away, high like an eagle, to the sun.

For five minutes or more, she stood like that, at one with nature. Time that was endless, the sounds of the trickling river receded, the birdsong became her song as she flew on the wings of imagination, soaring higher and higher. Her outstretched fingertips fluttered slightly, like the quivering wing tips of an eagle, soaring on the spiralling thermals. She took a final, deep inhalation, lowered her arms and dropped her head to her chest, feeling her spirit, her vital animus, flow slowly back into her body. She could feel her essences tingling along her arms and into her fingers, trembling through her nails.

At last, she opened her eyes; the glare was sharp and cutting and caused her to overbalance slightly and she tottered down the side of the hollow to its base. Slowly, she sank to the ground, like a dying swan at the ballet, and folded her arms about her head. Suddenly, she felt exhausted, drained but cleansed, pure, her restless soul at peace.

FIFTEEN

Nay. He's just a varmint.

'Hello, Isaac,' Molly Hindle said, coming up behind him as he walked down Whitton Lane towards Adlard's Forge. 'Where are you off to then?'

'Nowhere, really, just down to t'forge,' he answered, looking around to make sure that no one, especially Saul, could see him talking to a girl. 'Where's thee going?'

'My mam sent us out of the house. My Auntie Myrtle's come round, and she's got some problem with my Uncle Albert she didn't want me to hear.'

'Oh, aye, what's the problem then?' Although Isaac was not all that bothered, he was far more concerned with getting away from the highly public Whitton Lane, where just about the entire village could see him with Molly Hindle.

'Don't know really, except me Auntie Myrtle's crying all the time and I heard Mam say, well I never, the dirty beast, or some'at like that. Then she saw me on the stairs and sent me out.'

'Oh?' Isaac tried to imagine what sort of problems Mollie's

Auntie Myrtle could be having with Uncle Albert and could only assume he had been up to something rather like his brother Joe was up to with Ethel Poskit.

'Anyhow, what you going down the blacksmith's for? Getting yourself some new shoes?' Molly asked.

'New shoes? Oh, aye, dead funny, I don't think.'

'So, what you going for then?'

'Nowt, really. I just like to go and watch.'

'Can I come with you? I've got nowt else to do,' she stated and fell into step alongside him, giving him a big smile as she did so. 'I mean, Auntie Myrtle's going to be hours yet. She always stays forever, even if she's only come to say how do.'

'Well, you'd probably find it right boring.'

'I don't mind, Isaac. Not so long as I'm with you.' She briefly laid a hand on his arm, causing him to blush to his roots.

He felt funny, nervous and breathless, not knowing what to say. He liked Molly a lot and part of him wanted her to be with him, but the other half dreaded the prospect of being seen with her; he would never live it down if Saul saw him. He hunched down his head, into his shoulders, in the hope that he would not be recognised if anybody saw them together, trying to think where Saul might be. Isaac picked up the pace, almost running now.

'Hold on,' shouted Molly. 'Can't hardly keep up'.

'Girls can't. Shouldn't try.'

'Don't be so rotten, Isaac Garforth. If you don't slow down right now, I'll never ever speak to you again. Ever.'

'Alright.' Isaac slowed down slightly. 'Only, don't try and lag on purpose, else …'

'Else what?'

'Just don't, that's all.'

They walked further down the road, Isaac still hunched down, hoping to be invisible, when Molly suddenly clutched his arm. 'Ooh, look! Is that your Saul over there?'

'WHAT! WHERE? WHERE?' Isaac looked wildly around.

'Oh, no, sorry, it weren't. Must have someone else,' Molly said, all innocence, gazing at some distant nothing, her eyes sparkling, finding it hard not to burst out laughing.

'You did that on bloody purpose,' Isaac shouted angrily.

'You shouldn't swear. My mam says that people what swear only go to prove how ignorant they are. Lacking in ... voca-bal-berry. Goes to show, they don't know many words.'

'Near on freet me to death.'

'Are you that frightened of Saul, then?'

'Nah, gerraway. It's just ...well, you know. Being with a girl and all, he'll think I'm soft.'

'I don't think it's soft to be seen with a girl, Isaac.'

'Well, that's because you're a lass, that's why. Lasses know nowt.'

They had come up to Adlard's Forge now, and Isaac could hear the dull pounding of hammers on the anvil, and his pulse quickened. He loved to come down the Forge, loved the smells: the red and yellow glowing coke, the dull red-hot metal, the horses waiting to be shoed.

He could spend hours just watching, peering through the open window, listening to the crash of hammers on the anvil and the hiss of the bellows heating up the furnace, drawing in the sights and smells. Sometimes, when he wasn't too busy, Mr Adlard, the blacksmith, would let Isaac look around the Forge and he would show and explain things to him. Isaac soaked it all up, wishing that he too could become a blacksmith. The prospect of having to go down the mine, as he would have to any day, appalled him and he yearned for the Forge, ached for a chance to become a blacksmith.

'What do you come down here for then, Isaac?' Molly asked as he moved over to peer through the open window.

'Just like it. That's all. Just like it.' He bridled defensively. 'Nowt wrong with that, is there?'

'Never said there was, did I? Just curious, like why you want to come here?'

'I told you,' Isaac growled. 'I just like it.' Immediately, he felt sorry for having spoken so sharply. 'Well, actually Molly, I'd like to be a blacksmith, working with iron and that. Making shoes for the horses. Repairing ploughshares and the like. Far rather be doing that than going down the pit,' he explained, looking at Molly to see if she were laughing at him. He had never before told a living soul about his secret ambitions.

'So, why don't you?'

'Because of the 'prenticeship, that's why. Two bob a week or more it'd cost, and me dad'll not pay owt like that.'

'Have you asked?'

'Nay. No point is there? He's set his mind on Saul and me going down't pit with him. Says it'll keep us in order, but I wouldn't need keeping in order if I were doing what I wanted, would I? I mean, I only cause trouble in school because they always try to make me some'at I don't want to do. Or can't do.' There was bitterness in Isaac's voice, a sense of injustice that Molly could see cut him very deeply.

'Like what? What do they make you that you can't? You could do *anything* you wanted, Isaac. Honest.'

Isaac turned away and slid his left hand into his right armpit, a gesture that was obviously unconscious. 'I mean, it's like with the writing, in't it? Because I'm cack-handed. They won't let me use my left hand, and they force me to try and use my right hand. When I were little, they even tied my hand, my left hand, up behind my back. To make me use my right. Well, I couldn't. Not properly. So, all my writing were wrong.'

'I remember that, in Mrs Spurling's class. It's cruel. Right cruel. It's not your fault, is it?'

'No, course not. That's the way I was born, that's all. It's not some'at I do on purpose. Some'at I do to annoy them. But they wouldn't have it. Said I had to use my right, especially Mrs

Spurling, even when I couldn't. So, my writing, it's not very good. Because it's not natural, I suppose.'

'Must be dead hard. Like me try to write with my left hand.'

'Mrs Spurling said I were sinister. Always remember that. Sinister. And if I ever used my left hand, often as not without even thinking, she used to hit it, dead hard, with that metal ruler she had in her hand all the time. Said it was the devil's mark. I suppose that's why I got to be a big nuisance in class. Couldn't do the work because I couldn't write proper, so …' Isaac shrugged heavily. 'I made a nuisance of me'self.'

'But what about Saul? He's not left-handed.'

'Nay. He's just a varmint, a right little bugger, as me dad says.'

The two of them laughed and giggled at the use of the word 'bugger', not knowing what it really meant, but they knew it was a bad word that their fathers used a lot, but which children weren't supposed to.

Molly looked earnestly at Isaac; although she was almost the same age, Molly was that much wiser, that much more mature, the way that 14-year-old girls were in comparison to boys of the same age. Molly was already on the verge of womanhood, whereas Isaac, despite the fact he would be going to work down the pit at any day, was still a boy.

'Honestly, Isaac,' she said, pleading with her eyes. 'You can do anything you want. Anything. You can fly as high as the birds if that's what thee wants, but you've got to do it for yourself. Tha' says that you wants to become a blacksmith, but you've done nowt about it, have you?'

'There's no point, I tell you.'

'How do you know? You don't, not until you ask.'

'There's the cost of the apprenticeship. My dad'll not wear that.'

'So? How much is the apprenticeship?'

'Don't know exactly. Two, three, four bob a week.'

'So? Go and find out. Go on, get yourself in there right now and ask Mr Adlard.'

'He'll say no, bugger off out on it.'

'You don't know that. And even if he does say … that, what have you lost, eh? Nothing!'

''He'll still not take me, because of being left-handed. I couldn't work in there hammering with my right hand. I'd take somebody's fingers off.'

'If you don't ask, you won't know.'

'Why, aye, I suppose you're right.'

'Get yourself on in then.'

'Aye, right,' Isaac said without much conviction, shuffling his feet around in the dirt.

'You want me to hold your hand and go in with you?'

'Nay! Get off, don't be so daft.'

'Gan on in, then.'

'He … he might be busy, Mr Adlard.'

'And he might not.'

'Will … will you wait for us, Molly? I don't know how long I'll be.' He laughed nervously. 'Probably only about 10 seconds. Before he tells me to clear off for being so cheeky.'

'Aye, course I will. Now, stop dithering about and get yourself in there.'

'Aye, right.' Isaac took a deep breath. 'Fly as high as the birds, you said?'

He squared his shoulders, straightened his flat cap, gave Molly a nervous grin, and walked into the side door of the Forge.

SIXTEEN

The same type of nails would have been used for Jesus' crucifixion.

'Dad?' Isaac asked nervously, his apprehension so great his voice hardly carried across the width of the table. His heart beat furiously and he could only breathe in shallow pants. Ever since he had returned from the Forge, he had been trying to find an opportunity to talk to his father, but the right moment never seemed to come.

All through dinner he had waited, hoping that the conversation might give him an opening, but Mary Margaret and Eleanor were chattering away about nothing of importance and almost as soon as they had got up and left, Harold had come in late from his shift and sat at the table for what seemed like forever, and still showed no signs of leaving. Isaac wanted his mam to be there when he asked; he sensed she would be on his side, but he most particularly did not want Saul around, and would rather that Harold was not there either, but it did not look as though he was going to have a better opportunity than this.

'Dad?' he asked again as Jack Garforth laid down his newspaper and tapped out his pipe on the bricks of the fireplace, the tobacco dottle sizzling slightly as it fell onto the hot grating.

'Aye, lad.'

'I were down at the Forge today, this afternoon—you know Mr Adlard's—and he said he can take me on as an apprentice for only two bob a week ... that's all, as I'm dead keen and been going down for ages and I'd really like to do that, Dad, really, all my life I reckon, been wanting to do that. So, can I Dad? Please?' Isaac made his speech without drawing breath so that the words came out in a garbled rush, all tumbled up upon one another, gushing so quickly it was hard to tell where one word finished, and another took up.

'Hold on, son. Not so fast. Calm yourself down and take it a bit at a time.'

'Aye, right.' Isaac's initial nervousness had gone now, the die was cast, and he spoke distinctly and slowly. 'I were saying Dad, I went to see Mr Adlard this after ... this afternoon, tha' knows, Mr Adlard down at the Forge?'

'Aye, I know Henry Adlard, right enough.'

'I were asking him about an apprenticeship. To work with him at the Forge.'

When she heard Isaac say this, Mary felt a bound of relief. 'He's not to go down the pit,' she thought, her prayers answered.

'And you want to be bound apprentice to him, is that right?' Jack asked, not unkindly.

'Aye, Dad, I think that's what I've always wanted to do. I mean, I've spent hours, hours and hours down there at the Forge, sometimes talking with Mr Adlard when he's not busy. He knows I'm right keen, because of all the times I've been down there.'

'And he says he'll take you on. Without talking to me about it?'

'No, no, Dad, course not. He said I've got to talk it over with thee first, and if you agree, to talk with him.'

'I reckon this needs some thinking about. I've already told Mr Baker at the pit that you and Saul will be starting on as soon as he wants. Be any day now.'

'I know, Dad, I should have spoke to you sooner, I know, but …' He shrugged, unable to actually say that he was afraid of his father, afraid that he would get a belting for his cheek, and that it was only the prodding by Molly Hindle that had given him the courage to do anything about raising the question of an apprenticeship.

'I think it's a right good idea,' Mary said, wiping her hands on her apron and coming to sit beside Isaac, to give him moral support. She knew Jack was not a cruel man, would not force Isaac down the mines unless there was no other option, so she had to make sure that this alternative was well and truly aired.

'Maybe so, Mary,' Jack replied, 'but like I say, it needs some thinking on. Pass us down the jar, Isaac. I'll have another pipe and you can tell me more about it.'

'I never knew you liked the Forge, Isaac. How come you never said owt before now?' asked Mary when Isaac sat down again after passing Jack his tobacco jar.

'I don't know why. I suppose because it were always assumed, right from the start, that me and Saul were going down't pit, and I never thought there were no option else. And then, when I spoke to Mr Adlard, and he said he could take me …'

'Another one as ain't got the bottle to go underground,' sneered Harold, 'What with thee and fancy ideas, Nicholas, the whole village is going to think that the Garforths are going right soft.'

Isaac coloured, his nostrils flaring as got to his feet and prepared to launch himself at Harold. No one ever called him soft and he let it by. 'Who are thee calling soft,' he challenged, fists clenched in anger.

'Sit yourself down, Isaac,' his father ordered. 'We'll have none of that. Harold! If thee's got nought useful to say, you keep your flapping gob shut.'

'Aye, Harold, you take heed of your dad,' echoed Mary. 'Isaac, nothing can get decided with you flying off the handle like that.'

'Well, tell him, Mam, there's nowt soft in being a blacksmith.'

'Aye, it's a man's work alright and let there be no doubts about that,' Jack said as he got his pipe smoking heavily again. 'Stick the kettle on an all, Mary. We'll have us a cup of tea and try and talk things out, rationally.'

Harold got to his feet. 'Well, I'm away down to the 'Green Tree'. Can't spend all night listening to his soft talk. He'll be telling us next he wants to take up embroidery lessons or some'at.'

And Isaac, biting his tongue, felt a surge of relief at seeing him go.

'Aye, well. We'll not be missing the benefit of his valued opinions, that's for sure,' said Mary as Harold stomped out. 'The only thing he can ever do is sneer and pull folk down, and I'm right sorry, Jack, it's me who has to say that.'

'You're the only one as could and me not take you up on it. He's not a bad lad, Mary. He means well, I'm sure. Just he feels a bit left out sometimes.'

'For goodness sake, Jack, he's 21 years old. It's about time he was left out of things a bit.'

'Perhaps you're right, Mary, but none of that's got owt to do with what we're talking about here.'

'Aye, well, that's the thing with Harold. He always gets things stirred up, gets everyone at odds with each other and pulls your mind off the main track. He just loves to stir it up, and I tell you, Jack, sometimes he makes me want to spit.'

'He'd be a brave man as gets the wrong side of thee, Mary Garforth. And even then, he'd only do it the once.'

'Mam! Dad!' Isaac interjected. 'This is important to me.'

'Aye, Isaac. So it is. It's your whole life from now on we're talking about and it's only right that you should have all our attention,' Jack said. 'But us old folk have a way of putting off important matters. We ignore 'em and hope they'll all go away.' He spoke with a grin to tell Isaac it was his heavy-handed way of saying sorry, the nearest he could ever come to apologising to a 14-year-boy. 'Right then, Isaac, I'm all ears.'

'Well, Dad, Mr Adlard says he can take me on as apprentice for 2 shilling …' and he tailed away as Jack held up a hand to interrupt him.

'Before we gets to talking about the money of the thing, Isaac, that's the least on it, what I want to hear from you, son, is how you feel about blacksmithing. Why? Why is it so important for you to be doing this?'

'I can't express it dead right, Dad. I know, inside, that it's something I want to do. I've spent a lot of time down at the Forge and Mr Adlard, he knows how right keen I am, right keen, which is why he's willing to take me on … says he'd only take on a lad whose heart is in smithying.'

'What about it do you like, Isaac?' Mary asked gently, sensing that Jack had already decided to go along with the boy's wishes. There was a relaxed contemplative set to Jack's head and body, and she could sense no aura of conflict in him, usually a sure indicator of his mood.

'The best way I can say it, Mam, is to tell you about something that Mr Adlard once told me and I never forgot it. He said as how they had found some Roman nails up on the wall —you know, Hadrian's Wall, up the road a while past Consett?'

'Aye, son, I've heard of Hadrian's Wall,' Jack answered dryly.

'Let him talk, Jack. There's no need for thy two-penn'orth.'

Isaac rolled his eyes in exasperation, the train of his thoughts broken by the interruptions.

'Sorry, lad, I'll not say another word 'til you've said your piece.'

Isaac took another deep breath, and then carried on. 'They found these nails, see? Big ones'—and he spread his hand to indicate the size of the nails, six inches long or so—'Roman nails. Up by the wall, all bright and shiny, and Mr Adlard said they had to be hundreds of years old, but they were all bright and shiny, just as if they'd been hammered out yesterday. And I asked him how come they hadn't all rusted away and he said it was because they weren't made from steel but from Low Moor iron, that had been smelted from the iron ore with charcoal, not with coke like they use now. And he said some'at else, Mr Adlard, some'at else that really stopped me, made me think. He said as how the same type of nails would have been used for Jesus' Crucifixion, when they nailed him up on the cross.'

'Good Heavens above! Just think on that, Jack. The same nails as were used to crucify Our Lord.'

'Nay, Mam, not the same nails, but similar like.'

'And that made you decide? About being a blacksmith?' Jack asked, looking at Isaac, perhaps seeing him the first time, not as a trouble-making small boy, but as a growing youth, with ideas and opinions of his own, and he nodded slowly, as if in approval.

'Nay, not just that, Dad, but that were part of it. But you know, working with something that could last hundreds of years, well, it makes you think, don't it?' Isaac said excitedly, virtually the first time in his life being able to talk to his dad without the fear of a thrashing involved. 'You see, when you smelt iron ore with charcoal, with charcoal rather than with coke, it allows the iron to breathe.' His enthusiasm took flight. 'It's not softer exactly, but more'—he hooked his fingers into claws in frustration at his inability to articulate his feelings—'more ... it's got more *life* in it. Doesn't rust,' he finished lamely, knowing what he meant, that iron smelted by charcoal was more flexible but without loss of strength, more forgiving, was purer to the soul, but his 14-year-old vocabulary was inadequate to properly express his feelings.

Isaac sat forward, on the edge of his chair, almost wishing he had said nothing at all, the disappointment of failure would now be crushing, and he cursed himself for allowing Molly Hindle to stoke up his dreams.

Jack puffed slowly on his pipe and even Mary grew apprehensive, her earlier certainty that Jack would agree evaporating with every puff of smoke, afraid that Jack was merely contemplating the easiest way to let down the boy.

Finally, Jack took his pipe out of his mouth and turned to Mary. 'What does thee think, Mary?'

'The lad's dead set on it, Jack. Dead set. And I'd do anything to keep him from going down t'pit, you know that. We can manage the money and, whatever it takes, I'll go without ... only please, Jack, give him this one chance.'

'You go without more than enough already, Mary, I'll not have no more on it,' he declared, and her heart fell.

'Nay, Jack, there's allus some'at I can scrimp on.'

'Dad, I'll take on whatever jobs I can, after I've finished with Mr Adlard for the day. I'll do owt, anything at all to make a few coppers, a bob or two, to pay for it.'

'Any lad of mine goes as an apprentice, he gives all his time to it. You can't be serving Henry Adlard right if you're worn out from minding pigs all night, else digging ditches or whatever.' Jack scratched his chin as he thought for a short while. 'They have blacksmiths at the pit, you know, shoeing the galloways and making bits and pieces needed for the machinery. Have you thought of that? I could speak to Mr Baker, see if there's owt there?'

'It'd not be the same Dad, honest. Not the same as a proper apprenticeship with Mr Adlard. He makes all sorts down there, tools for farms, hinges for gates, fancy ironwork, not just horse-shoes and that. Working in't pit, well, it would be just that.'

'And he'd have to go underground, and you know how dead set I am against that, Jack. Not just for Isaac. For any of you.'

'Well, then, looks like I'd best be getting on down to see Henry Adlard, some'at about an apprenticeship.'

'Ohhh, oh, thanks Dad. Thanks. Thanks. Don't know how else to say it. Thanks Dad.'

'Aye, thank you, Jack, you don't know how much this means to me.'

'Oh, aye, but I do Mary, lass. I do.'

Isaac jumped up, his eyes shining with excitement, scarcely able to believe it had happened. He wanted to hug his mother and father out of sheer happiness. But did not know how. 'I'll just be off for a minute, go and tell Molly, she'll be dead chuffed.' He stopped in his tracks, his ears burning with embarrassment as he realised he had just spoken of Molly.

'Molly?' his mother asked quizzically. 'Would that be Molly Hindle? Freda Hindle's lass?'

'Aye. That's her.'

'Courtin' are you, then lad?' Jack bellowed with heavy humour.

'Nay, Dad, nowt like that. She just helped me, that were all. She's interested like.' Isaac fled before he could be interrogated further.

Mary crossed over to Jack's chair and put a hand on his shoulder. 'Thanks for that, Jack. You're a grand man and you've made our Isaac dead happy. He's a good lad and he'll make some'at out of himself now. Thanks to you.'

'I did it for thee, lass, as much as for the lad.'

'I know that, Jack, and I love thee for it.'

Jack tapped out his pipe again and leaned back in his chair, suddenly feeling very tired, and sighed. 'Eh, I don't know Mary, our Isaac seeing a lass. Where does the time go to, eh? Hardly seems like yesterday since him and Saul was born.'

'You know what this means, don't you, Jack? Isaac going to the Forge. And seeing Molly Hindle? It means that he and Saul are starting to drift apart. They are not just 'the twins' anymore, they're separate people now, in their own right'.

'Well, that's no bad thing. Isaac will do all the better for being out from under Saul's influence.'

'I only hope all this talk of a war doesn't spoil things for 'im, change things too much.'

'Aye, Mary, the world's going to change alright. There's no doubt about that, the world's changing. And I'm not so sure it's going to be a better place for it.'

SEVENTEEN

Where a murderous rookery of noisy crows discussed such world events.

August 4th, 1914

The dawn seeped slowly over the eastern slope of the valley, a sickly pale grey-yellow wash, so faint, so vaporous, that only the deep black shadow of the valley sides, standing stark against the diffused pale luminosity, could delineate where night ended and day began.

Jeb Fulcher tested the blade on his scythe again. He already knew that it was sharp, honed to an edge so keen that you could shave the fluff from the soft pale-peach skin of a baby's back and leave not a mark, but it gave him something to do, something to fill his hands with whilst waiting for the wan, sickly dawn light to thicken.

Vague grey shapes, mere outlines, of the other reapers swirled around the edge of the field, 24 or 25 of them, some from the farm, some from the village, some from other farms whose fields weren't ready yet. Next week, Jeb himself might be over at Col. Palgrave's fields, or up in the top fields if they were ready; sometimes the top fields took longer to come on. Jeb could never understand that. The top fields took the rising sun first and kept it most of the day, but often they still came on last.

He took his whetstone from his jacket pocket, a fat-bellied cigar of carborundum and stroked it along the edge of the scythe blade, caressed it as a lover might stroke the line of his lady's spine or thigh. Some men could never get the hang of it, no matter how hard you tried to teach them, could never get that clean easy slicing edge that could take off a man's head with a single sweep if you were so minded.

'Aye. You strokes it as you would a woman', Tackie Potter had told him, all those years ago when he had been a boy of 14 or 15, grinning at Jeb through toothless gums as he taught him how to hone an edge to his scythe. 'Any man's got to know how to stroke his woman, get her keen edged, you might say, else she'll not keep you warm at nights. Aye, you've got to learn how to keep you scythe sharper than a spinster woman's tongue.

Look on, you does it like this, top to bottom, all in one. Just like stroking a lass. Why aye, that's it, lad, gan steady like, gan steady'.

Tackie had been dead these many years now, the plough horses had bolted on him, dragging him under the harrow, cutting him to shreds like scrag ends through a mincer, but Jeb had never forgotten what he had taught him, not just how to hone his scythe but how to swing it in that endless steady rhythmic cadence that you could keep up all day if you did it right, allowing the weight of the blade to do the cutting, utilising the *pride* of the scythe in its work and so do the mowing. Fight it, try and force it and within minutes your arms felt as though they would fall off for aching.

The rasping hiss of the stone on the scythe blade was a soothing balm to Jeb's ears. Impatient to get off, waiting only for there to be enough light to mow in safety without cutting off feet and toes, which had happened more than once before now. Laurence Fletcher, pig man on Ashbrook Top, he had taken off his toes clean as a whistle, mowing up on Lord Exham's Lower Farm for Farmer Quantrill, what three or four years ago?

Had his mind on other things, on the Widow Ransome more than like and, if truth be known, there was a great deal about the Widow Ransome to fill the mind with. Laurence Fletcher had more than likely been thinking how he could entice her to his bed rather than keeping his mind to his work.

Not that there would have been much space in the bed left over, once she was in it, but that was by the by. Laurence had lost his rhythm, got out of step, and brought the wrong foot forward at the wrong time, and his scythe had gone straight through the leather of his boot like tissue paper and taken off three toes and half his foot before he even knew it; whatever else he might have been, Laurence Fletcher was another man who knew how to keep his scythe blade keen.

Whether he was able to keep the Widow Ransome keen edged was something Jeb had never found out. Laurence had been rushed to Dr Treddle's surgery, who had taken one look at the foot and sent him over to the hospital in Durham. Jamie Jope had gone with him and said that when the nurses took off Laurence's boot, they had poured more than a pint of blood out of it. 'Bled worse and squealed louder than his shoats when he cuts their knackers for 'em' was how he'd put it.

The dawn was sharper now, bleeding summer light across the dale side, a thin shard of sun; the merest sliver of an orange and gold-tinged yellow-white disc peeked hesitantly over the horizon, like a nosy neighbour peering over a fence.

The sound of clattering horseshoes on the lane echoed along the hedgerows and the men all turned toward the gate in the corner, by a stand of ash trees where a murderous rookery of noisy crows discussed such world events as the perennially prickly Irish problem and the shelving of the Irish Home Rule

Bill, the German invasion of Belgium, and the scandalously usurious increase in the Bank Rate to 10%. The reapers knew that the rider would be Hector Whitehead, owner of Highfield Farm, come to fix the rate for the harvest.

Jeb swung his scythe two or three times back and forth, practising his rhythm, loosening the muscles of his shoulders. It was a good scythe, his own, bought for 7s.6d in the market at Bishop. Many of the reapers owned their own tools because every scythe had its own feel, its own weight and character and pattern of swing. Before buying a scythe, a man should spend a deal of time testing the swing and feel of several. At 7s.6d a time (nearly a week's wages for some men), you only bought a scythe once in your lifetime, and you had to be certain that you found the right one, the one that *talked* to you, the one that whispered secrets to you like a lover, the secrets of its shape and the swing of its blade, the one that suited your height and length of arms and the way you walked.

So Tackie Potter had said, and Jeb believed him, not that he would ever have breathed a word about a scythe, whispering its secrets to any of the other reapers, but they knew nothing and, at the end of the day, it would be Jeb and his partner, Jamie Jope, who did the sheaving, who would have the greatest number of stooks marching in solemn line down the fields behind them, like guardsmen on parade at the Trooping of the Colour.

Hector Whitehead trotted into the field, a broken-barrelled shotgun across his arm, ready for the rats and rabbits that would be flushed out by the reaping. He was a tall heavyset man with a bulbous nose like an over-ripe strawberry that showed much allegiance to the port bottle. Jeb had worked for Hector Whitehead all his life, thought him a hard man, but a fair man. He would drive a rigorous bargain, no doubt about that, but you could as certain as could be that once the deal had been made over a handshake with Peter Longshaw, the senior mower, the 'harvest lord', he would stick to it and make sure that beer was on hand for all the reapers for as long as it took to clear the fields, at an allowance of 17 pints per man a day, and every drop brought to the fields had to be drunk. Once the barrels were there, standing at the back of the harvest wagon, they had to be emptied. Good, strong, home-mashed ale it was too, not like the thin weasel-piss they sold at the 'Tree' or up at the 'Victory' over towards Scanton on the top road.

Jeb ran his thumb lightly over the scythe blade again; even through the leather-hard skin and callouses on his thumb-pad, he could still feel the keenness, the *eagerness* of the edge.

The deal struck with Peter Longshaw, Hector Whitehead mounted his horse again and stood up in the stirrups. 'Right then, lads,' he shouted, 'let's get it done. And the quicker it's done, the better off you'll be for it. Beer wagon'll be along shortly, but let's get down to it now, half the morning's gone already.'

'And about bloody time an' all,' grumbled Jeb, swishing his scythe again. 'Come then, Jamie, let's get the bugger done. I can feel a bloody great thirst coming on me already.'

They walked over to their allotted place and, almost before they had reached it, Jeb started mowing, swinging easily into his rhythm, the hiss and swish of the blade as precise as a metronome. Behind him, Jamie Jope scooped up the fallen stalks of corn and gathered them together in armfuls, tamped them down to even height and swiftly bound them together with brown twine, standing the stook upright before moving on to scoop up another armful. He would have his work cut out to keep up with Jeb and could already feel the sweat starting a thin sheen, like oil, on his forehead and under his armpits. It was going to be a long hot day, they would be at it until night fall, 17 hours or more, and apart from breaks for dinner (slices of fresh bread the size of small books and chunks of cheese washed down with copious beer), and other short stops to empty the bladder so as to make room for more beer, they would be mowing and sheaving virtually without stop.

Tomorrow, and the days after, would be the same. And after mowing, came the stacking and the raking of the stubble and only then would the last stook, the 'policeman' stook, be removed, signifying that the field could be gleaned, and all the farm woman and girls and children would sieve through the stubble, salvaging all the wayward ears of corn that had escaped the sheaving and raking.

Jeb moved on ahead, like oiled machinery, every sweep of the scythe taking exactly 11 rows of corn onto the blade, every sweep the same, as precise as clockwork. Jamie stopped to mop his brow.

'Can you not keep up, idle bugger? You're no more use than a bloody soft lass,' Jeb complained, heavy droplets of sweat beading his giant conk like raindrops on a kerbstone. 'At this rate, I'll be away and gone, and tha'll still be on your second stook.'

Jamie said nothing, Jeb might be the best mower in the district, but he always was a miserable old bastard and had already turned his back to him, relentlessly marching on, almost running, scything down the ranks of ripe-eared corn that fell around him in a shower of gold.

In months to come, when Jamie Jope was to see companies of men fall to machine-gun fire like this, he would always to be reminded of the summer he sheaved behind Jeb the Neb Fulcher.

A rabbit started almost from under Jeb's feet, the swish of the scythe all but taking off the rabbit's cotton wool ball of a tail. Hector Whitehead let the rabbit jink and dart out of the sight line of the mowers and then raised his shotgun and, with the easy fluid follow of a hunter, quickly brought the sights to bear and pulled the trigger, stopping the beast dead in its tracks.

At the sound of the gun blast, the crows in the rookery broke off their discussions and swirled into the air, screaming insults and imprecations and swearing at the men below in a cacophony of vicious croaking caws, circling the field once or twice in aerial formation before setting down once again in the trees.

'Now then, brother crows, where were we before we were so rudely interrupted? Ah, yes. The Irish Home Rule Bill.'

Overhead, the sun climbed on remorselessly, scattering the thin cloud wisps and burning away the last few scraps of ground mist. Even this early in the morning, it was obvious that it was going to be a blazing hot day, a scorcher, and the 17 pints of beer to each man began to seem woefully inadequate.

EIGHTEEN

Not only losing his lands, but subsequently his head.

Hector Whitehead felt tired and headachy. He had drunk too much—far too much—of the beer he had brought up to the fields for the reapers, but had not sweated out of his system as they had been able to do.

The glare from the high sun was not helping his headache either, which seemed to be located right behind his eyes. He pulled his hat down tighter over his forehead to try and cut out more sunlight, but without much effect. 'Bloody fool,' he told himself. 'Ought to know better at your age, but you never learn.'

Every year it was the same at harvest time: too much beer under the heat of the sun and it always, *always* gave him a blinding headache. 'Stick to port, that's the best thing … stick to port … that only gives you the gout!'

Hector walked his horse slowly, anything more than that jarred his aching head too much, made it feel as though red-hot railway spikes were being driven into his skull. The three braces of rabbits, dangling from his saddle, bounced soggily against his thigh. 'Give them to Mrs Harper, let them hang for a day or two, cook them in cider, and they'll make a fine rabbit pie for lunch one day.' But at the thought of food, his stomach turned queasy and he had to pull his horse up at the side of the track until the spasm of bile had passed, tasting sour in his mouth.

The road up to Highfield Farm seemed longer than usual, the track more than usually pitted, causing his horse to jerk and bounce as he climbed around and over the deep ruts, rattling Hector's aching eyes in their sockets, and he began to feel that he would never make it back home.

Highfield Farm stood amidst fields away to the east of Ashbrook Stills village, high up on the south sloping valley sides, leading down to the wandering river below. The river sauntered along a soft-coiling route through willows and ash trees, a vagabond stream, following a serene path that took it under Bitchburn Bridge, past the 'Green Tree', through the back end of the village before turning sharply to the south, where it flowed through Quantrill's fields with Marley Hill and the copses to its left.

Highfield had been in the Whitehead family for generations, at least as far back as Henry the Eighth, who had granted Sir Oliver Whitehead all the lands to the north of the river. The lands had been a gift in recognition of Sir Oliver's support when Henry was divorcing Catherine of Aragon in order to get his lustful hands on Anne Boleyn.

Actually, the land in question had belonged to one Sir William Jacoby, who had vehemently opposed Henry's divorce and ended up not only losing his lands, but subsequently his head as well when Henry had him executed on a trumped-up charge of treason.

Jacoby had been distantly related to Catherine Howard, Henry's sixth wife, and when he separated her head from her shoulders after it turned out that she was not quite as pure and virtuous as a queen ought to be, what with the odd lover here and there, and a little bit of incest on the side, Henry had taken the opportunity to settle a few scores, amongst whom was one William Jacoby.

The original holdings had been much larger than they were now, but Walter Whitehead, a drinking crony of the Prince Regent, later George IV, had been an inveterate (and very incompetent) gambler, and managed to lose more than 70% of the family fortune over the card tables.

A chronic inability to count the cards meant that he almost always lost at whist and in the space of time from when he inherited the estate at the age of 27 to when he drank himself to death nine years later, he almost bankrupted the family. He signed away countless acres of prime lands and had to sell considerable property in order to meet his notes, most of which he signed when all but insensible.

Property lost this way included the Great Manor House, which passed into the hands of the Sawden family, the only child of whom, a daughter, married Lord Exham in 1823, and so the Great Manor became Exham Hall. Walter also managed to lose a street of Regency terraces in Newcastle, two farms and a coal mine, which also ended up in the hands of the Sawden family.

Walter Whitehead's untimely death in 1794 from a combination of drink and syphilis, was a great tragedy to his drinking friends and gambling cronies, who had intended to divest Walter of all his property and possessions before he departed this world. His premature death was of great inconvenience to them and they never forgave him for being so inconsiderate.

By one of those strokes of rich irony, so beloved of romantic novelists, the granddaughter of the luckless (and headless) William Jacoby, married an elderly but wealthy timber merchant called Thomas Sawden, the same Sawden family who later acquired most of the estate of Walter Whitehead. Nearly 300 years after Henry VIII had beheaded William Jacoby for some imagined slight or other, nearly all his confiscated property was back in the hands of his successors. If headless corpses could laugh in their graves, William Jacoby must have had many a chuckle to himself.

Over the next 100 years, the Whiteheads had made steady, yeoman-like if unspectacular growth, but never regained its pre-eminence as the leading family of the district; that honour was very securely in the hands of the Exhams, by way of the wealth of the Sawden's and the titles of the Lords of Exham.

If Hector Whitehead was perturbed by the family history and loss of fortune and position, he never showed it. Sometimes, his wife, Phoebe, alluded to it, particularly when important visitors came to Exham Hall and most particularly when Edward VII had stayed overnight on his way to Balmoral in 1907 (and who had put his hand on the thigh of Mrs Christabel Tanquery, seated next to him at dinner, so very high on her thigh that she had almost orgasmed under the touch of his chubby royal fingers, and all but choked on the poached salmon), but Hector told her there was no point in brooding on what had happened over 100 years ago and which could not be changed now, but she would not be mollified.

'If only Walter Whitehead had not been so stupid, we would have been entertaining His Majesty, do you realise that, Hector? *Do* you? His Majesty the King at *our* table.'

And no doubt he would have put his hand high on her thigh as well, which may well have been all she was after.

The hooves of Hector's mare clittered and skittered on the river-washed gravel of the drive as he slowly walked up into the yard, his head pounding fit to split. He slid gingerly from his saddle, trying not to jar his feet too hard, and passed the reins to Jennings, his head horseman, and nodded at the rabbits. 'Give those to Mrs Harper, would you please, Jennings? And you can unsaddle Easter. I shan't be needing her again today.'

'Aye, right then, Mr Whitehead, sir,' Jennings said. 'Off to sleep it off then, are you, drunken old bugger?' he mouthed to Hector's departing back, having caught a blast of stale ale on

Hector's breath. 'All right for some,' he thought to himself and led the horse off to the stables at the right-hand side of the main farmhouse building as Hector tottered over to the front door. 'Bet the missus gives him an earful an all, eh Easter?' he asked the mare.

She snorted and tossed her head as though in emphatic agreement.

Hector's boots echoed loudly on the polished millstone grit paving slabs of the hall and Jenny Pollack, the maid, looked up from her dusting and bobbed in a short curtsey as he walked across and then turned to face the wall, as all servants were taught to do when their masters come by, like naughty children at school.

'Where's Mrs Whitehead, Jenny? Do you know?'

'She went out, sir. Gone over to see Mrs Palgrave, sir. Col. Palgrave's wife, she's been not too good.'

'Right, thank you Jenny.' He sat down on a high-backed bench at the end of the hall, briefly holding his head in his hands before unlacing his calf-length boots, trying to keep his head upright as he did so.

'You all right, sir? Do you need any help with them, yer buits, I mean?'

'No, no thank you, Jenny,' he growled rather more harshly then he intended. 'I'm not so far gone in my cups that I can't unlace me own boots.'

'Oh, no sir, din't mean that.'

'That's all right, Jenny, I'm sure you didn't. Just please ask Mrs Harper to bring me a glass of water, would you? A large glass.'

After a short nap on top of the bed, shorter than he would have liked, Hector felt better, not much but some, and then found that he actually felt worse for lying down. After rinsing his face in cold water, he made his way downstairs and into his study.

He sat in his high-backed leather chair, leaned back and

closed his eyes, and felt better almost immediately. He sat like that for an hour or two, simply letting the strong home-brewed ale work its ravages out through his system, and mulling things over gently in his mind.

Hector often did this; he liked the solitude, and nobody ever disturbed him in the study. Once he had gone inside and shut the door behind him, nobody but nobody dared to intrude on him, not Robert Wilson his manager, certainly none of the servants, and not even his wife. The world could be coming to an end and the Archangel Gabriel standing outside the door to give warning of Armageddon, but Hector was never, *ever*, to be disturbed in his study.

Phoebe Whitehead occasionally asked him what he found to do in there for so long and he would tell her that he was going over the farm accounts or reading stock reports, perusing learned journals on improved methods of husbandry, or checking the Shorthorn Herd books that recorded all the breeding details for his prize herd.

And, sometimes, he really did these things.

But, most often, Hector would get his decanter of vintage port and a cut-crystal glass, and having placed these on his desk, would reach behind him and pull down from the bookcase a large, very heavy, leather-bound *Bartholomew's Atlas of the World*. The book was nearly 18' tall and 12' wide, bound in crimson leather, embossed with now faded gold and was so heavy and durable that it would almost have made an adequate substitute for the millstone grit paving slabs on the floor.

The book was a special limited-edition, printed in1897 in commemoration of Queen Victoria's Golden Jubilee, and was Hector's pride and joy. If there had been a fire and he had time to take only one possession before he fled, that atlas would have been the one.

His younger brother, Wilfred, now a Major with the Royal Durham Regiment, had given it to him as a present when he had been posted to South Africa during the Boer War, a sort of memento, just in case. Hector had given Wilfred a matched pair of Purley shotguns, beautifully balanced weapons, and Wilfred had made fine sport with them on the high veld with the result that many an antelope and gazelle and scores of ptarmigan and grouse had found their way onto the Officer's Mess dinner table.

When opened, the atlas covered half of Hector's desk, and he would have to push aside his papers and stock reports to make room. A well-worn crease down the length of the spine showed that the book was usually opened to only one or two pages and, as soon as Hectors throbbing head had subsided to a mere dull ache, he had once again lined up his port and glass, taken down the atlas, grunting as usual at the sheer weight of the beast and, almost reverently, opened it up and turned the pages over, gold-edged heavy vellum folios that whispered sibilantly as they turned, skimming them over until the whole book seemed to subside with relief into an accustomed position when he reached the shores of Africa.

Africa!

The very name had a magnetic pull on Hector. Ever since he had been a small boy, Africa had had a fascination for him. He had never been there, never expected that he ever would; the responsibilities of Highfield Farm were simply too great, but he could sit in his study and close off the rest of the world about him, turn open his atlas and lose himself on the high African veld or in the jungles and steamy heat of the Slave Coast.

With his fingers, he would trace the courses of the great rivers, flowing in his mind down the cascades of the Nile and Niger and Zambezi, or tracing the footsteps of Livingstone or Burton, John Hanning Speke or Mungo Park, wishing that he been one of them.

Or that he could have been with his brother, Wilfred, who had taken unpaid leave after the South African war and, in company with three fellow officers, had traversed southern and central Africa, from the Cape to Abyssinia, on horseback, before finally arriving at Djibouti, racked with fever and with a poisoned leg, almost dying. But even if he had died, Wilfred would have lived the life he wanted. He was back in England again now, stationed at Home Barracks in Durham City with his regiment and desperately missing the sharp, clear blue skies and the wide-open veld of South Africa.

Hector was the eldest son and so had inherited Highfield, and it had been tied as tightly round his neck as a yoke on a bullock. Apart from when he had been sent away to school, he had hardly ever left the district and it had been his brothers, Wilfred, younger by two years and Herbert, younger by four, who had escaped the shackles—the straight-jacket confinement—of Highfield and travelled the world.

Wilfred had been with his regiment in India and in Africa, and Herbert had joined a Missionary Society and had been sent to China, where he had been murdered during the Boxer Rebellion in 1902, crucified onto the rough mud walls of his tiny mission, and forced to watch as his wife Mathilda and two small children had been beheaded before his eyes. But, in spite of all his subsequent agonies, Herbert had broken out from Highfield.

Hector smiled to himself as he considered how conventional the lives of the Whitehead males had been, the eldest inherits; the second joined the army and the third, the church. Even his two sisters, Helena and Hortense, had escaped Highfield, although not so far as Wilfred and Herbert. Helena had married Sir Percy Drange and helped him manage his estates in Ireland and Hortense was married to John Jameson-Farr and together they ran a small, but select, public school in Bath.

And Hector stayed—trapped—at Highfield. As would be his eldest son, Leonard, tied by roots as deep in the soil of Highfield and the roots of the trees that surrounded the pond on the other side of the drive, by the roots that stretched back and had dug deep for almost 400 years.

Leonard was 20, studying in Edinburgh and Hector knew that, in his heart of hearts, he really wanted to become an architect, but Leonard accepted, as Hector had had to accept, that the responsibilities, the future of Highfield, was in his hands, in his blood.

The other sons, Giles and Herbert, could follow the dictates of their hearts, because the soil of Highfield, however much of it got ingrained beneath their fingernails, that soil could never be theirs. Highfield soil belonged to the bloodline and Highfield soil owned the soul of that bloodline. And nothing could change that!

With a sigh, Hector drained his glass of port, closed the atlas with a heavy thud and replaced it on the bookshelf.

NINETEEN

And Germany and Britain were at war.

Out in the fields, Jeb the Neb and Jamie Jope and the other reapers still worked; the scythe still swung in that same rhythmic cadence and a long line of stooks marched across the golden stubble like guardsmen.

By the time dusk fell, Jeb Fulcher's huge monolith of a nose was sunburnt and peeling, the British ultimatum had been dismissed by the Kaiser, and Germany and Britain were at war.

TWENTY

I'll not be telling you again, woman, get yourself up them stairs.

Norman Blackett, Mary Garforth's brother, staggered out of the 'Greyhound' and leaned against the wall for support, trying to clear the mists of alcohol that clogged his brain. The thirteen pints of Newcastle Breweries Mild and Bitter ale lay heavy on his stomach, distending his bladder like a barrage balloon.

'Need a piss,' he mumbled to himself and lurched across the road and into a dark narrow alley, the fading summer evening light barely penetrating into the narrow brick gennel.

He fumbled open his fly and urinated in a steady stream that seemed to last forever, a sharp fetid smell telling him that the alley was already well patronised by cats and dogs for the same purpose. He could feel a tingling running down into his fingers from the relief of emptying his ale-full bladder; a yellow Niagara Falls of urine ran down from the wall and flowed around his boots like a river around rocky outcrops.

With difficulty, he fastened himself up, managing to get most of his fly buttons done up and, feeling pounds lighter, carried on down the street, vaguely heading towards his home in the village of Mangdon Hearth on the outskirts of Durham.

Norman, a Regular with the Royal Durham Regiment, was home on short furlough. The barracks in Durham had been rife with rumours of war and as many men as possible had been rotated on four-days leave, just in case. Yesterday, from outside the barracks, Norman took a bus into town and then cadged a ride the four miles to home with Manny Vickers in the butcher's van.

His wife, Olive, had not been expecting him. She was dusting the front room of the narrow terrace house when Norman got home. She had inherited the house when her mother died in 1907. Norman hardly sent home a penny more than the allotment of 3s 6d automatically deducted from his pay. On top of the Government Separation Allowance she got when he was away from home, and if she had not got the little house, she and the children would have been out on the streets for all the support Norman provided.

Olive was a drawn thin-faced woman with sunken cheekbones. She had once, briefly, been pretty, but the years of a lonely and loveless marriage had not worn well on her. Her hair, prematurely grey, had thinned to bare wisps and she almost always wore a head scarf to hide the pink scalp that glistened through the sparse, watery hair.

She looked up in surprise when Norman stumped in through the back door. He had stopped off at the 'Bull's Head' at the corner of the street for a pint or two or three on his way home and it showed in the thickness of his voice and the way he leaned against the door jamb.

'Hello Norman, pet, I weren't expecting you,' she said soothingly, trying to gauge his temper. Norman could get nasty with drink and she always had to tread a bit warily when he had been at the 'Bulls Head'. 'Nowt wrong, is there?'

'Nay, just got four days, is all.'

'I were just dusting. Have you had owt to eat, I can fix you up with a bacon butty, if you like?'

'Nay, bugger that. Get yourself on upstairs and get you drawers off.'

'Now? What about the bairns? They might come on in.'

'Drop the latch on the door then, Olive, come on, use your common …'

'Aye, but …'

'I'll not be telling you again, woman, get yourself up them stairs.'

There was a menacing ale-edged ring to Norman's voice and with a sigh Olive put down her duster, locked the back door, and followed Norman up the narrow stairs to the front bedroom.

After he had finishing rutting on her unresponsive body, Norman said, 'Wake us up in a couple of hours,' and then rolled over and went to sleep, snoring lightly through his open mouth, lips moving as if he were blowing out a candle.

Olive slid over to the edge of the bed, located her discarded underwear, dropped her skirts and went on downstairs to finish her housework.

After his sleep, Norman had eaten some bread and bacon and cheese, and then took himself off to the pubs again. He rolled home around midnight and woke up Olive and the kids as he swore and cursed, trying to unlace his boots. 'Fucking bastards,' he hissed in frustration as the laces wilfully refused to untie.

He finally got them off, threw them into the corner, and then clattered and crashed his way upstairs and collapsed, fully clothed across the bed. Olive covered him with the quilt and trying to hold back her tears, slithered over into the far corner of the bed, and curled up into a tight ball, trying to take up as little room as possible.

TWENTY-ONE

The toe caps of his boots flapped open like gutted fish.

The next morning, the kids kept out of Norman's way, he was hungover and irascible, and he prowled around the house like a caged bear, liable to lash out at anyone who upset him.

Olive cooked up some ribs of lamb and mashed potato and cabbage, and after his lunch Norman said he was off, out again down to the 'Bulls Head'. Olive wondered how he had money to go out drinking all the time but did not dare to ask.

Actually, Norman had been a big winner on the 'Crown and Anchor' board run (illegally) by Dennis Stanley in the barracks, winning more than £5, enough to pay off his debts from all the times he had lost and still have £2.10s in his pockets.

After drinking all afternoon and early evening, he found himself in the 'Greyhound' again, not far from the town centre, where he nearly got into a fight with a drayman over who had won the FA Cup Final in April. Norman loudly insisted that Aston Villa had won, whereas the drayman, equally intoxicated, swore blind that it had been Sunderland.

In fact, both men had been wrong. Burnley had beaten Liverpool 1-0 at Crystal Palace. Nevertheless, the two men shouted and waved their arms at each other before squaring off in the middle of the public bar. Then some glasses got knocked over and the landlord had thrown Norman out, allowing the drayman to stay because he was a regular.

As he continued up the road, a street urchin, no more than nine or 10 ran up to him. The boy was thin and undernourished, short in stature and had a runny nose, which he wiped on the back of his hand. He was wearing only a thin grey shirt, short trousers, obviously cut down from a man's pair many sizes too big and held tightly cinched round his waist with a piece of rope. The toe caps of his boots flapped open like gutted fish.

'Hey mister,' he called as he ran in front of Norman. 'You want to fuck my sister? Only two bob?'

'What?'

'Aye, fuck my sister? Come on, man, only two bob. She's 14 years old and me mam's only just started her prossing so she's right clean. Come on, mister, what you say? Or has too much ale softened your cock?'

'Cheeky little bugger,' Norman snapped, but was still tempted, wondering whether he had too much drink in him to manage.

The boy-pimp, sensing Norman's hesitation, pointed across the road to where his sister stood by a gas-lamp. 'Look mister, see? She's right nice, juicy. she'll get it up for you and no mistake.'

The girl, so far as Norman could tell in the dim light, was thin like her brother but pretty, at least for the while, until the ravages of her trade took hold.

She waved a hand and then rubbed at her crotch enticingly and blew kisses at him. 'Come on over, pet,' she called. 'I've been keeping it nice and warm for thee.'

Somewhere, in the shadows, another street-whore cackled, rusty-voiced and bronchitic.

Remembering the unsatisfactory coupling with Olive, Norman was sorely tempted and scratched at himself unconsciously, but he knew deep inside that he would never manage it, not with the girl just backed up against the wall in the alley; he was far too drunk for that.

'Nay, nay,' he said at last to the boy, the words coming out almost as a sigh. 'Thee's right. Too much ale.'

'Gis a tanner then.'

'A tanner! What's thee what a tanner for?'

'For me time and trouble. Come on, mister, gis a tanner.'

'Give you the back on my hand, cheeky little sod,' he said, lurching towards the boy, hand raised for a backhand slap, but the boy danced away, boot toes flopping in derision.

'He's useless,' he shouted to his sister. 'The stupid old bugger's got a soggy cock. SOGGY COCK!' he shouted after Norman. 'SOGGY COCK! SOGGY COCK!'

Other shouts and taunts followed Norman as he scurried away, feeling angry and humiliated, wanting the girl even more now, but unwilling to go back, not daring to risk the humiliation if he did go back and still couldn't perform. He clenched his fists angrily, wanting to smash at something, anything.

He found his way back to Mangdon Hearth and stopped off again in the 'Bull's Head' for another pint.

'Thy Olive's been looking for you, Norman,' Jimmy Sullivan, the landlord said. 'She sent your Billy down here first to find you. Told him you'd left ages ago. Then Olive came down herself, seemed a bit agitated, like.'

'Bugger 'em, just give us a pint, Billy. I'll be away home when I'm good and ready and not before.' He downed his pint in three swallows and, still in a foul mood, headed home.

Olive was waiting for him by back gate, looking down the passage for signs of him.

'What's all the bloody fuss about, woman?' he demanded, belligerence swelling out of him in waves.

'Telegram, Norman. You've got a telegram. It come about five o'clock. I didn't know what to do, I've been right worried. Must be important, else bad news ... a telegram.'

'Aye,' Norman answered, his anger fading in trepidation. Telegrams usually meant one thing only: a death in the family.

Olive hurried on ahead of him and passed the little buff envelope to Norman as he came through the door. He looked at it a little fearfully, as if it might bite, and then slowly ripped it open, dragged out the telegram, and peered at it under the gaslight.

'Well, I'll be buggered,' he muttered.

'What is it Norman?' asked Olive, hand on mouth.

'War!'

'War?'

'Aye, war. All leaves been cancelled with immediate effect and I'm ordered to report to barracks as soon as I get this. We're mobilising. It's come at last, Olive, war. We're at war with Germany.'

TWENTY-TWO

We'll be facing Kaiser Bill and his bullyboys.

August 1914 France

Major Wilfred Whitehead mopped his brow and raised his binoculars to his eyes again, focussing in on the dirty-grey spirals of artillery smoke that swirled skyward across the other side of the town of Le Cateau, tucked away in the valley of the River Selle, down to the northeast.

His eyes felt heavy and gritty, from too much dust on the French country roads, from too much marching and too little sleep. He wondered what the date was, had to think back, counting out the days in his mind; it must be August 24th, he finally decided. Not even three weeks since war had been declared. No, that couldn't be right, he thought again. Puzzled, he worked it out once more, using the fingers from both hands, ticking off the days since the battalion had arrived in France.

They had disembarked at Boulogne on the 17th and had moved up to take up position by Mons. The 23rd had been a Sunday, he was sure of that. The 23rd was his wedding anniversary and he had heard the church bells of Mons in the distance amidst the gunfire and had thought of his wife, Kathleen. She too would have heard church bells, the bells of St. Andrews in the village of Castlebridge in the Dales of south Durham, close by the border with the North Riding, where they had set up home.

So, if the 23rd was a Sunday, today must be, what? Monday had been the 24th, Tuesday the 25th—today must be Wednesday the 26th August. That sounded more like it.

Something about the date, 26th August, stirred a vague memory, tantalisingly close to the surface of his brain, but as was usually the case, the harder you thought about something, the further it faded, and he could not track it down. 'No, can't think what it was. It can't have been that important.'

He scanned slowly across the gently rolling fields. Most of the wheat had already been harvested and the stooks lay strewn across the fields like golden pavilion tents, but he could see where some fields of sugar beet and clover were still standing, although he doubted whether much would remain standing once battle was joined.

To either side of him were the lines of his shallowly entrenched battalion, the 2nd Royal Durham's. The men of his own company were nearby: Sgt Anderson, Norman Blackett, Wilson, Stainson and others. Wilfred felt as though he had been on the move ever since landing at Boulogne, and the 10 days or so before that had been hectic enough, with the regiment mobilising and preparing for war.

All leave had been cancelled and there had been no time to make up the silly quarrel he and Kathleen had had the last time he'd been home. He could not even remember what the stupid argument had been about but wished he taken back all those harsh wounding words, so unnecessary ... so wrong to go to war like that ... with sour words festering between them.

He had not even been able to telephone her to say sorry and goodbye. Telephone lines had not yet been laid up to the village;

the nearest telephone was more than eight miles away, in West Fenton. He had written, of course, but he had been so frantically busy before they sailed, he hardly had had time for more than a few hastily scribbled lines.

Telegrams had been sent out all over the county, calling in the Reservists; they all had to be equipped, assigned to platoons, and their shiny new boots broken in. The organisation of all the vast paraphernalia of a regiment on the move was immense, time so short, and then the whole battalion had been transported by rail from Darlington to Southampton for embarkation and the journey across the Channel.

Packed like sardines in a P&O transport, they had moved out and down the Solent at about six o'clock, slowly sailing past the forts and Spithead, gliding through the heavy viscid night, silent like black-hulled ghosts in a dark, whispering sea.

All told, by the 17th August, one cavalry division, six infantry divisions, and two support divisions of the British Expeditionary Force, almost 90,000 troops, with all their ammunition, equipment and horses, had crossed to France in a highly secret operation—so secret that, almost up to the day they were confronted by the BEF at Mons, the German General Staff refused to believe that more than a handful of British soldiers had left the shores of England.

Never a good sailor, Wilfred had been more than glad to disembark at Boulogne, where it seemed as though the entire town had turned out to welcome them, a milling throng of babbling Gallic enthusiasms, flags waving, cheers and flowers, and kisses from soft (and not so soft) French lips. As they marched through the town to the transit camps, the town came along too, swirling around the marching men with more flowers and cheers and flags, chocolate, cigarettes, newspapers that few could understand, bread, sweets, bottles of wine or beer, yet more cigarettes, some pressing little red white and blue tricolours into willing hands, or pinning tricolour ribbons to jackets, a triumphal cheering gladiatorial parade.

More than one soldier was swept aside into a nearby cafe or estaminet to toast the *entente cordiale* and, for some, it was many vin-rouged hours later before they were led or carried back to their units by their ever-accommodating hosts.

Col. Colyer-Brown, the CO, instructed his officers to turn a blind eye to any such transgressions. 'The men are in good high spirits, gentlemen, so let us keep it that way. As long as they are all present and, more or less, correct at morning rollcall, we should not make too big an issue of this, eh, Whitehead?' He addressed Wilfred but encompassed all the assembled officers in the remark with a wave of his hand.

Wilfred disagreed but knew that his opinion was not actually being sought. 'After all,' the CO continued, 'within the next few days, we'll be facing Kaiser Bill and his bully-boys. Then we'll show them, give them the damn good thrashing they deserve and send them packing back to Berlin with their tails between their legs, eh? So, a little overindulgence with our convivial hosts will not go amiss for the men, for today at least. However, gentlemen, such will not be the case with the Officer Corps, standards still have to be maintained in this regiment and I expect all my officers to set a suitable example.'

Colyer-Brown permitted himself a thin smile, a rare indulgence, and then declared, 'Having said that, gentlemen, I trust you will join me in sampling some of this excellent brandy that the mayor has insisted on presenting to us.'

Pvt. Norman Blackett was one of many who could hardly keep his head upright the next morning, skull splitting; he swore that he would never ever touch a drop of alcohol again for as long as he lived which, judging by the way he felt, was not going to be very long. What on earth had he been drinking, for fuck's sake?

'Van blong' his drinking companion, wrapped his arms over

Norman 's neck and breathing garlic and wine fumes all over him, kept calling Norman 'mon ammee', pouring more van blong into his glass and shouting 'cheerio' and 'bonn sharnse' and 'veeve larntarnt cordial', which Norman presumed to be some sort of drink, and he responded with, 'Aye, doon the hatch, man,' and 'mud in your eye' and 'why, aye, pal, I don't mind if I do have another.'

'Never again,' he swore, swallowing hard as another rush of scalding bile surged up from his stomach. 'Never a-fucking-gain.'

The following day, the battalion had entrained and travelled east across France, arriving at a little village near the Belgian border called Bruyere-la-Mont, a few miles east of Valenciennes, and some 15 miles to the south of Mons.

Wilfred and the other officers travelled in some style, in the first-class passenger carriages and, although the journey seemed endless, there had been some diversion in watching the French peasants working their fields and endless discussion as to whether the war would be over by Christmas, and wasn't it a damned outrage that women suffragettes, convicted of assault on policemen, had been unconditionally released under the King's Amnesty, the consensus of opinion being that the war *would* be over by Christmas, and that rather than being released, the suffragettes should have been damn well horse-whipped. Votes for women, indeed! They'd be enfranchising dogs and lunatics next!

Comfort for the soldiers had been less evident, for they had travelled in horse trucks.

'Home sweet fucking home, I don't think,' grumbled Blackett, scraping mounds of horse droppings into a pile with his boot and sweeping the dung out of the truck and onto the ground beside the rails. 'And what the bloody hell is supposed to mean?' he asked, pointing at a sign by the door which read: HOMMES 40 CHEVAUX 8.

'Forty men, eight horses'

'Aye? Well bugger that for a lark. I ain't gettin' in there with eight fucking horses.' He jumped out of the wagon again, peering all around him, as though looking for equine travelling companions.

'Blackett, you useless pillock, get your arse back up there,' shouted Sgt Anderson. 'It means 40 men or eight horses, the reason being as how it takes 40 useless fuckers like you to match the intelligence of eight fucking horses.'

'Oh, aye. Then what's all this straw for then Sarge, eh?'

'That's your fucking rations, Blackett! What the bloody hell do you think it's for? It's to sit on, you pillock! Now, get the fuck in there and bloody well shut up. The Colonel would rather like to get off sometime today, if that's all right with you, Blackett, of course?'

''Why, aye, Sarge, tell him any time he's ready, that's fine by me.'

'Aye, well, he'll be right pleased to hear that, I'm sure.'

TWENTY-THREE

Here we are, come to save their arses for 'em.

Arrival at Bruyere-la-Mont caused great consternation and panic. Nobody had bothered to tell the French of the regiment's arrival and the sudden sight of a thousand strange and undoubtably foreign soldiers streaming out of the train, pouring out like rats through their little country station, had sent the villagers fleeing in panicked alarm, convinced that the dreaded Boche were amongst them, bent on pillage and rape.

'Well, ain't that bleeding typical. Here we are, come to save their arses for 'em and all they can do is fuck off out of it. Typical of these bloody frogs,' grumbled Blackett, his observations based on a lifetime of experience in France, gained over at least three days, and conveniently forgetting all about his highly enthusiastic and alcoholic welcome in Boulogne.

Soon enough, the villagers realised their mistake and set about making rapid amends. The village girls quickly made up bouquets of flowers for the officers and the mayor made earnest hand-wringing representations to the CO, all but demanding that the village be allowed to vindicate its honour by making a presentation to all 'les brave soldats Anglaise' and that the honour of 'tout la belle France' would be 'despoiled', spat upon, if he refused.

Mindful of the need to maintain good relations with their allies, Col. Colyer-Brown reluctantly agreed and ordered the battalion to be drawn up in the village square.

''Tallion … shun,'' bellowed the RSM and 947 pairs of boots stamped down as one onto the stone paviours of the square, the hob-nailed crash echoing around the walls like thunder and startling the pigeons and sparrows, as the beaming rotund mayor, best suit buttoned tightly across a well nurtured belly, waddled in great self-importance up to where Col. Colyer-Brown stood, his adjutant and other officers arraigned behind him with the battalion in ranks, in company formation, Wilfred Whitehead standing before A Company.

Behind the mayor, a bevy of young (and not so young) village girls, clutching bouquets, giggled to one another as they waited for the signal to make their presentations to the officers. Eager villagers pressed around on all sides, or hung out of windows, stood on cafe tables, or climbed into the trees of the square, perching in the branches like vast over-ripe fruit.

Much to Colyer-Brown's evident discomfort, the mayor gave him a huge bear hug, colliding belly to belly with him (the CO not exactly sylph-like in figure himself), following this up with a hearty, very wet, very audible, kiss on each cheek, waves of indignation and disgust radiating from Colyer-Brown like farmyard ordure. At this, the welcoming committee of girls hurried forward, jostling one another to get to the officers they had already decided were the ones for them, the best looking and the most dashing, most of the girls only too willing to give their all for the war effort.

'Look at 'em,' Norman Blackett muttered enviously to Dick Stainson, a reservist, lined up beside him. 'French popsies, officers only for the use of.' The eagerly expectant girls placed the flowers over the officers' heads, giggling and fluttering their eyelashes.

However, his envy soon turned to derision as the officers (under orders, it must be added) merely saluted in acknowledgement, stiff and unbending, while the disappointed girls, scorned and hurt-eyed, turned away.

'Useless fucking prats. You can't bloody believe it, can you, man? Offered up their greens on a plate like that and they turn 'em down.' He clucked his tongue in disgust. 'I always thought that officers were neutered bastards and this fucking well proves it!'

Determined to be compromised by at least *somebody*, the girls turned their attention to the rest of the battalion, handing out single blooms to the soldiers, who were only too happy to restore the honour of the British Tommy, more than willing to do their best to help the girls in their evident desire, their overwhelming anxiety to be compromised.

The estaminet was placed out of bounds, but that did not dampen the outpourings of mutual esteem. The officers, perhaps trying to overcome some of the ill-feeling caused by their pompous dignity, clubbed together and set up barrels of free beer in the square (Wilfred disagreed with this as well, but could not be seen to be a piker, and reluctantly added his share to the kitty).

By early evening, a short, quite chubby little farmer's wife had grown quite attached to Norman Blackett. Her husband had been called up from the reserve on August 1st, as had most of the younger men of the village, and full of burning patriotism and free beer, she was now feeling rather lonely and very amorous. Eventually, she led him away to one of the outhouses where the battalion had been billeted and, without much further ado, reached for his fly buttons, grasping for his stiffening erection, pushing her plump breasts against his chest.

'Now, there's a little sweetheart,' he whispered, trying to ignore the smell of cattle in her hair as he lifted her skirts to find her naked beneath, very wet and eager to his touch, and proceeded to enjoy an entente cordiale with her.

And he was by no means the only one in the battalion to cement good relations with the villagers this way, or at least with the female ones, that is.

The next morning, August 20th, was a scorcher. The sun beat down relentlessly, shimmering off the white-washed walls and cobbles in a furnace as the battalion lined up in the square once more, preparing to march out. The whole village turned out to see them off, sorry to see them go. They festooned the troops with flowers again, slipping the blooms under caps and behind ears, tucking them behind buttons of tunics or in breast pockets, thrusting posies into hands, draping wreathes around necks and over guns, single stems slipped down the barrels of rifles, thrusting more loaves, more cigarettes, and round soft cheeses at them, damp-eyed girls wiping away a tear or two, perhaps already wondering if the consequences of their welcome might not bear bitter fruit in nine months' time.

For half a mile or more, the villagers kept escort with the marching troops, cheering and waving. Blackett could see his eager night-time companion waving and scurrying along, trying to keep pace, blowing kisses and laughing and crying at the same time, and he felt a stab of remorse, not for the French farm wife but for his own wife, Olive, at home in Durham. He quickly dismissed it, however. 'Sod it, I could be dead tomorrow and what she don't know won't hurt her.'

He had been unfaithful before, with the camp whores in India and wherever else the battalion had been stationed. He had been with the whores, who plied for trade outside the barracks at home and, if he lived long enough, no doubt would do so again. He felt his groin stirring at the memory of Marie, that was her name, writhing under him like a warm, well-fleshed barrel.

Wilfred Whitehead marched at the head of A Company, staring steadfastly ahead, looking neither to left or right, ignoring the cheering and waving, thinking how disgraceful the behaviour of the villagers had been, most particularly the women, shameless hussies, throwing themselves at the men like that. Had they no respect for themselves? But, then, the French always did have loose morals and were renowned for their decadent behaviour, and their toilets were an absolute disgrace.

Just beyond the environs of Bruyere-la-Mont, most of the escorting townspeople stopped but continued to wave until the battalion was out of sight, although one or two boys kept track with the marching men for another hundred yards or so before dropping out.

Dick Stainson, a former miner only recently joined up, grinned at Blackett. 'Not a bad little billet that one, eh, Norm? A cushy number. If I'd known soldiering were going to be like that, I'd have joined up proper years ago.'

'You should 've been with us in the Shiny, man. That was a cushy number and no mistake, like that all the bleedin' time, all these brown Indian bintis with jewels in their nostrils, thought us white men were kings. And treated you like that an' all. Best poontang I ever had anywhere, I can tell you.'

'Oh, aye? How were that like?'

'Why, aye, man, they're trained like that. They've got these temples, see, all over the place, with statues and carvings, all of folk fucking. So, they can learn all about it, see. It's like a sort of religion to them, you see.'

'Gerraway man. Nobody has statues or owt like that, not on temples, well I mean, wouldn't be allowed. Stand to reason does that. Not on temples. You just codding, ain't you?'

'I tell you straight, man. Ask anyone what's been in the Shiny. You ask them about the carvings on the temples. And about the bintis. Ask about the bintis.'

'What about 'em?'

'Well, they're taught how to take care of a man, take care of all his needs like. They're taught to be … what's the word? … subservient, aye, that's the word. Subservient. Do anything you tell 'em.'

'Anything?' Pvt. Crawley, another recent arrival on the other side of Blackett, asked.

'Aye, absolutely anything. And everything.'

'Are, are they different like? You know, different?'

'What's you mean, different? Like have they got two heads or some'at?'

'Nah, you know, different? Down there? You know? *Different*?'

'Oh. Aye, of course. They all got two of 'em, one for every day and one for the weekend.'

'Really. Nay, you just codding me again, playing the old soldier, aren't you? They ain't really got two. Have they?'

'Course they ain't. Only difference is, none of 'em 'ave got any hair on it. Soon as they get to 12, 13 years old, it's all plucked out. Smooth as a baby's bum.'

'Why'd they do that then?'

'Hygiene, I s'pose. So's you don't get crabs or nowt. Aye lads, the Shiny's the place alright and no squaddie can say he's got his knees brown until he's done a stint there.'

'And you reckon it's a cushy number? Jack Bilson were saying as how the enemy women cut your balls off if they catches you?' Dick Stainson asked.

'Aye, and the rest, slice you up in ribbons they will, the Pathan women. So, you don't let them catch you and in any case that's only up on the Frontier. Otherwise, it is a cushy number alright. Everything gets done for you, you give a wallah a rupee or two, coppers only, and everything gets done for you-your washing, cleaning, and you even gets shaved as you lie in bed in the morning. I tell you, I could do with a few more little cushy numbers like that, and no mistake.'

'Talking of cushy little numbers, Norm, how about that little one that latched herself onto you, last night?' asked Crawley, a sneery leer on his face.

'Aye, well, she were a right little belter. Couldn't hardly wait 'til I got me trousers down, at it like a rat up a drainpipe. How about you, you get lucky?'

'Well, didn't really fancy none of them.'

'None of 'em really fancied you, you mean.'

'Nah, it's not that, but you don't know what they've got.'

'If you don't know what they've got by now, son, no wonder none of 'em didn't fancy you.'

'No, I don't mean that, I mean disease and that.'

Norman Blackett shrugged; to an old sweat like him, venereal disease was as much an occupational hazard as irascible sergeants or ponced up officers.

'What I can't understand,' Stainson said, 'is how she could fancy an ugly little bloke like you?'

'Because of me shy and retiring nature, that's why.'

Turning a bend in the road, they were finally out of sight of the village and somebody at the rear of the column, with a fine sense of occasion, began to sing. 'Who were you with last night, out in the pale moonlight?' and in no time the whole battalion joined in. 'It wasn't your sister; it wasn't your ma ...'

'Bastard, shit, bastard,' Norman Blackett swore as his hob-nailed skidded yet again on the slippery smooth cobbles of the pavé. Even soldiers hardened after years of route marches along roads and highways all over the Empire found it all but impossible to march, or even walk, properly over the cobblestone roadways. No matter which way you put your foot down, the angle of boot sole to road surface was wrong, throwing the weight of the body off line and onto the ankle, and in the oppressive August heat, feet began quickly to swell and blister. Newcomers like Dick

Stainson, in particular, suffered with blistered soft skin in still hard new boots, but even the old sweats soon began to suffer from blisters the size of half-crowns.

Ankles turned and twisted on the cobbles with rapid and depressing regularity and all the men were soon hobbling along as though walking barefoot on red-hot coals, every foot soldier in the BEF the same, convinced that cobblestones were an instrument of torture devised by the Spanish Inquisition.

The noonday sun was high overhead, beating down on the Durhams as they marched northwards to link up with the rest of the BEF over the border in Belgium. Sweat poured down their faces, attracting hordes of irritant flies. Packs dug deep into shoulders and rifles seemed to get heavier and heavier with every step and before long, every ounce of excess weight had been thrown aside, the line of their march was littered by a trail of wilted bouquets, crumpled flowers, (empty) bottles of wine and beer, cheeses, and just about anything else not strictly necessary.

The chorus of songs had very quickly petered out, at first becoming merely desultory, and then rapidly tailing off altogether. It was simply too hot and uncomfortable. The superheated air seemed deficient in oxygen, leaving none to spare for singing. But, despite their discomfort, the men were still in good spirits, the high holiday atmosphere of their French excursion still with them, and they were on their way to give the Germans a damn good thrashing and be home again for Christmas.

TWENTY-FOUR

Dismissed the BEF as 'a contemptable little Army'.

The BEF, under Sir John French, were taking up positions to the left of the French Fifth Army, holding the extreme left flank of the Allied forces, deploying on a 25-mile front, running northwards for 10 miles from the fortress town of Mauberge to Mons, and from Mons westwards along the Mons-Conde Canal.

By late morning of the 21st, the Durhams had entered Quiverain, passing by a squadron of highly polished Hussars from the 4th Cavalry Brigade stationed there, and Pvt. Norman Blackett once again had to scrape horse-dung from his boots.

'Why the fucking hell can't they pick it up and take it home with 'em? God only knows. Leaving it round here for decent folk to step in—bastards! Just because they're sitting up there on big fucking horses, they think they own the place.'

Continuing down the Mons road, they passed through Boussu and then moved up to the canal and, by late afternoon, finally reached their position close by the village of St Ghislain, six miles westwards of Mons, collapsing in exhausted heaps.

They were allowed a few minutes respite before orders were given and they began to dig in. Other troops from the 13th Brigade, the 2nd Hants and Dorsets, could be seen digging in on the other side of the canal, covering the road access from the north and the railway bridge.

Even though the Germans were rumoured to be close by, the Belgian girls from the village still took great interest in the Durhams as they dug their trenches and filled their sandbags. Throughout the evening and following day, they trooped down in droves, bringing with them beer and wine, baskets of fruit from nearby orchards, eggs, coffee, water, and salves to soothe blistered feet, and more than one girl had to be ejected from forward lookout posts as they joined in the jolly game of looking out for Germans.

Snaking wraiths of river mist seethed across the surface of the canal as dawn broke on the morning of the 23rd. Across the other side of the canal, ground mists hugged the terrain and the soldiers moving about there seemed disembodied (as indeed some of them soon would be), legless corpses floating on a grey, heaving swirl of hazy murk.

Wilfred Whitehead walked along the line of the shallow trenches, inspecting sandbag walls and lines of fire, talking to his platoon commanders and checking the disposition of his men, giving encouragement here and there to the nervous about to come under fire for the first time.

Aerial reconnaissance told the Corps Commanders that the Germans were moving closer, pushing forwards on a wide front. The BEF was ready, four divisions in all, with the full expectation of forming an offensive in conjunction with the French Fifth Army of General Lanrezac, stationed on the right flank, and sending the Germans packing.

But the best laid plans …

The Germans, more numerous than expected, were also moving in a wider arc than expected, and General Joffre's disposition of the French Fifth Army and, particularly of the BEF, had left them dangerously isolated, stuck out on a limb that could easily be severed as the German First Army under General Von Kluck and the Second Army under Von Bulow approached from the north, and the Third Army of General Von Hausen moved in from the east.

The French were attacked on the 22nd August and could no longer cross the River Sambre in offensive formation and, on the following day, General Lanrezac warned that the fortress at Namur had been pounded to rubble by heavy siege mortars and was about to fall and that the German Third Army had appeared on his exposed right flank; there was no option but to withdraw.

This left the BEF, already in a forward position, to face the full weight of the German First Army at Mons, and the Germans, having already dismissed the BEF as 'a contemptable little Army', expected to sweep aside the two divisions of II Corps facing them at Mons and along the canal with little difficulty. But the best laid plans …

TWENTY-FIVE

Able to lay down witheringly accurate fire at a rate of 15-20 rounds per minute.

Slowly the rising sun burnt away the last shreds of mist and the men of the Royal Durhams now had a clear view across the canal and the flat lands beyond, the woods and copses, the telegraph poles on the railway lines, the handful of red-tiled buildings at the road junction ahead, and the church tower at Baudour, all plainly visible.

Wilfred Whitehead checked his watch yet again—waiting was always the worst part—and then he closed his eyes and mouthed a silent prayer, imploring for the strength and courage to face the day, and praying that Kathleen should find future happiness if he should fall, and then he recited 'The Lord's Prayer' to himself. *Our Father, which art in Heaven, Hallowed by Thy name. Thy Kingdom come, Thy Will be done, on Earth, as it in Heaven …*

Norman Blackett scratched an insistent itch in his crotch and wondered whether Marie had given him crabs or the pox, but decided it was too soon to tell and that it was probably only an insect bite or the heat.

Nine o'clock and the weather was already hot, and the church bells in Mons began to ring out for Sunday Mass. The first shots of the battle were fired as forward outposts across the canal spotted a troop of Uhlan cavalry emerging from the woods and opened fire with rapid rifle volleys, driving them back with heavy casualties. More and more German troops began to emerge from the trees and down the roads, swarming across the open fields like grey ants by the hundreds, rushing to try to take the bridges and drive the British back.

Time and time again, they were driven back. The riflemen of the BEF were trained in peacetime to the highest standard in the world, able to lay down witheringly accurate fire at a rate of 15-20 rounds per minute. So concentrated was the fire that some Germans thought they were advancing against machine-gun fire. But, eventually, the sheer weight of numbers began to tell as six German divisions were brought forward for the assault.

'Rapid fire, rapid fire,' Wilfred shouted again as the Germans massed once more across the canal, trying to get to the bridge. Overhead, the divisional artillery laid down another barrage into the rear of the Germans, the shells screeching over, sucking the air as they passed, shrieking like mad things in the tortured air. He had lost count how many times the Germans had poured forward, each time to be thrown back with heavy losses.

German artillery had been brought forward by now, raking the British positions with deadly shrapnel, shells bursting in the air above, blasting down their lethal rain of resin-cased lead balls, and dozens of Maxim machine guns set up at the forward flanks were beginning to take their toll. Casualties in the Durhams were mounting, already Lt. Aust and more than 20 men had been killed in A Company alone, and many more wounded.

Blackett slammed home the detachable 10-round magazine box back into the stock of his Lee-Enfield Mk III rifle, adjusted the back sight again, drawing a bead on a heavy-bearded German NCO urging his men onwards again, and shot him clean through the chest, worked the turned down bolt to eject the spent .303 cartridge, and lined up another target—again and again, his actions so automatic as to be almost robotic, exhaling through his clenched teeth in a short punched gasp after every shot.

Beside him, Dick Stainson worked his rifle steadily, not as rapidly but to a good rate nonetheless, his eyes stinging from cordite smoke, grunting 'bastard, bastard, bastard' with each shot.

Away to the right, Wilfred could see thick pillars of black smoke rising as Mons burned, finding it hard to believe that barely hours ago, the church bells had been ringing for Mass and that Belgian citizens there had been about their devotions. More shrapnel shells screamed by overhead, this time to explode beyond their position.

Across the canal, he could see that the vastly outnumbered Hants and Dorsets were in danger of becoming overwhelmed and he directed more fire into the advancing Germans, but the position had become untenable and the defenders began a controlled retreat back to the bridge, moving back by platoons, each movement covered by another platoon in a leap-frogging manoeuvre. With a rush, the Germans swarmed up on them and, only by desperate hand to hand fighting, were driven back; the badly mauled Hants and Dorsets pulled back onto the bridge and over to the southern bank of the canal as the Durhams poured more covering fire at the onrushing attackers.

Had the French still held the right flank position, it was possible that the German advance could have been held up even longer at Mons, but with their flank unprotected and the German Second Army moving up, and the First Army turning around on the left flank, the BEF had no option but to pull back or risk being encircled.

The 'Contemptable Little Army' had inflicted stunning losses on an Army almost three times its size, stubbornly resisting attack after attack but it could do no more and, in a now dangerously exposed position, began to withdraw.

Col. Colyer-Brown received the orders to retreat by motorcycle messenger from Corps HQ, and the Durhams began to pull back slowly from the canal, company by company, as behind them the Royal Engineers blew the bridge. They fell back slowly and in good order, without panic, but Saint-Ghislain was silent as they passed through, no laughing girls with bouquets today. Fearfully, the villagers hid in their cellars, knowing that Mons had fallen and that the next soldiers to come down the streets would be Germans, hard on the heels of the retreat.

And so began the Retreat from Mons, an ordered fall back of nearly 130 miles, pulling back southwards from Belgium almost to the outskirts of Paris, a fighting withdrawal that took almost two weeks to complete as the BEF moved back in parallel with the French Armies to the right.

However, a retreating cat, even though wounded, still had claws and General Sir Horace Smith-Dorrien, Commander of 2 Corps decided to turn and make a stand at Le Cateau, 25 miles to the south of Mons, buying time with lives so as to allow the remainder of the BEF to continue to withdraw in good order.

So, now on the 26th August, the 2nd Battalion Royal Durham Regiment, reduced in numbers following the battle at Mons, but still a very effective fighting force, were shallowly dug in on the rise leading back from the Cambrai Road and awaited the assault as Von Kluck's First Army bore down on them from Le Cateau.

Pvt. Norman Blackett lit up another Woodbine, drawing in deeply and blowing the smoke through his nose so that it wreathed about his head and face, and then he swore as it stung already sore eyes. He scratched about vigorously in his pubic hairs again, convinced that Marie—was that her name -it seemed so long ago he could hardly remember her—had given him crabs. *The dirty fucking frog bitch*!

Captain Wilfred Whitehead raised his field glasses again, scanning the fields and slopes in front of the Durhams' position. Just ahead were three batteries of the 28th Royal Field Artillery with their 18-pounder howitzers and, to the left, the HQ of the 13th Infantry Brigade. At the bottom of the slope, close to the Cambrai Road, the 2nd Kings Own Scottish Borderers had dug in, whilst behind them, further back up the rise towards the guns, were the 2nd Kings Own Yorkshire Light Infantry.

Other batteries of artillery and the 14th Infantry Brigade stood to the right, whilst beyond, to the left, the remaining remnants of II Corps were positioned, reinforced by No 4 Division, who had not been present at Mons, all waiting for the First Army to continue their outflanking advance from Mons and Le Cateau, and bear down on their hastily deployed positions.

Up on the ridge, some 2000 yards away—near the ruler-straight Roman road that passed to the right of their position and cleaved over the hill ahead like a sword cut through a skull—Wilfred thought he saw movement and trained his glasses there, lightly adjusting the knurl to sharpen the focus. At first, he could not see what it was that had caught his eye, then he saw them jumping out large and menacing into the lenses—German heavy guns, 15-cm field guns—brought up along the road from Montay and now swiftly unlimbered and ready to be deployed.

Wilfred quickly turned his field glasses over to his left, over to the other side of the sunken road to Troisvilles, where 122, 123 and 124 Batteries of the 28th RFA stood, ready to send a messenger to them if necessary, but the gunners had already seen the Germans and, even as he watched, he could see them preparing to open fire.

The 18-pounder guns spat fire and smoke, rocking back in recoil, the spades digging deep into the stubbled soil of the fields as the guns seemed to rear back onto their trails before crashing back down onto the spoke wheels, the bark of the cannonade obscenely shattering the mellow silence of the early morning and echoing across the shallow folds of the valley as the smoke swirled back and around the gunners, briefly obscuring them as they run up to reload.

Wilfred turned to watch the fall of the shells; flames and earthy gouts of the hillside spat up to show that the shots had fallen well short of the German positions and gunnery officers quickly shouted orders to raise the elevation of the gun barrels by a degree or so. Other batteries opened to the right of the Durhams, better elevated, but still falling short and wide.

Then the German heavy artillery opened up in response. The 15-cm field howitzer was of much larger calibre than the light-weight 18-pounder British guns, laying down HE shells weighing almost 100lbs, five times heavier, and with a well-trained gun crew almost as quickly: five rounds to the minute as against eight per minute.

Grey white smoke, deadly powderpuff balls like sprouting dirty grey toadstools, began to spread across the fields, the air filled with the primeval banshee scream of shells and heavy crashing explosions as the opposing artillery battered each other's positions like fire-spitting dragons, a ferocious gunnery duel where helpless infantrymen could only huddle in their shallow trenches and pray, powerless at the moment to affect the course of the battle.

An infantryman needed a target, needed to be able to see his man in his gunsights, else he was impotent. Artillery duels fought over ranges of thousands of yards were not for him. All he could do was wait and die, trapped like a rabbit on harvest day on the shell ravaged slopes.

The Germans, on the high ground, quickly established the range to the British batteries and laid down constant heavy fire onto the guns whilst other guns sought out the ranks of soldiers hiding in the fields amidst the cornstalks and clover, and sowed a deadly seed of shrapnel into the furrows of their tight-closed ranks.

Whitehead raised his glasses again and saw smoke rising from the woods by Le Cateau, where British shells had gone wide, setting trees alight, and then saw the muzzle flashes as the German guns fired again. A field gun in the battery to the right was smashed aside as though it were matchwood and the gunners ripped asunder, and then more shrapnel raked the trenches. Casualties were high but, for the moment, so long as the British held ground, the Germans could not advance except into the rapid-fire fusillade that had exacted such a fearful toll at Mons.

Another shrapnel salvo straddled the Durhams' position, showering them with clods and dirt and its lethal rain, ringing ears with the blast, and Wilfred could hear high-pitched screaming further over to his right; somebody had been badly wounded in C Company. Over and over, the agonised wail cut like a knife across the hellish battlefield cacophony of gunfire, impossible to believe that human vocal cords could produce such hideous tortured anguish. It sounded worse than pigs being slaughtered at Highfield Farm, and he whispered a prayer for the poor wretch in such torment. 'How much longer?' he asked himself. 'How much longer are we supposed to stand this?'

And through all the chaos and din of the battle, the significance of the date, 26th August suddenly came back to him. It was the Anniversary of the Battle of Crécy, when Edward III and the Black Prince had crushed the French; he wondered if this was a good omen.

The 2nd Durhams hugged the ground tightly as another salvo rattled viciously about them. Dick Stainson had a haunted, waxen glaze to his face, and Norman Blackett guessed he was near to breaking and gave him a nudge. 'OK?' he shouted.

Stainson swallowed hard. 'We're sitting ducks,' he replied.

'Like rats in a fucking barrel. Rats in a barrel, that's what we are. Done for.'

'Think on it this way, Dick, lad: it's better than marching.'

'Aye, tha't right—almost owt's better than marching over them bastard cobbles.'

But there was little conviction about him, his remaining courage spread thin, and Norman wondered idly whether Stainson had shit himself, a lot did under heavy barrage like this.

For possibly the hundredth time that morning, Wilfred Whitehead scanned the battlefield, knowing that the German infantry must be advancing through Le Cateau, were probably already working round to the east to encircle their position and then, even as he watched, grey ant-like figures began to trickle out through the woods to the west of the town, taking up positions at the lip of the cutting by the crossroads.

'Machine gun crews!' Wilfred thought, looking across the Roman road to where the Brigade had but a single machine gun.

Further troops spread out beyond the cutting and reached the Cambrai Road. Within minutes, a firestorm of machine-gun fire rained down, scything across the fields to deadly effect, cutting down the gunnery crews as they worked the remaining field guns.

Gamely, the lighter-gunned RFA fought on, but it was like a bantamweight boxer taking on a heavyweight; sooner or later heavier punching was going to be decisive. All morning, the guns had fought and men had died, torn to bloody scraps or ripped to shreds by shrapnel. The smoke wreathed thicker, catching at the throat and nose in a choking acrid mist.

The batteries to the east began to shell the enemy, which was now beginning to gather to the south of Le Cateau, threatening to envelope the right wing of the British position, and the 14th Brigade advanced to cover the flanking manoeuvre. But the situation was becoming critical; so many guns were now out of action and the Germans were advancing to the front and around either flank.

By 14.00, it was obvious that they would have to retreat. All positions were in danger of being overrun and Brigade HQ gave orders for the guns to be retrieved. The horse teams were brought up from the rear, where they had been kept in relative safety, but Wilfred could see that the guns were now so fearsomely exposed, especially those of 122, 123, and 124 Batteries in front of him, that the attempt must be all but suicidal.

A captain of the RFA whom Wilfred vaguely knew, Captain Jones, called for volunteers and six teams of men and horses set off down the shell-racked slopes, towards the guns and into a storm of machine-gun fire and HE barrage so heavy, Wilfred thought it scarcely possible any living thing could survive. Within a minute, 20 horses were down, eight men dead, including Captain Jones, and a dozen or more badly wounded.

Unbelievably, the remaining teams reached the guns and in full sight of the German machine gunners, began to limber up the 18-pounders. More men fell, but three guns were limbered, and they set off back up the slope.

'Come on, come on,' shouted the Durhams, rising to their feet and cheering the gunners on. 'Come on!'

'Please God, they make it,' prayed Wilfred. 'If ever, brave men need Your Blessings today O Lord. Bring them through. Bring them through.'

'Jesus wept, the poor bastards,' Blackett shouted in anger as the first team was blown to shreds almost before it had got moving, men and horses and guns smashed to bloody, pulpy scraps and tatters.

The battlefield erupted into pustulating bouts of fire as the German guns ravaged the slopes, trying to stop the escape of the guns as the Durhams cheered and yelled like lunatics, swept away in the craziness of it, waving hats and guns, as through the hellfire and smoke the two teams galloped on, the guns bouncing and twisting as though alive, gunners crouched over the withers of the left-hand horses, flailing with whips to urge the terrified beasts on.

'Go, go, go,' Dick Stainson bellowed wildly, his fear forgotten in the excitement of the courage of the gunners. 'Go, go!'

'Come you bloody beauties, come on you bastards. Move, move, move,' Blackett, urged, clenching his fists tight around his rifle and waving it over his head as the gun team charged headlong toward them, Durhams scattering to either side as the nearest team, unable to slow down or stop, charged right up and through the ranks, the gun carriage bucking and rearing as though in sudden pain when the wheels lurched into shallow hip trenches.

The second team was nearly on them, aiming for the gap when an HE shell screamed down close by, blasting into them, scattering the gunners clinging to the carriage and bringing down the lead horse. Wounded men lay tossed around like rag dolls as the other horses in the team reared and struggled in the harnesses. An RFA officer hung around the neck of the second horse, blood streaming down his face and shoulders, blinded and in agony. Then, slowly, he slithered to the ground, to writhe and thrash in hideous pain.

'Come on,' Wilfred Whitehead shouted. Without thinking, he jumped out from his trench and ran to help. 'Come on, A Company, to me,' he turned and shouted again.

'Oh shit. Come on, Dick,' Blackett yelled, a blood-filled roaring in his skull.

He and Sgt. Anderson, Bilson, Crawley, Stainson and a few others ran down the slopes to the gun team. Dick Stainson was cut down within yards, machine-gun bullets stitching a bloody pattern across his chest in scarlet stripes, flinging him aside.

Wilfred reached the team and seized a bayonet from Bilson and hacked at the traces and harness, freeing the dead horse. The driver, although dazed and wounded, backed up the team and swung away to the right and on up the slope and through the lines as the Durhams looked to the wounded.

Anderson fell and then Norman Blackett was mortally wounded almost immediately afterwards as another salvo blasted the field, ripping him apart. He never regained consciousness and bled to death about 15 minutes later, never to know whether he had crabs or not. Bilson and Crawley went down and as Wilfred Whitehead struggled to lift the wounded gunnery officer, machine guns swept the field again and scythed them both down.

Wilfred lay in agony for a minute or so and then death settled slowly over him. He died with a prayer on his lips.

II Corps began to pull back along the full length of their front and, by 4.30 in the afternoon, had fallen back by three miles to a line along the Honnechy-Ligny Road, the 14th Brigade in a fighting retreat that slowed down the German III Corps and prevented the right flank from being turned. The order for general withdrawal was given at 17.00 and when the withdrawal was halted at midnight, they had fallen back some 10 miles from Le Cateau.

Where guns could not be recovered, gunners smashed the sights and withdrew the breeches, rendering them useless. All in all, II Corps had lost 38 guns and more than 8,000 men, but the stand at Le Cateau had seriously disjointed the German advance, and the time bought would enable re-grouping of the armies and the strengthening of the defences around Paris.

Pvt. Norman Blackett and Captain Wilfred Whitehead became the first men of the village to die. Norman Blackett had left his home in the village when he had been 14 years old. He had spent nearly all his life since with the army, and as he had married a Durham girl and occasionally lived there with her; at his widow's request, his name was entered on the Durham memorial.

Wilfred Whitehead had been born at Highfield Farm. Once

he had grown up and joined the army, he had not spent a lot of time in the village but, nevertheless, he was still a man of the village and his name could be found at the bottom of the Roll of Honour on the War Memorial. W.A. Whitehead. The first man to die, the last name on the Roll of Honour.

CODA

When 19-year-old Gavrilo Princip pushed his way through the milling crowds lining the roads in the Bosnian city of Sarajevo, and fired two shots from his Browning pistol into the bodies of the Archduke Franz Ferdinand of Austro-Hungary and his morganatic wife, the Duchess of Hohenberg on their 14th wedding anniversary, he unwittingly added the final piece to a highly combustible international jigsaw.

Princip, a member of the Serbian Black Hand Gang—which had a suitably melodramatic ring to it (rather like a 1930's thriller movie, 'Bulldog Drummond versus the Black Hand Gang')—did not, as is popularly supposed, light the fuse that led to the Great War. That fuse had already been smouldering away for a decade or more. Rather, he added to the last few inches of that fuse or, to take the analogy one step further: Princip was the one who inserted that burning fuse into the bomb that was shortly to explode all over Europe and much of the rest of the world.

To anyone studying the convoluted web of treaties and pacts and alliances that abounded in the early part of the 20th century, the reasons for war in 1914 seemed complex. They were not. Quite simply, it came down to greed. And railway timetables. Greed, envy, rivalry between empires, a massive inferiority complex, a massive superiority complex, nationalism, feudalism and yet more greed. And railway timetables.

By 1914, Germany was by far the most powerful state in continental Europe, both in military and economic terms. But

Germany had only become a unified nation in 1871 and had subsequently missed out on the great empirical land grab of the last part of the 19th century. By the time Germany had become a world power, there was precious little of the world left to grab and so felt cheated of what she felt was rightfully theirs.

After all, they argued, we had as much right as Great Britain or France to take over, by force if necessary, large chunks of Africa or Asia and subdue the local populace to our will.

But there was not much of Africa left to divide up. France had taken most of North and West Africa and Britain had cut a swathe from Egypt to the Cape and even King Leopold of Belgian had managed to bag for himself a sizeable chunk of central Africa when he claimed the Congo and Kaiser Wilhelm II was not happy; all that was left for Germany was a few crumbs, Togoland, Kameroun, Tanganyika and the dusty deserts of German West Africa. Although newcomers to the noble art of Imperialism, the Germans set about their new tasks with enthusiasm and quickly got cracking with the whips and shackles and gallows, exploiting the natives all for the greater glory of the Kaiser.

And it was the Kaiser, pompous, vain, weak and overbearing, with a penchant for ludicrous headgear, who had the massive inferiority complex.

And talking of his ridiculous headgear, there was a wonderful photograph of him wearing a highly polished helmet—with an enormous badge on the front—a chain-link chinstrap leading to what looked like headphones sitting above his ears and, to top it all, an 8' high bird wearing a crown, probably meant to be an eagle, perched with wings outstretched, right on top of the helmet, looking for all the world as though it was crapping down the back of the Kaiser's neck.

Britain was the world's major naval power and like a spoilt child, the Kaiser wanted big boats to play with as well, just like his uncle, Edward VII, and subsequently, George V, who couldn't stand his obnoxious little cousin, and so Germany set out to build a bigger and better navy than Britain.

So, there we have Germany, recently arrived on the world stage, aggressive, powerful and successful but inherently unstable, consumed with jealousy over Britain's empire, ruled by an egomaniac, with a feudal system of government dominated by the military and whose concept of international diplomacy fell little short of confrontation and bullying.

Germany's main ally was the crumbling, creaking empire of Austria-Hungary, archaic remnants of the once mighty Holy Roman Empire, a loose conglomerate of Germanic, Hungarian, and Slavic states ruled by the Teutons of Austria and the Magyars of Hungary, all of whom hated one another.

But nationalism was rife throughout the disparate peoples of this empire; the call of nationalistic freedom had spread far from revolutionary France across eastern Europe and by 1900 the Austro-Hungarian Empire was being torn apart at the seams and, together with the disintegrating Ottoman Empire of Turkey, had led to the emergence of several Balkan states, including Serbia, Romania, Albania, Bulgaria and Greece.

France had been humiliated by Germany in the Franco-Prussian War of 1870, losing the provinces of Alsace-Lorraine and, with the loss of that war, France also lost her pre-eminence as the most powerful nation of continental Europe and, so simmered with punctured Gallic pride, determined to recover lost territory and avenge the insult to French honour as perpetrated by the upstart Germans.

After the emergence of Germany in the late 19th century, Bismarck, the architect of German re-unification, had concluded a number of treaties to complement his victories on the battlefield. The Kaiser, on succeeding to the throne, immediately removed Bismarck and the whole carefully woven fabric of interlocking diplomacies and treaties fell apart like a rotting fishing net as the bludgeoning arrogance of the Kaiser rapidly made him more enemies than a temperance publican with the only bar in town.

As Germany grew closer to Austria-Hungary, Russia, previously bound by treaty to Germany, began to move away from them and towards an agreement with France, and so, at a stroke, the Kaiser had surrounded himself with two potential enemies—i.e. France and Russia, thus proving himself as inept at statesmanship as everything else.

Britain, meanwhile, traditionally stayed aloof from these endless European shenanigans, concentrating on the protection of her trade routes and on expanding the markets for the mass-produced output of her industrial might—and that was the real purpose of Empire—ready-made markets in which to sell her products.

Why else would Lancashire cotton be sent to India when it could be manufactured so much cheaper there? And that was why Germany was so upset about missing out on the empire. Envy! Pure envy of Britain's worldwide market for her goods and so, by 1914, economic rivalry had reached a peak.

However, although Britain wanted to remain outside these international treaty obligations, the emergence of Germany as a belligerent trading rival began to cause concern and it was Kaiser Willie's insistence that he had to have the biggest boats to play with—and so thereby challenging Britain's standing as the premier naval power—which led Britain led to an informal (and unlikely) alliance with her traditional enemy, France.

During the early years of the century, a series of international incidents, Morocco 1905, Bosnia 1908-9, and Agadir in 1911, heightened tensions and polarised the powers into their opposing corners. Germany and Austria-Hungary were shortly to be joined by Turkey. And, in the blue corner, France and Russia, with

Britain hovering in the wings, already dismissed by Germany as a potential military threat.

War plans were accordingly drawn up by the German General Staff, purely as an exercise in strategy, you understand —plans intended to avoid a war on two fronts—and, so, Count Alfred Von Schlieffen, Chief of the German General Staff, devised a plan designed to strike a swift and devastating blow on France and so knock her out of the war almost before it began, therefore allowing Germany to then turn eastward and bring her full weight onto the slower mobilising Russia.

As plans went, it stank. It was so horrendously inflexible, that no matter what scenario or threat was presented to Germany, no matter from where danger came, Germany had to immediately invade France and the plan depended completely on the speed of German mobilisation, a swift and total victory over the French, and the notorious slowness of Russian mobilisation. And it was dependent on railway timetables.

The plan could not be changed because of the railway timetables. The German General Staff refused to consider a revised or more flexible strategy and insisted that to change the railway schedules would throw the entire army into total disarray.

And so, when Gavrilo Princip fired his gun and assassinated the heir to the Austro-Hungarian Empire and his wife, he was merely the final cog that set in motion a chain of events he could not possibly have foreseen; he just thought he was striking a blow in revenge for the oppression of Serbs.

How could he possibly have realised that the German General Staff could not change their battle plans because of railway scheduling?

The age-old animosity between Teutons and Slavs became focussed on those two deaths, highlighting a rapidly deteriorating relationship between Austria and Serbia. And if it could be proven that Princip was working under Serbian influence or orders, then Austria would take very strong action indeed.

For a month after the assassination, it appeared that diplomacy might hold, that arbitration or negotiation would result in a settlement between Vienna and Belgrade, but then Austria, egged on by the Kaiser, delivered to Serbia an ultimatum with such drastic and humiliating terms, that if accepted, virtually deprived Serbia of her sovereignty.

Not surprisingly, Serbia refused, as she was meant to, and mobilised her troops against possible invasion, giving Austria a flimsy excuse to declare war, which she did on July 28th 1914, catching most of Europe's senior diplomats and politicians by surprise—and on holiday. Austrian troops actually began to move into Serbia before Austria had even officially declared war.

And then the other dominoes tumbled into place with astonishing speed, fanning the tiny flames of the Serbian issue into a mighty conflagration that swept all of Europe into war within days.

The Czar of all Russia advised his cousin, Kaiser Wilhelm, that Russia could not stand idly by if Serbia were invaded and ordered the mobilisation of 1,200,000 troops and, tit for tat, the Kaiser replied that if the Czar did not de-mobilise them again, then he, Kaiser Wilhelm II, would be forced to mobilise *his* Army.

To which Czar Nicholas replied, 'Go and stick it in your silly helmets, Willie.'—or words to that effect (called international diplomacy) and so, by August 1st, they were at war.

Which was where the Schlieffen Plan and the railway timetables came in. As you may recall, the Schlieffen Plan stated that no matter what, France must be invaded, and so even though Germany was at war with Russia, the railway timetables, which had dictated the form of the Schlieffen Plan, meant that Germany had first to attack France, who had a treaty with Russia.

And in order to attack France, Germany had to invade Belgium and violate her neutrality, a neutrality guaranteed by treaty by Britain, France and Prussia, now better known as Germany. The Kaiser overcame this small technicality of guaranteed neutrality, to which his country had been a signatory, by dismissing the treaty as 'a mere scrap of paper' and, convinced that Britain would do nothing about it, promptly invaded Belgium.

However, Britain told Germany that it *would* honour its treaty obligations in respect of Belgian neutrality and gave Germany an ultimatum, which was ignored.

By August 4th, Britain and Germany were at war.

Just to keep things all neat and tidy, Germany next declared war on France, Austria declared war on Russia and Serbia declared war on Germany, and then Germany and Austria threatened to invade Italy unless she denounced her neutrality, and for some reason I can't quite work out, on August 23th, the Japanese declared war on Germany and round and round the Mulberry bush we went.

All of which might lead to you suppose that Britain went to war in order to protect Belgian neutrality.

Not so.

Britain went to war because she thought that that Kaiser Wilhelm was getting too damn big for his highly polished goose-stepping boots and needed to be taught a lesson, and deserved a damn good thrashing and needed to be brought down a peg or two, and whatever other clichés you cared to throw in along similar lines.

And Germany went to war because she was jealous of Britain and her empire and wanted to play with the big boys and, in the process, grab territory anywhere it could ... Russia, France, Belgium ... she wasn't really too fussy.

Greed, envy and rivalry.

And so, when the newly appointed Secretary of War, Lord

GILES EKINS

Kitchener, called for the first 100,000 volunteers for his New Army, the men of the village of Ashbrook flocked to answer his call.

And men from the village were amongst the first to be engaged in combat against the enemy.

TWENTY-SIX

She'd bloody kill me, she knew I were here.

August 1914

The notice had been pasted onto the back of the post office pillar box that stood at the junction of Ashbrook Road and Whitton Lane. Arthur Morrison, the Council billposter, had ridden up on his bicycle with a bucket of paste strapped to the carrier at the back, and rolls of posters in the other basket, and pasted it up. The surprising thing was that nobody saw him, even though it had gone nine o'clock in the morning.

When he had finished he got back on his bike and rode around to the 'Green Tree' and pasted a notice on the wall there; for good measure, he put one on the stone pillar at the end of the bridge over the river at the bottom of Bitchburn Hill, another one further up Whitton Road past the junction, and one on the wall below the notice board that gave details of service times by the church lychgate. Another appeared on the wall by the chapel and yet one more on the side wall of the Co-operative Society store.

And nobody could ever remember Arthur actually pasting them up; it was though the notices had appeared overnight by some kind of divine intervention.

When he had finished sticking up all the notices, Arthur rode back the five miles to the Council offices in Bishops Shilton where he worked, put his bicycle in the shed, walked to the Drill Hall where the recruiting Sergeant was still setting up his tables, and became the first man from the village to respond to the notice, but then, he had had plenty of opportunity to read it.

At the head of the notice was the Royal Crest with the letters G and R on either side and below that the stirring words:

Your King and Country Need You.
A CALL TO ARMS
An addition of 100,000 men to his Majesty's Regular Army is immediately necessary in the present grave National Emergency.
Lord Kitchener is confident that this appeal will be at once responded to by all those who have the safety of our Empire at heart.
TERMS OF SERVICE
General service for a period of 3 years or until the war is concluded.
Age of enlistment between 19 and 30
HOW TO JOIN
Full information can be obtained at any Post Office in the Kingdom or at any Military Depot.
God Save the King

This last was in a beautiful Germanic Gothic script, which was actually rather ironic if you think about it.

Jeb Fulcher heard about the notice from Dennis Jennings, the head groom at Highfield Farm, and thought about it for a long time, but as was usually the case with Jeb, quantity of thought did not necessarily mean quality.

Jeb puzzled over it all afternoon, turning it over in his mind. The age of enlistment was a worry, he was well past 30, in fact he was well over 40, but he most certainly had the good of the empire at heart; after all, didn't he have a brother serving in the Army in India, or at least the last time he had heard, Jacob had been in India, but that had been in 1909, and Jeb supposed he ought to get round to replying to Jacob's letter sometime, but correspondence was not a strong point with Jeb.

But that was not the point; somehow, the Empire was being threatened and he knew he ought to do something about it.

But there was more to it than that. It was the best, if not the only, chance Jeb might ever get to get away from life as a farm-hand, even though the thought had only just occurred to him. Until he heard about the notice and the call to arms, it had never entered his head that that he might want something more out of life, that there might be something more to be had from life.

It was a matter that required great thought and giving matters much in the way of thinking was not normal for Jeb and he found it unsettling, most unsettling, to his peace of mind. He found it so unsettling, in fact, that he almost forgot to go out and check his traps and was in such a daze as he did so, that even 'blind-bugger Sam' could have caught him if he had been about that night.

All the next day, Jeb worried about the notice, gnawing at it like a terrier with a rat in the barn, before finally deciding he ought to find out more about it.

The next morning, on the way into the village, he came upon Jim Comby, sitting on a wall by the bottom of the hill. Jim had just had a big row with his wife and had gone out for a walk to cool off his temper, and he decided to go along with Jeb. They read the notice on the wall of the 'Green Tree' and agreed they ought to go to Bishops Shilton, to the Drill Hall there and find out more.

The four-mile walk to Bishop took just over an hour and they made their way past the market square and along Auckland Street. Outside the Drill Hall, there was a queue of over 50 men and, by the door, a soldier of the Royal Durham Regiment was directing newcomers to the end of the line, cajoling them like a bus conductor in rush hour.

'Come on lads, move along, move right down the bus please. Plenty of room on top, move right along.'

'Why, I only want to ask about it, man,' said Jeb, 'not joining up nor owt.'

'Move right along to the end there, son,' answered the soldier, who must have been all of 20 years old, pointing to the end of the line 'The Sergeant will see you when you gets inside. Answer all your questions then.'

'But I tell thee, only want to ask—about the notice, age of enlistment and all that.'

'Aye, and so do all of these others, and they got here before thee. Now, I div'ant got all day to gossip with you, so either get to the end of the queue, or else piss off.'

'Come on, Jeb.' Jim Comby took Jeb's arm and pulled him away. He could see him starting to bristle and Jeb Fulcher could be an obstinate old bastard when he wanted to be and the last thing they needed was an argument in the street.

'Stands to reason, Jeb, they've got to have a queue system, else they'd never get nothing done. Folks just walking in from t'street and asking questions all the time.'

'Aye, suppose you're right.' He turned to the soldier who was standing with his hands on his hips, watching them. 'Aye, but thy's a reet bugger, div'ant cost nowt to be polite.'

'Polite? What the fuck's polite got to do with owt? This is the army, man, the fucking army. See where polite gets you in here.' He turned away and directed another group of men who had walked up. 'Right down the end there, lads. Move right on down the bus. Plenty of room on top.'

They walked along the line, nodding and 'how doing?' to men from the village and others they knew: Jackson Wragg from Whitton Lane, Davy Pollack, father of Jenny Pollack, the maid at Highfield, Dick Wilson and Molly Hindle's dad, George. They touched their caps to Gordon Tanqueray, (son of Christabel Tanqueray on whose high thigh Edward VII had once laid his Royal hands at Exham Hall). 'Morning Mr Tanqueray.' And Dennis Jennings, who had told Jeb about the notice, Barney Kenyon, and Percy Edwardes.

Near the end of the queue they came across Edgar Garforth. As soon as Edgar had heard about the notice, he had known what he was going to do and had only been waiting for a propitious moment to skip his shift and hurry on over to the Recruiting Hall.

'How do, Edgar lad.'

'Jeb. Mr Comby ... Jim.'

'Does you dad know you here, Edgar?' Jeb asked, his big nose pointing accusingly at Edgar.

'Nay. Nor my ma. She'd likely bloody kill me, she knew I were here.' And that's the truth and no mistake, he thought.

'So, what you doing here, then?'

'Same as thee, I reckon, Jeb. Joining up, like it says. Only hopes we get to France before it's all over; they reckon it'll be over by Christmas. Besides me dad's got a poor cavil this quarter, and so did I, and there ain't much money coming in. So I thought, you know, one less mouth to feed, well, it might help out a bit.'

'Thee'd best get yourself on home, lad, before your ma finds out. They'll not take you anyhow. 19 it says and you're not 19.'

'Aye? And it says 30's top limit and thee's well over that, so thy'd best get yourself home an' all, Jeb.'

'Cheeky bugger, thee.'

'Well, making on like I'm a bairn or some'at. And anyhow, Micky Dickson, you know, from Alice Street, they took him earlier, and he's younger than me. And smaller.'

'Aye, but I reckon thy ma will take on more than Martha Dickson. She don't give a tuppenny damn about any 'o them kids of hers, be glad to see back on 'em,' said Jim Comby. 'But, Mary, your ma, she'll be right cut up about this, Edgar,'

Edgar shrugged with all the callousness of youth. 'So what? It's does not like she's my own ma, she's only my stepma.'

Jim Comby wagged a finger angrily in front of Edgar's nose. 'Now, thee listen to me, Edgar Garforth. Mary would be hurt, dead hurt, if she heard you talk like that. She loves you, loves all on you like you was her own. And if Jack, you Dad, heard thee he'd knock your bloody, ungrateful head off for you, big as thy are't. And serve you bloody right, an' all.'

'Aye, sorry. I shouldn't have said that, right enough, but stop treating me like I was a bloody kid. I'm 18 year old, and I've been working down't pit for four year, and I'm going in there to enlist and there's nowt that you or any bugger else can do about it. It's the right thing to be doing and by the time it's done, it'll be too late for me ma or dad to do owt about it, neither.'

'Aye, well, you've got to do what you think is right, that's for sure. That's all any on us can do.'

An omnibus pulled up on the other side of the road and a group of about eight or nine young men seated on top deck ran down the spiral staircase and jumped off, laughing and joking, pushing and shoving one another in high spirits. From the cut of their clothes, they were obviously clerks or bookkeepers; all wore suits with waistcoats and watch chains, crisp starched white shirts with high celluloid stock-like collars and ties.

'Look out, Fritzie,' one of them shouted. 'Here we come.'

'What's this then?' another asked Jeb, nodding at the queue of men. 'The Salvation Army soup kitchen?'

'It's the queue for the Drill Hall,' Edgar answered, caught up in their excitement. 'Queue for joining up. You come to enlist? I have.'

'Aye, that's for us. Come on then, lads, form up here.'

'How long's it going to be afore us gets in, that's what I want to know? We've only got half an hour for us dinner break and old Rat-Face Ransome will have some'at to say if we're late back,' declared the youngest of the men, little more than a boy really, anxiously looking around.

'Mr Ransome to you, junior clerk, or sir, and don't you forget it,' responded another of the men in a pompous tone of voice, obviously taking off their superior.

'Don't you worry about Rat-Face, Billy. We're doing this for the King; this is His Majesty's business, so what can Rat-Face say or do, eh?'

'Well, if we're late back, he'll dock my wages and me ma will go spare.'

'Billy, we're leaving that place to join the army. So, what can he say? What can your ma say? Nowt.'

'You don't know my ma. She'll kill me if I lose this job. Bloody well *kill* me.'

'Look, Billy, for the last time, once you're signed up, there's nowt anybody can do, your ma nor Ransome, nor anybody. Now, just up your mythering, the army wants men, not boys.'

Billy blushed in hurt pride, Jeb mumbled something unintelligible, and Edgar grinned to himself at the boy's discomfiture.

Slowly, the line shuffled down the pavement towards the entrance to the Drill Hall, all the men in good spirits, prepared to wait, their only worry being that Kitchener might have found his 100,000 men before they got to the door. More than one man in the queue had visions of queuing up all morning and, just as he got to the entrance, the recruiting sergeant would close the door, saying 'sorry, all full up'. Every minute or so, one of the clerks, or Edgar or Jeb, would lean out from the line, straining his neck forwards to see how many more were still left in front of them. The nearer they got, the slower the queue seemed to move.

'Well, I'll be buggered,' one of the clerks who had introduced himself as Robert Patterson suddenly shouted, pointing across the road at the sign over a shop. It read: WILLIE-HEINZ MECKLENBURG & SON Pork Butchers and Sausage Makers. 'Look at that. That sounds German, doesn't it? Willie Heinz Meck-len-burg?'

'Aye, look, bloody Germans, here in Bishop'.

'They should be fucking well locked up.'

'Should be fucking well shot, you mean?'

'Why, aye, I bet they're bloody spies, you knar. Spying for the Kaiser.'

'Watching to see how many on us have come to join.'

'They'll be up in the top room, counting us, you bet.'

'You watch. Tonight, there'll be a carrier pigeon, sent off to Berlin. With all the information on numbers of enlistments.'

'GERMAN SPIES!' Patterson yelled and pointed. 'SPIES!' And like a match put to a stream of petrol, a groundswell of anger rolled over the line of men in a wave, sweeping them along in a burst of collective fury and, in the blinking of an eye, the orderly line had become a mob, howling for blood.

'BASTARDS.'

'GERMAN-HUN BASTARDS.'

'GO ON, FUCK OFF. BACK TO HUNLAND!'

'SHITES! SHITES! GERMAN SHITES.'

A scared, white face appeared at an upstairs window, prompting another hail of shouts and abuse.

'Look there. BASTARD!'

'Telled thee. Spying on us.'

'SHITES. FUCKING HUN SHITES.'

The mob surged across the road with a howl of anger, hammering at the door, fighting to get closer, pushing and shoving. A screeching, ululating howl swelled around the ranks, a primeval feral roar that raised the hackles and heated the blood. Edgar Garforth jostled and pushed with the rest, blood pounding in his skull, his only thought to get at the Germans, tear them limb from limb. He stumbled on something at the paving edge and bent to pick it up, a broken half brick, lying there almost by providence.

A soaring red rage swirled through him, imbuing him with a strength he did not know he possessed, and he forced a way to the front of the press, shouting and screaming. 'Back!' he yelled. 'Stand back, stand back. I'm going to smash the bloody window in, stand back. Back!'

Men fell back to give him room until a heaving, panting semi-circle fell back away from the shop-front window as Edgar raised him arm to throw. 'Go on, son. Smash the fucker in.'

'Go on, Edgar. Right through the fucking middle.'

The collective venom of the mob seemed to flow into his arm as he hurled the brick at the centre of the window. There was a tremendous smash and crash of breaking glass as the window imploded and the crowd cheered, and someone whistled.

'Good on you, son,' someone shouted, 'serve the shiteing krauts right!'

And then someone, Edgar did not see who, threw another brick at an upstairs window, missing it to the right. The mob rushed forward in a mass scrum to finish the job, knocking out the rest of the glass with walking sticks so as to get at the window display.

Pork chops and bacon, and strings of sausages, were strewn onto the ground, strips of belly pork were hurled into air to be trampled underfoot, a pig's head display with an apple in its mouth was held high in triumph, like a battle trophy, and was then smashed to the pavement, to be kicked by scores of booted feet like some bizarre primitive football match or fertility rite. White china plates and trays loaded with meat and parsley garnish were shattered on the paving stones in an orgy of destruction, a communal will to wreck and destroy. It was not even looting, but sheer red rage, a wanton act of destruction, the need to smash and devastate, like the pillaging hordes of the Dark Ages.

Someone threw stones at the upper window, smashing it in and showering the crowds below with broken glass, but since they were almost all wearing caps and hats, few were cut.

A policeman shoved his way through the crowds, who fell away before him as though he was tainted by plague. 'All right. Al right. Come on,' he shouted, 'move aside, move aside or else some of you will be spending the night in the cells.'

He reached the shop front and surveyed the damage, a pursed look on his face as he gazed at the smashed window and the ruined food, and then glared at the crowd, which was already beginning to melt away. 'Aye, you lot must feel reet proud of yourselves, lads, I don't bloody think. What a disgrace. Shameful.'

A few looked sheepishly around. Already passions had subsided. Almost as quickly as the rage had risen it had gone, as though a sluice gate had opened, flooding all the anger away in a torrent.

He looked at the nearest faces, scanning over them and as his gaze passed over Edgar, he felt a surge of panic, sure his guilt must be written all across his face, and he could feel a blush of culpable blood bursting out on his neck and cheeks.

The policeman had another look at the damage before asking, 'All right, then, which one of you lot did this?'

Edgar was about to step forward when he felt someone grip his upper arm tight to restrain him. 'Do nowt, lad, else you'll end up taking the blame for all't lot on us.'

Clucking his tongue in disgust, the policeman dismissed them. 'If I had nowt better to do, I'd have the whole bloody lot of you down at the station. Then we'd see what's what. Now. Clear off, the lot of you, and be thankful I ain't booked you all.' Then he stood guard at the battered entrance to the shop, waiting until all the crowd had dispersed before calling up to the broken upper window. 'It's all right, Mr Mecklenburg, they've gone now, but I suggest you wait there a while and then get this window boarded up. And take down this sign. Next time I might not be around, and feelings is running right high at the moment.' Then he proceeded onwards, kicking a leg of pork gently to one side.

TWENTY-SEVEN

Provided His Majesty should so long require your service.

A few men trickled back over to the Drill Hall and began to line up again; some men had not gone to join in the riot and had benefited by jumping up the queue. Even so, there were still a good 30 or so men lined up by the time Edgar joined the end of the line and, shortly after, Jim Comby and Jeb lined up alongside him. Of Robert Patterson and the other clerks who had instigated the riot, nothing was to be seen. Perhaps they had decided to return to face the ire of Rat-Face Ransome. Edgar wondered idly whether young Billy would get his wages docked and what his ma would say.

Not one of them mentioned the attack on the butcher's shop. It was if it had never happened and Edgar was suffused with a wave of shame and self-disgust, bitterly sorry, deeply regretting his part in it, unable to explain to himself why he had joined in, why he had allowed himself to get so carried away.

Even Jeb felt a bit embarrassed and it took an awful lot to embarrass Jeb Fulcher. It was not as if Jeb didn't know that that

Willie-Heinz Mecklenburg had come to this country nearly 40 years ago, had married a local girl and settled down in Bishops Shilton long before many of the attackers had even been born.

Willie-Heinz had been a sailor on one of the many ships that plied the North Sea, bringing timber from Hamburg and the Baltic to Newcastle and the east-coast ports with coal cargoes going in the opposite direction.

As Willie-Heinz told it, there had been some trouble over a girl in a bar in Hamburg. A knife was pulled, not by Willie-Heinz, he'd always insisted, and there had been a stabbing, not fatal but serious enough to mean trouble for all involved. Willie-Heinz's ship sailed that same night and he had jumped ship in Newcastle, knowing the Polizei would be waiting for him when it returned to Hamburg. He worked ships out of Newcastle for three years or so, long as they weren't Hamburg-bound, but he had grown tired of life at sea.

Willie-Heinz saved as much of his money as he could and after he had met and married Anna Byers, he took British nationality and then bought the butchery business in Bishops Shilton from Anna's uncle, Albert, when the old man retired.

Willie-Heinz had grown up on a pig farm in Saxony, knew the business well and he quickly established a reputation as the finest pork butcher in the district. By August 1914, Willie-Heinz himself had been retired for more than two years and the business was now run by his son, Peter, born and raised in Bishop, helped by his wife, Susan, and their youngest daughter, Greta.

Jeb knew all this, knew that many Highfield pigs found their way to the shop and that it could very well be Highfield pork that was strewn all over Auckland Street, but even knowing all this, he had still allowed himself to be caught up in the madness, urging Edgar to smash the shop window. But Jeb said nothing, introspection was not a strong point with him, and what had happened was over and done with and so what was the point of talking about it? All the talk in the world would not replace the window or salvage the ruined meat, so best forget about it.

When they eventually got into the Drill Hall, the actual recruitment came as a bit of an anti-climax after all the excited buzz of anticipation and tension outside and the attack on Mecklenburg's.

At one end of the hall, four desks had been set up. At each desk sat a recruiting sergeant. Another soldier directed the recruits to a desk as it became free.

'Over there, son,' he said to Edgar, taking his arm and pointing to the furthest desk on the right. To Jeb he said, 'You go to that desk there as soon as that chap before you finishes. Alright?' He indicated another desk.

Edgar, feeling incredibly nervous, swallowed hard and walked up to the desk indicated and stood before it, desperately anxious to be accepted; he did not think he could stand the crushing despair of rejection. The sergeant took another swig at a tin mug of tea, looked up briefly to Edgar, gave him a cursory glance and picked up a fountain pen and tapped the pile of forms on the desk in front of him. 'Questions to be put to the recruit before enlistment,' he read out aloud from the form. He looked up at Edgar again. 'That means you.'

'Yes, er, sir.'

'Sergeant to you, son. Only officers get to be called sir.'

'Yes, alright … er, sir, er, sergeant.'

The sergeant tapped the form again. 'This is Army Form B2505A. Comes in two parts. This notice which I give to you, spells out what's known as the General Conditions of the Contract of Enlistment that you will enter with the Crown. Note that well. A contract that you enter with the Crown. That means *His Majesty*.'

'Yes … sergeant.'

'Second part is this Certified Copy of Attestation. This has the questions you have to answer. Understand?'

'Yes,' Edgar nodded, even though his brain seemed to be turning into a soggy mush.

'Right, let's get on. What is your name?' he read out slowly, as though talking to somebody whose mother tongue was not the English language.

'Edgar James Garforth.'

'Garforth, James Edgar,' the sergeant repeated slowly as he wrote it down on the form.

'No. Er ... Edgar James. Edgar's me first name, not James.'

With a look of disgust, the sergeant screwed up the form and wrote out Edgar's name again on both sections of the next form. 'Right, does that suit you now?'

'Yes, sergeant. Thank you.'

'Very good, sir,' the sergeant said with heavy sarcasm, and proceeded to read out the remaining questions, in full, as they were printed on the form, slowly enunciating each word.

'What is your full address?'

'13 Victoria Street, Ashbrook Stills. Co. Durham.'

'Are you a British subject?'

'Yes.'

'What is your age, in years and months?'

Edgar thought for a few seconds, adding a year on from his birth date of 23 May 1896. '19 years, three months.'

'You sure?'

Edgar could have sworn that the sergeant gave him a little wink. 'Yes, sergeant, positive.'

'19 years, three months.' He wrote it on the form and Edgar gave an inward sigh of relief, pleased with himself that he had fooled the sergeant, not realising that the recruiting officers got a bonus for each man signed on and didn't care too much whether Edgar was nine, 19, or 109.

The questions continued: are you married; what is your trade; have you ever served in any branch of His Majesty's Forces, naval or military, and if so, which; are you willing to be vaccinated or re-vaccinated; are you willing to be enlisted for General Service; did you receive a Notice, and do you understand its meaning and who gave it to you.

Edgar had, with a quick nod, because the sergeant had given him one just 10 seconds before asking the question.

'Are you willing to serve upon the following conditions, provided His Majesty should so long require your service for the duration of the war, at the end of, which you will be discharged with all convenient speed? If employed with hospitals, depots of mounted units and as clerks, etc, you may be retained after the termination of hostilities until your services can be spared, but such retention shall in no case exceed six months.'

To this last question, he answered in the affirmative and, after being warned about the consequences of fraudulent declaration, signed his name, indicating that he was willing to fulfil the engagements made. After that came a medical, which he passed with no difficulty and then with a group of other recruits, Jeb and Jim Comby amongst them, he was sworn in by an officer (of what rank, Edgar had no idea, except that he had a lot of pips on his shoulder and braid on his sleeve and looked old enough to be his grandfather).

This officer first told them they could be attested and sworn in now, or they had the option to attest to a magistrate, whenever that might be arranged sometime in the distant future, and to a man they chose to be sworn in now, fearful that delay might mean rejection. They held their right arms high as the officer asked them if they had all answered the questions and then swore them in. 'Repeat after me. I … then state your name, in full.'

'I, Edgar James Garforth … swear by Almighty God. that I will be faithful and bear true allegiance to His Majesty King George the Fifth, his heirs and successors and that I will, as in duty bound, honestly and faithfully, defend His Majesty, his heirs and successors in person, Crown, and dignity, against all enemies and will observe all orders of His Majesty, his heirs and successors … and of the generals and officers set over me. So, help me, God.'

And that was it. Edgar, Jim and Jeb were in. And Jeb had never even got round to asking his questions about the age of enlistment. Then they were all told to go home and wait, and that they would receive a letter within the next few days telling them when and where to report.

TWENTY-EIGHT

If you've made thy bed, Edgar, you'll just have to lie on it.

Most of the Ashbrook men set off back together—Edgar, Jeb, Jim Comby, Dennis Jennings, Jackson Wragg, Davy Pollack, Percy Edwardes and George Hindle—all in great high spirits.

All the village men had been accepted except Barney Kenyon and another man called Fred Ferrier, who had both been rejected as being below the minimum height of 5'3'.

'Bugger that,' said Barney. 'Just because I'm small don't mean to say that I can't bloody well fight.'

And together with Fred Ferrier and another short man from Etherington, who had also been rejected because of his height, or rather lack of it, they later walked clear across the country to Birkenhead and joined the famous Bantam Battalion of the Cheshire, all to die in France in 1916.

But high spirits began to pale with apprehension as they approached the village; most of the men had not told their wives or families they were enlisting and the irrevocability of their actions was beginning to sink in.

Edgar's father, Jack Garforth, was seated at the table in the back room, waiting for his tea when Edgar walked in, feeling very nervous again, despite what he had said outside the Drill Hall about Mary only being his stepmother. He knew she would be very, very upset, and the last thing he wanted to do was to hurt her.

She was at the sink, draining boiled potatoes. Harold was also at the table and he looked up and scowled at Edgar before stuffing a piece of bread in his mouth.

'Ma. Dad. Harold,' Edgar said as he hung his cap up on the hook on the back of the door.

'Edgar,' his dad greeted him. 'You missed you shift this afternoon … you should've been on at two?'

'Aye, Dad, I know. Thing is, I went over to Bishop.'

'Got a lass, have you, over there?' leered Harold.

'Thee keep you big nose out, Harold,' Jack growled at him.

Mary tumbled the potatoes into a bowl and then divided rather more than half of them up again onto three plates, and put a cover over the remainder, to be kept for Nicholas and the twins. The girls, Mary Margaret, Margaret Mary and Eleanor had already eaten and gone over to Mrs Brayford's, the seamstress on Whitton Lane, for a final fitting on Mary Margaret's dress for her wedding on Saturday—not a 'wedding dress' as such, but rather a 'best dress' that could be worn for other 'posh frock' occasions (nobody could afford to have a special wedding dress that would be worn on a one-and-only occasion).

Mary added some cabbage and turnip onto the plates and then poured oceans of thick brown steaming onion gravy all over. It being Thursday and near the end of the fortnight since Jack and the boys had been paid and so there was no meat, nor would there be until Sunday. There was plenty of fresh home-baked bread though, and this would be used to mop up the gravy and fill any nooks and crannies left in the men's stomachs.

'Here you are, Edgar, get yourself sat down and get stuck in.

You can tell us what you've been up to once you've eaten,' she said to him, passing the other plates to Jack and Harold.

'Aye, right, Ma, thanks.' He was glad of the short respite.

The three men ate in silence as Mary hovered around them, sensing something in the air and not liking it much. Her feelings of doomy premonition had never left her, although they had never been as strong as they had that night last month when they had swept over her like a black tidal wave but, nevertheless, they were always with her. She knew something terrible was about to befall and that it must have to do with this awful war.

Jack finished his meal first and pushed his plate away from him, took a sip of tea and then wiped his mouth on his napkin, tossing it onto the table rather harder than he needed to. 'Right then Edgar, you'd best be telling us what's so blasted important that sends you all the way over to Bishops Shilton rather than going about your work. I can tell you that the over manager were not best pleased, and not just with thee, either. Seems like a goodly number on you all took it to you heads to bugger off for the day.'

'Aye well, Dad,' Edgar started to say, then paused as his mouth seemed to dry up, gluing his tongue to the roof of his mouth. He had to take another drink of tea.

'Come on, lad, spit it out. If it were worthwhile losing a day's wages over, it's worthwhile the telling of it.'

Edgar took a deep breath. 'Ma. Dad. I've enlisted! Joined the army. To go to France and fight.'

Mary gasped and held a hand to her heart, and Jack said nothing; he just carried on, looking straight at Edgar.

'Jack,' Mary said, 'now, you just stop him. Tell him he's not to go.'

'Is that right, Edgar, you've joined up?'

'Aye, Dad. Me. And all the others that were not on shift today: Jackson Wragg, Davy Pollack, and others, and even your marra, Jim Comby.'

'I don't care about any others,' Mary stated. 'They can do as they please, but you just tell him, Jack, you just stop his blather. He doesn't go!'

'Make more room in't bed if he does go,' Harold interjected.

'I've told you before, Harold, I'll not be telling you again,' Jack said menacingly. 'You just keep you big nose out of things that don't concern you. This business is between your mam and me and Edgar. So, you just keep it hushed.'

'If it were me as said I were going, there'd be none of this, would there? You'd all be right glad to see the back of me,' Harold retorted petulantly.

'You can stop that kind of talk an' all, Harold Garforth,' Mary declared angrily. 'I'll not have it. It doesn't matter which one of you it is. There's lots of others that will go before any of my boys go. Now, Jack, you just tell him. He's not to go. For a start off, he's not even old enough, so you'd best get down to Bishop and the Drill Hall, or wherever it is, and tell 'em, because if you don't, *I* shall. I shall be in to see the Chief Constable or the Chief General or whoever. Because he's *not* going.'

'Seems to me, like what he's done, is done,' said Jack, standing up to get his pipe and tobacco jar from the mantelshelf.

'Aye, Ma, can't be undone now. I've signed a contract. A *Contract of Enlistment*. With the Crown. With His Majesty. It's like treason or some'at if I don't go now.'

'And suppose you get you killed, like your Uncle Norman, eh? Or like Hector Whitehead's brother, eh? The poor man, his wife must be distraught, poor soul, just like your Auntie Olive? How do you think your dad and me would feel if that happened to you, eh? Don't you ever think about such things? Don't you care?'

'Mam, 'course I do!'

'Or suppose you come back, and you've lost an arm or a leg? Else your sight? And then what?'

'Ma, I haven't even gone yet and you're talking about me coming back like that.'

'Well, you're not even going in the first place. So, that's an end of it. Jack, you tell him.'

'Edgar, are you sure you know what you've done?'

'Aye, Dad, dead sure. The King has asked for men and I'm going to be one of 'em.' Edgar turned to Mary. 'Ma, if you try and stop me … if you go on down to Bishop and tell 'em I'm not old enough … I shall only go on off and go somewhere else and do it all over again.'

'You don't know what you've done, Edgar. You don't know,' Mary cried, the tears streaming down her distraught face unheeded. This was a worse nightmare than her boys going underground.

'But I do know, Ma, honest. I do know what I'm about.'

'Well, then,' Jack said as he cut off slices of his twist of black tobacco against his thumb with his penknife. 'There's nowt more to be said, is there. If you've made thy bed, Edgar, you'll just have to lie on it.'

'Aye, Dad, I will. And thanks.'

'That's it then, Mary. No more to be said. The lad will do what he thinks he has to do and there's nowt any on us can do to make it otherwise.'

'I might have known you'd take his side, Jack Garforth. Men! You always stick together, no matter what. No matter that I'll be worried sick about him all't time, it's always you men as sticks together.'

'That's the way the world is, Mary, love', he said quietly as he crumbled the slices of tobacco between his palms, breaking them up, and then rolling the tobacco up into a ball. 'Ever since time began, young men have gone off to fight the wars as their womenfolk wept and waited for them to come home again.'

'And is that supposed to make me feel better about it? Why

don't we just shoot him here and now, and be done with it? Do away with all that nasty worry and suspense?'

'Look, Mary, it'll all be over by Christmas. Chances are he won't even have had time to get his boots broken in, let alone get over to France for any fighting.'

'Don't say that, Dad. I want to get into the fighting.'

'Then you're a bigger bloody fool than I took you for. No man wants to fight, but sometimes he has to. That's his duty to his king, and that's the real reason you should've have enlisted, not because you want to go and kill another human being.'

'Why aye, you're right I suppose, Dad. It's just I'd not thought of fighting as killing other people, I suppose. Not as you put it like that.'

Jack tamped the ball of tobacco into the bowl of his pipe, struck a Swan Vesta, let the sulphur flare out and then put the flame to the tobacco, drawing in and puffing out rapidly to get it going, filling the little room with thick, acrid smoke. When he was satisfied, he threw the dead match into the fireplace, pulled at the pipe again, and then asked casually, 'Anything unusual happen in Bishops Shilton when you was there, Edgar?'

Edgar felt the blush of guilt rising up his neck and he turned away so his father could not see, pretending to cough from the smoke. 'No, Dad. Nothing. Nothing out o't ordinary at all, except for joining up, of course. I suppose you could say that were a bit unusual.'

'Oh, aye? Is that all? The way I heard it, Mecklenburg's butcher's shop got smashed up. You see aught of that?'

'What? Mecklenburg's? Smashed up?' Mary exclaimed.

'Aye, now you come to mention it, I did see some'at like that,' Edgar mumbled, not meeting Jack's eye. 'But it were nearly all over by the time we saw it.'

'To be hoped you weren't involved in owt like that, Edgar? Smashing in shop windows?' Mary asked apprehensively.

'What me? No. No. You know I'd not do nothing like that. No, course not.'

'Nay, wouldn't be him,' Harold sneered. 'Not got the bottle for anything like that.'

Jack glared at Harold. 'I told thee to shut it. Right now I'm talking o Edgar. When I want thy smart comments, I'll tell thee.'

'What are you saying, Jack?' Mary intervened. 'Edgar's a good lad; he'd not get into any sort of gallop like that.' As she spoke, she put her hand protectively on Edgar's shoulder. 'Would you, pet?'

'That's not the way I hear it. But then, perhaps folks is mistaken? You've been brought up to tell the truth, Edgar, so, as I say, perhaps I heard wrong.'

'No, Dad', Edgar sighed. 'You heard right. I were involved. Got carried away with it all. Somebody were saying as how the Mecklenburg's must be German spies and everyone were rushing over and hammering on the door and the windows, shouting awful things and that. Everybody, me, Jeb Fulcher. Jim Comby. Others. All shouting and swearing. I don't know what came over me. It was as if I was, I don't know, if I was like somebody else. Then I had this brick in my hand and I threw it. It were me what smashed in the window and I'm right shamed of myself.'

'Edgar. You don't mean it? You've always been such a good boy!' Mary exclaimed, keeping her hand on him as Harold snorted in derision.

'Sorry, Ma, but, aye, I did it. Can't for the life on me think why.' He turned to face Jack. 'Sorry, Dad. For lying to you.'

'Aye, well, it's not some'at you'd want to be boasting about.'

'I know that wishing can never change things, but I wish with all my heart that it had never happened. Been thinking that from as soon as I did it.'

'You knew all about this, Jack?' Mary demanded. 'You knew all about our Edgar smashing Mecklenburg's window?'

'Aye.'

'And you knew that he'd been to join the army?'

'Aye.'

'And you said nowt to me? All that time you've been sitting here, and you said nothing to me about Edgar's going to join up? You even didn't think to tell me that? You didn't even think to tell me?' Mary cried as her voice rose in hysteria.

'There's some things a boy, a man, has to tell his ma himself. Like getting wed, leaving home. Like joining the army. He has to do it for his self.'

'And that's your excuse, is it? A man's got to do it for himself?' Mary's voice was full of scorn.

'Aye.'

'Arrrggh.' Mary ground her teeth in frustration. 'I can't talk to this manly maleness thing. It's just an excuse and this … manliness … it sounds more like childishness to me. Stamp your feet and hope to get your own way and say that a man's got to do it for himself.'

'Aye, that's about the strength of it, right enough,' Jack replied calmly, pulling deeply on his pipe and blowing a contemplative stream of smoke into the air.

'Edgar!'

'Yes, Ma?'

'I don't like what you've done, joining the army, but I suppose a man's got to go wherever his life takes him. And I especially don't like what I've heard about you breaking Mecklenburg's shop up. I don't like that one bit. I thought I'd brought you up better than that.'

'I'm sorry, Ma, truly. I don't know how else to say it.'

'It's not me as you should be saying sorry to, is it?'

'No. Sorry, Dad.'

'I don't mean him neither. He's as daft as you are, or the other way about. Given the same set of circumstances, he'd probably have done the same stupid thing. Got no more sense than he was born with. But I'd have thought better of you.'

'I've said I'm sorry to you, I've said sorry to dad. What else do you want me to do? Say sorry to Harold?'

'Smart cheeky comments aren't going to help you, Edgar. I meant the Mecklenburg's. It's them you should be apologising to. It's them tha's got to make amends to. Isn't that right, Dad?'

'Aye. Lord knows how old Willie-Heinz must be feeling. I've known him on and off for 30 odd years now. You'd never get to meet a better man anywhere on this earth. Give you his last shilling, he would, give you the shirt off his back, and it saddens me to think that a boy of mine could get involved in aught like that. So, Edgar, what does you intend to do about it?'

'Tomorrow. I'll go over tomorrow. Apologise. that's all I can do, I've got no money to pay for a new window, but I'll see if there's anything I can do to help.'

'Tomorrow be buggered! Get yourself over there now. There's plenty of light yet, it's only just gone five o'clock, and it's now when they'll likely need help.'

'Dad! It's four miles or more. And back!'.

'Aye, and it was only four miles this morning when you went over there and took it into your head to break that window. Go on, be off, and don't come back 'til thee's redeemed thyself.'

'Besides, now that thee's in the army, you'd better get used to marching,' Harold leered, sticking in his two-pennorth of bile, as usual.

'One day, Harold, you're going trip over that long nasty tongue of thine,' said Mary with exasperated sharpness.

'Aye, that's right. Take his side, thy always has done.' Harold got up and stormed out the door as Mary held her head in her hands.

Edgar lingered for a minute or so over the few dregs of tea in his mug of tea. 'I'd best be off then,' he said at last, hesitantly, as though hoping that Jack or Mary might change their mind.

'Aye, you'd best,' Jack answered, not looking up from his pipe as Edgar took his cap from the peg and opened the door.

Mary waited until she heard the click of the gate latch before turning to Jack.

'What's to be done, Jack? I don't want him to go to fight, don't want anyone to go off and fight, you know that. What if he gets killed, like Norman?'

'You'll only get yourself worked up, Mary, love, going on like that. What's done is done and can't be changed. Be proud for him, Mary, that's the best thing you can do for the lad. Be proud.'

'Aye, I am proud, dead proud of him, apart from that other nonsense, that is. But scared an' all, Jack. This thing seems to be getting out of hand, this war. Seems to be taking on a mind of its own. And it's an evil mind, I can feel it, feel it deep inside that it won't be satisfied 'til it's taken all the young men. Taken them all for soldiers. I'm frightened, Jack, frightened of this war, frightened of what it's going to us all.'

'Nowt's going to happen, Mary, take it from me, nowt,' Jack answered, tapping out his pipe on the grating.

To Mary's ears, his words sounded as hollow as his empty pipe.

TWENTY-NINE

Stop tormenting and gloating on us like this.

Edgar could hear the birds singing excitedly as they flew into Moreden Woods to settle down for the night, and he whistled jauntily along with them as he walked back along the road towards Bishops Shilton. He squared his shoulders and tried to march, swinging his arms as he did, imagining himself already in his uniform, marching off to battle the Hun, to return in a blaze of glory, his chest full of medals and all the girls of the village eager to take his arm and walk with him.

The summer evening was fine and the sun, a blazing orange ball, was still several degrees from sinking away below the valley rim, and Edgar thought of when he had been a small boy, asking where the sun went at night and his fad telling him that the sun was on a long piece of string and that God lowered it down out of the sky every night and pulled it up again next morning. It was such obvious nonsense, even a child could see it to be nonsense, raising basic questions such as to why didn't the string burn and why did the sun come up on a different side of the world from the one it went down on, but he had never questioned it, never. Children didn't question their parents, he supposed. What your dad said went, and that was the end of it.

As it turned out, he quite enjoyed his walk back to Bishops Shilton, although he began to feel nervous as he got closer to the centre of the small town. Turning down, into Auckland Street, he could see the black-stained brick outline of the Drill Hall, sitting squat and toad like at the junction, and just opposite, Mecklenburg's Butchers.

The street was almost deserted and the few men that were walking down the road seemed to cross over to avoid Mecklenburg's, as if it were a plague house. Even at a distance, Edgar could see that glass and other debris still littered the pavement in front of the shop, although he could also see planks of wood propped up against the wall.

He stopped for a minute and straightened up his shirt and jacket and combed his fingers through his hair. He felt very nervous at approaching the shop and wanted to look as presentable as possible. Edgar looked around him to see if there was anyone he knew watching and then, with his heart beating furiously, he slowly crossed over to the same side of the street as Mecklenburg's, walking as slowly as he reasonably could, telling himself that the longer it took for him to get to the shop, the more chance there would be that nobody would be there. Irrational thinking, he knew, but he really did not know how to begin to face the man whose windows he had smashed.

Almost as he came up to the shop, the door at the side suddenly opened and with a lurch to his heart, Edgar thought it must be Willie-Heinz Mecklenburg come to berate or even attack him. He had visions of the old man coming at him with a meat cleaver and took an involuntary step backwards.

A young girl stepped from the door and she looked up with a start of surprise at Edgar as he overcame his apprehension and stepped, a little hesitantly perhaps, up to her.

'Excuse me, Miss,' he asked, taking off his cap, rolling it up and putting it into his inside jacket pocket. 'I … I wonder, like, if it's possible to have a word … a word with Mr Mecklenburg, old Mr Mecklenburg that is?'

'Why?' There was a brittle anger in her soft voice.

'I, er … I don't really know how to say this. I, er, excuse me Miss, but are you part of … well, part of Mecklenburg's, like?'

'Yes. Why?'

'Why, I wanted to see Mr Mecklenburg, if I could, and I weren't sure if I were right in asking you about it, that's all.'

'Yes, you can speak to me. I'm Mr Mecklenburg's grand-daughter. What did you want to see him for? As you can see, this is not a very convenient moment.' The peremptory tone of her voice didn't help Edgar's nervousness at all.

Edgar waved a hand in the direction of the broken window. 'I was here, like, when it happened and—'

'And that's why you want to see my grandfather?' she inter-rupted angrily. 'So you can gloat some more? Haven't you animals done enough to him already?'

Edgar could see indignant, angry tears sparkling the corner of the girl's bright eyes, and he was suffused with a wave of embar-rassment and regret again. 'No, Miss, you got me wrong. I come to apologise.'

'Bit late for that, isn't it?' the girl answered bitterly.

'Aye, perhaps it is. But I would still like to see him. And apologise. I know that nowt I say going to change any of this.' He waved a hand at the damage again. 'But, like I say, I want to say I'm sorry.'

'Aye, just so's you can ease your conscience, no doubt. Say sorry and all it's all forgotten and forgiven, is that it?'

'Miss, you're not making this any easier.'

'Is there any reason why I should?' she retorted bitterly, her irate eyes flashing at him like daggers. 'Do you know where my grandfather is right now? Do you?'

'Why no, Miss.'

'He's in the hospital! Where you put him.'

'Hospital?'

'Aye. The hospital. So, now you can go and tell the rest of your brave, marauding friends and have a good laugh about it, can't you? Tell each other what a good job you've done on the German spy. My grandfather is 73 years old ... 73 years old and in poor health. When he saw what you animals had done, he collapsed. From a heart attack. In all probability, you've killed him. Well, I hope you are satisfied, and I can tell you what you can do with all your meaningless sorry.'

'Miss Mecklenburg, I'm sorry, I really am. Dead sorry. Please, believe me. Nobody meant to hurt him. Honest. To tell you the truth, I don't even know why we done it, but you got to believe me, nobody was meant to get hurt.'

'No, well how about this then?' she almost shouted and one or two passers-by turned to stare before hurrying on as she pulled back the long sleeve of her blouse to reveal a bandage on her forearm, darkly stained with dried blood. 'When you animals threw the brick through the upstairs window, this is what the flying glass did, and don't say you didn't know I was there because it was not until somebody saw me at the window that they threw the brick. I could have been blinded. Or was that the idea, eh? Blind the spy so she couldn't peep on you anymore?'

She was almost sobbing now, her anger turning to tears that trickled down her face. Edgar took another pace forward, not knowing what to do, 'Please, Miss, don't take on so. Please, is there owt I can do?'

'Yes, you can go away and stop tormenting and gloating on us like this.'

'You got me wrong, Miss, honest. I've not come to gloat. I come to say sorry and to see if there was anything I can do. The only reason I'm here is that I wanted to speak to your grandfather, say how sorry I was. I've walked all the way from Ashbrook to do that.'

'And now you can just walk all the way back again, can't you? We don't want your 'sorry', whoever you are. Just go away and leave us alone.' The girl turned on her heel and made to go back indoors.

'Please, Miss,' Edgar pleaded, taking her arm to hold her back and then jumping back as if scalded when she turned and snatched her arm away, blazing at him with her eyes again.

She was only a small girl. In fact, Edgar was surprised just how tiny she was, no more than 5'0' or 5'1' but, what she lacked in size, she more than made up for in spirit.

'Sorry, Miss. Sorry. Look, I know as how you can't be talking about it in't street like this, but, there's all this … mess to be cleared up and them planks to put up at the window. If you need to get off to the hospital, why, aye, I'd like to help … you know, clean up this mess. And I'll put these up for you,' Edgar said eagerly, desperate to atone as he pointed at the wood.

Greta Mecklenburg hesitated, torn between her practical need for assistance and despising the man who offered it to her, despising herself for needing his help.

She looked at Edgar again, trying to gauge his sincerity. Could she trust him not to do further damage if she went to the hospital to be with her father and grandfather? Her mother was away and knew nothing of this yet; she had been away all day, visiting relatives in Darlington, 25 miles away, and there was no-one else nearby she could turn to.

Mr Avelin, who ran the grocers next door, he would help, but would want something in return, and she had seen the way he looked at her and she had a good idea what that something might be. He was a widower and had twice already asked her father for her hand. If they were beholden to Avelin, her father might, just might, accept his offer.

On the other side of the shop was Mrs Prater who ran the

haberdashery. Greta had always thought Mrs Prater to be a friend, if not of her, at least of her mother and father, but she had turned away, spitting with hate as she hissed 'Hun' and shut the door in Greta's face when she had gone to ask for help.

Greta had to assume that other neighbours would also be caught up in this collective anathema for things Germanic.

Or things that merely sounded Germanic. She had already heard that Wilhelm Kruger's dachshund dog had been hanged from a lamppost as a spy and he was not even German but Swiss. Why had such evil craziness come to the world?

'How do I know I can trust you?' she at last demanded harshly, hating herself for asking.

'Aye, well. You don't, not for right sure, and I don't know as how there's ever going to be a way thee's going to know, excepting to let me prove it.'

'Or otherwise,' she snapped, unwilling to unbend an inch.

'Aye, or otherwise.'

'Well, since you caused all this mess, I suppose it's only right that you should clear it up.'

'Thank you, Miss Mecklenburg, er … it's Miss Greta, in't it?'

'Miss Mecklenburg, if you don't mind.'

Edgar grinned at her, amused at the idea of this tiny girl, scarcely older than himself, putting him in his place like this; he felt as though he were back at school.

'Aye, as you likes, Miss Mecklenburg.'

'I'm glad you find this so amusing; you'll be able to have a grand laugh at all our expenses once you get amongst your cronies in your drinking dens.'

Edgar sighed. There was obviously going to be no appeasing this little hellcat, pretty as she was, in fact. She was just like a cornered cat, pretty to look at but ready to sink its claws into you as soon as you got too close.

'Give us the brush and a bucket of water. Hammer and nails

and that, and I'll get on. Can't spend all night in idle chat with you like this.'

'There's no need to be offensive.'

'Miss, I come here in good faith to apologise and to offer what help I could, and all you've done is sneer and put me down. Fine, you got no call to be grateful to me, after all I were one of them that did this, but if you don't want me to get on with this, say so and I'll get on out of your hair, since it's obvious that nowt I say has the slightest effect. You obviously don't believe that I'm genuinely sorry for this and that I'm trying to make amends as best I can, so there's nowt else to be done, is there?' Edgar declared in exasperation.

'Perhaps you do mean for the best,' Greta answered, but still uncertainly. 'I'll bring you the brush. The hammer and nails should be down there with the wood. I'd asked Mr Oxminton to bring them as well.'

'Right, oh, then, Miss Greta. I'll make a start with sorting out this wood.' He noticed, with a quiet smile to himself, that she did not correct him this time, although she must have heard him.

Greta Mecklenburg went back through the door as Edgar checked out the lengths of planking, running his eye along the length of window, trying to assess if there were enough. There seemed to be enough. Just! As he worked, Edgar wondered why Oxminton the carpenter had not offered to fix the window, rather than just delivering the timber.

Greta Mecklenburg came back out again, struggling to carry a long-handled stiff-bristled broom, a bucket of water that slopped over her ankles as the handle of the broom got caught in the doorway, a hessian sack, newspaper, and a dustpan and brush.

'Here, Miss, let us take that,' Edgar said, hurrying over to take the broom and the bucket from her.

'Thank you. I never realised before how awkward it is to carry a broom under your arm like that.' She smiled briefly at him before remembering that she was not supposed to. He was one the 'animals' responsible for the mess.

'Aye, and it's a right narrow corridor down by the stairs, an' all, in't it?'

'You can sweep up the rubbish and put it in the sack,' Greta said brusquely. 'Do you think it will be enough, or will you need more?'

'Well, Miss Greta, we'll need more than that one sack and it might be better to put it in separate sacks, like. One or two sacks for the glass and stuff and some others for the spoiled food. That way you can feed the food to the pigs, maybe.'

'Won't there be glass, fragments and that, in the meat?'

'Aye, no doubt in some of it, but not in all of it, I reckon. Worthwhile trying to salvage summ'at out of this mess, in't it?'

'Yes, I suppose so,' she replied uncertainly, still not sure whether she could trust Edgar.

Edgar took the brush and walked to the far side of the shop front and began to sweep, working the brush with an easy rhythm, shepherding the shards of broken glass and plates before him like a sheepdog working a flock. He carried the sack with him and picked out the least damaged pieces of meat and, after checking to see whether there was any embedded broken glass, placed it in the sack. He did the same out in the road, gathering all the debris and wheel-squashed sausages and bacon into a pile in the gutter, and then swept the heap up into the dustpan and into another sack.

Greta had now put on a hat, and hovered close by, watching him work for a moment or two, nibbling at her lower lip as she did so. Finally, decided, she said, 'I'll be off now, down to the hospital, to see grandfather. Will you be alright?'

'Yes, Miss Greta. I … I hope he's alright. Honest I do and if you get the chance will you apologise for me? And give him my best, best wishes for his recovery, like?'

'Strange words from the would-be assassin of a German spy,' she answered tartly. 'I am quite sure my grandfather can manage very well without your hypocrisy.'

And with that parting shot, Greta turned and walked away from him. Edgar stood and watched her go, sorry that she had gone. Despite her prickly reaction to him, which was understandable, he found that he liked her and wanted to see more of her. But rather doubted that he ever would. Or that she would ever want to see him.

He picked up the brush again and quickly finished the sweeping up. Then he got to work with the hammer and nails, securing the window. It was almost dark by the time he had finished, and he looked hopefully up the road to see if Greta Mecklenburg were returning before he set off to walk back to the village.

THIRTY

Sentences simply got trampled underfoot and lost in the avalanche of creativity.

Nicholas Garforth sharpened his pencil with a penknife and then opened the red cover of the exercise book that he had bought at Wilson Stationers with money he had saved from his jobs.

He sucked on the end of the pencil for a minute or two, wondering what to write, and then in a small neat hand wrote: *My mother is a right confused combination.*

He read the words again and crossed out *My mother* and *combination* and replaced them with *My Mam* and *mixture* and carried on writing.

My Mam is a right confused mixture. On the one hand, she is dead proud that our Edward has joined up, answered the call to fight for our King, but on the other, she is afraid, worried as any mother must be when a son goes off to fight for his country.

He liked the sentence and the way the words ran together; he had no real idea what he was going to write when he had sharpened his pencils, but he thought he ought to make a start on his literary career and write something, even if it was rubbish. He decided he would write a short story based on Edgar's enlistment and the reactions of his family but changing the names, of course. He had even thought of a title: *The Call to Arms*. He wrote it out in block capitals at the top of the page and then, underneath, he wrote: *A Short Story by Nicholas Garforth*.

He liked the sound of the that and ran it through his mind a few times, changing it to 'a novel by Nicholas Garforth', and 'a novel by Nicholas James Garforth' and 'the novel by N J Garforth', before deciding that he simply preferred Nicholas Garforth as the author name.

He started to write some more, expanding on how Mary has reacted to Edgar's enlistment, adding his own feelings, pride in his big brother, and the mixed reactions of the sisters: Mary Margaret pleased and proud, Margaret Mary worried but understanding and Eleanor, who became almost hysterical in her fear for Edgar (or Edward as he was called in the story).

Words flowed across the pages of the exercise book as he bent nearer and nearer to the paper, so that his nose almost touched the back of his hand as he wrote. And as the words soared in his mind, his writing deteriorated to a barely decipherable scrawl, and he found he could not get all the words and phrases down quickly enough, and many ideas and sentences simply got trampled underfoot and lost in the avalanche of creativity.

After an hour or more of feverish writing, his hand began to cramp and then, as suddenly as the flood of words had poured into his brain, they dried up again. The story was not yet complete, and it would require polishing and re-writing, but as he re-read his scribbles through again, he felt that he had captured something.

'I really am going to be a writer,' he thought aloud and then carefully went upstairs and into the bedroom he shared with the girls. He lifted the bedcover and hid the notebook under the mattress; the last thing he needed was for Harold to get his hands on it. He would never hear the end of it and would probably have to fight him to get it back and get beaten to a pulp again for his trouble. He smiled inwardly to himself at the corollary between the pulp that had been used to make the paper he had written on and being beaten to a pulp to get it back again.

'Bugger you, Harold, and all who sail in you,' he thought to himself and wished that he could show his story to someone, anyone, wished that there were somebody in the family he could talk to about it, but he did not feel he could even confide in Eleanor. Old Man Parsons? No, the only reaction he would get would be another basket full of irrelevant quotations and platitudes. Sarah Treddle? No! She would probably laugh at him and he did not think he could stand that.

No, the half-formed story would simply lie there under the mattress forever, to be found in some distant future epoch by a curious archaeologist who would strain to decipher the scribbled words and wonder at what manner of creature could produce such a marvellous sense of the time and feeling of his age.

Smiling inwardly to himself at his foolishness Nicholas went downstairs and out through the backyard to the privy. 'More likely the bloody thing will end up on the nail on the wall here,' he thought wryly as he pulled off a square of yesterday's *Daily Sketch* from the nail and screwing it up to soften the paper before wiping himself.

'Best place for it, really.'

THIRTY-ONE

Suddenly feeling like a piece of meat on a butcher's slab.

Eleanor lay back against the side of her secret hollow, wanting more than ever to be able to fly away with the birds, or to let the river carry her away to where it would.

All this excited talk of war had disturbed her. Ever since the invasion of Belgium and the declaration of war against Germany, the only talk in the house had been of war, war and war, particularly by Nicholas and the twins. Even Edgar had become affected by the madness and had joined up, carried away by the collective madness that seemed to be sweeping the world away. She had always thought of him as being more solid than that, unlikely to be so impulsive.

The idea of war was abhorrently hateful to her and more and more often she came here, needing to escape. At home in Victoria Street, she felt more and more like a wild bird trapped in a cage.

She lay back quietly for some minutes, enjoying the warmth of the sun on her face, even though she knew it was supposed to be very bad for the skin, very ageing, 'leather-making' as her mother called it.

And then, she suddenly heard the sound of hoofbeats nearby and wriggled up to the lip of the hollow to investigate; if it were the Hunt she would probably die, but no, it was only a single horse by the sound of it, although hard-ridden.

She could see the rider now, galloping along the ridge in the opposite direction she had come from, and she winced as she saw him whip the beast on the flanks. She felt the surge of anger raging through her, as it almost always did when she saw cruelty to animals. 'How would you like someone to do that to you, you swine?' she thought, and would have been only too happy to have shown him how it felt.

He passed by within 50 feet or so of her position without seeing her. She had ducked down well before he got to her, but Eleanor had already seen who he was: the 2nd son of the local land and mine owner Lord Exham. He was the Honourable Gerard Barclay-Milnes and it looked as though he were headed back towards Exham Hall itself. Eleanor felt unaccountably relieved to see him disappear from sight.

After a few more minutes, she slowly got to her feet and headed back towards home. Lost in her thoughts she climbed back over the stile and continued along the path.

'I say! And what do we have here, eh? Popping up out from nowhere like a damn rabbit out of a hole?'

The man's voice, suddenly intruding, startled her to such an extent, she felt as though she had been shot and she clutched a hand to her heart. She looked up to see Gerard Barclay-Milnes standing nearby, partially hidden in a copse of trees. He was holding a cigarette in one hand and the reins of his horse in the other. From the way the horse was holding its foreleg, Eleanor guessed that it had gone lame.

'I'm sorry, er, your, er … sir.' She wasn't certain how to address him. 'But you startled me. I didn't see you there and you

GILES EKINS

made me jump.' She wanted to see to the horse's injury and took
a step or two over. 'Your horse, sir. Is it all right? The poor
thing.'

'Damn beast has gone lame on me, blast him.' And he
swished angrily at the horse's legs with his crop, causing him to
back away.

'Oh, don't do that, sir. Don't hit him, he can't help it.'

'The damn stupid beast should look where he's going'.

'He can't help it. You shouldn't hit him like that, mister. The
poor thing.'

'And who might you be to tell me what I can or can't do with
my own horse? His voice held a drawn-out, languid, nasal drawl.

'Me, sir? Nobody, sir'. I'm not anybody, sir.' And she could
feel his eyes on her body, and she turned away from him,
suddenly feeling like a piece of meat on a butcher's slab. 'I'd best
be getting off then. Sir, I hope your horse is going to be all right
… only, please, don't hit him no more.'

'I said, who might you be? And don't be so damned insolent.
What's your name?'

'Eleanor Garfield, sir. My name's Eleanor Garforth, sir,' she
answered in a small voice, looking down at the ground.

'Garforth? A miner's brat, no doubt, aren't you?'

'Sir?' Eleanor shook her head in confusion, not understanding what he wanted of her.

'Don't be stupid, as well as insolent, girl. I'll ask you once
again. Are you a miner's brat?'

'Well, aye, I suppose. Me dad, Jack Garforth, he's a miner. A
hewer,' she added with pride. 'Top hewer at Ashbrook pit'. She
began to edge away. 'Er, I'd really best be off, now, sir. My mam,
she'll be worried.'

'And what's the damned hurry?' Barclay-Milnes inquired as
he threw his cigarette to the ground and trod it out, and then
looped the reins of his horse over a branch of a tree and took
several steps over towards her. 'You know that you are trespass-

ing, don't you? Trespassing on Exham lands? *My* lands. And trespassing is a serious offence.'

'No, sir, it's not trespassing. This is a right of way, this path. Always has been.'

'And how would you know that? You've seen the land deeds, have you?'

'No, sir, how could I possibly have seen owt like that?'

'So, you don't know anything of the sort, then, do you? Just because a few damn trespassers and poachers use this path from time to doesn't make it a right of way, you know?'

Even though very confused, Eleanor knew well enough that it would only make matters worse to argue. 'No, sir, I'm sorry, didn't know that. Sorry, sir. It won't happen again, mister, sir. Honest.'

'You're damned right it won't happen again. It's going to be the courts for you, my girl, and I'll make sure they throw the book at you. It's about time we made an example of people like you. Troublemakers. Strikers. Poachers.'

'I'm no poacher, sir. Honest! Just taking a walk along't river. That's all.' Eleanor was very frightened now, especially as he had moved closer and cut off her route back towards home. 'Please let me go now, sir. Please. It won't happen again. I promise.'

'And we all know the worth of a promise from people like you, don't we? As soon as my back is turned, you would laugh at me and take advantage of my good nature. Well, it just won't do, you hear? You must be made an example of. Or else you will just simply do it all over again, won't you? Perhaps take a pheasant or two, next time, eh.?'

'No, sir. I'd never take a pheasant, or anything else. I could never hurt any creature like that.'

Barclay-Milnes had now moved right up in front of her, swishing his crop against his leg, staring hard at her, a predatory glint in his eye that she found very unnerving. She kept looking beyond him, and around, praying for someone to come along and help her out of this predicament. Eleanor knew she was in some sort of trouble, she didn't know what exactly, didn't know what it was she was supposed to have done, but could tell deep inside that things were going to get very much worse before they got better, and she suddenly burst into tears.

He clucked in indignation. 'You can just damn well stop that nonsense right here and now, girl. All you women are the same. Think if you shed a few tears and say you're sorry, then every-thing will be forgotten. Well, it might work on my father when you come before him on the bench—he's far too soft with the likes of you anyway—but it won't wash with me.'

'Please, sir. Please, sir, let me go,' she sobbed, unable to think straight, 'I don't know what else you want me to say, honest.'

The Honourable Gerard was enjoying himself, obviously the girl was faking her tears, but he would act out the play with her, and then he would take her; all these girls were the same. They all had the morals of the streets and that could be the only reason she had followed him out here, perhaps hoping to earn a shilling or two.

He felt his erection stirring and reached out to touch her breast, surprised how full it felt under the cheap clothes. Eleanor jerked away as though burned, so shocked that she was not even sure that he had touched her, her confusion so great she was not even sure she trusted her own senses anymore.

Suddenly, she tried to dart past him and get away, but he was far too quick for her and seized her by the wrist, bringing her up sharply, jerking her arm and making her cry out in pain. 'Not so fast, girl. Here's a little matter of trespass still to resolve and running away only makes things worse, doesn't it? Goes to prove your guilt.'

Perhaps she hadn't been faking after all, he thought, but no matter, he still intended to have her. She was quite pretty, really.

Very pretty in fact, and the hurt sensibilities of a mining girl meant nothing. In any case, no respectable woman would be out here on her own; she obviously had no morals or decency whatsoever. None of these people did. She deserved all she was going to get.

'Where do you live, girl?'

'Please, sir, you're hurting my arm.'

'I asked, where do you live?' And Barclay-Milnes pulled her in closer to him and dropping his crop, wrapped his other arm around her, seizing hold of one of her breasts in his left hand.

Eleanor struggled and fought to get away, kicking at his shins, but he merely laughed and squeezed harder, making her cry in pain again. She flailed at him again, catching him a glancing blow on the nose.

'Damn bitch', he hissed through his teeth. Then, suddenly, he let her go, stood back one pace and slapped her hard across the face, snapping her head back, cutting the inside of her cheek on her teeth and then backhanded her on the other side, hitting her so hard she thought her head was exploding. She could taste the salty blood on her tongue mingling with her tears as she wiped the back of her hand across her mouth.

Eleanor was very frightened now, convinced her was going to kill her. Like a rabbit transfixed in a beam of light she could only stare at him as he walked around her, swivelling her head to follow his movements as he passed around behind her, afraid of what he might do. Her heart pounded in her chest as she sobbed convulsively, lungs heaving as she shuddered and shook like a little lost kitten confronted by a savage dog.

Barclay-Milnes rubbed at his nose where she had hit him; he too was breathing hard, his excitement intense. 'This is going to be so much better than I thought,' he told himself, feeling himself tight within his riding breeches. 'The little bitch is going to pay and I'm damn well going to enjoy every minute of it.' And he thought he knew the key that would unlock her.

'Tell me, once again, where do you LIVE?' he shouted, making her start again in fright, as she stood there, elbows clinched into her body, hands shaking as they hovered around her face, her head tucked down onto her chest.

'I ... I don't know!' she squealed in confusion, shaking her head violently in agitation. 'I ... can't ... think. I don't ... know. Please, please let me go.'

'What do you mean you don't know where you live?', he asked as he took Eleanor's chin tightly in his hand and lifted her head, peering into her eyes. 'You can't really be that damn stupid, can you? Can you?' he persisted when she didn't answer.

'You got me all ... muddled. I don't ... know what ... I'm saying,' she sobbed.

'Well, I'll help you then, shall I?' he asked in that condescending tone that adults use when talking to small childrn or animals, moving in closer to her again.

She tried to back away, but he held her arm tightly, transfixing her with his eyes.

'You live in Ashbrook? Correct?'

Eleanor nodded.

'Your father's a miner? Correct?'

Another nod.

'Works at Ashbrook Pit?'

One more nod.

'You live in a colliery house? In Ashbrook?'

Eleanor nodded again, wiping her eyes as she did so.

The Honourable Gerard nodded with her. 'Good. Good. Now, we're getting somewhere.'

His cajoling voice seemed to give some small reassurance to Eleanor and her highly tensed body relaxed slightly, as if someone had slackened off the guy ropes of a tent.

Barclay-Milnes noticed and nodded to himself. He placed the back of his hand against Eleanor's throat and then slowly ran his hand down her body, lightly running the knuckles of his fingers over the swell of her breasts.

She tried to squirm away, but he held her fast to him by her arm.

'No, no, no,' she protested. 'Not to do that. Not to do that. It's not right. What will me mam say?'

'She won't say anything because you won't tell her, will you?' He cupped her breast more fully now, the bulge of his erection straining hard against his breeches as he pushed himself against her thigh. He was breathing heavily now, his breath whistling through his nostrils.

'No, sir, please,' she pleaded again, pulling away from him again.

'Listen to me, girl,' he snapped. 'If you don't keep still, you know what will happen, don't you?'

Eleanor shook her head.

'Your father loses his job, that's what! He loses his job and all his rights, and it will all be your fault.'

She shook her head violently, mute appeal in her doe-like, frightened eyes.

'Yes, all *your* fault. When any member of the family of an employee breaks the law, the employee automatically loses his job. Automatically. It's company rules. The same day. And you are trespassing, breaking the law.'

Eleanor had a haunted, hunted look about her now and she tried to shrink within herself. She closed her eyes, imagining she were at home in bed, warm and cuddled up to her sisters. Within herself, Eleanor reverted to a six-year-old child again. She could make the bad things go away by hiding her head under the blankets; if you stayed like that, under the blankets, for long enough, all the bad things, like thunderstorms and nasty men, would go away. She tried not to notice the hands on her, clutching her breasts and then a hand slid down over her stomach and pushed into the top of her thighs, touching her there. She tightened her legs closer together. 'No, no, no, it's not happening, no,' she thought frantically.

She heard his voice, muffled, distant. 'And if you have brothers or uncles, anybody else at all in the family working at the pit, they'll all lose their jobs. All of them. All of them will be out of work. And your house. By tonight, you will all out on the street. Beggars!'

She felt herself being led along, dragged by her arms. She kept her eyes closed tight, keeping her imagined blankets tightly wrapped around her head as her pulled her under the trees in the copse. She felt his hands pushing at her shoulders and she staggered back. He pushed again, and she stumbled and, off-balance, she fell backwards when he pushed her for the third time, hooking his leg behind her calves to trip her. She landed heavily, winding herself, bruising her hips, and then he was on her.

Eleanor screamed as he grabbed at her skirts and tried to wrench them up. 'Keep quiet, bitch,' he hissed as he clapped a hand over her mouth. 'Make any more noise and it's the poorhouse for the lot of you.'

'No, please. it's not right. Not to do that,' she begged as he held her down with his elbow across her chest, dragging up her clothes with the other. She could feel him scrabbling at her underclothes and she tried to close her legs even tighter.

Then he slapped her again. 'It's up to you, girl,' Barclay-Milnes gasped as he dragged her skirts even higher. 'Either you keep still or else you're out on the streets tonight. You and your whole damned family. Do you think your mother could ever live with the shame of the poorhouse, eh? Think of it, girl, the shame of the poorhouse?'

Eleanor said nothing, the enormity of the threat was simply too great to comprehend. All she knew was that, somehow, she had got into a situation where her whole family would be evicted unless he did what he wanted. After all, he was the son of the man who owned the house she lived in. Who could say he could not throw them out on the streets if he wanted? She could never live with herself if she were instrumental in their losing their home.

She felt his hands between her legs, and she thought she would die of the shame. He seized a hold of her cotton drawers at the baggy crotch and tore them apart, exposing her as brutal fingers probed and prodded at her. She kept her eyes screwed tightly shut, but she could tell from the rustlings that he was unfastening his own clothes.

The worst thing was that Eleanor did not even know what he wanted to do to her. She knew he should not be touching her breasts or touching her down there, but she had no idea what else he was doing, except that it was rude and disgusting and forbidden, the rude thing that Harold and Edgar used to snigger about when they were boys.

The Honourable Gerard had finished unbuckling his breeches and took hold of her legs, just above the knees, and with a sudden wrench forced them apart and she felt his weight come down on her, fumbling with his hands on her thighs and in between and the most searing piercing pain tore through her. She thought she were being ripped apart and she arched her back with a scream of sheer agony.

Faintly, she could hear him grunting as he thrust at her, tearing her even more; she felt as though her flesh was ripping into shreds. For how long he thrust at her she had no idea. All she knew was the searing burning agony of his thrusts. He grunted even louder and she thought he was moaning as well, then all his weight came down on her until she thought her back was breaking, and then mercifully it was over, and Eleanor felt him rise up and away from her.

With a start, Barclay-Milnes noticed the blood between the girl's thighs and on himself. 'Well, I'll be damned. The bitch was a virgin after all,' he thought, but felt not the slightest remorse at his violation of her virginity. 'Ah well, I've saved someone else the job. No doubt now she's tried it, she'll get to like it, the slut. Be out on the streets next week selling it.'

He lifted up the hem of her underskirts and wiped himself on it, and, almost with contempt, threw them back down onto the sobbing girl. 'Clean your damn self up, girl!' He set about pulling his own clothes together, noticing with distaste the dirt and grass stains on the knees of his breeches and he felt a burst of anger towards the girl over them. 'Damn stupid bitch,' he thought, as if it were her fault.

Eleanor lay sobbing on the ground, curled up like a foetus, wishing she were dead as she hugged herself tight, the pain still cutting like a knife. But, worse than that, was the utter humiliation she felt. She felt so dirty, so unclean, she thought she could never ever get clean again; even the touch of her soiled clothes on her legs and lower body was a defilement, a contamination. A surge of bile and vomit scalded up her throat and she began to heave, throwing up where she lay, thick flecks of sick and drool splashing onto Barclay-Milnes shiny riding boots and he jumped back in disgust.

'Watch what you are damn well doing, girl,' he snapped angrily, tempted to kick her for her insolent clumsiness, and then he strode away to look for his riding crop, brushing at his clothes with his hands as he did so.

Slowly, Eleanor got to her knees, rocking back on her heels, arms clutched tight about her stomach, strings of phlegm and vomit slaver hanging from her mouth and staining her blouse. Slowly, she rocked back and forth as the pain gripped her again, she had seen the blood on herself, and felt sure that something must have been torn loose within her insides. 'I'm going to die,' she thought, and the idea of death was almost comforting. 'I'm going to die,' she repeated over and over again, setting up a cadence in time with the rocking to and for on her heels, tears still trickling down her lovely, despoiled face.

Barclay-Milnes found his crop and swished it back and forth

in the air and chopped at some stalks of tall grass, wondering whether to give the girl a thrashing as well with it. He felt in fine mettle, revelling in the power he had over the girl. He could make her do anything he wanted now and wondered briefly whether to take her again, but no, she would keep for another day.

'Get her cleaned up and she could be quite presentable,' he thought, wondering whether Mrs Fordham, the madam of the brothel he went to in Newcastle, might be interested in her, but then decided that pimping was not really the style for a gentleman. He lit a cigarette, drawing the smoke deeply into his lungs, savouring the taste of it, remembering he had heard that at Eton they once used to whip boys who had not smoked a pipe before breakfast. Quite right too. He had been at Rugby himself, but he could appreciate the thinking behind the Eton regulations.

The damned girl was still snuffling and snivelling. Blast her, anyone would think he had hurt her for God's sake! For a second or two, the Honourable Gerard had a pang of worry. Not that he was concerned that he had hurt her, or had any fears about what the blasted girl might say; after all, who would believe the word of a miner's daughter over that of the son of a Peer of the Realm?

It was just what the 'old man' his father, Lord Exham, might think about it; he might get a bit shirty. He could be a bit stuffy at times, especially after that other affair.

There had been a bit of fuss over some girl at Mrs Ormroyd's, another Newcastle brothel he frequented. He had beaten her, nothing wrong in that. He had paid good money to beat her, but then he had got a bit over-enthusiastic about his hobby and had injured her quite severely. There had been talk of police involvement, but he had bought his way out of it; still, his father had got to hear of it somehow. Perhaps he went to the same place, Gerard thought sourly, and there had been an unholy row, lots of pious prattling about the good name of the family and all that sort of nonsense.

Perhaps he had better give the girl a sovereign or two, just to keep her quiet? He didn't want to lose his allowance, for God's sake, just because some slut of a miner's daughter told tales about him. Even as he thought of it, he began to feel irritated by the idea and decided the girl ought to be reminded exactly what was what, the poorhouse threat, and the shame of it seemed to be a very effective deterrent.

He tossed aside his cigarette and stomped over to where Eleanor still crouched. She was muttering something over and over and seemed unaware of his presence and another surge of anger swept over Barclay-Milnes as she continued to deliberately ignore him—damned insolence. He bent down to her, intending to give her a good thrashing if she didn't pick up her ideas and pretty damn smartish at that.

'Why? Why? Why?' she was muttering. 'Why? Why? Why?' Rocking backwards and forwards, eyes fixed and glazed, staring at the ground about five or six feet in front of her, she reminded Barclay-Milnes of a caged animal he had seen somewhere in somebody's private zoo, he couldn't remember exactly whose, but the beast, wherever it was, some monkey or other, had sat and rocked back and forth like that all day long. Damned unnerving.

'Cut that out', he snapped, swishing at her buttocks with the crop, the whip making a heavy thwacking sound against the thick material of her skirts and layers of petticoat. It probably didn't hurt much, but it had got her attention and she turned dull eyes towards him.

'Why?' she pleaded, needing to know. 'Why? I ain't done nothing, mister. Why, why'd you hurt me like this? I'm bleeding.'

'Of course, you're bleeding. All girls bleed the first time, it's natural. So, just shut up your damned whining and listen to me.'

Eleanor turned away and started to rock again.

'Now, just damn well stop and listen to me,' he shouted angrily, smacking the crop onto the ground in front of her. 'Just listen,' he ordered furiously as she turned back again, looking at him as if he weren't even there, looking through him almost, and he felt a peculiar sensation run through him. 'Perhaps I'm not really here at all,' he thought, before dismissing the idea as nonsense. 'Listen! What did you say your name was?'

'Eleanor.'

'Eleanor! Yes, that's right, Eleanor.' He spoke as though she had been the one who had forgotten. 'Now, you had better remember, Eleanor, that you are still in a great deal of trouble. Trespassing is a serious business, you know, and the magistrates take it very seriously indeed. It could mean prison. And then, of course, there's your father's job to consider. Jack Garforth, you said?'

Eleanor nodded in mute anguish.

'Right, Jack Garforth, I'll take good note of that and if I hear anything at all about what happened here today, he is out of a job the same day and it'll be the magistrates for you and the poorhouse for your mother. I should think the shame of that would kill her, wouldn't you? I bet she's a proud woman your mother, right?'

Eleanor nodded, there was no denying it. Mary Garforth was as proud a woman as any Eleanor knew. Poorhouse shame would kill her, without a doubt.

'So, you had better just think on. You hear me?'

'Yes,' she whispered.

'Good. Now, say thank you to the nice man for not putting your family out on the street.'

'Thank ... thank you.'

'Thank you for not putting my family out on the street,' he persisted, enjoying himself again. This was almost as much fun as watching kittens drown in a bucket.

GILES EKINS

'Thank ...you ... for ... for not putting ... putting my family out in the street.'

'Now, there's a good girl,' he said, patting her benevolently on the shoulder, wondering whether her should make her come back another day but finally deciding against it. This hold he had over her would not stand for repeated usage, or close examination. 'Damn it,' he thought savagely, and knocked her backwards again, pulled up her skirts and threw himself down on top of her again.

As soon as he was finished, he stood up, fastened his breeches again, lit another cigarette, walked over to where his horse still waited patiently, took up the reins and walked away, leaving Eleanor's life in ruins. And not giving a damn about it.

After the Honourable Gerard had left her, Eleanor slowly got to her feet, half expecting all her insides to spill out in a heap about her feet. The worst of the pain had gone, but she still felt ripped apart, as though by the claws of an animal.

She wiped her face on her sleeve, smudging the tear tracks gouged down her cheeks, and unsteadily she walked over to the river and slumped down into the bank, wishing the cold waters had been deep enough to carry her away forever. Only then did she think she could ever get clean enough, and perhaps not even then.

Her handkerchief was lost, probably dislodged from her sleeve when she was trying to fight him off and she had no intentions of going back there to look for it. Her petticoats were torn and soiled from both dirt and from him, and she tore the innermost one apart and bent down to soak it in the gelid waters of the stream, shivering as the cold water raised goosebumps on her arm. With the wet cloth, she wiped her face and the back of her neck, wincing at the swollen bruise on her high cheekbones where he had hit her.

How many times had he hit her all told? She tried to remember, but the hideous events all seemed to blur together, like in a dream and she could not pick out the details one from the other except, of course, for the one blinding detail when he had ripped into her, *that* she could never ever forget. Then she shook her head; no matter how many times he had hit her, it had been too many, even one blow had been too many.

Slowly, she made her way home, almost unconsciously, the way a wounded animal returns to his lair, to lick his wounds and escape from the dangerous world outside. If her secret hollow had not been so close to the scene of her humiliation she might well have gone there, but as it was, she could not.

THIRTY-TWO

There'll be some reckoning to be done.

Mary was hanging out clothes. It was not washday, but her wash load was too great to keep until Monday. 'Oh my goodness, Eleanor, what's happened, pet?' Mary exclaimed when she saw her and ran over to her as she came in through the gate, putting arms about her and leading her indoors, away from prying eyes and ears, particularly Nellie Spearman's.

'What is it, pet', she asked again when they were safely indoors, but all Eleanor could do was shake her head violently as tears started to run down her face again. 'Are you hurt? Has there been an accident, pet? Eleanor, tell us love, what is it?'

'Looks like she's been run over by a horse and cart, don't it?' Harold, sitting at the table, asked and Mary wondered at what sadistic quirk of fate always had Harold nearby to sneer and pass comment whenever anything happened within the family, such as when Edgar had enlisted, or Isaac talked to his dad about his apprenticeship.

'Harold, show a bit more concern for you sister … some'ats

wrong with her, you can see that.' A hard note of asperity tinged her voice. She couldn't cope with both Eleanor and Harold at a time like this.

'P'raps somebody's killing badgers again. That turned her dead queer last time.'

'That's it, Harold,' Mary rounded on him. 'Get yourself off out of it!' She ordered, pointing a finger dramatically at the door.

He only shrugged, an insolent sneer on his face, and slouched off out.

Mary sighed. 'Well, he's out of the way now, Eleanor, so come on, love, tell us. Has there been an accident?'

Holding up her face, Eleanor just shook her head, sniffling and wiping her eyes.

'Has something happened? Tell me, Eleanor. If you don't tell me what's wrong, I can't help you, now can I? Come on, pet, you can tell me.'

Eleanor shook her head vigorously, and then burst into racking sobs and flung herself into Mary's arm. 'There, there, Eleanor, pet, there, there,' she murmured, holding Eleanor's head onto her shoulder, rocking her as she stroked her hair. 'There, there, it's alright now, pet. Nothing can hurt you now.'

Mary could feel Eleanor's tears through her blouse, cold and damp on her shoulder as Eleanor heaved and sobbed against her. 'Shushh. Shushh, pet, shushh, it's alright, alright.' She spoke to her as she might a baby. 'Whatever it is, love, there's nothing you can't tell me. I'm your mam, pet, and you can tell me. Tell us what it is, and I can help.'

'I can't,' Eleanor sobbed, her voiced so choked Mary could barely understand her.

'What love? I couldn't hear you for the tears.'

'I can't, Mam.'

'Can't what, love? Tell me? Course you can, you can tell me owt you want, only just let me help you.'

'I can't. He said.'

'He said? Who said? Why can't you say, love? Who said?'

But Eleanor could only shake her head in anguish again, torn between the need to tell her mother and the fear of the downfall of the family and eviction if she did.

'Has somebody hurt you, pet? Is that it? Is somebody threatening you? Frightened you with something terrible?'

The haunted look that flashed across Eleanor's face was answer enough and the horrible conviction began to steal over Mary as she held and solaced Eleanor. Margaret Mary came in then and helped to give some comfort to her sister, but only after Mary had cautioned her against asking questions of the distraught girl or making comment.

Jack, her dad, also came home, to be told only that Eleanor had had an accident. He could stay in the house on condition he kept out of the way, but Saul, who had been on the same shift, was dispatched round to his Auntie Jessie's to ask if he could eat there.

Mary's worst fears were realised when she and Margaret Mary led Eleanor upstairs and helped her undress for bed and saw the blood and torn underclothes and the livid bruising on Eleanor's thighs as they helped her on with her nightdress.

'Margaret, get on downstairs and boil up a bowl of water, not too hot mind, and bring it on up, and I'll give our poor love here a nice wash. Put the kettle on an' all. And then we'd best send for Dr Treddle.'

'Shouldn't I go for the Doctor first?'

'Nay, what's been done has been done and all the doctors in the world can't change that. The most important thing is to get her cleaned up and into bed.'

Edgar and Nicholas came home about that time and were sent away again in their turn to go and eat at their Auntie Jessie's, to be followed some minutes later by Isaac and then Harold was summarily sent away again, to go where he would.

When Margaret brought up the bowl of hot water, Mary

gently washed Eleanor as she would a baby, crooning softly to her, and without questions. Then she gave her sips of strong sweet tea, held her again and then rocked her gently until the poor girl slid down into the bed and seemed to fall asleep.

'Aye, pet love, you sleep. Best medicine of all.' She wiped away a damp tendril of hair from Eleanor's face and bent over to kiss her on the forehead. 'Sleep, pet. Sleep and your mam'll take care of it all for you.'

She turned to Margaret Mary, sitting anxiously at the side of the bed. 'Margaret, pet, go and ask you dad to pop down to t'shop, get a piece of stewing beef. About four ounces tell him, and we'll make up some beef tea for our Eleanor, maybe she'll feel like some later. See if there's any Bovril and, if not, ask him to get some an' all.'

'Aye, right oh, Mam.'

When Margaret came back up to take away the bowl of dirty water, she asked, 'Mam? Who do you reckon done this?' She nodded at Eleanor as she curled herself round a bolster.

'For sure I don't know, pet, but I'm going to find out,' Mary answered. 'And happen when I do, and I tell your dad, there'll be some reckoning to be done. Accounts to settle.' Mary's face was set and grim, a cold implacable fury settling about her. Her sweet favourite Eleanor had been brutalised and someone would have to pay for it. 'But whoever it was, and if I ever get hold of the swine, I'll strangle him with my own hands. Whoever he was, he's got our poor Eleanor right frightened about some'at.'

'What about the police, Mam? Perhaps they can help? They might be able to find him, him what done it? They should know About this, in any case. They ought to be told.'

'No, no police, Margaret. This is a family matter and the law will only muddy things up. They'll be questioning our Eleanor, confusing her the more, bringing back bad memories that had best be laid to rest in their own good time. You know the police; they'll clomp all over her with their clodding great buits and try and make out it were all her own fault. No, we'll not be getting the police in on this. We'll not be making a circus for all the village to know our business.'

Wearily, Mary walked back downstairs, leaving Margaret to sit with Eleanor until the doctor came. Jack was in the back room, puffing agitatedly at his pipe and he jumped to his feet as Mary came in.

'How is she, Mary? What's wrong with her? I've been imagining all sort of terrible things. Is she hurt bad?'

'Bad enough. And whatever you've been imagining probably isn't terrible enough.'

'What's you mean? Tell me, Mary, what's wrong with her?'

'Sit down, Jack and I'll tell you, best as I can'

'An accident, you said? I'm going up see her.'

'Nay, Jack. She's asleep now. Let her be. Sit down.'

'What's up with her? I want to know, she is my own daughter,' Jack demanded angrily.

'And she's every bit as much mine, except not by blood,' Mary retorted, but not harshly. She knew that Jack was only concerned for Eleanor. 'Let her sleep, Jack. Sit yourself down and I'll tell you all I can.'

Jack's face turned to thunder as Mary him told she believed Eleanor to have been raped. 'I'll kill the bastard. Who is it, Mary, tell us, who's done that to my little Ellie? Who is it, eh? I'll rip the bastard's throat out, see if I don't!'

'I don't rightly know, Jack.'

'What's you mean, you don't rightly know? What did she say?'

'She didn't say who it were.'

'Don't she know who it were? Were it a stranger? Maybe's a tinker or gypsy? Never did trust them bloody didicoys.'

'I don't think so Jack. But whoever it is, he's got some kind of a hold on her. He's frightened her silly. Scared her so much she can't say who it was. In fact, that's about the only thing she has said. 'I can't. He said'. They are the only words she's said about it. 'I can't. He said'.'

'By God, Mary', Jack said, clenching his fists in impotent rage. 'Who could do such a thing to sweet little Ellie? Who? I swear, Mary, when I find him …'

Mary hesitated slightly before making her next remarks. 'Let me talk to her about this, Jack. Don't you say anything to her. You'll only upset her. When she's had time, in the next day or so, I'll find out. She'll talk to me.'

'She can talk to me, for God's sake, I'm her father.'

'Aye, but you're a man as well and it was a man as done it to her.'

'I'm her FATHER!' he exclaimed in anguish.

'Aye, Jack, and a good one. But this business needs a woman. She needs to talk to a woman. To her mother, or her sisters, but not a man.'

'Aye,' he sighed. 'Perhaps you're right, Mary, but I can't stand it, not being able to do anything.'

'Just be there for her, Jack, that's what she needs from thee.'

'Of course, I'll be there for her.'

'She's going to think you blame her, Jack,' Mary said quietly. 'You know that, don't you?'

'Of course, I don't blame her. I know my Ellie; she's good girl. A *good* girl.'

'She's going to take a lot of reassuring on that.'

Jack sighed deeply again, suddenly looking old. 'Whatever I need to do for her, Mary, you tell me. You tell me what I 'ave to do. All I want is for her to be well again. I love that little girl, Mary, more than life itself. If she asked me to, I'd tear out my own heart for her.'

'I know that, Jack. And so does Eleanor, but you leave it to me to talk to her. You just give her all that love, Jack. That's what she needs most from you. All that love.'

Over the next three days, Mary slowly eased the story out

from Eleanor, bit by bit, like drawing a stubborn cork on a bottle of champagne until, suddenly, with a pop, it was there, and the wine coursed freely, spilling from the neck of the bottle and pouring down the sides. Once Mary had coaxed out the cork, Eleanor told her tale in a flood of tears and self-recriminations, now convinced that she was going to be the ruination of the family and that soon, within the day, they would all be jobless and out on the streets.

Mary told Jack when he came off shift. He took his pipe and his problems out for a walk to think it over and, on his return, he got out his best suit and put on his best cap and walked over to Exham Hall.

'Leave this to me now, Mary, love. Whatever is to be said and done to Lord Exham, it's best it's said by me.'

THIRTY-THREE

No thank you, Your Lordship, this is not a social call.

They said that on a clear day you could see the twin towers of Durham Cathedral, 12 miles away, from the tower on the corner of the south wing of Exham Hall, and presumably vice versa.

Although the only time, recently, I climbed to the top of the tower of the Cathedral, I couldn't see Exham Hall at all and very nearly got blown clear across the county for my pains, the wind fairly whistled up the Wear Valley from the east coast and so if you ever planned on climbing the tower at Durham Cathedral— and it's well worth the climb, and the coronary—make sure your wig is well glued on.

Having said all that, I do not believe that you could have seen the Cathedral at all from Exham Hall; the city of Durham was wrapped around itself in a bend in the River Wear, in a steep sided valley and it is not until you are actually coming down Gilesgate, about a mile away from the City centre, that the vista bursts open like a ripe peach and the Cathedral comes into magnificent view, standing proudly on the promontory overlooking the town, the greatest feat of Norman architecture in the world. So, I consider it rather unlikely that you could have seen the Cathedral from Exham Hall.

Exham Hall, located some four miles beyond the village, is an overpoweringly ugly edifice, a monument to bad taste, a mansion without grace or favour, which is a pity because the site is superb and deserves so much better. Standing on the southwest, facing slopes of the glacially formed valley which, combined with the meandering flow of the river, has produced a flattened Y-shaped valley. The locus of the house commands magnificent views across the whole Durham dales and over the wandering course of the river, flowing like a silver thread through the green and gold baize cloth of the fields below.

The Hall itself is a curiously brutal hodgepodge of period and style. Of the original Tudor Great Manor House, which had been confiscated from William Jacoby and granted to Sir Oliver Whitehead, very little remains except part of the stable block to the rear, which has now been converted to garages and workshops. The walls of the main hall of the original building are reputed to be original, but so much was knocked down and rebuilt when the estate fell into the hands of the Sawden family during the Regency period, courtesy of Walter Whitehead's nine-year run of bad luck at the card tables, that I rather doubt anything really remains, except perhaps that the stones recovered from the demolition were probably re-used.

When Emily Sawden married Sir Edward Barclay-Milnes, the second Baron Exham, in 1823, she decided that the old manor house was insufficiently grand to go along with her lofty new status as Lady Exham, the second Baroness, and set about rebuilding it as Exham Hall.

Her husband, who had inherited the title from his father but very little money to go with it, was only too pleased to agree, being very enamoured with his new bride's wealth, which should have become his on marriage. Unfortunately, for him, the money and property were so tied up in trusts and covenants that he could not directly get his hands on it and so, therefore, was obliged to keep her happy in order to get his allowances, very galling for a chap, but what else could one do, eh?

Lady Exham employed a Newcastle architect, James Braithwaite, to draw up the plans for the new house. She proved an incredibly difficult client to please, and Braithwaite was greatly relieved when she removed him from the commission and completed the designs herself in conjunction with her builders.

The house consisted of a barn-like main block, double storey, with steeply pitched gable roofs that formed an end on central hub to which the two side wings butted up. At the end of each of these wings, two further ends on blocks were placed, so forming a blunted E-shape in plan. To the gable end of the main block, Emily Sawden, Lady Exham, added a double storey, angular bay window with a red-tile pitched roof, which did nothing at all for the overall proportions of the house.

The windows in the two wings were originally well proportioned, but then she spoiled the pleasing effect by adding single storey, square bay windows, two on the north wing and three on the south, which broke the facade up into a series of irregular ill-balanced blocks.

She then laid out a terrace, which ran the full length of the frontage, and sloped ornamental lawns stretching down to the artificial lake she had dug (after considerable and very expensive levelling works), complete with an island and a classical style gazebo.

Within the lawns, she placed kidney-shaped flower beds and then, as if ashamed of the whole effect, planted rows of elm trees in front of the Hall.

Her final act was to build, totally unconnected to the main building, a tall circular tower, with a balconied observation gallery at high level and a domed roof. The proportions of this unfortunate folly were exactly those of an erect penis, which may well have been her source of inspiration, for certainly it became known locally as the 'Cock Tower' or 'the Prick of Exham Hall', but I suppose, in the latter case, they could equally well have been referring to Lord Exham.

What Lord Exham himself thought of all this was not recorded.

The third Baroness Exham extended the south wing to enclose the cock tower in a style displaying all the delicate articulation of corporation public lavatories, with large areas of blank wall interspaced with tiny windows at high level and completely out of line with the Georgian windows of the rest of the house (incidentally, true Georgian windows are not the fussy shallow bay windows with tiny 6' square panes of glass so beloved of property developers in the suburbs).

She also added a classical portico to the gable-ended central block, complete with Ionic columns, extended the terrace, adding carved lions on every other pedestal, and unicorns holding shields on the others. She then thinned out the elm trees.

However, she did have the good grace to build a high brick wall all along the road, so screening off the monstrosity from public view, so she couldn't have been totally without sensitivity; she must have had some regard for the feelings of others.

The north wing was extended shortly after this by the next lady of the house, who decided that 17 bedrooms were totally inadequate. The north wing extension comprised of a slab-sided box with large bay windows at ground floor level, with disproportionately smaller ones, like pimples, at the first floor, deranging an already disturbed facade to the point of schizophrenia. She also extended the terrace again, which by now had reached a size roughly equivalent to the seafront promenade at Brighton.

As somebody at the time said, the Hall had become as ugly

and as bad-tempered as old Mrs Lankester, which was a bit cruel really; no building was that bad.

By 1914, the orgy of building and reconstruction had long ceased; in fact, Lord Exham had carried out no further alterations after the death of his wife in 1897 (she of the feeling of inadequacy over the numbers of bedrooms) although, from time to time, he toyed with the idea of demolishing both wing extensions and so bringing the proportions of the Hall back to something more domestic in scale, and remodelling the facade, but nothing actually came of it.

Sir Ralph Barclay-Milnes, fourth Baron of Exham, had had a long day. The meeting at the Coal Mine Owners Association in Newcastle had been endless, the only two topics of conversation being yet another post-mortem over the recent strike which, to listen to most of the owners, had all but bankrupted them, and what would happen to coal prices if the war continued for any length of time, which would most likely finish the job.

In fact, by dint of marvellously convoluted argument, the owners had managed to convince themselves they would be bankrupted whatever happened; if there the war continued beyond Christmas, it would mean ruin and if the war stopped tomorrow, the effects would be disastrous.

As he listened to the endless talk of imminent ruin, he wryly recalled the heated grumbling of some of the mine owners three years ago, as they bitterly complained that the effects of the 1911 Coal Mines Act, which made certain safety measures compulsory, and had all but bankrupted them.

Sometimes, he wondered why he attended the meetings at all, but as one of the leading mine owners the area, he supposed he was duty-bound.

After lunch, he had a meeting with Harrison, the agent who managed his various properties in and around Newcastle, and who insisted on going through all the accounts with him in person, 'Just to show that everything is all above board and ship-shape and Bristol fashion, your Lordship.' A further meeting took place with his solicitors and, to cap it all, his train had been late following a derailment just outside Edinburgh.

Jackson, the doorman, ran down the steps to open the car door and Brindley, the butler, had the front door of the Hall open for him as the car pulled up the drive.

As Sir Ralph stepped out of the rear of the Daimler and looked up at the house, he winced as usual at the hideousness of the building, wondering once again just why he allowed his wife, Lady Constance, Lord rest her soul, to extend it yet again.

He had been young and in love, he supposed, ready to grant her any little favour she craved, and every new Baroness of Exham had wanted to add her own touches, to personalise her domain.

And by the time the love had dried up, the deed was done. He doubted he had ever even been in most of the rooms of the new addition, apart from the billiard room, of course.

Brindley's white-gloved hands took Sir Ralph's hat and brief-case as though they might be contaminated and then ushered him through the hallway and into the library, where the sherry decanter was already set up as usual.

'A good day, your Lordship, I hope?' Brindley enquired obsequiously.

'Yes, thank you, Brindley,' his Lordship replied, sinking into his favourite high-backed wing chair by the windows, with the view across the lawns to the lake and the stand of trees along the road, falling away to encompass the magnificence of the entire dale, framed in the window like a painting by an old master.

'Very good, sir. Dinner at eight o'clock, as usual, your Lord-ship?' Brindley asked as he handed his Lordship a glass of Amontillado.

'Yes, that will be fine, thank you, Brindley. That will be all.'

The last thing he needed was Brindley hovering around him like a pale-faced ghoul. Brindley had been at the Hall for generations it seemed, certainly during the latter part of Sir Ralph's father's time, all through his own childhood, so he must be well past 70 now; time to put him out to grass.

Gently sipping at the sherry, rolling the taste around his tongue, Sir Ralph sat back deeply into his chair and closed his eyes. This half an hour or so of rest and contemplation, with a glass of sherry as an aperitif before his bath and dinner, had become almost a ritual with him.

Most evenings he would play one or two of his phonogram recordings, recordings by Caruso from Puccini or Verdi, allowing the vibrant richness of the music to resonate through him like a sounding board. Tonight, he thought, 'It has to be 'Tosca.' Enrico Caruso's rendition of 'E Lucevan Le Stelle', Cavaradossi's farewell to Tosca from Act III.

He walked over to the phonogram, refilling his sherry as he passed, and then sorted through the stack of records on the table, reading the titles through the round hole in the brown paper sleeves. 'Ah, here we are.' Sliding out the black disc onto the palm of his hand, he then carefully slotted it over the spindle on the turntable. 'And afterwards? What next, more Puccini? Musetta's 'Waltz Song' from 'La Boheme'? Or Verdi's Rigoletto, 'Questa O Quella'? Ah, that's the one!' he thought as he read another label: 'Nessun Dorma' from Puccini's unfished masterpiece 'Turandot'.

Exham lifted the arm of the phonograph and inserted a new needle into the round head from the box that swung out from the side of the case, sucking in his breath as an errant needle pricked his finger. He then cranked up the handle that drove the clockwork, slid the mustard spoon-shaped lever to the left to start the turntable spinning, and carefully lowered the head onto the disc, lining up the needle with the wider spaced leader grooves at the very edge. There was a rasping hiss and then the solo flute introduction, followed a few bars later by the sublime voice of Caruso, and the full genius of Puccini flowed, a little scratchily, around the walls of the library and into his soul.

He sat again in his chair, adjusting the bell mouth of the speaker so that it played more directly to his ears and closed his eyes, to be lost in the music, feeling a shiver run through him as usual as Cavaradossi sang out his heartbreak.

Sometimes, he wished he had married again; his wife, Constance, had not shared his love of opera and he would dearly love to share these intimate moments with a beloved companion. But after she had died in the riding accident, there had been no-one else, apart from an occasional casual dalliance.

Well, no, that was not strictly true. There had been another, but the relationship had been impossible, doomed from the start and she had left. The boy, his son, must be, what, all of 15? Or even 16 by now, and he resolved to make enquiries about him, just to see if he was alright, if there was anything he might need.

He would send for Baker, the mine manager, to come and see him. But could Baker be trusted to keep his mouth closed? No, probably not. No, there was only one man whom he could ask, and he would probably want to spit in his face.

He played 'E Lucevan Le Stelle' once more, the music matching his mood exactly, wondering if records could ever be made large enough to record the whole of an opera, 'Tosca' say, two hours or more, and then dismissed the idea as ridiculous, a quick mental calculation telling him that such a disc would need to be some thirty feet in diameter.

He sat with his thoughts for a few minutes more and then, with a sigh, he drained his sherry and rang for his bath, suddenly feeling very old and very lonely.

Brindley, the butler, coughed discreetly as Lord Exham dozed in his chair in the library. Brindley could see that the sherry had been well attended to. His Lordship seemed to be drinking more and more these days, ever since the start of the war, really. 'Don't know what he's got to worry about,' Brindley thought, 'it's not going to be him as has to go and fight the Germans. Or his precious sons.'

Brindley had never married but he had nephews of whom he was very fond, and the youngest had just enlisted and his mother, Brindley's sister, was worried sick for him.

Brindley coughed again. 'Harrumph! Excuse me, your Lordship.'

Lord Exham snorted and started in his chair, coming awake with an eye-blinking disorientated jerk, looking around the library as though surprised to be there at all. 'Sorry to disturb you, your Lordship, but there is a person to see you.'

'A person, Brindley? What person and what the devil is his business at this time of the evening?' Lord Exham asked irritably as he arched himself in his chair and stifled a yawn, wishing he had not had that third sherry.

'A Mr Garforth, sir. By the cut of his clothes, I would say he is a pitman, your Lordship. I tried to send him packing, sir, but he insists on seeing you. Even though I told him you were not available, he said he would wait. He insists that he *has* to see you, sir. On a personal matter, he says. I know that it's your policy to always grant audience to your employees, sir, but if you wish I can get Jackson to forcibly evict him. Or send for the police.'

'Garforth, you say?'

'Yes, sir, Jack Garforth he says. Says that you will know of him, sir … er … harrumph.' Brindley coughed once more, as if to indicate he had better things to do. 'Shall I send for the police, your Lordship?'

'No, Brindley, there'll be no need for the police, I'm sure. You had better show him in. If I know Garforth, he'll stand out there all night, otherwise.'

'Yes, your Lordship, very good, sir. I, er … left the … person standing outside the back door, sir. I hope that was in order, only, er, the silver, you know?'

'Yes, Brindley, that was perfectly correct, although I am quite sure that the silver would have been safe.'

'Very good, your Lordship. I'll show him in.'

'What the devil could Garforth want?' Sir Ralph asked himself. 'He is the last man I would expect to come knocking at my door, asking for an audience.'

Brindley ushered Jack Garforth, Eleanor's father, into the room. 'Garforth, your Lordship.' And then he backed out again, bowing like a courtier, and closed the doors behind him.

Jack stood quietly, waiting for his presence to be acknowledged. His best suit was tight on the shoulders and the top buttons of his too small waistcoat strained in protest. He held his cap in both hands down in front of him, as if surprised when naked and seeking to cover himself with the first thing that came to hand.

'Garforth?' Lord Exham asked, barely glancing up at him.

'Aye, good evening, your Lordship, sorry to be disturbing you at this time of an evening, but it's a matter as can't really wait,' Jack said. His tone of voice was polite and deferential, without being servile. He spoke as man to master, but not unduly so; Jack Garforth bowed and scraped to no man.

'Let me be the judge of that, Garforth.' He got to his feet and walked over to the drinks tray. 'Sherry? Or I am sure that Brindley could find you some ale from the kitchen?'

'No, thank you, Your Lordship, this is not a social call.'

'No,' Lord Exham drawled the word out into three syllables. 'I did not suppose that it was. Well, then, Garforth, you had best state your piece.'

'It's about my daughter, your Lordship, my daughter Eleanor.' Jack paused to try to phrase his next words correctly and Exham thought he had finished his sentence.

'Your daughter, Garforth? Why, you want to put her into

service here? If so, speak to Brindley for that. I never get involved in the hiring of domestic staff.'

'No, sir, it's not that, and in any case, I would not be putting any daughter of mine into service here.'

'Well, spit it out then, man! I don't have all night.'

'Eleanor, she's sixteen, nigh on seventeen, my youngest daughter, aye, and as pretty as a picture.'

Exham snapped his fingers in impatience, but Jack could not be hurried. 'Eleanor, well she's trusting, believes what she is told, without question.'

'If there is a point to all this, Garforth, for goodness sake, get to it.'

'The point is, your Lordship, is that my Eleanor has been molested, abused, and I am sorry as to have to say this, sir, but she was molested by thy son. By your son, the Honourable Gerard, your Lordship. He raped her! Beat her and raped her!'

The ugly words hung heavy in the air, swollen and ripe with accusation. *He raped her. Beat her and raped her!*

Lord Exham was about to drink from his glass but stopped mid-air and slowly, as if unsure that he could control himself, put the glass back onto the silver filigree tray, next to the cut glass decanter.

'Rape? That is a most serious accusation, Garforth. Most serious. I hope you can substantiate it?' His voice was steady, but with a heavy underlying threat only too implicit.

'My girl, she said so, and that's good enough for me.'

'Your girl said so?' Exham asked, arching his eyebrows in disbelief. 'That is hardly proof of such an outrageous allegation, is it Garforth … an allegation made against my son?'

'There's proof enough she was raped and beat, bruises, blood, stuff like that. Mary, my wife, can swear on that.'

'Medical evidence? A doctor's report? Police statements? It takes rather more than the word of a girl and her mother to bring about a charge of rape.'

'Aye, the doctor came to see her, he'll say what he found, no doubt. As for the police, no, your Lordship, we didn't get the police involved. The girl has suffered enough, without that.'

'So, you have no proof, none whatsoever? You come to me with this monstrous tale, without evidence, claiming my son raped your daughter? This could be serious, Garforth, very serious indeed.' He stared hard at Jack, trying to intimidate him.

'I realise that, my Lord, but I would not come here with wild tales if I weren't sure on the truth of it.' Jack stood his ground, not looking directly at Lord Exham, but not looking away or down at the ground either, refusing to be browbeaten. 'My girl said so, and that's good enough for me. She's a good girl and has been brought up to tell the truth.'

'My son, would of course, deny any such allegations and damn your eyes, likely give you a thrashing for your impudence.'

'I would expect nowt else from such a man as could do what he did to my lovely Ellie,' Jack retorted, trying to hold onto his temper.

'Just remember who you are talking to, Garforth, and mind your place.'

'And what about the place of my daughter, my Lord? Raped by thy son?'

'You certainly seem sure of yourself about this, Garforth. Do you intend to bring this matter to court?'

Jack laughed bitterly. 'Why, aye, that's for sure!' he answered ironically. 'The whole world knows there's one law for the rich and another for the poor. If we did bring it to court, what chance would we stand? You being a lord and a JP and a rich man. You'd hire some fancy-talking lawyer from London and he'd tie our poor Eleanor up in knots, destroy her to save thy son, and your friends on the bench would not take the slightest bit of notice of us anyhow; you'd make sure of that. No, your Lordship, we'll not be going to court. The girl has suffered enough, not just bodily, no doubt she'll get over that, but she was always a happy trusting soul, innocent and sweet and the 'Honourable Gerard' has taken that away from her forever.' His voice was full of contempt when he spoke the name.

'Garforth, you just speak with more respect when you talk of my son,' Lord Exham snapped.

'I give him the respect that's due to him.'

'That will do, Garforth, this has gone on quite long enough.'

'You'll have to have me thrown out bodily, your Lordship. I come here to say my piece and say it I will.'

'And what makes you so damned sure I won't have you thrown out and charged with trespassing?'

'If you were going to do that, my Lord, you'd have done it as soon as I said anything about thy son having raped and beat my Eleanor. You didn't. So, I reckon you know the truth as to what kind of a man he is already.'

'Don't be so damned impertinent, Garforth. That sort of behaviour won't do you, or your daughter, any good whatsoever.'

'I'm not here for my own good, your Lordship.'

Lord Exham stared hard at Jack, unused to being spoken to like that by a mere employee, but miners were proud men, and Jack Garforth as proud as any there was. 'Well, since you are here,' he said at last, 'you had best finish what you came to say. Although I give you fair warning, Garforth, if you continue to make unsubstantiated allegations, I will have you thrown out and bring down upon you the full weight of the law.' He pulled out his heavy silver hunter from his waistcoat pocket. 'You have five minutes, Garforth. Five minutes.'

Outside, Jack could a horse's hooves on the gravel of the drive and wondered angrily if it were the Honourable Gerard coming back home. 'Coming back from the rape of another poor innocent,' he thought sourly, wishing he could get his hands on the man. He'd not be molesting girls for a long while if he ever did.

Jack took a deep breath and straightened himself and addressed a spot somewhere to the right of Lord Exham's shoulder. 'My daughter, Eleanor, she came back home t'other day, broken and beat and raped, sobbing into her mam's arms, crying fit to break your heart. Beat and raped by a fiend of a man who give not a toss for her. When I saw my Ellie all broken and bruised, I wanted to cry for her, take her pain myself. Mary tried to talk to her, find out what had happened.

'Oh, I mean it were dead obvious she had been raped, don't get me wrong on that, your Lordship. She were raped and nothing you or I say will change that fact, but my wife couldn't get nowt out of her how it had happened. Or who. Eleanor were frightened, terrified of some'at, scared half out of her wits. All she could say was that she couldn't tell, couldn't tell.

'But eventually Mary got her talk about it, tell her what it was she were frightened of. He, the man as had done it, he threatened Eleanor with what would happen if she ever told about it.' Jack paused to get control himself again, breathing heavily with emotion.

Lord Exham said nothing, simply stared at Jack and sipped at the glass of sherry that he had picked up again.

'He said, this man … he said that if Eleanor ever said a word, he would see to it that I lost my job at the pit. That my sons would lose their jobs at the pit. Everybody in my family who worked at the pit would lose their jobs. He threatened her that if she ever said a word, we would all be thrown out of our house, and that her mother would be sent to the poorhouse. So, you tell me, your Lordship, just who could make threats like that, if not your son, the Honourable Gerard?'

'I've told you before about the tone of your voice, Garforth,' Lord Exham snapped, obviously shaken by the revelations. He got up from his chair and slowly walked up and down the length of the library before coming back to stand before Jack.

'You still have no proof, Garforth, none at all. All you have is unsubstantiated gossip. I would be well within my rights if I dismissed you out of hand for making these unfounded accusations against one of my family, in which case you *would* lose the right to your company cottage, you realise that, don't you?', he stated ominously, as though refusing to accept any truth in the allegations and intending that the thinly disguised threat would result in them being withdrawn.

'I have always believed thee to be an honourable man, your Lordship. You've always treated us workers fair, let us come to thee with grievances and that. Should it be you decide to dismiss me for this, even though you know the truth on it, aye well, no matter, for then you're not the man I thought you was and not be the sort of man I'd want to work for anyhow. With so many miners enlisting in the army I'd have no difficulty finding a place at another pit. But sacking me won't change the truth, your Lordship, and deep down thee knows that.'

'You're damned sure of yourself, Garforth.'

'There's no hiding from the truth, your Lordship, like it or not.'

'So, what do you want from me? Money?'

'No, I'd spit on your money, your Lordship,' Jack said, his nostrils flaring with indignation.

'Yes, Garforth, I rather imagine you would at that. So, why are you here? You said yourself that you are not taking this to court.'

'Aye, that's right, your Lordship. I've got no … what's the word … recourse? Aye, no recourse to the law, you'll make sure of that. And I've no way of taking matters into my own hands, either, on account of who it were that attacked my Ellie. So, what can a man in my position do? I'll tell you, nowt. Nothing! Thy son will walk away from this as pure as the driven snow whilst my poor Eleanor, she's damaged for life. She was a good girl, pure and chaste, and that has been torn away from her and there's not a blind thing I can do about it. Except, your Lordship, except, that I can tell you what kind of a man your son really is. Whether you believe it or not, it had to be said. I've got nowt else to say, your Lordship, so if you'll excuse me, I'll be on my way.'

'Garforth?'

'Your Lordship?'

'I understand what you have said to me, and I shall give it due thought and attention. But understand me on this, if you repeat one word of these unproven allegations to anyone outside the four walls of this room, then you may rest assured that I shall dismiss you instantly. And I shall also ensure through the Mine Owners Association that you do not find another place, as you put it. I shall make sure that there are no other jobs in any other mine, most certainly not in the North East. Do I make myself clearly understood?'

'Aye, abundantly so, your Lordship.'

'I have listened to you, Garforth, because it has always been my policy to listen to the grievances of my employees. Always! However, in your case, do not presume that I shall do so again. You may go now.'

'Right, your Lordship.'

'I shall ring for Brindley to show you out.'

The two men stood at opposite ends of the library, nothing more to say to each other.

'You rang, my Lord?', Brindley asked as he came through the door, grimacing at Jack as though there was a bad smell about him.

'Yes, Brindley, be so good as to show Mr. Garforth out.'

'Very good, my Lord. This way, sir,' he said to Jack with barely disguised contempt.

Lord Exham sat for some minutes whilst he digested what Jack Garforth had told him. Not for one moment did he disbelieve it. He had known it to be true from the very first, as soon as Garforth had said that Gerard had beaten the unfortunate girl; the absolute veracity of the story had hit him like a blow between the eyes.

Everything he had said from then on had been camouflage, since not for one minute could he let a man like Garforth, an employee, a miner in one of his pits, know that he could believe his own son, the son of a Peer of the Realm, capable of such a despicable act. But he knew it to be true. God knew he realized it to be true.

All his life, Gerard had been a cruel and wilful child, a sadistic boy who liked to watch mice and rats drown in buckets of water. Later, he had once tied the tails of two stray cats together and hung them over the bough of a tree and laughed and clapped with glee as they clawed themselves to shreds in their pain and panic.

Family dogs had been mistreated, horses whipped so much that their flanks had bled when Gerard rode them too hard, and then there had been the wretched affair of the girl that he had beaten half to death in Newcastle. And, no doubt, there were other incidents that he had not heard of.

And now this.

No man likes to admit that his one of his sons is an unprincipled brute, a bully, a man without morality or sense of common decency, but the facts could not be denied any longer. Sadly, Lord Exham sighed in resignation, for the good name of the family, something would have to be done. He walked over to the telephone and made a series of telephone calls.

Then he rang for Brindley.

'Ask Mr Gerard to come to me, would you please, Brindley? I shall be in the study.'

'Very good, sir.'

THIRTY-FOUR

They lie as a matter of course.

'You said you wanted to see me, Father?' the Honourable Gerard said after he had been shown into the study and Brindley had closed the door behind him.

'Yes Gerard, I do. A most important, and distasteful, matter has come up,' replied Sir Ralph.

'Well, if I can help,' Gerard drawled, screwing an Abdullah cigarette into an ivory holder and lighting it, blowing a stream of bored smoke up to the ceiling. He felt a slight twinge of apprehension, something was up, he could see that from the set of the old man's sour face. Mind you, he looked like that most of the time, humourless old duffer, but it could be nothing serious, Gerard was quite sure of that, convinced that the girl was too frightened to say anything. And if she had, who would take her word over his, the little trollop? No, if he kept his head, there was nothing to be concerned about.

'I've had a complaint, Gerard, from one of our miners at Ashbrook. A most serious complaint.'

NEVER SUCH INNOCENCE AGAIN

'Don't tell me, he's grumbling because he has to actually work for his money?'

'Don't be facetious, Gerard,' Lord Exham said peevishly. 'It doesn't become you, and this is not a laughing matter.'

'Sorry, Father,' he said, not meaning it in the slightest. 'A complaint, you said? Anything I can assist you with?'

'The complaint, Gerard, is that you attacked and raped his daughter.' Lord Exham looked hard at his son as he said this, looking for signs of reaction or guilt, but Gerard had composed himself well.

'Stuff and nonsense,' he blustered. 'The man is obviously lying. I trust you sent him packing. If it had been me, I would have set the dogs on him. Teach him to keep his place. And to mind his manners.'

'The man who made this complaint is one of our most trustworthy workers. He has been with us for many years.'

'You know what these people are like, Father, they lie as a matter of course. What was he after? Money, no doubt.'

'No, Gerard, he was not after money. Jack Garforth had far too much dignity for that.'

'Garforth? Garforth? No, never heard of him. Nor of his lying daughter,' the Honourable Gerard said, furiously seething inside, the little bitch, telling tales on him like this, not that anyone would believe her, but the indignity of having to defend himself like this was humiliating.

'But is she lying, Gerard?'

'Of course, Father, don't tell me that you actually believe this nonsense?' he asked, stubbing his half-smoked cigarette out in the ashtray on the desk.

'Actually, Gerard, I rather believe that I do.' Lord Exham spoke quietly, but the force of his words struck Gerard like a blow.

'You can't mean it, Father. You mean to say that you actually believe the word of this trollop over that of your own son?'

'The girl is no trollop, Gerard. By all accounts, she was a good and virtuous girl, and the medical evidence proves that.' Lord Exham had no such evidence, of course, but he knew that Gerard had no means of knowing that.

'It's still her word against mine, Father, and I would expect you to accept the word of your own son against that of a miner's daughter, a nobody.'

'Your word, you say? In that case, do you give me your word, your word as a *gentleman*, that you had nothing whatsoever to do with this assault?'

Gerard suddenly felt trapped. His father had mentioned evidence. Was there more proof that could link him to the girl? If he gave his word and it was then proved he had had the girl, maybe roughed her up a little, the old man would probably get very shirty about it, very shirty indeed. He had these quaint, inconvenient notions about honour and the word of a gentleman. Gerard could see his allowance being cut if he were not careful.

'I don't think it's really necessary for all this melodrama, do you father? As I say, the girl and her trouble-making father are so obviously lying that I don't think there is much more to say,' he answered stiffly, hoping to brazen it out, but he was not sufficiently bold enough to walk away.

'There is a great deal more to be said. You have not yet answered my question, Gerard. Do you give me your word that you did not assault this girl?'

'I ... I did ... er. I don't think this ... is ... necessary,' Gerard mumbled, unable to look his father in the face.

Lord Exham got up from his chair and eased himself out from behind his desk. He found the whole business utterly distasteful and now simply wanted to get it over and done with as soon as possible. Gerard was lying through his teeth and that was all there was to it.

'Gerard,' he began carefully. 'Regretfully, I have to say that I have no doubts whatsoever that you were responsible for the attack on this poor girl. That you did in fact beat and rape her as alleged.' He held up his hand for silence as Gerard tried to interrupt, cutting him off with a furious hard-faced scowl. 'Nothing you have said here tonight has changed that conviction in the slightest.'

'Father, I … I—'

'Be quiet, boy,' snapped Sir Ralph, and Gerard subsided back into silence. 'Finally, I have had to face up to the fact that you are a wastrel and a bully. Worse, a common rapist, bringing down disgrace on both yourself and the family name. And it is not as if this is the first incident, is it?

'There have been indications of your … nature ever since you were a small child. There have been numerous incidents of your cruelty to animals, that sort of thing, reports of bullying when you were at school. But I tried to make allowances, tried to make excuses for your behaviour by the fact you were without a mother to give you moral guidance. But then there was that business with the girl in Newcastle. And now this, this disgraceful affair.'

'I told you, Father, it's all lies. And in any case, the girl was willing enough at the time. She is just trying to stir up trouble, dun us for money,' the Honourable Gerard blustered, condemning himself out of his own mouth.

'That is enough, Gerard. Only moments ago you said you did not even know the girl.'

'I … I, er, was unsure which girl you meant at first,' Gerard fumbled, searching for excuses.

'Be silent before I knock you to the ground. More lies will only make matters worse for you. My only concern now is to ensure that you do not besmirch the good name of this family any further. For that reason, this affair cannot ever come to court or public attention. Garforth will say nothing more, I'm sure of that, but only if he can see that action had been taken.'

Lord Exham paused as Gerard tried to hide his agitation by

lighting another cigarette. 'Equally, I cannot let it be said that I have abused my position by allowing this matter to be swept under the carpet. Our position in society is dependent not only upon our wealth and standing, but upon the moral rectitude of our behaviour and the respect that we earn.

'If we do not command that respect, the respect of those who place us in high position, then we have nothing, and that will bring about the downfall of our society, Gerard, and the evils of socialism and communism will sweep down upon us like the barbarians of the Dark Ages.'

Despite his apprehension, Gerard almost burst out laughing. 'Pompous old fart,' he thought, reassured by his father's pontificating, that anybody who spouted such nonsense could not possibly be taken seriously.

'We have a duty to keep our house in order, Gerard. Position brings with it an obligation of responsibility which we cannot shirk. I simply cannot let the assault on this poor girl go by; it would be a dereliction of that duty. For the good of the family name, Gerard, you will have to leave Exham Hall. For you to do otherwise would only give the impression that I condone your vile acts.'

Gerard wondered how his father could be seen to be derelict in his duty when at the same time nobody was to know what had happened, but he said nothing, sensing that it might only make matters worse. As for his banishment, he was more than ready to leave Exham anyway. He found it restrictive and provided his allowance was maintained, it could actually be a turn for the good.

'In days gone by,' Lord Exham continued, 'profligate sons of the gentry were sent out to the colonies, to further the good of empire, but these are times of crisis and circumstances have changed. Men are actually returning from the colonies to fight for their King and as His Majesty has an urgent need for men, Gerard, I have decided that you shall answer his call.

'Perhaps the army might make a man of you; God knows I
have failed in that. As the son of a gentleman, you shall, of
course, take His Majesty's Commission, which I shall arrange
for you.' He paused for a second or two to let his words sink in.
'You can refuse; in that case, you will leave this house tonight
with the clothes you stand up in and I shall disinherit you
without a penny. The choice is yours.'

'You give me no choice, Father, none at all, do you?' Gerard
answered bitterly. The army was not at all what he had in mind,
but then he brightened. 'The Brigade of Guards, Father. I'm sure
your influence would get me a Commission in the Blues and
Royals, or the Life Guards.' If one had to join the army, at least
join the regiment with the most social cachet. Gerard could just
see himself trotting down Horse Guards Parade in his burnished
breast plate at the head of a troop of Guardsmen.

'If you think for one minute, Gerard, that I am rewarding
your foul behaviour with a Commission in the Brigade of
Guards, you are most seriously mistaken. You will join the Royal
Durham Regiment and be proud to do so.'

'The Durhams?'

'Yes, Gerard, the Durhams. I have already spoken with
General Maxwell-Miller. You report to the Drill Hall in Bishops
Shilton tomorrow morning. You will see a … Col. Williamson,'
he said, reading from a note he took out from his jacket pocket.
'He will swear you in and then you will be sent for Officer
Training at Sheffield University. You will then be commissioned
into the 8th Battalion of the Durhams.' Sir Ralph read from his
notes again. 'The 8th Battalion is in the … 33rd Brigade, which
is part of the 11th Division. The 11th Division has been formed
under the command of Major-General Hammersly. Is that
understood?'

'Yes, Father, I understand.' The *Durhams*? That was worse
than being exiled to the … Patagonian Desert, wherever in Hell
that was? And wherever it was, it could not be more of a rural

GILES EKINS

backwater than the Royal Durhams. They were Infantry? For goodness sake! Foot soldiers!

'This might be the making of you, Gerard. Let us hope so. At least in serving your country, you go some way toward redeeming yourself. I don't believe I have any more to say. Do you have anything you wish to say to me before you depart?'

'Father … I … I … er.'

'Yes, Gerard?' Lord Exham asked, hoping for an apology, some sign of remorse from his son for his behaviour.

'Father … er … what about my allowance?'

'Is that all this means to you? Your allowance?'

'A man has got in live to the manner that he's expected to, Father, especially in the army. For the good of the family name and all that, it would hardly do for the world to think we were paupers, would it, Father?'

'Your allowance will continue, Gerard, very much curtailed I'm afraid, but it will be sufficient enough for you not to renege on your mess bills. That will be all. You had better go and pack. Goodbye, Gerard.' He did not offer to shake hands.

'Goodbye, Father,' Gerard replied, not offering his hand either. 'Goddamn you to Hell,' he muttered angrily under his breath as he stormed out of the study. 'And that little tittle-tattling bitch … the next time I see her, I'll thrash her to an inch of her life and damn the consequences. Just see if I don't.'

After the door had clattered noisily, Lord Exham sat down heavily at his desk, sighed deeply, and then reached behind him for the bell cord hanging at the wall.

'Your Lordship?' the butler asked when he entered, appearing so quickly he must almost have been waiting outside.

'A brandy, please, Brindley. A large one.'

As he sipped his brandy. he thought fondly of his eldest son, Edmund, Lord Barclay-Milnes, who had been studying Classics at Oxford, who had immediately enlisted and was now commissioned as a Second Lieutenant, undergoing training with the University and Public Schools Brigade.

A fine young man, destined for great things, such a contrast to his wastrel younger brother. 'Perhaps,' he thought to himself again, 'the army might make a man of Gerard.' But in his heart of hearts, he doubted it.

How could two sons, born of the same parents, be so drastically different? He sighed and took another sip.

THIRTY-FIVE

'Get away out of it, you old goat,' she answered.

'Did you tell him? His Lordship?' Mary Garforth asked anxiously as Jack came in through the back door.

'Aye,' Jack said, walking straight past her and through the kitchen to the front room.

'So? What did say, Lord Exham? You did tell 'im about his son and our Eleanor? What he did to her?' she asked again, following him into the front bedroom.

'Aye, Mary. As I say, I told him. But he said nothing. But, then, I never expected anything else, after all … no man in his position is ever going to admit the truth of such things to a man like me. Aye, never in a million years. Chances are he won't even admit it to himself. But that's of no matter, it had to be said.'

'Are you sure, right sure, Jack, that it was the best thing to do? I'm not criticising or owt like that, I just want to be certain in my own mind that we've done the best for our Eleanor.'

'As sure as any man can be,' Jack answered as he sat down on the bed and untied the laces of his best boots, 'sometimes you have to do things no matter what the consequences might be. I could not be sleeping at night knowing I had not done what had to be done.'

Mary felt a chill settle over her. 'Consequences, Jack? What consequences? You're not saying we're going to be thrown out of here, are you?'

'No, Mary, no, I'm not. Lord Exham said nothing about that. Well, no, that's not strictly true. What he did say was that if I said anything to anybody else, then he'd see we was thrown out.' Jack had taken off the jacket and waistcoat of his suit and carefully folded and wrapped them up again in tissue paper, and then he unhooked his braces, unbuttoned them from the waistband of his trousers, unbuttoned the fly buttons, and slid the trousers down his legs and onto the floor.

'Oh, Jack! That's means he didn't believe thee. He's going to throw us out, in't he?'

'I told you, Mary. No!' He picked up the trousers by the bottoms, lined up the seams and, holding the trouser bottoms under his chin, picked up another sheet of tissue paper from the bed, tucked the end of that under his chin as well, and then folded the trousers and the tissue paper down over his arm. 'He said nothing like that … said he would think on what I told him, that's all.'

He crossed over to the other side of the small bedroom, pulled open the second drawer of the heavy chest of drawers, releasing a heavy pungency of mothball naphtha into the air and carefully laid his best suit to rest therein.

'Aye,' Mary said bitterly, 'he'll think about it long enough to tell Mr Baker to throw us out. And where will that leave our Eleanor? Out on the streets without a home.'

'This house isn't really ours anyhow, is it? Never has been, never will be. We're here by the grace and favour of the mine owners and if we has to leave, well, we 'ave to leave and that's all there is to it. I'll readily find another job, makes it easier really, and Eleanor will be all the better for getting away from bad memories.'

'You can't mean that, Jack? About Eleanor being better off away from here? The poor bairn blames herself enough as it is. How's she going to feel we lose our home an' all, eh? You know how sensitive she is. She'll blame herself forever more ... she'll never get over it, *never*.'

Jack had a stricken look on his face. He had been so sure of the righteousness of his actions in confronting the father of the man who raped his daughter, that he had given no further thought as to the possible corollaries or consequences.

Every action created a reaction and he was only just coming face-to-face with this fact. Pride and principles could be dangerous allies. It had simply never occurred to him that he could make matters worse for Eleanor. Losing his job and home meant little to him compared to his pride—his pride in the propriety of his conduct. To Jack Garforth, a man stood or fell by the strength of his integrity, but the farthest thing from his mind had been to cause more problems for his poor, brutalised daughter.

'You don't think that, does you, that she'll blame herself? I mean, how can she blame herself for some'at I did?'

'I don't know, Jack. Who can say for sure how she'll react? But I don't see how she's not going to believe it's her fault if we lose our home, and you and the boys lose their jobs, because it's exactly what that swine told her would happen if she told anyone. And she did, she *told*. And you know our Eleanor—she takes everything as gospel truth, without questioning it too deep.'

'God knows, Mary, that were the last thing I intended when I went to see his Lordship. I never gave it no thought. I just felt that it were the only thing to do, that Lord Exham had to be told what kind of son he had sired. I mean, what else was there we could do? Nothing! Nothing, absolutely nothing, and so I couldn't just let it lay unsaid, could I?'

'Aye, I know you meant for the best, pet, but I don't know. It seems to me that sometimes doing for the best means the exact opposite. Take our Edgar joining the army. I know he thought it was for the best, but what if it means he gets hurt? Wounded badly. Else crippled. Or worse?'

'Edgar will be just fine, you'll see, Mary, love. Don't fret yourself over it, leastwise not 'til it happens. As for the other, losing us jobs and the like, if it happens, well, we'll have to just make the best on it, won't we? Same as we always have. You and me together.'

Mary straightened herself up. Jack was right; whatever befell them, they would face it together, with fortitude, as they had always done. 'Aye, p'raps you're right,' she said with a nod. 'But best you get some more trousers on first, eh?' With a small tight smile on her face, she nodded towards his hairy legs poking out of the bottom of his long-johns. 'Else folk'll think we've been up to hanky-panky.'

'Well, I'm game if thy art.'

'Get away out of it, you old goat,' she answered, but there was love and laughter in her voice as she said it. 'I'm a respectable married woman.'

'Aye, more's the pity. You should see the old bat I've got to put up with,' Jack jested as Mary threw his trousers at his head.

THIRTY-SIX

The biggest problem was going to be how to tell Mary!

The weather had changed very much for the worse, raining down in heavy sleeting sheets; the wind had picked up and whistled in from the northeast, a cutting wind that felt all the colder because it was still nominally summer, the sudden storm sweeping in from the sea with a speed that had caught everyone by surprise.

Jack Garforth huddled deeper into his jacket, pulling up the collar, shivering as he trickled water down his back as he did so. He set his cap further forward and, holding his jacket lapels closed tightly, scurried up the drive of 'the Big House', Exham Hall, wondering apprehensively why Lord Exham had sent for him.

'Garforth, do come in,' his Lordship said as Jack, feeling rather damp and squelching in his boots, was shown into the library. 'Come in.' Turning around behind him to lift up the arm of the phonograph from a recording he had been listening to, Enrico Caruso's 'Vesti La Giuba', from 'I Pagliacci', the first recording in history to sell more than one million copies.

'You sent for me, my Lord?'

'Yes, Garforth, good of you to come at such short notice, especially with the weather having turned so quickly like this.'

As if there had been any real choice in the matter.

He did not offer Jack a chair. 'I sent for you, Garforth, because I felt you should know that my son, my son Gerard, has decided to answer His Majesty's Call to Arms. He left the night before last; he has accepted a commission in the Durhams and is now at Officer Training Camp.'

'Aye? I see, your Lordship, aye. Thank you for telling us.'

'I think that is all I had to say, Garforth. Now, if you will excuse me.'

'Very good, your Lordship.'

Nothing more was said between the two men, but Jack Garforth understood very well what his Lordship was telling him, that the Honourable Gerard's enlistment had been a banishment, and this was as close as Lord Exham would ever get to admitting the truth about the attack on Eleanor. Jack felt as though a great weight had been lifted from his shoulders; he had been fretting and worrying for days about what effect his precipitous action might have on Eleanor.

She was not over the rape, not by a very long way. She had withdrawn into her own little world again and rarely spoke, staring at things that only she could see, but the relief that Jack felt that he was not going to adding to her burden was enormous.

He hurried back down the drive, barely feeling the lashing rain now, anxious to get back to Mary, to take the worry from her mind as well.

As he passed the church lychgate on the other side of the road, a striking poster on the notice board caught his eye. He stopped and hopped around, between the puddles, as he crossed over the potholed road to read it. It was so striking he was sure that it had not been there when he walked up the hill on his way to Exham Hall little more than an hour ago. He could not possibly have missed it, but who on earth was out posting up bills in weather like this?

BRITONS

The word BRITONS was printed in blood-red letters, almost 8' high. Beneath that was a picture of Lord Kitchener, staring straight at you. At *you*; nobody else. From whichever angle you looked at the poster, Kitchener stared unflinchingly, moustache bristling in patriotic fervour, as his gloved hand, seeming to stick right out of the poster, pointed a forefinger straight at you, so there was no mistake who he meant.

Jack wondered briefly how it could be made to look so life-like, and actually squinted at the poster sideways on, just to see if the finger did protrude or not, and then felt very foolish as he did so.

Under the head of Kitchener, were the words: WANTS YOU. It was as if it were Kitchener saying it, the words 'wants' very small, sitting on top of the O of the giant sized YOU.

Beneath that clarion call, again in large blood-red letters, the poster read: JOIN YOUR COUNTRY'S ARMY. Beneath that were the words, still in red print: GOD SAVE THE KING.

The very simplicity of the appeal struck a chord in Jack Garforth and he suddenly knew with great certainty what he had to do. He could not explain it, not even to himself, but he thought he could sense the intervention of a divine hand showing him the poster so soon after hearing that the rapist of his daughter had just enlisted—he knew that he had to join up as well, as if his own destiny were drawn inexorably into the same rite of passage as that of the Honourable Gerard. He could not rationalise it any further than that but knew that tomorrow he would be going down to Bishop's Shilton to enlist.

The biggest problem was going to be how to tell Mary!

THIRTY-SEVEN

The only way he could see of getting out of the shit pan.

September 1914

Joe Garforth also saw the notice, not long after his father, and he almost immediately decided that he was going to enlist.

His resolution was so immediate that he could give no real reason for it; it was simply the right thing to do. But the more he thought about it, the more it made sense. He had no great burning patriotism. He believed in God and the King and the empire and thought that to be born an Englishman was the greatest blessing that God could bestow upon an ordinary man but, beyond that, he had no great animosity towards Germany and her people.

Germany threatened the empire, that was reason enough to go to war, but his reasons for enlisting were, like most men, I suppose, far more personal. His home life was unsatisfactory, Lizzie had become more and more withdrawn and distant from him and, if he was honest with himself, he had done little on his side to overcome that and reduce the emotional chasm between them.

And his affair with Ethel Poskit was becoming more and more enmeshing, entangling him in an emotive and sexual net that grew tighter every day. He liked Ethel, liked her a lot, loved her even. He found her sexually exciting, in a way he did not know was possible; she devoured him sexually, but he was beginning to feel depraved when he was with her and it seemed as though there was nothing, but nothing, that she would not do.

It was this feeling that he was no longer in charge that was beginning to worry him. Ethel had become utterly obsessed with him and he could not see where their affair was headed, except into very deep trouble.

But even so, Joe knew that as long as he was around, and she was still avid for him, he would go with her; the musky sexual allure she permeated would have him trotting along up to Woodfield Copse behind her like a dog after a bitch on heat. Even when it was too damp to lie down, they still fucked, leaning up against a tree.

So, by joining the army, he might get some breathing space to think things over, and the separation might cool off Ethel's desperate hungry ardour for him. But even just thinking about her like this had set his pulses racing and he knew he wanted her very badly even now and he could feel the familiar tingling in his groin.

He wondered what shift Sammy was on and whether he dare go round to their house and see her. No, he decided, it was far too dangerous. They were living on the edge as it was, with visits to Woodfield Copse two or three times a week. To go see her at home would set a very hazardous precedent. He adjusted his long-johns around his tautened semi-erection and set off to Bishops Shilton and the recruiting office. He was due on shift at two, but ah, bugger 'em … things were a mess, and this was the only way he could see of getting out of the shit pan.

THIRTY-EIGHT

The Sergeant give him a quick hard look.

'They rejected me,' a still stunned Jack Garforth said to his wife, Mary. 'They bloody well *rejected* me.' Feeling as though it was the King himself who had told him he wasn't wanted, Jack stomped around the kitchen, an impotent anger brooding inside of him. He felt insulted, outraged, his very manhood had been found wanting. His King, and he glanced up at the portrait of King George and Queen Mary where it hung over the mantlepiece. His King had spat in his face. Rejected as not being good enough to fight at his side.

Mary commiserated with him, but inside she laughed and cheered, ecstatic that he had been turned down. He was too old anyway, and she did not want to lose him, not now, not ever. She could live with his bruised pride. He might go around and kick the furniture and stamp and swear, and take one or two pints more than he ought down at the 'Green Man', but she could happily live with all of that, just to keep him home. If she had

her way, Edgar would be the only Garforth the army got, and he
had only slipped her net because he caught her by surprise.

Mary had known that Jack was planning to go and try to
enlist. He said nothing about it, not a word, but there was something about his attitude towards her that had told her. He was
shifty-eyed and acted guiltily; he kept looking at her sideways,
not quite meeting her eye, like one of the children when they had
been naughty.

It had been transparently obvious to her what Jack's intentions were as soon as he told her about Lord Exham and the
Honourable Gerard's reluctant enlistment in the Durhams. Mary
could sense it in Jack even then, knew that for some perverse
masculine compulsion that she would never ever understand, that
he would have to go as well. 'Just like squabbling kids,' she
thought, 'anything you can do, I can do better! Men! And they
call themselves the superior sex? The only sex supposedly
capable of rational thought? Huh!'

Deeply fearful inside, she had said nothing, not even when
Jack took his cap off the peg at the back of the door and said to
her, 'Right oh, then, Mary, love, I'm just popping on over to
'Bishop' for an hour or so. I'll not be long.'

She knew that nothing she could say would dissuade him, in
fact quite the reverse; he was as stubborn as the most pig-headed
donkey on this earth and whatever she said would only make
him dig his obdurate heels in even deeper.

'Aye Jack,' she had answered, trying not to betray her agitation. 'Will you be back for owt to eat at lunch?'

He grunted at the stupidity of the question, when a man was
off to answer his Sovereign's call to arms, how can he know
whether he was going to be home for lunch? And to think that
women claimed to have the same intellectual capacity as men?
The country would go straight to the dogs if ever, God forbid,
women got the vote.

Mary saw him off to the gate, as casually as if he were going to the corner shop to buy his black-shag tobacco, but as soon as she was back indoors again, she went through to the front bedroom and knelt by the bed to pray that he would be deemed too old to enlist, even though she knew that Amory Blackburn from Alice Street, who worked as a clerk in Miller's Gents Haberdashery, had been accepted and he was a good two years older than Jack.

She added a prayer for the rest of the family, especially for Eleanor, who seemed to have reverted completely to childhood, talking, when she spoke at all, in a childlike monosyllabic speech. It was as if by reversing the years in her mind, she could pretend that the years on her body had been reversed as well so that, therefore, the rape had never happened, could never have happened.

Mary then prayed for Edgar to be kept safe. He was still living at home, although he reported daily to the Drill Hall, and the Battalion marched up and down and around and about; they went for route marches across the valleys and the moors up beyond Wolsington, but every night, or most nights, he came home again, still in his civilian clothes, deeply disappointed that he had not yet been issued with a rifle or uniform. In fact, he had not even seen a rifle, let alone held or fired one, and all his small-arms drills had been carried out with a broomstick.

But Mary did not mind, for as long as he, and the rest of the boys of the village who had volunteered, were still at home, they could not be shot at and killed by the Germans. And if the war really were over by Christmas, the chances were that they would never even get the chance to be sent to France and into battle. And Mary prayed mightily for that as well.

All morning, she waited anxiously—waiting for Jack to return, unable to concentrate fully on her housework, so much so that she scalded her hand on a steaming kettle. She could not bear the thought that he might go from her. Jack Garforth had been her rock. Her foundation. Without Jack, she would have gone under long ago.

Her heart lurched when she heard the back gate open and she knew from his face as soon as he came through the door that her prayers had been answered.

'Bloody well turned me down.' He swore again, shaking his head, as if still unable to believe it.

'Were it your age, Jack?' Mary asked. 'I mean, you are 55 year old and the notice did say 35 were tops.'

'Amory Blackburn were tekken and he's got a good few years more than me.'

'What is it, then?' she asked solicitously. Not that she minded —any reason that kept him out of the army was a good reason so far as she was concerned. 'Why did they not take you then, pet?'

'Aye, right, put the bloody kettle on and we'll have a cup of tea and I'll tell you. I'm dead parched.'

The Drill Hall had been full when Jack got there mid-morning. The walk from Ashbrook to Bishop's Shilton had taken him a lot longer than he had anticipated and he found that it had taken a great deal out of him; he felt quite exhausted by the end of the four-mile walk. He went across to Furmoil Park and sat on a bench by the pond, watching the ducks for half an hour or so to recover. The years and years of swallowing coal dust made him short-winded and he did not want to appear before the recruiting sergeant panting and wheezing from his exertions.

When he felt rested and composed again, he walked slowly down Auckland Street to the Drill Hall, glancing across the road to look at Mecklenburg's butchers. The window had been replaced, but the sign had been repainted to simply read Pork Butchers. Everybody knew it was still Mecklenburg's, but nobody seemed to mind so long as the German ancestry of the shop was now longer blatantly paraded in the street, not now that the first casualties from the district had taken place. The casualties from the battle at Le Cateau: Wilfred Whitehead, Hector

Whitehead's brother, and Norman Blackett, whose widow, Olive, lived in Durham, just a few miles up the Cansdale Road.

Like Edgar before him, Jack waited in line until he was eventually directed to one of the tables. The recruiting sergeant sitting there was bored and obviously uncomfortable on his hard, wooden folding chair, and he stretched and cracked his knuckles as Jack stood before him. He then lit another cigarette, dropping the burnt-out match into an already overflowing ashtray and then carefully balancing the cigarette on the ashtray edge whilst he sorted out another B 2505A form. Jack stifled an urge to cough as the raw smoke from the cigarette rose up in a blue, curling spiral and tickled the back of his throat.

He answered all the questions on the Attestation Form, hesitating only slightly when he gave his age as 43 years, 11 months. The sergeant give him a quick hard look and wrote down the age, but in such a way as to be almost illegible. After Jack had answered the last of the questions and had been duly warned as to the consequences of false declaration, which gave him a momentary start of unease, he signed the form as directed and was sent behind the screens for his medical.

The stethoscope felt cold to Jack's chest as he stood before the M.O. with his braces dangling about his thighs, shivering slightly as chill air rippled across his unaccustomedly bare chest.

'Breathe deeply, take a deep breath and hold it,' the doctor ordered, listening intently to the inner workings of Jack's chest. 'And again. Hold it. Now, exhale slowly,' the M.O. requested as the end of his stethoscope slithered over Jack's skin like a steel beetle. 'Turn around, take a deep breath again, and hold it.'

As Jack breathed in deeply. He could feel a cough beginning to stir deep in his lungs like a disturbed dragon in a cave. He fought to hold it back, feeling his chest constrict as he did so; his shoulders tensed and quivered with the effort of subduing his traitorous chest, but struggle as he might, the fire breathing beast in his lungs won and a tattoo of dry rigid coughs pattered in his throat. He kept his mouth tightly closed, so that the coughs exploded from his nose like dry gunfire as little tears started forming in the corners of his eyes.

The M.O. listened carefully to the little volcanic spasms, waiting until they had ceased before instructing Jack to turn round again.

'Sorry, chum,' he said, not unkindly, 'but we can't take you, I'm afraid. You are medically unfit.'

'What?' Jack demanded indignantly, as though someone had insulted him mortally. 'What's tha' mean, eh? What's tha mean you can't take me?'

'I'm sorry, Garforth,' the doctor replied, consulting Jack's papers. 'But you have pronounced pneumoconiosis with very severe emphysema and chronic bronchitis. The army couldn't possibly take you like this.'

'And what's new-mow-whatsis when it's at home then, eh? And emphy-oosis?'

'Pneumoconiosis. It's a very common disease among miners. Coal-dust inhalation over many years causes damage you see, leads to fibrosis of the lungs and susceptibility to infections such as emphysema. That's an abnormal presence of air in the lungs and it's what makes you so breathless. Pneumoconiosis can also lead to chronic bronchitis and TB, sometimes cancer.'

'Aye, I see. I always knew the dust were doing me no good, but it can't be that bad, surely? After all, I'm still working, aren't I? Can't be that bad if I'm working. I must be alright for the army if I'm working, mustn't I?' Jack pleaded earnestly.

'I'm sorry, Garforth, really I am, but there is no way I could possibly pass you as fit. It's more than my job is worth. In your state, you could barely march to the end of the street, let alone march across France. You are actually a very sick man.'

Jack sat down heavily on the stool, far more concerned that he had been rejected than the fact that the doctor had said that he was a very sick man. He felt crushed with disappointment, belittled.

'What's … what's to be done then?' he asked after maybe half a minute. 'About them things you said. Emphy-seema and the other newmowconny thing. Is there a cure? If I get cured quick, I could still join up, couldn't I?'

'There is no cure I'm afraid, Garforth. The damage to the lungs is irreversible. The only thing you can maybe do is stop smoking. And to get out of the mine and away from the dust.'

'That's what I'm bloody well trying to do, get out't pit, but you won't let me,' Jack answered tartly.

'Yes, I suppose you are at that,' the MO said with a slight smile, 'but I meant get out of the mine so you can rest. The army is not a rest cure.'

'How can I get out of the bloody mine and rest? I got a wife and family to support.'

The doctor shrugged. Not his problem. 'Get dressed now, Garforth, quick as you can. There're others I've got to see. Sorry and all that.' He turned away to write up his notes.

'So, there you have it, pet,' Jack said as he sipped disconsolately at his tea. 'Tossed aside like an old shoe. Not bloody good enough for them. Bugger 'em, bugger 'em'. Jack put down his tea and stood up, as if wanting to hit something. 'You know, Mary, it makes me feel about this big.' And Jack held his hooked finger and thumb about 2" apart. 'This big!'

Mary came and stood by Jack's side and hooked her hand about his waist. 'It's not thy fault, Jack. You can't help it if the mine has made you badly. You shouldn't blame yourself.'

'Nay, well who should I blame, then? I felt so … helpless, useless. Worthless. Like I say, I felt this bloody big. Oh, aye, he were nice enough about it, the doctor, but it made me feel like nowt. Absolutely bloody nothing!'

'You'll never be nothing to me, Jack. Nor to the kids. You tried to do your bit, that's what counts. You tried. That's all anybody can expect of a person. That they try. And you did and I'm proud of you for it. Dead proud.'

'Aye,' he said with a sigh of frustration. 'Maybes you're right, Mary love, but my God, it still bloody hurts.'

'Course it does, Jack, pet. A proud man like you, I'd expect nothing else,' she said, trying to massage away the hurt to his feelings by stoking up his self-esteem.

'You knew I was going to try to enlist, didn't you? This morning, when I went out, you knew?'

'Aye, Jack, it shone out of you like a lighthouse beam.'

'And you said nothing?'

'What's to say? You'd not be the man I thought you were if you let a prattling woman come between you and what you think is right. But what's more important now is you, and your chest. Can you not come out from underground now? Ask Mr Baker for a job above ground?'

'That's charity, Mary, and I'll have none of that. As long as I'm capable of doing my job at the seam, that's what I'll do, and I 'll hear no more about it.'

'But Jack!'

'Nay, but nothing. With so many men away to the army, they'll be needing more skilled men at the face, not less. So, I'll hear no more of it and that's that.'

'Aye, Jack, if you say so, but at least give up on the pipe, if that's what the doctor says. Give it up. It always makes you cough, anyhow.'

'It's come to a pretty pass when a man can't even have a pipe after his day's work.'

'I'm asking for me, Jack. I want you around for as long as I can and if asking you to give up the pipe makes even one day's difference?'

Jack smiled. 'By God, woman, you'd try the patience of Job with all your mythering. I reckon I'll get no peace unless I do give it up, will I?'

'Not for one minute.'

'Aye, alright then, I'll try, like you say. It always makes me hack me lungs out anyhow.' Jack shook his head and then smiled at her. 'Sometimes, I think thee must be a witch, Mary Garforth, tha's got me bewitched. A man's got no mind of his own around you. You should be burned at the stake.'

'Don't be silly, Jack, we've got stacks of coal.'

Jack lightly smacked Mary's buttocks. 'Take that for your sauce.'

And she watched as Jack got his pipe rack and tobacco jar down from the mantelshelf.

'No time like the present, I don't suppose,' he said and, with a sigh a farewell resignation, threw them all into fire, pipes and rack together, and then emptied the tobacco jar as well, watching transfixed as the tobacco was quickly consumed in a thick blue column of smoke. But the briarwood pipes took a long time to even catch alight.

'Jack?' Mary asked, when he turned away from the fire.

'Aye?'

'You know, with all the money you save on pipes and tobacco?'

'Aye?' Jack answered suspiciously.

'Why don't we buy our Eleanor a new dress? She might like that. Help her along a bit?'

'Aye, let's do that. And owt else she fancies. Breaks my heart to see her like this. Fair breaks my heart.'

THIRTY-NINE

You're all bloody fools, every single one of you.

It was if the men of the village had been subjected a to a common will, enthralled to the dictates of a master puppeteer who inexorably pulled the strings of the men towards the Recruiting Office. It was a constant flow, every day at least four or five men found their thoughts and then their footsteps drawing them towards Bishops Shilton and the Drill Hall.

It was not patriotism or bravery that drove them on, nor was it love of their King or hatred of the Germans. Nor was it a need to escape from an unsatisfactory marriage or because a miner had drawn a poor cavil that quarter, although all these factors played a greater or lesser part in the decision of the men to answer the call to arms.

It was rather the sense of being left out of the village collective will, the sense that a destiny was being created and the need to be part of that destiny. It was the fear of missing out on an experience that would shape the world forever. It was the gnawing anxiety of being excluded from the magic circle of those who had been, not to have been 'one of the boys'.

Probably few of the men could have articulated this feeling, but this was the unspoken, often unrealised magnet, that lured Jack Garforth and his sons, and the other men of the village, to the recruiting sergeant. Even though Jack had been driven by other, personal, factors, he too had been bound up in the inexorable village resolve. His disappointment at rejection was very much conditioned by the overwhelming feeling that he had been excluded from this select fraternity.

Like the small boy who was not picked to play on the football team and told to go away, Jack had become an outsider.

Joe, Jack's son, he had no such difficulty, passing all hurdles easily. He told his wife Lizzie, however. She seemed indifferent to the prospect of him joining up, but actually she was not. Lizzie did not want to become a widow, did not want her husband to go off to war, but she and Joe had so fallen out of the habit of talking to each other on anything like civil terms, that she no longer knew how to speak to him, to tell him she would miss him.

But she knew that she would miss him, miss him terribly, and would worry incessantly for his safety, and for once did not turn away from his advances when he placed his hands on her hips in the night.

After they had made love, most enjoyably, Joe felt severe twinges of guilt, realising how much he regretted cheating on Lizzie; she could be a fine loving wife if only they could work at it.

But he was honest enough with himself to know that the very sight of Ethel would set his pulses racing and the thought of her lying, spread-eagled, waiting for him with that hungry gleam in her eyes, would send him scurrying up the path to Woodfield Copse without a second thought.

Daniel Garforth, Jack's second son, was a quiet introspective man, a man who said little but listened a great deal. Unlike his elder brother, Daniel had no problems in his marriage; he had been happily married to May for three years now and they were as much in love with each other as the day they had wed.

May had given him a fine son, James. There was another child on the way and Daniel was well content with life. He had drawn a good cavil with a high rich seam, and he was making good money, very good money. He felt no yearnings to visit foreign parts and would never be able to see going to war as an adventure, as many of the others did.

He was no more or less patriotic than his brothers, but Daniel was as sure of himself as any man could be. He told himself that if he did not believe that answering the call was right, he would not allow himself to be intimidated by the need to keep the regard of his fellows. Peer pressure would never force Daniel into anything he did not wish to do. Any decision to enlist would be his and his alone, unaffected by outside influences.

Only if he were convinced of the absolute righteousness of his decisions, then and only then, he said, would Daniel Garforth act. And it was possible that he even believed some of this, but as much as anyone else, he was still drawn into the collective will, and however much he told himself that he had not been influenced by his 'marras' in the pit joining up, there could be no doubt that it exerted a powerful leverage on him. Quite simply, Daniel did not want to be left out, however much he told himself otherwise.

Others who answered the siren call of war included Hector's son Leonard Whitehead, who enlisted the day after he heard of the death of his uncle, Wilfred, at Le Cateau. His brother, Giles, followed suit some days later and Hector Whitehead could sense that the roots of Highfield were beginning to creak and split apart. Leonard would not return and work his inheritance once those roots, roots that had grown deep for more than 350 years, had been torn up in the turmoil of war.

Nicholas Garforth also tried to enlist but was turned down because of his age, and it was probably a good job his mother never got to hear of it; as it was, Mary was in a bad enough state. Despite all her best intentions, her family seemed to be falling apart around her, first Edgar, then Joe the eldest lad, Daniel, Margaret Mary was talking about becoming a nurse, of joining the VAD. Eleanor had retreated so far into herself that Mary doubted whether she could ever come back again and, for the only time in her life, Mary wished evil on another human being, desperately praying that the Honourable Gerard would come to some harm.

Her husband brooded about his rejection and more than once voiced his regret at giving up his beloved pipe, blaming Mary for all his problems. She had to tread very warily around him. He knew he was being irrational and unfair in taking it out on Mary, but like a tormented bear, he lashed out at the nearest and most vulnerable target.

Only Harold Garforth resisted the call, sneering at those who did, decrying their patriotism as a betrayal of the working man. 'You just see how much bleeding thanks you get once this is all over. Nowt. Absolutely sodding nowt. The bosses and the nobs'll just say ta very much for your help. Now, get back under my heel so's I can keep on grinding you under. You're all bloody fools, every single one of you. Fools, fools, bosses' tools!'

To Ethel Poskit's immense relief, Sammy, her husband, had also volunteered and she had fond visions of him falling to German gunfire, leaving her free to marry Joe Garforth, (quite what she thought would happen to Lizzie Garforth, I didn't know, but first things first).

She saw nothing wrong in wishing for her husband's death;

she wanted Joe Garforth and no other considerations came into her mind. If Sammy had to die in order to achieve that, well, so be it.

But when she heard that Joe had volunteered as well, she was so overcome, she felt ill, physically ill, vomiting in her wretchedness.

She was even more upset when Sammy told her that he and Joe were in the same battalion, the same platoon even, which meant that whatever danger Sammy was exposed to, Joe would be there as well.

Mary Margaret was in tears.

'Why, Mam?' she sobbed. 'We've only been wed four week, less than a month. Why's he want to go off and leave me?'

Mary Margaret and William Hindle had married on 15th August. They had married in the church, up on the hill along Whitton Lane. In her best dress, only just finished the previous evening by Sarrie Whitlock, Mary Margaret had taken her father's arm and walked the half mile or so to the church from Victoria Street. It seemed as though the whole village had come to the church to greet the couple when they emerged again as man and wife.

Mary Margaret would never be described as pretty, she was too heavyset and plain-featured, but she looked radiant that day, and everyone agreed that she would make a fine wife and a good mother, just like her own stepmother.

After the ceremony, friends and neighbours and anybody else who happened to be passing joined in at the reception in Victoria Street. The front door was open for the first time in many years, not since Jack's first wife Mary had died in 1897, and everybody was welcome to come and wish good luck to the bride and groom.

There had been cakes, buns and mountains of filled stotties

and sandwiches for the guests, all contributed by friends and neighbours. Despite her penchant for malicious gossip, Nellie Spearman was a superb cake-maker and so she had made the wedding cake as her present to the couple. Jack had laid in a barrel of best bitter from 'The Green Tree' and a case of brown ale, with a bottle of port for any ladies who might like to drink, but not many did, although Mary had a thimble-full just to wish the bride and groom good health.

Billy Edwardes had brought his squeeze box and Charlie Spearman wheeled the piano out from the front room onto the path next door, and they struck up with a jig and there was a high old time, what with dancing and singsong. The children had jelly and cakes and more than one or two felt sick afterwards from too much rich food, but didn't they have fun as they raced in and out and around and about?

And now, four weeks later, Mary Margaret was in tears.

'I don't understand it, Mam,' she sobbed. 'I've tried to be a good wife to him, honest. Even, you know?'

'I know you have, Mary Margaret, pet. I know you'll have been a fine wife to him, none better, but this has nowt to do with you being a good wife or not.'

'What then? Why does he want to go off and leave me so soon if it's not because he thinks I've not been good to him?'

'The only certain thing about all this, pet, is that thinking, any kind of thinking, doesn't come into it at all.'

'He must have thought. I mean, a newly wed man just doesn't up and off to war without thinking. Without thinking how I must feel about it all?'

'Mary Margaret, lovie. He's a man. Men don't think. Ever! I often wonder what the Good Lord thought fit to put in their heads in place of brains and common sense. Take your Dad, 55 year old and the daft beggar thinks he can go off and join the army. Jack, Edgar. Daniel. The whole village has gone daft. Same thing your Billy.'

'William. He prefers I call him William. Billy's for his marras. I'm his wife, so he likes me to call him William.'

'Billy, William, whatever, your dad; none of them *ever* think. Not one of 'em has got the brains they was born with.'

'William, he said as how we had to fight German militarism. He was saying something about the German menace. What does he know about the German menace? He knows nowt about Germans. So, why does he want to go and fight them? It must be because he wants to leave me. It has to be, because nothing else makes any sense.'

'Mary Margaret, the last thing, the absolutely last thing you look for in men is sense. You try and make sense out of what a man says he's got to do, and you'll drive yourself doolally. Believe me, pet, it's nothing to do with you, or what you've done or not done to be a good wife, it's all part of this universal madness. I could tell you to be proud of him, going to fight for his King, but pride in your man is a matter for you and you alone.'

'Are you proud of our dad, I mean, for trying to enlist? And of Jack and Edgar and Daniel?'

'Aye, and that's the big question, isn't it? No wife or mother wants to see her men go to war but, aye, I'm proud of your dad, daft old beggar that he is. And Edgar and Jack and Daniel. God knows I did everything I know to try and stop them, but I wish them well and hope it never comes to them fighting, but I'm dead proud that they answered the call and dead fearful for them all at the same time. Your dad says it's always been the lot of women-folk to wait on their men as they go to war. But I think that's just an excuse.'

Mary Margaret wiped her eyes. 'So, you don't think that it's because he wants to get away from me? Our Billy, our William?'

'Nay, pet. He's just caught up in it all, all this madness, that's all. He'll not have given owt else a thought.'

'It's all so … stupid, in't it, Mam? Stupid!'

'Aye, you're right enough there, pet. Stupid just about sums it all up.'

'What's going to come of it all, Mam?'

'Lord, I don't know, Mary Margaret, pet, but you just get ready to welcome your Billy home, and all the others. This war is all about some'at and nothing and it'll be over by Christmas, just you wait and see.'

But even as she spoke, she suddenly recalled the words that had leapt from the page of Jack's Dickens the day of her blackest mood those few short weeks ago: *something will come of this, I hope it mayn't be human gore.* And she felt a shudder rippling down her spine.

I hope it mayn't be human gore.

PART TWO

FORTY

April 25, 1915 Gallipoli

Forever in the annals of brave but foolish endeavours.

The sky over Cape Hellas and the village of Sedd El Bhar at the foot of the Gallipoli Peninsula, was purple-hued and bruised, a sullen sky, dark and heavy, and the fetid humidity of the night clung around the old converted collier troop ship like a warm wet blanket.

Even so, Edgar Garforth shivered slightly as the ship slopped into the weighty oily sea that swelled back from the closing coast, feeling the hard knot of apprehension tight in his stomach. All around him, other soldiers from the 8th Battalion of the Durhams, part of the 29th Division, shuffled and swayed, nervousness rippling along the ranks like wind through a cornfield as the impending invasion and assault on the beaches of Gallipoli loomed ever closer.

Gallipoli was a barren peninsula, jutting out into the Aegean Sea on one side and the narrow channels of the Dardanelles leading to the Sea of Marmara, the Bosporus, Constantinople and the Black Sea on the other.

The Dardanelles, 40 miles long and from one to four miles wide, were strategically important, separating European Turkey from Asia Minor, the only route from the Black Sea to the Mediterranean, the route through which Russian ships could bring much needed supplies of wheat to the Allies, and receive weapons and ammunition in return.

In October 1914, Turkey, hoping to gain territory from long-standing enemy Russia, joined the Central Powers of Germany and the Austro-Hungarian Empire. Bulgaria would also later join.

If the Allies could seize the Dardanelles and occupy Constantinople, Turkey could be knocked out of the war. In March 1915, a joint British and French naval fleet attempted to force the narrows, but after two ships were sunk and three holed by mines, Vice-Admiral de Robeck lost his nerve and ordered a withdrawal of the flotilla. Had he held his nerve and pushed on, he could very well have taken Constantinople and brought about the overthrow of Turkey.

That missed opportunity was to have tragic consequences.

Still determined to seize the Dardanelles, Lord Kitchener despatched the Mediterranean Expeditionary force, 70,000 men, to make landings on the Gallipoli Peninsula.

Gallipoli was part of the Ottoman Empire which, before 1915, most people in Britain had probably never heard of. But the name was shortly to be etched across the imagination of the nation, never to be forgotten, forever in the annals of brave but foolish endeavours.

The strategic concept for the invasion had everything in its favour, provided the planning was efficient. As it turned out, the preparations for the landing were woefully inept. The landing sites were not thoroughly reconnoitred, the dispositions and strength of the Turkish Army were not studied, and the maps largely copied from tourist guides.

The Aegean coastline, where the landings were to take place, consisted mainly of steep sandy cliffs rising from the sea to heights of 100-300', ideal terrain to defend, providing cover and artillery sites, whilst leaving the landing troops dangerously exposed.

Landings were to be made on four beaches, designated V, W, X and Y, whilst the French would land troops on S beach, on the Dardanelles side of the peninsula,

The Australian and New Zealand troops, ANZAC, who would gain immortal glory at Gallipoli, were to land some 15 miles further up the Aegean coast near Gaba Tepe.

V beach, Cape Helles, now awaited Edgar Garforth and the rest of the Durhams.

The high spirits of Mudros Harbour on the island of Lesbos had evaporated like sea mist under the sun during the 17-mile voyage across the Aegean to the Turkish coast. The troops, packed tight in the rusting transport, began to feel the tension stretching drum-taut in the empty pre-dawn hours.

Only Jeb Fulcher seemed unperturbed by the advancing battle, but only, as Edgar surmised, because he had so little imagination. Jeb was pulling slowly on his pipe, chomping bucolically on the pipe-stem between his teeth, like a cow chewing its cud, big nose twitching as stray curls of smoke swirled up into his cavernous nostrils, staring impassively out across the dark water as though watching corn grow. Edgar nudged Dennis Jennings, standing beside him, and nodded towards Jeb.

'Look at him, Jeb the Neb, daft old bugger. You'd think he was going to the Miners Rally in Durham instead of going to war.'

'Aye, I've seen cows going to the slaughterhouse look more worried than him.'

Edgar paled slightly at the use of the word slaughter and

swallowed hard. 'Slaughter? You don't think that this is going to owt like that, do you?' he asked, trying to keep his voice light-hearted.

'Nay, lad. Johnny Turk! Why, he'll not stand and fight, man. He's never had to face an English army afore—he'll take one like at these guns of ours and be off across them hills quicker than shit after a bellyful of green apples, you just see if'n he don't. I mean, it's not like we're fighting a real army, is it? Just a bunch of Turkish wogs.'

'Aye, course. Soonest we get this lot over and done with, we can get back to France where the real fighting is.'

'Brave words, Edgar lad,' he told himself as he ran a finger around the inside of his collar; the material of his tunic was rough and scratchy, and the fear-sweat on his neck only made it worse.

He gazed around at the mill-press of soldiers packed up close about him, and then grimaced with anger as he caught sight of his platoon commander, standing by the railings next to a rusting ladder, none other than Second Lieutenant the Honourable Gerard Barclay-Milnes, the violator and rapist of his little sister, Eleanor. Edgar's eyes slitted and his innards curdled with hate as he eyed Barclay-Milnes.

'What bastard quirk of fate made him our platoon comman-der?' Edgar asked himself yet again. 'Just look at the smug-faced bastard, parading around for all the world like a perfect gentle-men.' He sneered inwardly at the idea of Barclay-Milnes as a gentleman rather than the vile rapist bastard that he was, the evil shit-faced animal who had defiled Eleanor.

At least the bastard had not got her with child, Edgar thought; he would have killed the Honourable Gerard if he had of done, except of course that he would have had to fight his way past his father and brothers Joe and Daniel, to get at him before they did. 'Bastard,' he muttered again and turned away before anyone could see the loathing on his face.

286

'Say summ'at, Edgar?' Dennis Jennings asked, quizzically noting Edgar's reaction to the officer.

'What, me? Nay. Talking to myself, I guess. Do it all the bleedin' time. Must be the heat that's got to me brains. Puddled 'em,' he replied and lit up a Woodbine to conceal his agitation, wincing as the smoke caught at his sore sleep-deprived eyes, then passing the packet over to Jennings.

'Ta, I'll take one for after an' all.'

Edgar winced again, kicking himself for forgetting what a sponger Dennis Jennings was.

Edgar touched his breast pocket again, reassuring himself that the letter from Greta Mecklenburg was still there, even though he had only checked for it a few minutes before, still scarcely able to believe that she would have agreed to be his girl.

After he had first met her outside the smashed ruins of the butcher's shop window in Bishop's Shilton, Edgar had not been able to get the sight of her slight figure out of his mind, the sharp wounds from her lacerating tongue cut deep in his heart. He had gone back to Bishop the next morning and the morning after that, hoping to catch a glimpse of her, but knowing that even if he did see her, he likely would not have enough courage to go up to her and strike up a conversation.

Greta Mecklenburg had him obsessed. And he knew it. And he knew, deep inside the purple-profound recesses of his rational mind, that she most probably would have nothing to do with him, even if he did see her again. He was, after all, the man who smashed her shop window and helped to put her grandfather in hospital.

He became so preoccupied with thoughts of Greta Mecklenburg that even the letter from the War Office, ordering him to report to the Drill Hall on the Monday morning for battalion training, paled in significance and he tossed it aside in frustration, worried that he would be sent to France without having seen her again.

Turning the buff envelope from the War Office around and around in his hands, he calculated how many more opportunities he might have to see her before the army dragged him deep into its gaping maw. And to think, only a few days ago, it had been his greatest wish to get into the army and, now, the prospect filled him with a sick anticipation of loss and missed opportunity.

'What's the matter, eh, soldier boy? Lost you bottle for it has you, Edgar? Eh?' Harold hissed in scorn. 'Now that's come?' He nodded his close-shaven head at the envelope; he had had a bad case of head lice and his skull had been scraped bare.

Curiously, no one else in the family had been afflicted. 'Always knew you'd shit yourself rigid once it came to it,' he said, sneering behind a cupped hand so that Jack or Mary would not hear him.

'See you outside later, Harold, and we'll see whose got the bottle for owt.'

Across the table, Nicholas watched the whispered exchange between his half-brothers, his eyes flickering from one to the other, storing it in his mind, wondering if he could write a story about it, a modern variation on Cain and Abel maybe, or David and Absolem, but other than the fact that Harold was his usual bloody objectionable self, he had no idea what they were squabbling about.

Mary Garforth glanced up quickly from the sink, sensing the antagonism between the two brothers. 'I don't know what it is between you two, forever knocking heads like stags in rut, but whilst you're under this roof, I'll have none of it, you hear me. Tell 'em, Jack, tell 'em I'm sick and tired of it, sick to death of it, and if it don't stop now, I'm out that door and you can all fend for yourselves … and then see how far your bickering will get you.'

'You heard your ma, you two. Now stop. Else I'll start knocking a few heads together.' Although both Harold and Edgar stood a good head taller than their father, they both knew he was more than capable of carrying out his threat.

'Aye, right', Edgar mumbled, 'I'm off out anyhow.'

'Me an' all.'

Outside the back door, Edgar and Harold immediately turned their backs on each other and headed their respective ways, Harold down to the 'Green Tree' and Edgar to Bishop's Shilton once more to try to see Greta Mecklenburg.

A light patter of rain skittered across the valley sides, gone again almost before Edgar had time to pull his collar tighter around his neck, and then the sun burst out of the clouds again, just as if it had been waiting in ambush. Along with the abrupt burst of sun, Edgar had a sudden premonition that this time he would be lucky. That this time he would get to see her again, and his heart began to beat faster in the anticipation of it, his stomach twitching in apprehension in case she ignored him, or worse still, humiliated him with her astringent tongue.

He had made the walk across to Bishop's Shilton so often of late that his boots seemed to find the way of their own volition, and it was with a start of surprise he looked up to find himself at the head of Auckland Street, with Mecklenburg's shop only a handful of yards away.

Nervousness swept over him again and his heart was pounding so much in trepidation that he actually turned away and took several steps back down the road, toward the village, before chiding himself that he was being stupid. 'After all,' he told himself, 'the worst she can do is to tell you to bugger off, so thee's got nowt to lose. Not as if it's the first time in your life you've been told to bugger off, is it, son?'

He looked up and suddenly there she was, barely yards ahead as she came round the corner from Sutherland Street. His heart beat so rapidly that he thought it would burst from his chest, his palms sticky and sweaty.

Swallowing hard, his stomach a seething knot of snakes, he

strode up to her. It was obvious she could see him, but she looked straight past him, as if he were not there, and he felt a sudden stab of fear that she would ignore him totally, which would be worse than a rejection.

'Er ... hello, Miss ... er ... Mecklenburg,' he mumbled as he stepped in front of her, whipping off his cap so quickly that she flinched.

'Yes?' she answered peremptorily, as if she had no idea who he might be, although it was apparent to Edgar from the look that flashed fleetingly across her face that she certainly had recognised him.

'Er, it's me ... Miss Greta. Edgar ... Edgar Garforth.'

'Yes?' she said again with that infuriatingly quizzical look on her face again, her eyebrow arching so high that it threatened to disappear under the fringe of auburn hair that framed her lovely petite face.

Her nose wrinkled slightly, as if he smelled bad, and as she had already reduced him to such as nervous state, he almost had to restrain himself from sniffing at his armpits, even though he knew he had had a good wash at the kitchen sink before leaving the house and that, if anything, he would smell of C.W.S Soap and Shaving Stick.

'You remember miss? Edgar Garforth. I fixed your window.'

'Oh yes, the animal who helped put my grandfather in hospital.'

'Look, I've said I'm sorry about that, and genuine, I mean it. If there was owt I could do for it not to 'ave 'appened, I'd do it. Swear to God I would.'

'Yes, I rather believe you would,' Greta responded. 'Anything to salve your conscience,' she added tartly, drawing a grimace from Edgar.

'You're never going to let me forget this, are you?'

'Mr ... Garforth, is it?'

Edgar nodded miserably. This was going far worse than he ever imagined.

'Mr Garforth, I cannot foresee any circumstances whereby forgiveness or allowing you to 'forget it' will ever be of relevance to me. Our paths simply do not cross. If you truly do wish to forget about the incident, then might I suggest you make your way to the nearest alehouse?'

'Greta,' he pleaded. 'Miss … Mi-iss Greta,' he stammered as her furious scowl at his familiarity scorched him like a torch. 'Please, please. Just hear me out. You owe me that, at least.'

'I owe you nothing except my contempt.'

'Please …?' he beseeched, a stricken look across his face, like an unjustly punished child.

'Mr Garforth, you are nothing if not persistent. Annoyingly so.'

But there was something in Edgar's earnest puppy-like appeal that touched Greta and she glanced over towards St Peter's church tower to check the time. 'I can give you two minutes, Mr Garforth, two minutes to say whatever you feel you have to say to me. After that, I have to go and see my grandfather.'

She peered meaningfully over at the church clock again and Edgar realised that it was all or nothing. This was his only chance. 'If I bugger it up now,' he told himself, swallowing hard. His mind suddenly went blank. He had rehearsed in his mind all manner of imagined conversations with Greta, witty, clever talk that would sweep her off her feet. But now he could not remember a single word and he found it hard to breathe, the mere proximity of Greta seeming to solidify his lungs and vocal cords.

'I … I … er … I,' he gasped out at last, feeling like a fool, wishing that the ground would split and swallow him up, together with his stammering stupidity.

'Take a deep breath. That might help,' Greta suggested,

surprising even herself. She wanted to be hard and peremptory with Edgar, but he looked so crestfallen as he stood before her, tongue-tied and squirming, twisting his cap around in his hands from nervousness, that she almost felt sorry for him. 'Take a deep breath and count to ten.'

He did as he was told, her quiet words calming him more than the deep breaths.

'That's it,' she said.

He took another deep breath and tried once again, his tangled tongue suddenly freeing itself from the knots of nervousness. 'Miss Mecklenburg, I don't really how else to say this, so I suppose the best way is to just come out with it and not beat about the bush any longer.' He paused, feeling a strength flowing through him like a tidal wave.

'Yes?'

'When we met, you know, the other day?'

'Yes, I remember. It's hardly a day I'm likely to forget, is it?'

'No, I don't suppose it is. And nor for me neither. It's a day I'll remember for the rest of my life. You see, Miss ... you see, Greta, I was ... I don't know any other words for it, but I was smitten. Aye, that's the word, smitten. With you. I didn't think such a thing could be possible.'

He laughed softly, tossing his head back. 'Smitten? More like thunderstruck really. I've not been able to think of anything else; it's like a dream. All the time, you're on my mind. Can't sleep for thinking of you.' The words tumbled from Edgar like an over-flowing rainwater butt. 'Never thought that any lass ... any girl ... could ever make me feel like that.'

'The thing is,' he continued as Greta stared up at him in dumbstruck amazement. 'The thing is, might I 'ave permission to call on you. Formal ... formally?'

'You ... want to call ... on me?'

'Aye. Yes, that is if you give me leave to do so.' A sudden

thought struck Edgar like a blow to his midriff. He had no idea whether Greta already a 'young man', someone already calling on her. He did not even know if she were married or not, as she wore gloves and it was impossible to tell. She was so attractive that it seemed to him improbable that there could not be someone in her life and he felt a bigger fool than ever before, his temporary assurance draining away as quickly as it had appeared.

'Bloody Hell, Edgar lad,' he told himself. 'Thy's making a right bloody pillock of yourself. God Almighty knows what she must be thinking on you.'

'As to whether I give you permission or not, that rather depends does it not,' she answered finally, an expression on her face that Edgar could not decipher.

Wonder? Contempt? Pity? He knew not.

'On what?' Edgar asked gingerly. At least she had not dismissed him out of hand.

'On what you think we could possibly have in common. You are, after all, an uneducated miner, are you not? Given to violence and strong drink.'

'As to strong drink, Miss Greta, you have no knowledge at all as to my drinking habits, none whatsoever. As to violence, aye, well you maybe have some cause enough to say that, except I reckon that if you look into your heart of hearts, you'll know how much I regret that. As to being a miner, well that's it you see, I'm no longer a pitman. I've joined up. I'm a soldier, one of the King's men.'

'A soldier?'

'Aye, a soldier and proud of it.'

'Which means that not being content with putting my grandfather into hospital, you have actually volunteered to go and try to kill his kinfolk. *My* kinfolk. I am, as you are very well aware, of German ancestry,' she added haughtily.

Edgar sighed, feeling defeated and drained, humiliated by his

GILES EKINS

own failure, battered by her obduracy and the unfairness of her remarks.

'Well, I've taken the blame for a great deal, Miss Mecklenburg, but bug ... blessed if I'm going take the blame for England and Germany being at war. As you say, I'm just an uneducated nobody, but there no way you can lay that one at my door. I know your grandfather's German, which was what caused all that ruckus, but you are going to have to decide for yourself where your loyalties lie.

'Seems to me that thy's a Durham lass, born and bred, and you mother and father before you, and that makes you English, and you should be proud of the lads who're going to fight for you. As are going to die for you. But as I say, that's for you to decide upon. In your own mind.'

He took another deep breath and raised his hand in a half-salute. 'I'll bid you good day, Miss Mecklenburg, I'll not be troubling you again.' And, with another heavy-hearted sigh, he turned away and put back on his cap.

He had taken a couple of leaden footed steps when she called him back.

'Mr Garforth! Mr Garforth. Please come back. I'm sorry,' she said, shame-faced as he stood before her again. 'I have been less than civil to you and I had no right, absolutely no right at all, to speak to you the way I did about volunteering. Of course, you should be proud of doing your duty for His Majesty. And, yes, you may have leave to call on me.'

'What?', Edgar gasped, not sure that he had heard correctly.

'I said, Mr Garforth, that, yes, you may call on me. Might I suggest Sunday afternoon? About four?' A devilish little gleam crept into her eye.

Greta Mecklenburg had decided she quite liked Edgar Garforth. Her father had always indulged her whims and tantrums and she had ever been sharp of tongue; until now, very few people had stood up to her and she found that she admired

Edgar for it, together with his quiet hurt dignity. And he was quite good-looking, in a rough-hewn sort of way, and she particularly liked the fact that, despite his trade, he kept his hands clean with nails trimmed and free from grotesque half-moons of deeply ingrained dirt, so common amongst working men.

'Sunday? Afternoon? Aye, right. Why, aye. Aye,' he mumbled, his heart soaring with pleasure. If he had to walk barefoot across broken glass to get to her, he would be there.

'Now, you really must excuse me,' Greta said, 'I do have to get to my grandfather. Until Sunday afternoon then, Mr Garforth … Edgar.'

It had been a strain, that Sunday afternoon, as Edgar in his best (and only) suit, too small for his growing frame, had sat on the uncomfortable edge of his seat, trying to make polite conversation to Greta's mother and father.

He felt utterly wretched and inadequate as Peter Mecklenburg, Greta's father, asked him what his plans were after his army service; after all, everyone knew that the war would be over by Christmas at the latest. Did Edgar intend to return to the pits, he asked, as Greta's mother sniffed loudly at the notion of a mere miner becoming involved with her only daughter. Celia Mecklenburg had enough airs and graces to do justice to a countess, and if Greta insisted on taking up with a military man, she expected nothing less than a major as being good enough. And a wealthy one at that.

As he looked down at his boots, he could see an area on the right heel that he had not shined properly, a dull irregular patch the size of a florin, and he surreptitiously tried to tuck that heel further away from view, so that they would not think him a bigger clod than they already did. If such were possible.

Edgar squirmed as he confessed to having no plans, other than he saw the army as a way out of the mines, but beyond that he had no ideas. He blushed to his roots and he could feel Greta's contemptuous eyes on the back of his neck as Celia Mecklenburg made a remark about the shiftlessness of the working classes these days. His early euphoria had long since evaporated and inwardly he seethed. Greta had done this to show him up and humiliate him.

However, although he did not wish to be rude, Edgar was damned if he was going to let this woman, who after all was only the wife of the local butcher, treat him like something unpleasant stuck to her shoe. He had been polite and well-mannered and had given Greta's mother a cake that he had persuaded Mary to bake for him and saw no reason why he should allow her to belittle him this way.

'Aye, I'm a working man and proud of it. And, it seems to me, that without us pitmen, yon fire,' he said, pointing at the unlit coal in the hearth, 'would likely have nowt to burn in it.'

'Well I never. Such rudeness,' Greta's mother stated, jerking back dramatically as though slapped.

'Well said, Edgar,' Greta said to his surprise. 'Mother, now you leave him be.'

'Aye, no doubt the lad's right,' added Peter Mecklenburg.

But Celia Mecklenburg was determined to have the last word. 'Really, Greta, have you no pride, not when Albert Tweedy's son, Alfred, has been asking after you?'

'That's enough, Mother,' Greta remonstrated. 'And you can forget any notions you might have that I would ever consider a proposal from Alfred Tweedy. Edgar, I believe that we need to take a short constitutional. The atmosphere in here has become quite unpleasant.'

Edgar got to his feet. Even though still angry, he was determined that his manners would not give cause for further antagonism.

'Thank you, ma'am. Thank you, Mr Mecklenburg, ma'am, sir, for your kind hospitality. I hope I will have the pleasure to meet you again. Good day,' he said as affably and as politely as he could and hurried along to open the door for Greta.

Once outside, Greta took Edgar's arm, which gave him a tingle of pleasure.

She was pleasantly surprised that he had stood up to her mother, who could be overbearing to anyone she considered to be from the lower classes.

'What was all that about?' Edgar asked. 'I mean, I was polite. Didn't pick my nose or scratch myself. Tried to be pleasant and conversational.'

'Mother feels that her life has been a disappointment. Her family, the Markhams, were once monied, had status in Newcastle, but some scandal, or bad investments, I'm not totally sure what, Mother has not said, but the family were reduced financially and socially. Mother is resentful, feels her rightful place is in society. Marrying my father, a butcher, is not what she envisaged from life.'

'Your father's a good, well respected man. And so is your grandfather, 'though I've not met him, but my father speaks highly of him. What is there to be disappointed about in life there? There's many as would give their right arm for such a life.'

They sat down together on a bench, close against the wall of St Peter's churchyard, the evening sun casting sharp shadows across the gravestones and memorials.

'She wants me to vicariously live the life that she feels was denied to her.'

'Vicariously? Now there's a word, I don't know the meaning of. But, how did you put, it? I am after all, an uneducated miner, given to violence and strong drink,' Edgar said, a smile across his face.

'Did I really say that?'

'You did, but I can probably guess what vicariously means— watching others do the things you wanted to do? Your mother wants you to have the life she's feels was denied her, which is why she wants you to consider a proposal from Mr Alfred Tweedy. Who ... whomever he might be.'

'Alfred Tweedy, son of Albert Tweedy, is rich, educated, dull and boring with the conversational skills of a stuffed badger. Whereas I find you easy to talk to, Mr Edgar Garforth.'

'Private Edgar Garforth, if you please.'

'Yes, Private Garforth,' she responded sadly. 'One day, you will leave me go to war. Won't you?'

'Aye, but hopefully it will all be over soon. Before Christmas, they reckon.'

'Nothing is certain about that, is it? Germany will not easily be defeated.'

'Aye, p'raps you're right. It's only what they say in the papers. The only certainty in this life is uncertainty. Life in the mines is like that, never knowing if the pit's going to go off whilst you're down there. I suppose war is the same. Never knowing if that bullet is for you so, as I say, the only certainty is uncertainty.'

Greta shivered, not only from the cold of the evening. 'I think I had better be going back home now, Edgar.'

'Aye, right. I'll walk you to your door.'

At the door, they shook hands formally. 'Might I see you again, Miss Mecklenburg?' he asked, suddenly tongue-tied again.

'Of course, Private Garforth. Shall we say next Sunday afternoon?'

Private Edgar Garforth thought of all those Sunday afternoons and other times that he had called on Greta as the Gallipoli Peninsula and Cape Helles loomed ever closer.

Even though it had only been eight months since he had enlisted in August of the previous year; so much had happened that it seemed as though he had lived through an entire new life, that the village and working down the mine had been mere preludes to his real life, and he thought back to those first days as a soldier of the King.

So many men had answered the call to arms that the army had simply been unable to cope, not only in Durham, but throughout the length and breadth of the country.

It had been weeks before Edgar, Jeb Fulcher, Dennis Jennings, Dick Wilson and the others from the village, who had answered that first call, were issued uniforms, and even then, they had not been proper uniforms. At first, they had been issued with blue smocks and trousers, worn with blue field service caps whilst they waited for khaki to arrive. There had been no badges either, no insignia, nothing to distinguish them as soldiers, and so Gordon Tanqueray (who had refused an offer of a commission) ordered and paid from his own pocket, cap and collar badges that showed the sanctuary knocker from Durham Cathedral as an emblem, with the words Royal Durham Regiment, 8th Battalion wreathed in scrolls beneath. And he refused any payment for them.

And, as for boots, they rarely fitted properly and Jeb Fulcher who had very large feet, complained that the boots issued him were the wrong size.

'Nay, son,' replied the quartermaster sergeant, 'it's thy feet that's the wrong size.'

There had been no rifles to train with and so early drilling had been carried out using broomsticks.

And, all the while, Edgar reported for duty every morning, and every night went back home again to Victoria Street to a chorus of sneers from Harold.

'Here comes the broomstick warrior.' Or, 'Thee'll not be shooting too many Germans with your broom, will you, eh Edgar?' Or, 'Sweeping all the enemy before you, are you then, Edgar?'

And, once Edgar had begun seeing Greta Mecklenburg, Harold's insults grew worse.

'Consorting with enemy spies, that's treason.' Or, 'Swept her off 'er feet, did you, then, Edgar?' Or, "Has you practised any flanking movements on your German spy yet, then?'

Then there was, 'D'you reckon your Hun spy has told the Kaiser that all he's got to face is a few daft lads with broomsticks? Scare him witless, I should think.'

Several times they almost came to blows, only the intervention of Jack and Mary keeping them apart, but the bad blood between them grew ever more rancorous, more gangrenous day by day.

It had been a relief to Edgar when a temporary camp was established in Bishops Shilton and he no longer had to go home at nights.

Apart from getting away from the taunts of Harold, Edgar had another reason to be pleased to be now based in Bishops Shilton: his ongoing relationship Greta Mecklenburg.

Tents were set up in Furmoil Park and, despite the discomfort, the men finally began to feel as though they were at last on the way to becoming soldiers. There was almost a perverse pride in the discomfort. Heavy rain throughout October and November of 1914 made the conditions in Furmoil Camp almost insufferable; there were no floor boards in the tents and so the sixteen men had to lie on a floor of mud, the dirty smeared tents sitting like squat grey brown toads in the mire. But although the men grumbled and groused, they did not really mind; after all, now they were soldiers.

Training begun in real earnest with route marches of ever-increasing distances, five miles, nine miles, 15 miles, the men returning to their camp with blistered feet and knotted calf muscles. They dug trenches across the verdant green grass of the park, ran across from trench to trench as though advancing across enemy territory, and crawled under barbed wire obstacles. They were soldiers and proud of it.

That first draft, the first men to enlist, were assigned to the 8th Battalion, Royal Durham Regiment, 34th Brigade, 29th Division, part of what became known as the First New Army, the first of the five Kitchener Armies to be raised.

The battalion was commanded by Lt. Col Walters, an old 'dug out' who had retired after the South African War, but who had been dragged back to cover the acute shortage of experienced officers ... in fact, never mind experienced, the shortage of any kind of officers.

The platoon sergeant was another grizzled old veteran; Sgt. Hanson had first seen action as far back as the 1860's, as a 14-year-old boy recruit, fighting Pathans on the northwest frontier of India and then, later, Fuzzy-Wuzzys in the Sudan. He too had retired after the Boer War to what he thought would be a comfortable old age. He had taken over as landlord of a little public house on the outskirts of Hartlepool.

When the weather was wet or even only threatened to be wet, Hanson could feel a heavy aching throb in his right thigh where one of the Mahdi's spearmen had driven his assegai deep into his leg during the capture of Khartoum in 1885. The wound became infected and he had been lucky not to lose the leg.

And now, after more than 10 years retirement, he had been called back to try and lick these raw recruits into shape as quickly as possible so that they could be packed off to the trenches of France or the beaches of the Gallipoli Peninsula.

FORTY-ONE

men were going to die this day

April 25, 1915 Gallipoli

Five o'clock, in the uncertain pale light of an Aegean morning, the village of Sedd El Bahr was now clearly visible. The beach below the village had been scanned and studied from the sea and was known to be entrenched and strewn with barbed wire. However, the invasion planners assumed that a heavy barrage from guns of the battleships *HMS Albion* and *Cornwallis* would so devastate the beach and demoralise the defenders, that little resistance would be met as the troops waded ashore.

The *SS River Clyde*, converted into a troop carrier with 2000 troops aboard, slowly eased towards the beach, the sea calm and placid.

Then the barrage commenced, gunfire crashed out, heavy naval gunfire, screaming over Edgar's head, making him jump as he and the others ducked in surprise, huddled together into tight groups up against the rusting steel plates of the old freighter … as if there were safety in numbers, like kittens huddled up against their mother's flanks. The hair on the back of Edgar's neck began to bristle and he could feel his heart pounding frantically as more salvoes from the escorting battleships crashed onto the beaches and the Turkish trenches set into the slightly rising dunes.

'Fucking hell,' gasped Dick Wilson. 'Where the bloody hell did that come from?'

His face was pale and pinched, but Edgar could find no breath in his lungs to answer; he felt as though all his innards had fused together in a tightened scarlet knot.

'Over there, look, them battleships!' Dennis Jennings pointed, and they all craned to peer through the gloom towards the ships.

The light was thin, uncertain, dark enough still for the searing gun-flashes from the battleships *Cornwallis* and *Albion,* to shriek out of the purple-grey blackness, yellow-orange beacons of death, followed in less than a heartbeat by the screaming rush of tortured air as the salvo hurtled over their heads. The dawn air grew thick with the gun smoke as the bombardment continued, pounding onto the Turkish positions surrounding the small gravel beach. For more than an hour, the barrage rained down, with not one shot in reply from the shore.

Certain that the Turks could not possibly have survived such a torrent of gunfire, Edgar felt slightly better, but he could still taste the metallic acid of his fear and panic bubbling around, like blisters in a hot tar barrel, just below the surface of his mind, and he swallowed harder again, trying to force down the hard knot of fearful apprehension and trepidation that gripped at his innards like a vice.

The soft dawn air felt thin and sparse in his lungs, unable to satisfy his need for oxygen as the clear daylight gradually seeped across the panorama of the landing beach.

The old collier shuddered on towards the beach and Edgar idly wondered if any of the coal he had once hewed in Ashbrook, a lifetime away, had ever been loaded onto the rusting steamer. Across the rusting bows, he could see the beach on which they were to land.

The beach, designated as V beach, was no more than 300 yards wide and only about 10 yards deep. To the right, was the ruined medieval fortress of Sedd El Bahr, heavily battered, whilst just beyond the tiny village was huddled up close to the raddled walls. They had been told that the fortress had been damaged beyond repair during a bombardment as far back as last November, but the walls still looked strong and formidable to Edgar and, even in his short months as a soldier, he had learned enough to know that the whole beach, crescent-shaped and alluring, with the surrounding high ground and the dominating fort, presented an absolutely clear field for defensive fire. Despite the intensity of the naval barrage, his earlier fears crept over like a black shroud. He was suddenly mortally afraid; a lot of men were going to die this day and he felt certain that he was destined to be one of them.

The beach shuddered and wept, screaming in torment as it was ripped asunder. The noise was incredible, physically battering at the senses in pandemonic bludgeon.

Slowly, the *River Clyde* crept closer to the shore, across a sea that was now as smooth as a turquoise mirror, sun-splashed and pale.

'This is it lads,' Sergeant Hanson shouted. 'Brace yourself for impact!'

The plan was to run the *River Clyde* aground and disembark onto lighters through holes cut in the side of the ship.

The small boats, slung to the side of the collier, were now crammed full of men, huddled up against the rusting flanks like piglets at the teat. Other lighters, despatched from the rest of the fleet, scurried like water beetles across the limpid sheen of Homer's sea.

With barely a shudder, the *River Clyde* slid wearily onto the beach, settling down with no intention of ever moving again, like an old woman finally laying down a heavy load of shopping. The guns stopped.

Tangible silence, dense and impenetrable, settled across the Aegean morning like a shroud, a silence so deep that the clamour of the guns seemed almost angelic by comparison. With the stillness came an insidious fear, fear that crept around the heart and bowels with icy fingers, chilling the blood even in the warmth of the morning, filling the stomach with a hard knot of dread. Edgar felt his bladder swell, urgent and bursting, and he almost wet himself from the fear of it. Slowly, the need to urinate eased and he breathed more freely.

With the silence a faint breath of breeze came from the sun-shimmered cape, fragrant with the whispered hint of wild apple trees in blossom, of flowering broom and wild plum, of corn-flowers and scarlet poppies, tulips and wild thyme, the scents curiously untainted by the stinks of gunfire and smoke that drifted up from the bombardment of the beach. Through his fear, Edgar had time to wonder at the sweet smells, scents so alien to the bloody purpose of the day, and resolved to make a note of it, to tell Greta about it in his next letter. 'If you ever get to write another,' his traitorous fear whispered.

'Move on. Move on. Come on lads, get a bloody move on!'

Whistles blew and the soldiers began to shuffle forward, tightly packed on the decks and passageways where there was no room to move except to shuffle along with the thronging, heaving mass.

The lighters alongside began to head for the beach as the soldiers on deck lined up to disembark down the Jacobs ladder slung from the side of the ship, troops pouring out through the holes torched through the rusting flanks of the vessel to allow easy, swift access to the lighters and the beaches beyond, pouring out from the bowels of the ship like deserting rats in a shipwreck. The boats, 20 or so, packed full of troops, were within a handful of yards from the shore.

Then the Turkish machine guns opened up from the beach. Dense rifle fire, frightful in intensity, crashed out from the trenches where the Turks had lain hidden during the bombardment. From point-blank range they poured a storm of bullets into the packed mass of screaming, dying men in the boats and on the exposed decks and ladders of the River Clyde.

By the hundreds, the packed mass of the Durhams, Munster Fusiliers, Hampshires, and Dublin Fusiliers in the boats and on the collier standing shoulder to shoulder, died where they stood, too tightly packed to even raise a rifle. The sailors and young-boy midshipmen in charge of the boats were cut down and, steerless and out of control, the corpse-laden boats drifted away on the tide. Streaks of blood ran down the strakes of the boats like red paint, deeply staining the turquoise of the sea like a crimson dye.

Edgar watched in horror as one young sailor resolutely poled his boat up to the beach and then turn to urge his passengers ashore—to find that he was the only one still alive. All the soldiers were dead, the planks and seats of the boat awash with blood.

Then the boy was hit and slid slowly onto the thwarts, his body seeming to ripple as he fell. His corpse balanced precariously for a second or two by the bows; the head fell further forward and, with barely a splash, toppled over to lie half on the shore, half in the sea, as the lighter slid away from under him and back into the blood-stained sea. A black puddle, like tar, flowed around the boy's head, soaking into the sand like a dirty smear.

Shuffled forward by the weight of men behind him, Edgar could see the attack was failing. The men in the small boats had been torn apart and, although grounded, there was still too much depth of water under the bows of the *River Clyde* for the men to get ashore.

'Shit, shit, shit,' Edgar moaned to himself as the Turkish guns began to pick off the tight-packed men on the decks and gangways.

The attack fatally stalled.

'Look man, they're bringing more boats around,' Jeb Fulcher shouted.

They watched, hearts hammering in fear, as two men, chest deep in water and under heavy fire, dragged two lighters around from the rear of the vessel to form a causeway to the beach.[1]

Fearsomely exposed, the men came pouring out from the sallyports and down the gangways strung along the sides of the ship, presenting the Turks with more blank-range targets, like shooting ducks the rifle range of the village fare.

The gangways soon clogged up with dead and dying, but still they pressed forward. Edgar reached the head of the gangway and, feeling horribly naked and exposed, stepped out onto the ladder, hearing the zing and ring as bullets smacked and ricocheted off the rusting flanks of the ship. Behind him, he heard a grunt as Dennis Jennings, the next man out, took bullets to the head and chest, and toppled over to plummet down into the bullet-churning sea below.

The Jacob's ladder rocked and swayed, and Edgar felt sure he was going to be pitched out after Jennings. Almost paralysed with fear, he clung to the greasy wire of the handrail, oblivious to everything except the smack of bullets around him, rattling against the steel plates in a drumroll tattoo of death.

His feet seemed glued to the steps, unable to move; he stared out glassy-eyed across the crimson smeared sea to the beach, his mind seized solid, filled with the roaring fear-pulsed blood. He knew he was going to die and filled his lungs to scream out his death song, waiting for the bullets to rip him apart. Shouts. Bellowed orders. Through the cocooned mists of dread, he heard voices, insistent and loud, muffled. A blow to the back between his ribs. 'This is it, man,' he thought, 'I'm dead.'

'Move yoursen, daft bugger!'

'Leave me be,' he thought. 'I'm dying' and felt another blow into his ribs.'

'Get yousen out't bloody way, Edgar Garforth,' he heard Jeb Fulcher shout in his ear. 'Daft silly bugger! Move your arse else I'll kick you down't stairs!' None too lightly, he punched him again.

'Aye, right on, Jeb,' he answered slowly as his wits seeped back into his brain. 'Just admiring the view, that were all. It's right pretty over there,' he shouted as he scurried down the gangway; it was doubtful whether Jeb could hear above the cacophony of gunfire and screams.

Corpses clogged the foot of the gangway as Edgar and Jeb scrambled across and onto the first lighter. Edgar stumbled and fell across a body and pulled back in horror as his hand sank elbow deep into the chest and intestines of Jim Comby, his dad's marra, staring at him with death-still eyes.

He lurched away, scrambling more on his hands and knees than on his feet, everything slick with blood, the lighter filled and overflowing with the dead and dying, thick blood sloshing in the scuppers of the boat like beef gravy around a beef joint. A young midshipman at the bow of the second lighter urged them on, his thin piping boy's voice strangely in keeping with the howling screams of artillery and the rattling smack of bullets, his arms straining as he held onto the rope that tenuously anchored the lighters to a spit of rock jutting from the shore.

The beach, red-splashed and corpse-strewn, loomed ahead as Edgar and Jeb clambered crab-wise and breathless from the lighter onto the Gallipoli sands of Sedd Al Bahr.

Sgt. Hanson, bleeding profusely from a wound to his upper arm, pointed to a thin bank of sand at the head of the beach, against which a handful of soldiers huddled for shelter from the gunfire the raked the sands. 'Go on lads,' he panted, pain etched in the creases of his old-soldier face. 'Get on up there and out't bloody way, gan on, move! But gan canny, mind, but get off the beaches. Get off the beach!'

They scurried on like mice through the sands, jumping and hurdling over a litter of carcasses strewn over the beach, broken bloody puppets tossed aside as Hanson directed the next batch of Durhams to have to run the gauntlet of the gangways and lighter. Impelled by the need to get off that murderous beach, the troops pushed forward and drove the Turkish defendants from the trenches and secured the beachhead.

Edgar never saw Hanson again. Never even found out what happened to him; after 60 years of soldiering for King and Queen, Sgt. Belford Hanson disappeared into an unknown grave on the shores of Cape Hellas.

Of the 1,500 men landed on the beaches, 1,000 were killed or wounded by machine-gun fire. However, despite the tremendous losses on V beach and the adjoining W beach, forever after known as Lancashire Landing, where the Lancashire Fusiliers lost 500 killed and wounded out of a landing force of 950, the landings at X and Y were virtually unopposed, as were the landing by the French troops on S beach on the Dardanelle side of the peninsula.

Linking up, the invading troops pushed forward, their objective the village of Krithia.

FORTY-TWO

Mary, asleep in her rocking chair, did not hear her go.

Eleanor Garforth did not want a new dress. Or anything else except to be left alone in her misery. Mary's comforting words were just an irritant, as were those of her sisters, Mary Margaret and Margaret Mary. 'Just leave me alone to die,' was her unspoken thought.

'Why? Why? Why had that man, she could not give name to him, done that to her?'

She wanted her innocence back, her belief in goodness, in innate kindness and pity. All that had been torn away, the very bastions of her sheltered soul had been ripped asunder, torn from her being as casually as a butcher plucking out the innards from a chicken's carcass.

To compound her misery, her brothers, Joe, Daniel, Edgar and many men from the village had been caught up in the collective craziness of war. They would die, every one of them, she knew, could feel it in her waters and in the depths of her ravaged soul.

She could not bear that thought. Life without her brothers, silent in the strength they gave her in her darkest times, how could she live when she knew, knew in her deepest feral instincts that, Edgar, Joseph, Daniel, Nicholas and the twins, Isaac and Saul would all be caught up in the voracious maw of deaths in pitiless war ... when only Harald, revengeful, spiteful, evil Harald and 'that man', would survive. Eleanor could not live in a world if only those monsters, and others like them, still inhabited it. All would be infinite darkness.

The thought was just too fearful to comprehend.

She got up from the bed where she had been lying, heart-wrenched with her morbid soul-paralysing thoughts, walked into the kitchen, picked up the basket as if going to the shops, and made her way out through the backyard.

FORTY-THREE

Her numinous home, sanctuary for a restless soul.

The river, so long her private sanctuary, was despoiled. No longer did it provide her with peace and tranquillity; the riverine restfulness and serenity had gone forever, tainted by the memory of what had occurred beside those pristine waters.

The overhanging willow from where a majestic kingfisher perched and fished, diving in a flashing turquoise streak to take hapless minnows and guppies in the river below, held no peace of mind.

The river had been her numinous home, sanctuary for a restless soul, but now a soul in torment. The idyllic peace of her inner sanctuary had been foully desecrated, her paradise raped as surely as had her body.

Now, crossing over the stream by the dam, Eleanor slowly made her way to the shallow hollow—so long her favourite of all her secret places, so overpowering had been the feelings of peace it had once brought her, but no more.

She made her way to the bend in the river where the deepest

pools lay, dark and forbidding in the shade, and slowly she let herself slide into the water.

As the waters received her, she felt cleansed, pure, her restless, tormented soul finally at peace.

Mary Garforth wrote: *My dear son, it is so difficult to write this letter. I have tried so many times to put pen to paper but each time the weight of the terrible news overcomes me, and I have to stop. Edgar, our dearest Eleanor is dead. On Sunday 6th June, our own sweet girl went to the river and there took her own life. Drowned. She was broken inside, we all us knew that, but I thought with time and our deep love, she might recover and find her own sweet dear self again, but no it was not to be. Jesus has taken her into his loving arms, it is only in that thought I find comfort. We are all heartbroken. Take care my dear son. I pray to God he brings you home safe again. Your loving mother.*

'No-oo!' Edgar screamed inside. No, no, his sweet gentle beloved sister dead at her own hand but killed by the bastard Gerard Barclay-Milnes as surely as if he had dragged her to the river and held her head under the water until she drowned.

He brushed at the flies that flocked to the tears flooding down his face. As he leaned against the parapet wall in the trench beneath, under the fierce Turkish sun of Gallipoli, amidst the heat and dust and the stench of death, the endless swarms of flies and rampaging, fearless rats, Edgar Garforth swore on the pocket *Bible* that Greta Mecklenburg had given him their last afternoon together before he left for the war—swore that he would kill the Honourable Second Lieutenant Gerard Barclay-Milnes by his own hand.

If it was to last thing her ever did.

Even if it cost his own life.

'Eleanor, this I swear,' he vowed as he pressed the *Bible* to his lips. 'This I swear!'

The End

In Death's Grey Land will continue the story of the Garforth family and others of the village.

Dear reader,

We hope you enjoyed reading *Never Such Innocence Again*. Please take a moment to leave a review, even if it's a short one. Your opinion is important to us.

Discover more books by Giles Ekins at https://www.nextchapter.pub/authors/giles-ekins

Want to know when one of our books is free or discounted? Join the newsletter at http://eepurl.com/bqqB3H

Best regards,
Giles Ekins and the Next Chapter Team

NOTES

Chapter 41

1. The Commander of the *River Clyde*, Commander Unwin, and a boy midshipman called Drewry were awarded the Victoria Cross for this deed. Four others were also awarded VCs for their bravery during this action.

ABOUT THE AUTHOR

I was born in the northeast of England and qualified as an Architect in London. Subsequently, I spent much of my career living and working in Northern Nigeria, Qatar, Oman and Bahrain, working on various projects including schools, hospitals, leisure centres, royal palaces, shopping malls and, particularly, highly prestigious hotels.

I have now returned to England and live in Sheffield with my wife Patricia. Amongst other books, I am the author of *Gallows Walk*, *Murder by Illusion*, *Sinistrari*, *Dead Girl Found* and *Alpha and Omega*, as well as the children's book, *The Adventures of a Travelling Cat*, in which the cat in question travels the world, having various adventures.

I like travelling, reading, the countryside, and sports (and, for my sins, support Newcastle United FC).

Never Such Innocence Again
ISBN: 978-4-86747-420-4

Published by
Next Chapter
1-60-20 Minami-Otsuka
170-0005 Toshima-Ku, Tokyo
+818035793528

18th May 2021

Lightning Source UK Ltd.
Milton Keynes UK
UKHW010201070223
416581UK00004B/270

9 784867 474204